Enemy Storm

by

Marcella Burnard

Chronicles of the Empire, Book 3

This is a work of fiction. Names, characters, places, and incidents are either the product of the author's imagination or are used fictitiously, and any resemblance to actual persons living or dead, business establishments, events, or locales, is entirely coincidental.

Enemy Storm

Contact Information: info@thewildrosepress.com

Cover Art by *Jennifer Greeff*

The Wild Rose Press, Inc.
PO Box 708
Adams Basin, NY 14410-0708
Visit us at www.thewildrosepress.com

Publishing History
First Fantasy Rose Edition, 2020
Print ISBN 978-1-5092-3143-0
Digital ISBN 978-1-5092-3144-7

Chronicles of the Empire, Book 3
Published in the United States of America

Dedication

In Memory of Mandy, who would appreciate the dedication of this book

~

For Gnomeregan

Chapter One

Holy Gods, don't know what I did to piss you off, but dropping a starship on my head is overkill.

Vibration sliced Edie's sternum. She registered the data flashing down the ballistic-glass lenses of her Sensory Enhancement Module.

Adrenaline stole her breath.

She flung a glance skyward. No mean feat standing at the dusty bottom of the two-kilometer-deep slash in the planetary crust. The optics on her enviro-helmet flared, then darkened to shield her eyes as she scanned the narrow, heat-bleached strip of sky. Dust from the charred rock walls sifted past her visor.

She studied the angle of descent and engine frequency readings.

"Aw, c'mon," she muttered as trajectory projections flashed red, driving sharp-edged alarm through her breastbone.

Incoming mass. Right on target to squash her.

Bad.

It was smoking a hole through the already broiling atmosphere. From the data on her SEM, and from the ache lodged in her chest in response to the advancing pressure wave, it looked like the radioactive star drive was intact and still powered up.

Worse.

Blood pounding in her head, Edie ran in the killing

heat of a planet about to be consumed by its dying, expanding star.

The sky, her SEM, and the canyon lit like a supernova. The flash overwhelmed her optics. Blinded, she clenched her eyes shut, too damned late.

Reactor core explosion.

Brilliant. Now the atmosphere was radioactive as well as roasting.

Shockwave rattled the canyon and ripped the breath from her lungs. It shoved her straight into the unforgiving stone wall.

Her helmet struck rock, slamming her head against the inside. She tumbled to the ground. *Why the bleeding Gods hadn't she padded the helmet*?

Sonic vibration rattled the canyon again.

No time to be on your back, Edie. Radioactive wreckage incoming.

She scrambled for the only shelter she could reach and dove face first into a hole in the canyon wall.

The ship hit.

Ground heaved, rumbling and rolling beneath her. Debris pelted her.

A piece at a time, the crash-quake stilled.

Itching to rub away the sweat running between her breasts, she struggled to get her breath in the overheated, stale air inside her environmental suit, which was doing a piss poor job of controlling the environment.

Opening her eyes, she risked lifting her head. She'd taken shelter in one of the caves honeycombing the cliffs.

By reflex, she checked sensor readings only to stare into an empty projection field. SEM offline. She sat up.

Dust, gravel, and fist-sized stones tumbled from her enviro-suit. At some point in the proceedings, the face plate in her helmet had cracked. Another bit of gear she couldn't afford to be without, yet couldn't afford to repair.

At least the helmet wasn't strictly necessary on world. Still. Until she fixed it, she risked losing suit integrity in a critical situation elsewhere.

Unless she put aside a thus-far-fruitless bounty hunt in favor of salvaging the wrecked ship. Never look a superheated, radioactive gift Orhait in the mouth, right? Even one solid piece of salvage would pay for suit repair. Maybe even Seeker bombs.

First things first. She reset her SEM. The ballistic glass lenses winked to life. A faint twinge of discomfort at her temples assured her the sensory stimulator had come online, too.

Her handheld vibrated. A couple of well-practiced inputs on the unit and data fed into the SEM's visual field.

Stellar. Back in business.

Her SEM picked up the pops and pings of cooling metal, translating audio signals Edie couldn't hear into visuals she could read. Good. The crash had touched down nearby. Impact fires were burning out.

She'd have to move fast. The United Mining and Ore Processing Guild had a base within the warren of tunnels on world, and she wouldn't be the only one with an eye for profit. Edie crawled out of the tunnel and climbed to her feet.

The smoldering hulk of twisted, fragmented alloy, still glowing from re-entry, rested a kilometer up the canyon. It towered halfway up the rock wall. The UMOPG had shot it to all Three Hells. She couldn't even place the vessel class.

As she trudged closer, her suit's bio-system judged her in need of hydration therapy. A quick pinch over her femoral artery spread cool through her. Her pulse slowed. Breathing became easier.

Fortified, she picked up her pace. By the time she'd made her way down the impact scar, blistering re-entry heat had dissipated to something nonfatal. Edie kept a close eye on radiation levels, though, because there were all kinds of hot.

Readings didn't fluctuate. Amazing. She'd have sworn no one could survive the kind of damage she was looking at, much less the plunge into atmosphere. But the more she stared at steady radiation numbers, the more she believed someone had lived inside that disaster long enough to eject the reactor core *before* it had blown.

As she closed in on the ship, she noted structural supports shredded like wet ceremonial paper. She hadn't yet seen any weapons' emplacements. Those would tell her which government had built the ship, not to mention that salvaged weapon tech commanded the best credits, even shot up.

She rounded the wreckage.

A shattered, and, in places, molten view screen dripped in great oily globs to the dust. This section had been part of the command deck structure of a much larger vessel.

Her SEM flashed a familiar rhythm. Heartbeats. Several of them.

Twelve Gods. Survivors.

Chapter Two

Edie bolted for the charred emergency hatch.

She ducked under a dying piece of electronics. And found herself staring at an emblem perversely untouched by fire or re-entry heat. A spiral galaxy stylized into a gold and black, bird of prey on an emerald field. The insignia of the Claugh nib Dovvyth Empire.

Her chest constricted.

She jerked upright. Sneering, she spun on her heel and stalked away. She'd be damned before she rescued Claugh. She'd spent too many years fighting their invasion of her home world. Too many years watching monsters dressed in khaki uniforms torture and murder her family and friends.

Audio data registered as a visual wave on her SEM. It grabbed her by the sternum and stopped her in her tracks.

Weeping.

Edie squeezed burning eyes tight. Someone aboard that disaster was crying—sobbing in messy, frightened child-like gulps. From deeper in the structure, fainter audio signals mingled with the first. Screams. Moans.

This was the disadvantage of Sensory Enhancement. She couldn't see the audio signals on her screens, not since she'd closed her eyes, but the SEM fed the data into the nerves and fibers communicating directly into her brain. Edie opened gritty eyes.

The evidence of anguish twisted around her throat. She hadn't cried since the day she'd watched her parents die. Fifteen years ago. The terror, the pain, the unrelenting rage and grief hadn't gone away. It lingered beneath the surface of her skin, a poisoned canker, waiting to erupt, already rising in response to the tears someone else shed.

Gritting her teeth, she sighed, turned, and stomped to the access hatch as a pair of UMOPG ships buzzed the top of the canyon. The engine signatures shifted, receding, and banking for landing.

Great. The carrion-eaters coming for the corpse. Landing far away, though. Made sense in rocky terrain. She tagged the approximate location for investigation.

She'd have a few short hours. Three, maybe, based on the landing data her SEM fed her.

Fine.

Calculating the psychological advantage, Edie took off her helmet. Humanoids trusted faster when they could look another humanoid in the eye. Unreasonably relieved to be free of the stifling confines, she set the helmet in the dust at her feet.

Edie pounded the emergency releases beside the hatch with gloved fists. Only one of the charges embedded at the sealed edges of the door blew. She grabbed hold of that edge and pulled.

****

The noise of someone retching wrested V'kyrri to consciousness. The metallic tang of blood mingled with the reek of charred flesh bit the back of his throat. He was supposed to be dead.

Dread crawled inside his skin.

He commanded his eyes open. No response. Come to think of it, he couldn't feel anything except rising anxiety over whoever gasped with what sounded like dry heaves. Instinct kicked in. He sent out a tendril of thought, seeking telepathic ID on the person.

White-hot wires dug into his head, setting fire to every nerve. He groaned.

"Captain." Relief sounded in a raspy female voice. "Rest easy, sir."

His sluggish, aching brain supplied the speaker's identity. Commander Parqe, his second-in-command.

"Stim," he croaked.

Parqe hesitated. "Sir?"

"Stim."

"No," she grated. "It's too dangerous. Every combat first aid class…"

"Stim. On my belt."

"Dammit, this is a bad idea," she said. "You've been unconscious since you ejected the core. Unconscious and hallucinating. Screaming. You're injured. A stim could kill you. I thought you'd died once already. I can't do it again."

Suppressed terror in her voice stabbed through his skull. He fumbled for her hand, squeezed when she took it. "Parqe. Stim. That's an order."

She jerked out of his hold. "I'm lodging a formal protest, Captain."

"Noted. Belt. Right side."

She retrieved the medication, pressed the applicator against his skin, and triggered the mechanism.

Acid poured into his blood. He groaned, again.

His second-in-command drew a ragged breath.

The burn pumped into his brain where severed

psychic filaments writhed, bleeding some vital aspect of him out into the silence inside his skull. Bones, beset by the mounting pressure of the drug, creaked.

Praying for the pain to subside, he rocked. It merely changed. Energy trickled through him, building to a flood. As he woke, so too, did nerve fibers. They communicated physical hurt he hadn't noticed while he'd crippled himself telepathically by ripping apart his connections to his friends so he wouldn't kill them when his ship crashed.

He should have died.

"Sir," Parqe said, "stay still. Don't…"

By sheer dint of will, and to escape the sharp-edged metal digging into his back, V'kyrri sat up. Hurt slashed every fiber. His breath froze in his chest.

"…move," the woman said. "You might have suffered spinal injury."

"Considering the pain," he wheezed, "I haven't broken my back." He opened his eyes, then wished he hadn't.

The ship had crashed on its side. Light and dust trickled through cracks in the hull. His restraints had failed, dumping him into the panels above the communications station. Dark, gruesome fluids dribbled down the now vertical deck plating, the chairs, and instrument consoles. The mangled bodies of his bridge crew lay in tangled, obscene heaps against the crumpled hull. Rock poked through a jagged tear in the alloy.

A different kind of agony seared him. His skin and bone would knit. This memory wouldn't. For the rest of his life, he'd live with this bloody, bone-shattered image of the last mortal remains of his crew splattered across his bridge.

He initiated a mental pain-suppression routine. To save and serve his remaining crew, he had to bury his psychological and physical wounds. Training kicked in, walling off pain receptors. The loss, the deaths, the belated, useless flood of adrenaline and panic, those he pushed aside for later. If any of them had *later*.

He levered himself to his feet battling a sense of futility. None of them should have survived. Maybe they hadn't. Maybe they were just taking longer to die.

Until they did, he had a job to do.

"Report."

His officer flapped her hands and choked back what might have been a sob. Soot and blue rock-flour covered her, rendering her nearly unrecognizable. "We're down. Systems offline. No instruments. A few of us survived. I don't know how."

"The Gods of all Three Hells rejected us again," V'kyrri muttered.

A young lieutenant curled into a ball among the bodies burst into noisy sobs. Blood stained her khaki uniform nearly black. She'd been the one throwing up, he could guess. She'd had reason, regaining consciousness half buried by her dead friends.

"Just the three of us?" he asked.

Parqe averted her gaze from the remains. "We may find others aft, but on the command deck, we're it."

V'kyrri sagged and rubbed his forehead. The pressure against the bones of his skull did nothing to soothe the hot pain.

"Full protection protocol," V'kyrri said. "Get me weapons. We're not out of danger yet. Once we can protect them, survivors and a way off world have priority. Make this quick."

Parqe turned her head and winced. A red, angry burn marred half her face and neck, showing through the dust coating her.

V'kyrri hissed a breath between his teeth and looked up the vertical surface of the deck. He had a first aid kit at the base of his command chair and no way to get to it.

A thump sounded on the edge of the ship.

They froze, staring at one another. The sobbing lieutenant pressed her hands over her mouth to muffle the sound.

A scream from somewhere in the depths of the wreck twisted hot adrenaline into V'kyrri's system.

Survivors. Wounded. Trapped. He could do not a damned thing about it with someone knocking at the escape hatch.

Parqe gasped.

An emergency charge fired. It should have reverberated through his ship like a bell, summoning survivors. Instead, it plinked, a stone hitting an empty can. He'd expected more time before their attackers came to finish the job.

He drew his gun and traded a look with the commander.

Fear dulled her too-wide brown eyes. She'd pulled her weapon with a shaking hand and glanced at the door into the rest of the ship.

"The enemy's at the door. Focus." He jerked his chin at the emergency door while metal creaked as the attackers worked on forcing the hatch.

The commander took cover behind the shattered corpse of the communications station, weapon trained on the glimmer of daylight showing through the opening hatch.

V'kyrri climbed the skeletal remnants of a station he could no longer identify and hauled himself into a corridor.

A narrow gash in the aft bulkhead where the bridge had ripped away from the rest of the ship bled daylight into the passageway.

By some twist of sick cosmic humor, with everything trashed and offline, the manual door-release pulled open with well-oiled ease. The door moved without a sound.

Heat clubbed him. The sour stench of charred soil competed with the bite of gritty smoke. He choked back a cough and edged out the door.

Powdery sand deadened his steps. Acrid, blue-gray haze hung in the air. Rock towered overhead. The *Rhapsody* had scored a bright line in the stone and come to rest leaning against the cliff wall.

V'k scanned the dull rocks and dust. Nothing moved. Not even the thin, over-heated air. He edged around the ruined vessel. There. Voices. Correction. A voice.

"Shift your butts." Female. Speaking Tagrethian, colored by a dialect he didn't recognize. "Unless you intend to wait for the guys who shot you down to come finish the job."

From the dubious cover of a rock fall, V'kyrri surveyed the soldier at his bridge escape hatch. Shorter than he by no more than a few centimeters. Lower body mass, undoubtedly armed.

"Ident." Parqe's voice, hollow coming from inside the ship.

V'kyrri frowned. The soldier couldn't have been sent alone.

"Name's Edie. Let's go. You got to get out of there."

"We haven't even scanned for survivors," Parqe protested.

"The guys who shot you down are incoming. Get out of there, now."

"I'm not leaving," Parqe said. "Not while I have wounded screaming in the lower decks."

V'kyrri holstered his weapon, and silent in the sand, crept behind the lone soldier.

"Well, okay…" The soldier shrugged.

V'k clamped an arm around her ribs and yanked her against his chest. Hard muscle and lush curves shot a whisper of awareness through his blood. Definitely female. Definitely dangerous. He dug the fingers of his right hand into her windpipe.

Her squeak of surprise ended in a rasp. The fight went out of her.

"Captain?" Parqe barked.

"Under control." He spun to face the canyon so the soldier's asleep-at-the-trigger compatriots would realize they couldn't shoot him without killing her, too. If they cared.

"Where's your squad?" he demanded.

"What?" she wheezed.

He tightened his hold on her windpipe.

A tremor moved through her, and her knees buckled.

V'kyrri braced her against his aching body. "No games. Your squad. Location. Number."

Her breath came in an agonized rasp.

He had to support most of her weight. Breathing hard, he blinked sweat out of his eyes, and loosened his grip on her throat. She'd be no use to him unconscious.

"Alone." She made it sound like swearing.

"Lie." Rage shattered his grip on pain suppression. Hurt scraped him.

She sucked in a noisy breath and shifted as if his hold burned. "Bounty hunter."

Closing useless eyes, V'kyrri marshaled dwindling resources and slammed his mental doors to pain. He'd pay for the dangerous practice later. Or he'd die. Better him than any of his remaining crew. Physical hurt ebbed. Awareness of his prisoner's body clamped so tight to his didn't. It should have.

V'kyrri opened his eyes. He could see again. He had his face buried in her flame-bright hair. His mother's voice whispered in his memory. *'A fire-haired woman is either a curse or blessing to our kind. Rarely do we get to choose which. We are either redeemed or damned by her touch.'*

Dread strolled his spine. Impatient with his reaction to an old superstition, he released the woman's throat.

She didn't tense, didn't gulp for air. She drew an audibly deep, shaky breath through her nose.

Suspicion chilled him.

Somewhere, she'd learned to relax into the immobilization hold he'd used. Most people, when released from a choke hold, panicked, bolted upright, hyperventilated, and passed out.

'Bounty hunter', she'd said, but her slow, deliberate inhalation suggested specialized training. Still. While she might have lied about her profession, it appeared she hadn't lied about being alone.

"Where's your ship, Bounty Hunter?" he asked.

She snarled, a thin wisp of sound, cut off mid-protest and snapped, "Might as well be on the central star."

V'kyrri gathered a fistful of her collar before pressing the muzzle of his gun into her back.

She didn't stagger for balance when he set her on her feet. She'd feigned nearly passing out, too. She'd kept her head while he'd had her airway in his hand. That took discipline. It also suggested that she'd kept her muscles supple so she could launch a counterattack if he'd committed a single mistake. As he clearly had done in underestimating her.

"Try again," he said.

"On the surface. Fourteen hours," she muttered, her tone pressed flat.

Too far for a quick rescue. If he couldn't use her ship, he could still use her.

"Move," he commanded.

Edie's breath seared her bruised windpipe.

"My gear!" she protested before she could suppress it.

His grip in her collar tightened.

Edie grimaced. You didn't provoke the vicious, unpredictable Claugh. Her mistake not leaving every one of them to die.

The madman at her back hesitated. "Pick them up."

"Either finish strangling me or let me go," she said as she grabbed her pack and helmet. She hadn't even managed to straighten before he hauled her around, tried to poke the gun through her right kidney, and shoved her up his back trail.

He maneuvered her to a bulkhead door. "Inside."

Watching the radiation numbers ticking steady in her Sensory Enhancement Module readout, she went.

Heat-stressed metal stank. Lingering electrical-fire smoke stung her throat. Shredded metal and impact dents, originating from within the ship, made her swallow hard. This much damage should be soaked in blood and gore.

It wasn't.

Meaning the ship had torn itself apart before it reached atmosphere.

Space travel had become such a fact of life. No one thought about the horrors of dying in a vacuum. Quick? Yes. Painless? Where did suffocation land on the pain scale? Not that she'd ever gotten to ask. Once someone breathed vacuum, they weren't generally up for Q&A.

Imagination was enough. She suspected that anyone who made a living in space, and who survived on the edge of life in the first place, had more than their fair share of nightmares.

A data line on her SEM brought Edie up short. Vitals. Strong. Regular. She hissed in a breath when her captor jabbed the gun into her back.

"Quit or pull the trigger," she grumbled. "I'm going to be pissing blood, thanks to you. Might as well cauterize the kidney."

His grip on her collar tightened.

"Did you want to know about the survivor behind you?"

The gun in her back retreated. Her enviro-suit collar released.

"Where?" His single word, translated from Claughwyth by her SEM, carried the impression of terrible hope mingled with fear.

She turned.

He didn't stop her. His blood-stained, pale khaki uniform set Edie's heart knocking against her ribs. Her body still remembered fighting wave after maddened wave of invaders dressed in Claugh nib Dovvyth uniforms.

Stop it, she ordered her runaway pulse. *You lost that war years ago.*

Then why am I still staring up the barrel of a gun?

He'd pointed his weapon at the center of her chest, his copper-colored knuckles paling as his grip tightened.

She set down her helmet and pack and spread her fingers wide. She made certain she wiped rage from her expression before glancing into his face.

Pale green eyes glared at her. Cropped close, light brown hair contrasted his burnished copper skin. His long, lithe body slumped as if dogged by pain. He had the kind of wiry build most people underestimated in a close fight. Her aching throat attested to his strength, even when he was bent by injury. Bleak lines of ruthlessness and agony surrounded his generous mouth, washing color from his complexion. Fury and determination lit his eyes.

Volatile combination. Internal alarms flared. Edie slid her gaze away from his.

One of his insignia had been ripped from his collar. The other was intact. That solitary insignia squeezed the breath out of her overheated lungs. The Claugh knot and wings.

She had the ship's captain on her hands.

Chapter Three

Scanning the twisted corridor she suspected led to the bridge and the rest of the survivors, Edie jerked her chin at a door beneath their feet. "Your survivor is down there."

"Open it."

Edie knelt and put her weight against the override lever.

It creaked, the noise ragged data on her SEM. The handle gave. She landed on her butt, and sat, waiting for her heat-elevated pulse to settle. It didn't. She hauled herself to her knees and pried the door open a few centimeters at a time.

The mad captain set a boot against the edge and shoved.

Edie marked it as the first sign of rationality she'd seen in him. *Possible tactical advantage to playing on concern for his crew.*

The stench of death pummeled her. Holding her breath, she peered into the shadowed compartment. Edie didn't need more fuel for her nightmares, but she needed light unless she wanted to fry her gray matter with extra SEM processing. "Need light."

Without looking, she shoved a hand into the thigh storage pocket of her suit.

"If anything other than a light bar comes out of there…" He left the threat hanging. But not his H7 pistol. Standard Claugh military issue. Short range. High power. Tended to lose accuracy at distance. Like that would matter with it pointed right between her eyes when she glanced up at him.

"What? You'll leave my brains splattered all over your ship? Don't you have enough of a mess without having to sift my DNA out of your crew's remains?"

The muscles in his jaw worked. From the pallor outlining his lips, she guessed the reek of the compartment was making him queasy. Bad enough for her, but those were his crew smeared all over the bulkheads.

He eased back.

Edie brought her hand, clutching her light bar, out of her pocket.

With a jerk of the gun, he indicated that she should resume rescue efforts. She amused herself calculating how much explosive would be required to reduce him to constituent particles. She lowered the activated light bar into the gloom.

A pile of something rested against the far wall. Her eyes refused to resolve the image. Logic did it for her. Bodies. That's how space battles and decompressed ships played out.

Except for the young man huddled in one corner. He sported a shock of bright blue hair. Bruises covered the right side of his face. The bars on his collar made him an ensign.

He squinted into the light. He blinked rapidly, repeatedly, as if trying to erase an internal visual buffer. Sweat stood out on the kid's forehead and upper lip. He shivered.

Edie's chest tightened.

The kid was slipping into shock.

She set the light bar to one side and looked for her captor.

He crouched across from her, gun propped on one knee while he stared into the compartment, gaze locked on the carnage. Shadows pared the flesh from his face, leaving him looking haunted. Almost human. Almost sane.

A twinge of sympathy rose. Rubbing her bruised, aching throat, she stomped on the tendril of empathy.

"He's in the corner," she snapped, hoping to break him out of counting the dead.

She edged farther into the hole, head down, almost within reach of the young man. "Hey. Are you hurt? Do you speak Tagrethian?"

No response.

"Whose blood you wearing, kid?" Not that she wanted to know, but she couldn't suppress the murmur.

"The chief's," he whispered as if the tally played over and over in his unfocused vision. "Kalvie's, and Juspil's. The captain ordered engineering evacuated. I couldn't leave them, but I—I don't think I got all the pieces."

Edie squeezed her eyes shut and choked back the memories of her first space battle against this boy's people. It didn't work. The ghosts of mangled friends and fellow revolutionaries wrapped clammy fingers around the back of her neck.

He was in for a lifetime of nightmares. She would know.

"No," she croaked, opening her eyes to fish through another pocket. "You couldn't leave them. You did the right thing. Here."

Head pounding, she shoved a wrapped bit of candy into his line of sight. “Go on. You’ll feel better.”

He took the sweet with a grimy, trembling hand. He stuck the candy in his mouth and the first hint of color returned to his cheeks.

She’d wasted precious survival calories on a Claugh soldier. Out of sympathy. *Sympathy*. Her parents must be weeping in their graves.

No.

They’d always preached the virtue of service to others and of forgiving ones’ enemies. Not to mention that he’d have been in diapers while she’d wasted her youth fighting his people. He didn’t deserve her hatred. Not like his captain.

His captain. The Claugh madman dangled next to her reaching for his ensign. “Ensign. Stand up.”

She returned her attention to the baby-faced young man.

He shuddered.

“Come on,” Edie urged. “Won’t be long before the bad guys come to clean up the mess they made. You going to able to evac?”

His gaze found her and came into focus. “Ma’am?”

“Name’s Edie. We’re going to get out of here so we can look at the hand we’ve been dealt. You in?”

He flushed, glanced at his captain, and straightened against the bulkhead. “Yes, ma’am. Yes, sir. I’m in.”

“Got a name?”

“Ensign Scalte Fuller, ma’am.”

“We’re getting you out of there, Ensign,” the captain said. “Give me your hand.”

“Left arm’s broken, sir,” Fuller said, reaching with his right.

"Hang on. Anti-grav," Edie said. She shifted out of the hole, taking a second to let the pounding pressure in her skull dissipate, then dug a tiny anti-grav unit from a pack pocket.

When she turned back, the madman lay across the reeking, open doorway, gun pointed at her head, his gaze prying.

For a breathless second, she imagined he saw into her, hunting for parts of her she didn't want anyone to have.

He scowled.

The impression vanished.

She flattened herself face down on the edge of the doorway and said, "Catch. Hook it to your belt."

Edie switched on the anti-grav. Fuller's feet left the floor, and he started to tip. His captain steadied the ensign out of the compartment. Edie climbed to her feet and followed as the captain guided the younger man to a nearby bulkhead. She set the kid down.

On her handheld, Edie tagged his speech pattern with his name. She didn't have a name to attach to the captain. She itched to tag him as 'madman'. It would amuse her, but it could get her killed if he got a hold of her SEM or handheld. She hated it, but the wisdom of tagging him as 'Captain' won.

"Edie." The captain.

She glanced at him.

Again, that green gaze bored into her. Dizziness swept her.

He paled and swayed.

For a split second, agony shot through her head. Then it was gone. She gulped in a breath. Indication of the atmosphere turning toxic? Or had she exceeded her

SEM limit in some critical fashion? Sure, it fed visual and tactical data to the screens before her eyes, but the extra boost of nerve stimulation that came from Sensory Enhancement was addictive. She would know.

It was insidious and attractive because of the heady, nerve-buzzing high that came from so much information getting dumped through merely mortal neural networks.

Blinking away a fading headache, she arched an eyebrow while her nerves arced at his proximity. She frowned.

"I owe you an apology," he said, "but my coping mechanisms are offline, and I find I don't have one to offer. Thank you for getting my ensign out of that horror chamber."

She stared at him, unable to make an apology coming from a Claugh make sense.

"I'm going to have cause to apologize again. You can't keep that handheld." He plucked her little computer out of her hands and shut it down.

"Hey," she yelped. "I need…" Her SEM went dark. The buzz of sensory stimulation died. She shuddered and glanced at Fuller. The kid sat against the hull, knees drawn up, elbows propped on them, and his forehead on his clenched hands.

The captain gestured with the gun, reclaiming her attention. His lips moved.

Without the SEM to translate, she turned her gaze to his mouth. She could read lips, but it took time. She needed to see someone speaking over time to catalog their mannerisms, their unique way of forming sounds and words. With a nonnative Tagrethian speaker, it took even longer as she parsed out accent.

He was saying something angry. She couldn't tell what, but the pissy nature? That was clear. He hurled rapid-fire demands in her face.

Frowning, she concentrated, trying to work out what words he expected her to catch. It struck her that he'd switched from Claughwyth, which her SEM could translate, to Tagrethian, which he'd heard her speak.

She began to catch familiar sound formations as he spoke.

He said them oddly. Claughwyth was a tonal language. Was that what lent such a sensuous curve to his speech?

Her pulse picked up speed.

He closed a fist in the shoulder of her enviro-suit.

Edie started and lifted her gaze to his.

Ire burned in his icy green eyes. His jaw muscles clenched, but the skin over his cheekbones darkened. Blushing?

He spoke again, demanding, angry. "…answer…"

She caught that word and choked back a laugh. "I'm deaf, you Orhait's ass."

He froze. His eyes widened, then flicked back and forth as if he scanned a mental file marked *recent past*. The fight drained out of him. He closed his eyes and let her go, giving her an opening, kilometers wide, to ambush him. Caught by the recrimination pressing lines into the corners of his eyes, she hesitated.

Rubbing his forehead with one hand, the captain opened eyes filled with chagrin. "…sorry…"

"Yeah, yeah," she said. Cue pity for the poor deaf woman. "I should wear a sign. Give me my gear so I can turn on my SEM."

He studied her, his gaze probing. He said

something else.

"You're wasting your breath until I get this turned on," she replied, tapping the frame at her temple.

His gaze flicked to the slender frames supporting ballistic-glass lenses. He didn't extend her handheld. For a second, the shadows under his eyes deepened. He twisted his head one way then the other and winced before straightening.

At least two injured, traumatized Claugh. Edie frowned, her illusions of a quick rescue and quicker getaway flashing off.

He powered up her handheld. She'd packed the thing with customizations. Most of them not legal. His lips puckered in a whistle.

Of course he couldn't return the unit. She wouldn't in his shoes, and no way could she let him keep it.

"Sorry," he said again. He poked around the main screen.

Her SEM lenses lit.

"Better?"

She shot him a wary glance. "I understand what you're saying. Leave it at that."

He grimaced.

Edie resisted the urge to roll her eyes. "You took me hostage. What'd you expect? To win me over with charm and good looks after crashing a dead ship?"

"A guy can hope," he retorted.

He surprised an unwilling laugh from her. She managed to squash it into a snort. Probably not at all attractive. As if she cared.

Her SEM indicated footsteps incoming from behind her. One set steady, a second set that stepped and dragged.

The madman's gaze slid past her. He holstered his gun.

Edie turned.

A young blocky woman with short black curls and a gash on her forehead favored one leg as she dragged a stretcher full of body condensers. Her eyes widened.

"Fuller," she gasped, released the stretcher, burst into tears, and hobbled to embrace the ensign.

The young man, expression slack, climbed to his feet and patted the lieutenant's shoulder with his one good hand.

In the young woman's wake, covered head to toe in gray dust, a tall, wiry woman trudged. Even her short-cropped hair had been turned blue-gray. A bright red burn slashed through the dirt on the left side of her face and neck. She caught sight of Edie. Her weapon came up. The woman's lip curled.

"Status," the captain said.

"One working handheld," the gray woman said. "Twenty-three other survivors. We don't know the extent of their injuries."

"We'll search as we exit," he said. "This is Edie. Edie, Commander Parqe, and Lt. Chavolgen. You've met Ensign Fuller. My name's V'kyrri. Commander? Cover me."

The short-haired uniform rack gave the handheld to the lieutenant and turned her gun on Edie.

"Stand down," Edie said. "I don't have a gun on me."

"Which isn't the same as being unarmed," V'kyrri noted. He holstered his pistol and patted her down.

Edie sneered. "And here I thought we were friends already."

"Stow it," he commanded. He ripped open the seal on one of her thigh pockets. "My wounded don't have time."

"Neither do you. That pocket's the first aid kit," she said. "Take it. Put the regen unit on the lieutenant's leg."

"Fuller," the captain said, snagging and pocketing her supply of stim doses, "requisition Edie's medical supplies. Parqe. Get me locations on those survivors and a plan for extraction. Move, people."

Edie shook her head. "You have four mostly mobile survivors. If you intend to make it off world, you have to move fast."

"And wounded will slow us down," he said. "No one gets left. Alive."

She'd sucked in a breath to argue, but his final word pulled the plug on her protest. She firmed her lips. Beige lines at the corners of his mouth and the haunted light in his eyes stuck a knife of sympathy into her gut and twisted.

Fuller, his expression still dull, crawled to her side. He rummaged for the release tabs on Edie's first aid kit, while her pulse hammered at her. G*et out, get out, get out*.

Edie forced her expression blank. "You have your survivors and a plan. You don't need me. Let me go."

"No." The damned madman didn't bother to look up from his useless extraction plan.

She clenched her teeth. "Then give me my handheld so I can tag speech patterns enough to know who's speaking and when."

Fuller took the first aid kit and went to the dark-haired lieutenant standing on one leg. Parqe joined them.

V'kyrri handed over Edie's unit while Parqe found and downed an analgesic packet from Edie's supplies. The commander's shoulders settled lower. She blotted tears from her eyes with one filthy sleeve that left muddy smears on her face.

Edie added names, including the captain's, and auto-holstered her handheld.

He tugged it free and put it back on his belt without comment. The weight pulling his features lightened, suggesting he wanted her as an ally.

She could play on his wishful thinking. Should. Never mind that she'd kill to have someone she could trust at her back. Especially on this rock.

They were Claugh. They couldn't be that. Not ever.

"Fuller!" Parqe barked. "With me, now."

The ensign jerked upright, terror in his too-wide eyes.

"Belay that," V'kyrri commanded. He laid a hand on his commander's wrist.

Edie's gut twisted.

"It's over," V'kyrri said. The visual readout of his speech pattern broke. "Four crumpled decks between us. We won't get to save these people. We can't get to them."

Fuller buried his face in his hands.

"Our overriding duty is to get at least one of us to the Empire to report," V'kyrri went on, his vocal quality rasping a wide and spiky visual signal on her SEM. "Edie. What are we up against out there?" He tipped his head to indicate outside.

"Killing heat. Atmosphere being sheared away by the dying, expanding star," she said. "Your biggest problem begins and ends with the UMOPG. They're the ones who shot you down."

Parqe sucked in a breath and turned a hope-lit face upon her captain.

"They aren't going to take prisoners, much less treat your injured," Edie said.

The commander scowled at her. "They signed the same treaties we did."

"Right," Edie shot. "That's why you know the name of this world. Because surely, per the treaty you cite, the UMOPG filed all the appropriate claim documents."

The commander sputtered, "We have to try."

V'kyrri rubbed his forehead. The faint lines around his lips reminded Edie they were walking wounded. In shock. And in mourning. She had to jolt them into doing the one thing she couldn't afford to have them doing: Thinking like Claugh soldiers.

She strangled a sense of misgiving. If any of them were going to live through this, she couldn't be the only one thinking rationally. Or ruthlessly.

"This is a UMOPG military operation," Edie said as if her mouth had made a decision her brain hadn't yet been let in on. "The world is crawling with miners hopped up on their own importance."

V'kyrri reared back. "They don't have a military."

Right. End tactical briefing.

"Didn't have," he amended. He studied her with a gaze that peeled her back layer by layer. "Based on a previous mission and a couple of unanswered questions, it makes sense. Even if the UMOPG have militarized, their essential nature remains the same."

"They'll come looking for profit," Parqe said,

resignation in her voice. "We can't be here when they do. If we can't afford to be captured—"

"We have to go on the offensive and avenge our crewmates," V'kyrri concluded. "Or we have to escape."

Edie started. "Go on the offensive?"

"Baxt'k," Parqe whispered.

"Where are they holed up?" he growled. His weight moved forward, and his shoulders hunched like one of the bukkim, fierce, heavy-hooved ungulates from Edie's home world. The flash of white teeth against dark skin as he snarled set her back.

"Revenge?" Edie prodded.

He met her eye, madness and determination glittering in his. As if his madness were contagious, his crew's gazes went flat and hard. If he intended to go after an entire military with three wounded soldiers, those soldiers had his back.

Edie spread her fingers wide. "I am a firm believer in taking the hurt back to its roost, with the application of overwhelming force. You don't have that. You have a traumatized, injured crew whose odds for survival plummet with every minute's delay. You want out of here and a map to the base where you can sow chaos? I've got you. But this ship has to be destroyed."

Along with the wounded you cannot reach, she didn't say aloud.

The commander snarled.

"Edie's right," the captain said. "The *Queen's Rhapsody* can't fall into enemy hands."

"The ship *is* destroyed," his commander argued. "There's nothing left—"

"Automatic locator beacon for your data core going

off," Edie said.

The captain cut her a look that made her clench her fists, but he said, "I lost self-destruct when I jettisoned the core."

"Properly motivated, your trigger charges will blow and burn hot enough to destroy everything," Edie said. "Quick. Clean."

Blanching, all four stared at her.

The captain's eyes narrowed.

Edie stayed very, very still. You didn't imply you could blow up a ship and then make sudden moves.

"A bounty hunter who's a demolitions expert?" V'kyrri surmised.

With a shrug, she glanced around the semi-circle. Hope, pain, and weariness in the kids' faces. Hostility and contempt in Parqe's. That bone-chilling watchful thing V'kyrri did.

She swallowed hard. Twelve Gods. She was considering allying with the enemy. An enemy. One of a growing number. Edie sighed.

"Look. It's a religious thing for me, keeping people out of enemy hands. If it matters to you, I can help."

There went her mouth before her brain. Again.

She had to be insane.

Chapter Four

"Help," V'kyrri echoed. He rubbed a hand down his face. It did nothing to wipe away weariness. "Help would be a flight of Claugh heavy bombers and a medical ship."

Edie's lip curled as her gaze skimmed his uniform. When she met his eye, she shifted back and forth on her feet. "Yeah. If stars were wishes, we'd all breathe vacuum."

Training took over because, Gods knew, he couldn't think past the pain in his head. He set a hand on her forearm and squeezed, anchoring whatever impulse had made her commit to allying. "I have to stop that locator beacon and take out the main data store."

And murder the last of his crew who weren't going to get a chance to escape the ship. He couldn't get his breath.

Offering her handheld, he released her.

She didn't take it.

He pressed the unit to her chest. Her eyes widened. She sucked in an audibly unsteady breath.

"I've given you reason to hate us," he said. "Fine. Take it out on my ship. Just promise you'll make it a clean kill."

Chavolgen's tears transformed to sobs.

Edie's gaze slid to the weeping lieutenant. Her

brows lowered.

"Lieutenant," V'kyrri said. "Perimeter."

Parqe made to hand her sidearm to the younger woman.

V'kyrri lifted a hand. "You'll need that."

The blood drained from the commander's face.

Edie shifted to her pack. His reluctant ally produced a pistol, along with an extra charge. She took them to Chavolgen.

Wiping tears with a filthy uniform sleeve, the sniffling lieutenant smeared gore across her face.

"Accurate to three hundred meters," Edie said, putting the gun in the younger woman's hand. "Safety here. Pressure sensitive trigger. Half pull, single shot. Hard pull, spray plasma. If you exhaust the charge, eject the energy pack here. Slots in nice and easy."

"Yes, ma'am. Thank you, ma'am."

"Edie."

Chavolgen cut a glance at V'kyrri.

He lifted a brow.

She looked away. "I'd be demoted, ma'am."

Even in this ship of horrors, the two women were able to smile. V'kyrri turned away.

"Good cover out there. Use it." Edie tapped the Sensory Enhancement Module she wore. "You shoot, I'll know."

Jaw bunching, his lieutenant limped out the aft door.

Edie met his eye. The muscles of her face tightened, pulling her expression flat.

"Go," he said to Parqe.

Fists clenching and unclenching, the commander nodded. "Fuller. Let's go, son."

Hope shining from him, the ensign scrambled to his feet.

V'kyrri looked away from the burn of it and caught Edie blinking swiftly. She averted her gaze and pressed her lips taut.

Ice trailed his gut. He couldn't warn Fuller's hope away. Nothing he could say would prepare the younger man for the weight about to crush him with the fact that he and Parqe were likely going to have to execute wounded shipmates who couldn't be saved.

V'kyrri shifted.

Edie shook her head and activated the exit seam of her enviro-suit.

"You're going to need that," he said.

"I need mobility more. If we run out of time, the enviro-suit won't stop UMOPG laser fire, anyway." She peeled out of the bulky suit. Sweat stains darkened her brown fatigues, but the elaborate, loaded tool belt around her waist caught and held his attention.

It was something to focus on. Something besides death and pain.

She registered, then followed, the line of his stare.

"Twelve Gods, Edie," he said. "I have tool belt envy."

"I bet you say that to all the women you hold at gun point."

The snide rejoinder surprised a laugh from him.

She smiled, her brown eyes alight.

The air went out of his lungs.

Edie tore her gaze away from his, wadded up the enviro-suit, secured it to the outside of her pack, and fished the interior. She brought forth a cluster of explosives.

Every mote of humor drained from him.

"Unarmed," she said. False cheer colored her words. "Never know when you might need to force entry somewhere. Or exit."

Or when it might be necessary to coax a mortally-wounded Claugh battle cruiser to self-destruct.

Edie hooked the bombs to her belt. She fastened a climbing harness over the top.

"Okay," she said.

"This'll be clean," he said, turning away before she could respond, not wanting to face her answer or the weight of the lives he couldn't save. Hands shaking, he led the way deeper into the ship.

"Self-destruct triggers are vastly overpowered," she said, treading on his heels.

Her statement sounded final as if she'd settled the matter. Then the sharp edge went out of her tone as she added, "Used to think it was dumb. But it's so you can assure the destruction of your data and your weapons, even if an enemy isolates your reactor core. Anyone still alive in here will die instantly. They might hear the initial kicker charges fire, but it'll be the last thing. I swear."

V'kyrri marked the speech as the longest she'd volunteered thus far. What was behind that? Compassion? Pity? He snuck a glance. Her face steadily leaked color. It couldn't matter. Not while he plotted to destroy his crew.

The farther into the ship he directed her, the grayer his brain became, as if the destruction visited upon the vessel was being taken in toll from him.

Edie and he spilled out into what had once been the bridge. It hadn't decompressed. The stench of death pummeled him. Foul, stinking humidity made the air nearly impossible to suck down. The reek assailed him. Blood, intestinal contents, and the oily, clinging scent of terror cooked off in the heat.

He swallowed hard to keep his gorge where it belonged. He glanced at his prisoner-turned-ally.

Sweat beaded her pallid face. She pressed her lips into a grim, white line.

V'kyrri blew out a shallow breath. He had no business bringing her into this kind of horror. He swore that memory showed in the crinkles around her eyes.

He'd give anything to scan her, to find out which military she'd served. Until he could, he gambled their lives on a woman he'd nearly strangled, and who he'd coerced, mostly at gun point, into lending an unwilling hand.

Edie studied his command chair where the bridge trigger charge lived. She coiled a climbing line for a throw.

"Give me the handheld," he said. "I'll take you up."

"I got it."

"No." He plucked the handheld from her belt. "*I've* got you. My ship. My crew. You're part of my team, now. You need your hands for tools."

Expression tight, Edie clipped a charge to her belt.

"Then you'll have no issue holding these for me." Her syrupy-sweet smile did not reach her eyes. She handed him her other explosives.

He hesitated.

Edie grinned.

V'kyrri stiffened his spine.

Fear, so subtle and so swift he couldn't be sure he

hadn't imagined it, flashed through the brief widening of her eyes. Then her expression shuttered. "They're not armed."

"Fine."

Her brows lowered at his clipped response.

V'k rolled his neck to break up tension. He needed her cooperating, not plotting his demise. "Sorry. Bad day."

"Yeah." Her gaze swept the slaughter-house his command deck had become. "Hard to know friends from enemies when everyone is shooting at you."

Edie flung her climbing line for the base of his chair.

Missed.

"Is that what you are?" he pressed. "A friend?"

"Nope," she said, coiling the line for another try.

Her anchor caught.

V'kyrri hefted the handheld and opened the anchor. Instinct spoke before he'd consciously examined the words. "You aren't an enemy. What are you then?"

"The lesser of a great many evils." She set her weight against the line. The anchor held.

"Meaning that's what we are."

She glanced at him. Whatever Edie saw in his face struck her like a pebble plunked in a pool. She jerked her gaze away. "Ready."

He took her up, stopping the ascender before he brained his hope of survival against the jagged, broken arm of his chair.

She palmed tools, her motion competent and swift.

"Who do you call your friends, then?" He forced his question into an easy, casual arc keeping time with her movements. Matching and encouraging her focus so interrogation slid right under her defenses.

"Don't have any."

He shifted his shoulders lower and mirrored her light, tossed-off tone. Hers was forced. His couldn't be. "Liar. You're using a Skeppanda silk line. No one buys Skeppanda silk line."

"No, they don't," she said.

"They awarded it to you," he said.

"That's right. All you need to know is that the UMOPG and the Chekydran aren't on my friend's list." She wrenched open a panel.

He allowed himself a moment's satisfaction. She'd lost that round and recognized it. If they weren't wiring his ship to blow, and if he could get the razors in his brain to let up, interrogating Edie could be fun.

She freed the emergency medical kit. "Catch."

Good. More stim shots and another regen unit. V'kyrri caught the kit and studied his captive bounty hunter. Pressure mounted inside his skin. He'd seen Edie somewhere before. Frustrated recognition twisted him, stretching, reaching for the connection that would complete the circuit and tell him where he'd seen her before.

She juggled a charge and tools all while dangling from a line made of silk that couldn't be bought.

V'kyrri frowned. It hurt less. Edie's practiced ease belied the *bounty hunter* title she'd awarded herself, even one who specialized in explosives.

"Done," she said. "Bring me down."

He lifted an eyebrow and winced. "Awfully fast work."

"Not if you don't get me down."

He punched the button on her handheld with more

force than necessary.

Her boots clunked on the hull.

He released the anchor.

Edie tugged, then caught it. “I don’t have to tie into your self-destruct charges. Can’t anyway…”

“No power,” he finished for her. Suspicion eased. “Of course.”

She shouldered her pack and held out a hand for her handheld. “Next.”

He studied her.

Her expression remained placid. Flat.

He’d asked for her help. She’d given it. However reluctantly. Trust, or the appearance of it, had to start somewhere. He put the unit in her hand, trying not to notice that she’d given him the charges and taken possession of the device that would arm and detonate them.

She put an anti-grav unit in his hand. “Might find a use for that.”

If he had more survivors than stretchers. Or more survivors trapped in compartments like Fuller had been. His mercenary was an optimist. “Good thinking.”

Edie scrambled up the ladder of shattered stations, V’kyrri on her heels.

She strode aft. His bounty hunter knew the layout of his prototype. V’kyrri narrowed his eyes and stared at the back of her head. He needed in there. Both to work out his sense of recognition and to assess the threat she represented. A tiny slip of thought—slide it right through the cracks.

Agony slapped him back into the confines of his creaking skull. Nausea sloshed. He heeded the warning and forced himself to relax. The hard way, then. “You seem to already know where my destruct trigger is. Who are you that—"

"Why the interrogation?" Her gaze darted back and forth, processing whatever data her SEM fed her. "I said I'd help. You ensured it at gun point. Sorry if I don't think it entitles you to my life story."

"You have to trust someone sometime, Edie."

"It's just not your day, is it?"

He should have shot her.

They reached the bulkhead.

With the heel of her boot, she punched open an access panel. She crawled headfirst into a crumpled maintenance tunnel and stuck out a hand. "Charge."

V'kyrri set an explosive in her palm. He relaxed against the hull. It would be an all-too-brief respite from maintaining command presence for his crew. And for Edie. Especially for Edie.

But he couldn't forget that she was wiring his ship to kill the precious few of his crew who'd survived the firefight and then the crash. He'd been through a similar situation once before. He shouldn't be surprised by this outcome. Shouldn't have to fight down the searing heat behind his breastbone.

Dying would have been so much easier.

A *thunk*. Edie wriggled backward.

He grabbed hold of her ankles and pulled.

When she cleared the tunnel, her expression twisted. She tugged out of his grip. "Hands off. I work alone."

"Not today, you don't. Move out."

She climbed to her feet, slapped another anti-grav into his hand, and jogged out of the main corridor.

"Intcom or Armada?" he demanded.

Her brows drew together. She slid her gaze sideways. Evading, or trying to.

"Edie—"

"Don't 'Edie' me," she flared. "Or make the mistake of thinking it's my name."

"Isn't it?"

"Initials." She stalked to the first of three redundant trigger charges for data storage.

"For?"

"Explosive Device."

"A beautiful and resourceful one at that."

Edie met his gaze, eyes wide. Then she glowered. "Beautiful? How would you even know? I have muddy brown eyes and hair red enough to make me look like a building on fire. Spare me the charm. If you're going turn a weapon on me, make it one I can steal and use against you."

She scooped up the charge he offered.

"My culture has a legend regarding a fire-haired goddess protecting us. As far as I know, I'm dead and in heaven. You are the answer to a prayer I never got to say."

She snorted. "Give me any more grief, Captain, any at all, and I'll turn heaven into the lowest level of Hell."

"I'm counting on it."

Chapter Five

Flustered, and hating both the smirk on his lips and the fact that the mad Claugh had her wits momentarily scattered, Edie took refuge in ire. She slapped her charge against the first data store trigger charge, then spun and stepped over an obscene-smelling wet patch on the hull, heading for the next trigger.

"Intcom or Armada?" the flattened audio wave of V'kyrri's tone on visual suggested he wouldn't ask again.

A shiver struck her. Even in the stifling heat. Edie put out a hand for another charge. It shook. *Don't make a Claugh ask a third time*. "Intcom."

"I hesitate to ask how they got the layout of my boat, much less what they meant to do with it."

She sagged. She'd given the right answer. Lucky her. "That was above my paygrade."

Wriggling headfirst into a spot where bed rock poked through the shredded fabric of the vessel, she registered a low-level audio signal on her data feed. A survivor.

Edie pulled herself hand over hand. A meter in, stone had ripped a gaping hole in the alloy.

The audio signal spiked.

She peered into the hole.

Dusty fingers of light brushed a man's bloody face. He moaned.

Edie started. Gasped. She made to pitch herself into the hole, then hauled up short. The ship had him pinned, crushing his legs and at least one hip between wreckage and planet.

Her heart slid sideways in her chest. She placed her charge, hands shaking again. Stupid, because it couldn't matter, but she made certain to put it where the doomed man wouldn't see it.

"Help," he groaned. "Please, help me."

Edie's breath caught. Only one way to help, but to this point in her life, killing Claugh had meant people who were on their feet, hunting and hurting her people. Not this begging mortally-wounded husk.

With infinite time and a laser cutter, she could get him out. Even then, without a fully staffed medi-bay and stasis, nothing would save him.

She could only offer the mercy of a faster passing than this miserable rock had planned. Which meant getting out of the tunnel to fetch a weapon.

"Hold on," she said. "I'm getting help."

A momentary hitch in the moans. He was conscious enough to register what she'd said. Eyes stinging, Edie wriggled backward. She had no clue what showed on her face to make V'kyrri rock on his heels when she emerged.

"Survivor," she gasped. "Pinned. Lower body crushed."

Muscles in his jaw working, he drew his gun and ventured into the tunnel.

Edie tensed against the instinct to escape. She couldn't get her breath. Gritty, heavy air caught in her throat. Sweat stood out on her face doing nothing to cool the heat in her eyes. She squeezed them shut.

Long-dead friends paraded across the insides of her eyelids. Limbs missing. Bodies torn and seeping. Faces gone. The contents of their open skulls spilling. Bubbled, blackened flesh. Fire. Always fire. Clenching her fists, and opening her eyes, Edie swallowed rising bile.

Over the steady stream of moans, her SEM shoved shards of V'kyrri's murmur into her nerve fibers where she did not want him.

He fired a single shot. The SEM rendered it an icy-hot nail that scorched deep into her brain. Edie broke on a single sob. Too late, she ripped the lenses from her face.

No. No crying. Unconscionable waste of water.

Blotting her face with one sleeve, she grappled for control by counting. Miseries. The number of missions she'd run for Intcom. Anything for emotional distraction. She didn't want the Claugh seeing her…

Pressure against her wrist. The familiar pinch and squirt of cooling hydration flowed through her body. Her knees gave. She slid down the wall, eyes still shut. She did not want to see his face, read his trauma, nor let him into her haunted past.

He took hold of the SEM lenses in her grip. Tugged.

She declined to give them to him. *Get it together, Edie.* She forced her head up and slid the glasses into place.

He spoke.

Couldn't read it because she hadn't gathered the courage to look. She was getting too old for this. She opened eyes rubbed raw by the sandpaper of her eyelids.

He crouched before her. Deep canyons of grief carved the corners of his eyes. Concern creased his forehead.

That smote her conscience. He'd been forced to destroy his crewman, and here she was falling apart.

No useless questions about either of them being okay. She levered to standing.

Last trigger. She held out a hand.

He holstered his gun like he never wanted to see it again, pulled the charge from his belt, and gave it to her.

While V'kyrri leaned against her legs, providing counterbalance, Edie dangled head down in a chamber filled with more stinking remains.

She tossed the charge against the wall hiding the destruct trigger. "Done."

He hauled her free.

Weight—the entire weight of his destroyed starship and doomed crew—settled on V'kyrri's chest. One step closer to vaporizing the bloody bones of his first and last command.

Memory chose that moment. It unfurled an image of a younger Edie. Different hair color, but the shape of her eyes and the full, sensuous lips were unmistakable. So was the mix of rage and challenge firing her gaze as she glared at him from a decade old Claugh Most Wanted notice.

She hadn't been called Edie, then.

Ice gripped his breath.

"Firestorm."

She drew up short. Her spine straightened a vertebra at a time, as if shedding the mantle of weariness and heat exhaustion. She pivoted, her face smooth, serene. Behind her SEM, her eyes were alight.

"I should shoot you," he snapped, gun already in his hand. "The empire and my survivors would be safer."

"Probably," she allowed. "With the swarms of UMOPG on the planet, one shot more or less won't make a difference."

A snarl he couldn't control twisted pain straight through his misused soul. The breath he hissed tangled in his clenched teeth. "You murdered *thousands* of Claugh soldiers."

After the war, she'd turned on her own people. Heat and futility swarmed his chest. He'd been relieved to have an ally. Someone to trust.

"Why?" he threw out. "Why rescue us at all?"

She lifted one shoulder. "I wasn't. I was salvaging."

"You could have wired the ship to blow with us in it."

"Waste of resources. All I had to do was let the planet and the miners have you," she said. "Which is still an option if we stand around long enough."

"A common enemy. That's your story?"

She flung her hands wide. "What is your problem? You're still breathing. With a little luck, you might keep it that way. The choice you have to make isn't simple, but it is binary. You want this ship and your trapped survivors destroyed, or you don't. If I could get your people out, I would. These children you call crew hadn't been thought of when you people were destroying my world. They don't deserve this."

"But I do? Your world is thriving," he snapped.

" 'Thriving?' Kind of like how I'm 'helping' you?

Wearing deep bruises on my throat and right kidney? Or is the heel of the Imperial boot a much larger and more oppressive chokehold when an entire world is being coerced?"

Nose wrinkled and gaze turned inward, she waved away a reply. "Skip it. People are in agony. We're wasting time. Kill me or let me do my job."

He snatched her handheld from her grasp and shoved her by the shoulder. "Get out there."

They bolted out the aft door into the midst of V'kyrri's wounded.

"All survivors we could access accounted for," Parqe said, her tone dead. She wouldn't meet his eye, but she could and did point her weapon at Edie.

Eight stretchers. One of them held body condensers containing the last mortal remains of the few bodies they'd been able to recover.

Chavolgen sprawled in limp abandon against a stone the same wan color as her face. Gaze unfocused, she stared at nothing. Slow tears tracked the dust and gore crusted on her face.

Fuller had folded in on himself, shoulders trembling.

Rubbing his forehead, V'kyrri slumped. *So few surivors.* Sixteen, no, fifteen after he'd killed Lieutenant Striltor. Fifteen they couldn't reach to put out of their misery.

Firestorm, his semi-captive Claugh killer, made sixteen, but he hesitated to count her among their number. Ironic. His commanders would reward him handsomely for apprehending her. Yet he couldn't arrest her. He needed her to do what she did best—destroy Claugh.

He blew out a shallow breath. What did it mean that Nol Jakze's most notorious resistance fighter surfaced here and hadn't walked away to let a bunch of Claugh die? It was too much to hope she'd developed a soft spot for khaki uniforms since she'd escaped after the war and created a new identity. One that didn't murder Claugh soldiers out of hand.

He pressed fingers to his temples. The bones creaked. He glanced at Fuller and Chavolgen. They'd know the name Firestorm from stories. Only he and Parqe were old enough to have been on Nol Jakze.

Parqe's weapon trembled in her grime coated hand.

He shook his head. He had to keep Edie's secret. For now. He needed her. His doomed crew needed her. No one else needed to know who she'd been.

"You have a ship, E.D. for Explosive Device. Far away and well hidden. How many can we evacuate?"

She eyed him, hands at shoulder height, lips twisted as if she tasted something sour. That's right. Parqe had a gun on her. He declined to change the situation. Yet.

"Ship," he prodded.

"*t'Achreides-myn.* It's a one-and-a-half man," she said. "Useless."

Hope of swift rescue crashed and burned. His temples throbbed. He met Edie's gaze. Whatever she saw in his face, the stark lines around her mouth eased. Her gaze slid past him to the anti-grav stretchers hovering above the dust. She flipped up her ballistic alloy lenses and rubbed her eyes.

Repositioning her lenses, she marched past him. She rounded a stretcher and crouched. The blood ran out of her face—her lips went white.

He surveyed the burn victim on the stretcher. An Isarrite band locked his ribs. He'd seen an injury like it before when he'd been aboard a Claugh recon vessel that had run afoul of the Chekydran. Eight of the twelve crew had died. Just not right away. His boss had worn the same death's head look Edie did.

More dying to come.

Edie blotted perspiration from her upper lip. She stared at what remained of the badly burned woman on the stretcher before her. The scent of burning flesh hit like a fist. Nausea surged. Vision blanked.

Her parents' skin reddened, then bubbled, the subcutaneous fat sizzling as it rendered. Skin blackened and curled. Muscle fibers cooked. Her parents screamed. Begged. But she couldn't hear them. She never had. Not even in her dreams.

Gasping, Edie wrenched free of memory. Yellow dust registered. Brown rocks shot through with blue. Data dripping down her SEM lenses. The rainbow sheen of heat-stressed alloy in starship bulkheads. Khaki Claugh uniforms. Parqe's gun.

She shuddered. No more memory.

One. Two. Three. Focus, Edie. Four. Five. Breathe. Six. Seven. Eight stretchers. Seven survivors. Eight stretchers. Five of us.

The woman moaned a ragged audio wave.

Edie's stomach lurched. "Hydration. Pain killers." She clenched quaking fists and met V'kyrri's eye.

He paled. "One dose. Enough to keep her comfortable."

"Aye, Captain." Chavolgen's voice cracked.

Edie took the dosing units from Chavolgen and administered the drugs to the burn victim. "Rest. This will help. Rest now."

The gut-wrenching audio feed faded. The woman stilled.

Edie struggled to breathe past loathing. When she lifted her gaze, it stopped at the mad captain's insignia. Claugh. Always the Claugh. Her eyes burned. Twelve Gods, she hated them, all of them, for putting her in the position to have to remember.

She dumped her pack, sank to the ground, and yanked every hydration dose from the pockets of her environmental suit. No help for it. Not if she wanted to live through the next several hours. She tucked them into the empty thigh pocket of her trousers, then rose and dodged stretchers to get to Chavolgen's side.

The lieutenant glanced up, her face pasty, and eyes dull.

Edie popped a dose into her.

The young woman's respiration eased. She straightened. "Wow. Thanks."

"Save those," Parqe said. Her tone lacked bite. She'd put her weapon away at some point.

Edie gave Fuller a shot.

He groaned into his hands. "I don't want to feel better."

"You aren't living for you anymore," Edie said. "Hard to hear. I'm sorry. All you can do now is survive so you can carry your friends' stories to their loved ones."

The words had been said to her once. She'd been seventeen.

Fuller's red-rimmed, brown eyes met her gaze. The haze of pain didn't clear, but he became more present, as if he'd returned from a great distance.

Edie turned to Parqe. “It’s the water in your body that matters. The injured can’t have you passing out.”

Parqe stiffened, took the medical unit, and dosed herself.

One of the wounded moaned.

Edie clenched her fists. She glared at V’kyrri. “I need a word.” She stalked around the side of the wreck. Her nerves pinged.

V’kyrri.

And Parqe.

The captain pressed his lips into a challenging line.

“You’re in enemy territory with limited resources and no sure means of rescue,” Edie said.

“Make your point,” he countered.

She swallowed a snarl. “Terminal sedation for the two wounded who can’t survive this.”

Parqe had her gun pointed at Edie’s chest again. “That’s murder. These people are helpless.”

“Did you not have to execute people trapped in that wreck?” Edie snapped.

“They were trapped. There was no hope. These people are free. You want them dead because they’re Claugh. It’s obvious you hate us. You’re a monster.”

Ice trickled into Edie’s veins. It had been eight years or more since she’d had the accusation leveled at her. No matter that it felt right, like the natural progression of everything Edie touched, it still cut.

V’kyrri paled. He blew out a slow breath. The muscles in his jaw flexed.

“Did you think this got easier after going down with your ship?” Edie prodded. “Dying is easy. Staying alive on this broiling pile of rock is long odds.”

V’kyrri put a hand on Parqe’s wrist.

Edie didn't stand down. She'd broached a taboo subject with a bunch of strangers from a culture she didn't—and never wanted to—understand.

"Stop," V'kyrri ordered. "Evaluate. We're walking wounded. We have no food. Minimal water."

Relief blew through Edie. He'd worked it out, had maybe thought of it before she'd broached it. Only, he'd missed her main takeaway.

"There's not enough pain medication to keep the injured who do have a chance comfortable," Edie said.

"And quiet?" he snapped, his expression rigid, angry, but not directed at her. He had thought of it, then, and hated it as much as she did.

Edie dipped her chin.

"You don't know anyone will die," Parqe protested.

"No one survives burns like that."

"It isn't your call," Parqe insisted.

"No. It isn't."

V'kyrri glanced from his second to Edie. His sea green gaze lingered on her face, turning over memories.

Edie broke eye contact. Mistakes she'd made long ago screamed along her nerves with the voices of dead friends. It took her breath.

"You've had to make this choice," he said as if he'd picked the voices out of her head.

"Once." It emerged a broken fragment of a word. She cleared her throat. "Made the wrong one."

"You killed them," he said.

She shook her head. "Should have. By the time they begged to die, I no longer had the means. They died alone. In such pain they couldn't even scream anymore."

His expression went wan and smooth. “You had to abandon them to save the rest.”

She didn’t bother answering.

He shook his head. “These people are my responsibility. Not when it’s convenient. Not when it’s easy.”

Edie clenched her fists. “Unto death. I get it.”

“Hydration and half doses of pain medication. It’ll buy us time.”

Edie snorted. Half doses of medication weren’t going to cut it when the man with the gaping belly wound woke screaming over his spilled intestines. She stomped around the corner of the ship.

Chavolgen and Fuller recoiled.

Edie couldn’t care. Caring would crack her open if she let it. Instead, she retrieved dosing units.

Because she was a coward, she began with a young man, bandaged. Leg missing. Hands and arms mangled. Hydration therapy, half dose of pain meds. Second stretcher. Older male. Gaping gut wound. Horrifying stench seeping through the stained bandages. Unconscious. Small mercy. Hydration, half dose of pain meds.

Stasis and a full medi-center might save him if he got there in time, time she couldn’t possibly buy him.

“Gods ease your way,” she murmured.

Third stretcher. Female. Head injury. Broken bones. Possible internal injuries. She’d been the one moaning.

As Edie finished dosing the woman on the stretcher, Parqe and the Claugh captain rounded the corner. Parqe came at her, snarling, face mottled.

Edie’s temper blew. She slipped a hand into a

pocket and palmed a soft, damp ball. She flicked a fingernail against a device hidden in the wrist cuff of her shirt. It generated a spark, which lit the accelerant-soaked fabric in her hand…ah. Heat.

Edie tossed the palm-sized ball of blue flame at Parqe's chest.

Chavolgen and Fuller yelped.

A fizz of nerves warned her a split second before V'kyrri yanked her against his chest from behind. He clamped her arms at her sides.

Her fireball arced to the dust, flickered and died.

"She's killing them," Parqe accused.

V'kyrri shifted his grip, spun her to face him, and then shoved her against stone. He followed, pinning her body with his.

"Oof." Chemicals dumped into her bloodstream. Adrenaline. Hormones. Edie's heart tripped to staccato.

"What the Three Hells was that?" he demanded.

"A child's trick," she snapped, burning everywhere he touched her. "Get off. I'll show you."

"My injured?"

"Hydration. Half pain. You made the call. Your responsibility. Your guilt when they start screaming. And now, your problem. I am done."

Metal hit her wrist. *Click.*

Neural cuff. Edie drew breath between clenched teeth.

"You aren't going anywhere."

She growled and shoved. His weight didn't shift. "If you're determined for me to die on this rock with you, just shoot me. You'll save me a lot of pain and suffering."

"You're no use to me dead," he said. "Without

you, my trapped and wounded don't stand a chance. You'll help them, whether you want to or not. You aren't the only deadly one here."

She stilled, breath trembling. "You're Claugh. Of course you're deadly. Too many fringe worlds know that. If you meant to shoot me, you'd have done it already. Pick another threat."

His gaze went to her mouth.

She started and registered the uneven clip of his respiration rate flashing on her SEM. Heat dumped straight through her core.

The self-satisfied quirk of his lips, combined with Parqe's gaze filled with expectation centered on him, shot misgiving through Edie. They had another threat. She just didn't know what it was, only that their secret left the pair supremely confident.

Edie sagged.

Plucking the dosing unit from her fingers, V'kyrri eased away from her.

Neural cuffs dangling from her left wrist, she slid sideways along the canyon wall, away from Parqe, who'd turned her back to check the people Edie had already dosed, and away from her pack and everything she needed to survive on this rock.

After examining the dosing equipment, V'kyrri gave the injector to Parqe.

"Where'd you leave off?" he asked without looking around.

"Here, sir," Chavolgen said. "Tamiya next."

Edie slid another meter, watching the signs in her brain flashing *disengage! Disengage!*

"Ma'am?" Fuller murmured. "Please don't go."

Edie stared at him. Dark smudges shadowed his

eyes. Creases marred his young face, aging him. His plea translated through her SEM into a boulder lodged in her windpipe.

Pressing a fist against the ache behind her sternum, Edie folded until her butt hit the rock flour.

Edie had once been this young man. Lost. Hurting. Not caring whether she lived or died. An emergency medic had helped her all those years ago. Until the Claugh had captured the woman and murdered her by stacking weapons crates upon her until they'd crushed her. They'd taken bets, laughing while she'd died.

Edie had brought their barracks—the enormous building that had once been her world's largest university—down on their heads.

It had not been a clean kill. On purpose. They'd been so fond of suffocating someone, Edie had been only too happy to serve the experience up to them.

That job still stood as her highest kill count. And the first time someone had said the word *monster* in reference to her.

She hadn't thought of it in years.

Or of the kind-eyed medic who'd found her wandering the streets, bloody, burned, and half-delirious after her parents' deaths.

Now that she had, she couldn't betray the charge the woman had given her. "Someday, you'll help someone else like I helped you. That will be the only payment I'll need."

Had Fuller remained silent while she'd slipped away, Edie could have ignored the memory.

"I can't help them or me," Fuller said. "Not without you."

"Who's going to help me?" she whispered.

Prickles walked her nerves.

V'kyrri crouched beside her. "Are you all right?"

"What about this situation seems all right to you?"

Battered by the emotion surging in Edie's voice, V'kyrri's mental control fractured. He staggered. Agony, the sum of his physical and mental injuries, pierced him. He doubled over.

"Captain." Parqe. She closed a hand around his upper arm. Contact gave her fear a direct path into his injured nervous system.

He groaned.

Parqe snatched her hand away. Her voice trembled. "Sir? Pain meds?"

Edie rose. Came closer. Every step nearer she came, she trod the soil of him. Awareness of her burned into his soul. His mother's voice whispered inside his memory. *She brings salvation or destruction in her hands. Often both at once. She will deliver us if we let her.*

"Shoot me or get out of the way," Edie snapped.

Were goddesses supposed to sound aggrieved?

She pressed a dosing unit against the bare skin of his forearm.

"What are you…" Parqe shrilled.

A pinch startled him. Cool spread from that momentary sting. His vision cleared. Pain receded. His knees buckled. V'kyrri landed in the dust.

"Hydration," he said, his voice a thread-bare whisper. He eased one hand into his pocket and shot a stim dose through the fabric into his thigh and closed his eyes waiting for the energizing fire. "Helping."

Parqe snorted. "Help from one of her *kind*?"

Alarm jerked his eyes open and his head up to stare

at her. "As you were, Commander."

Edie spun on her heel, eyes narrowed behind the ballistic glass of her SEM. "No, no," she said, a volatile potion of rage roiling beneath her deceptively amiable tone. "What *kind* is that specifically? I'd like to know."

"A SEM addict," Parqe spat.

V'kyrri glanced at Edie.

Surprise sat in her wide eyes and in her mouth, caught open as if ready to respond. The corners twitched in an aborted smile. "You got me on that one."

Staggering to his feet, he drew deliberate breaths. With his hands braced on his thighs, he forced his pulse to slow. The aches in his body receded. He canted his head to keep an eye on his reluctant-rescuer/alleged-SEM-addict.

A glint of spite in Edie's eyes suggested there was more to the SEM story than she let on.

"We've got nothing on you." V'kyrri straightened. He wiped sweat from his forehead. He should have shot her. "I have to get these people off this rock. Despite my commander's animosity, Edie, I recognize I can't do it without you."

Her amusement drained. "Then let's get out of here."

She stalked to the nearest pair of stretchers and pulled a pair of clips from her tool belt. Edie secured the stretchers to her harness, one before her, one behind, and started walking.

He and Parqe hooked stretchers to their slack-featured junior officers. His exec shot him a look. He lifted a shoulder and let it fall. They'd been through something none of them should have survived. They needed medical facilities, counselors, and their families.

Things he could only provide if he got them off this rock.

He caught up to Edie. His people strung out behind him.

"What are our options?" he asked Edie between gulps for breath.

"The caves. Cooler." She waggled a hand. "Crawling with UMOPG."

"What's the bad news?"

A snide twist of her lips crinkled the corners of her eyes. "It's a damned labyrinth, and I don't have a map. It's not all bad. We'll get to pick off miners and steal their stuff."

She paused and looked back, face tilted upward. Light glinted on her SEM lenses, obscuring the line of her gaze.

Frowning, V'kyrri stopped. His crew shuffled to a halt and looked back.

"The rock face?" Chavolgen essayed.

"See the color shift?" Edie pointed.

"Old seafloor folded by metamorphic rock," Chavolgen said. Her voice caught and tears began tracking her filthy cheeks once more.

V'kyrri's nerves bumped. "Translate."

"When the ship blows, the pale part of the cliff will come down," Edie said.

He slumped as if the mass of crust had landed on his shoulders. His mercenary had planned for everything.

Chavolgen turned away, sniffling. Nothing he could say would make it better.

From the way she hunched her shoulders and shoved her hands into her pockets, Edie couldn't think of anything to say, either.

They trudged to the subdued groans from the wounded and the sound of Chavolgen trying and failing to stifle her weeping. The noise seemed to take the starch out of his captive revolutionary. Her shoulders hunched.

V'kyrri glanced at Edie. "How do I get them off world?"

She slanted a wary look at him. "There's no way to get everyone in my one-man. Life support isn't rated even on emergency rationing to handle this many people."

"But?" He prompted.

Every time the Claugh madman looked at her—really looked at her the way he was now—Edie's head buzzed. She shook the irritation away. Evac. She needed to coordinate an evac.

"*t'Achreides-myn* is all I have. Only option I see is to hole up until sunset. Anyone who survives the climb gets triaged. Pack the three most likely to live into my boat with one able body and straight shot them out of here."

"Ensuring that every single one of them dies when these Carozziel slime-bats shoot down your POS," Parqe snapped. "Not to mention that the rest of us get left behind to die."

"By all means, Commander. If my ship won't do," Edie said, flinging her retort and her hands in a snide arc, "why don't we just go find one that will?"

"One that…" V'kyrri echoed before breaking off. He blew out a breath noisy enough to register as data on her SEM. "You're suggesting stealing a ship?"

"Why not? My ship can't handle the job," she said,

warming to the charge of having disconcerted the enemy and to the ship theft idea in general. "One of theirs would solve a bunch of problems."

He stared at her. His color rose. His pain-dulled eyes brightened. "You're going to walk into a secret, militarized UMOPG base that wants us dead."

"You wanted revenge."

"Something you know a lot about. How many of us could your ship take before the engines fail?"

"Five. If you rip out everything but engines and life support."

He scowled.

"I'm not happy about it, either."

"That's not even half of us," Parqe protested.

"So I steal a ship." Edie rubbed the heel of her hand up her forehead. With every instinct screaming against it, she'd committed herself to a long-term campaign with these people. She'd started to lose track of who was supposed to be insane. "Some of your wounded aren't going to survive the night. Some won't survive tomorrow. Your hard choices aren't over."

Parqe drew herself up, chest expanding as if she meant to explode.

"Enough," V'kyrri growled. "We're leaving crewmates to die because we have no hope of getting them out. Have some damned respect."

Edie huffed out a breath and pushed the pace. She couldn't outrun recrimination. Galling, having to admit a Claugh officer was right. Sweat stung her eyes. Her chest ached. She didn't need the SEM telling her V'kyrri kept pace beside her. The goose bumps prickling her skin did the trick.

She didn't know where the odd awareness of him

came from. In another time and place, she'd care that she seemed to be hooked in a strange way to a Claugh officer. Right now, neither of them had the luxury of giving a damn about anything but staying alive.

Chapter Six

"Up there." Edie pointed at a ledge a meter up. Her pulse pounded in her head. Misery hung from her limbs.

Theirs, too, if their stooped-shouldered, slack, and swaying postures were any evidence.

"Up," V'kyrri ordered. He helped Parqe unhook her wounded. The commander scrambled up the rock face while V'kyrri released the stretchers he carried. He passed his pair to Parqe, then her survivors, then Fuller's, Chavolgen's and finally, Edie's.

He urged his crew ahead of him before scrambling to join them.

As Parqe and Chavolgen grabbed V'kyrri's arms and pulled him to the ledge, Edie climbed.

Struggling to fill burning lungs, she focused on the stone to avoid seeing an offered hand she wouldn't take. She couldn't bring herself to build trust. Not with Claugh. First chance she got, she'd bail. The longer they clung to her, the closer to dead she came.

She flopped belly first to the ledge. Her quivering, heat-exhausted muscles refused her effort to stand.

V'kyrri hooked a hand beneath her arm.

A jolt of awareness shocked her. She squeaked.

He assisted her to her feet, pulled at her thigh pocket, and dug a hand in it. The muscle jumped at the spark communicating through the fabric.

He pressed something to her forearm.

Medical dosing unit, her sluggish brain supplied. Hydration hit her system. Edie sagged.

He caught her.

Her aching chest eased. Respiration slowed. Her nerves arced, firing sparks into the gaping dark place where her heart should have been. Fluid warmth settled low in her belly.

Gasping, Edie jerked upright, out of his grasp.

Business. Time to blow up a Claugh asset. *That* was worth getting het up over.

She activated her handheld and glanced around. She'd led them to a cleft in the canyon wall that accessed the deeper caverns honeycombing the world. Her eyes couldn't penetrate the darkness inside. Daylight didn't filter much farther into the tunnel than where they'd gathered.

Fuller and Chavolgen had collapsed in heaps against the rock in the shade, heads tipped back, eyes closed. Parqe had arranged stretchers in the deep, marginally cooler shadow, and stood at their feet.

V'kyrri lingered on the shadow side of the knife-edge of sunshine. His respiration rate remained fast. Sharp.

"You're breathing too fast," Edie said. "Wasting water."

He whispered a curse that the SEM couldn't translate. He took a breath and held it. His respiration rate fell to zero for several long seconds.

On the SEM, his pulse climbed, then eased.

He exhaled a slow, steady stream, and then settled into a breathing pattern approaching normal.

Edie bent over her handheld, fingers flying.

V'kyrri's hands closed around hers.

She stilled and met his gaze. He pinned her with a look like he saw all the way to her stained soul. Old sorrow opened within her. *Oh, all Three Hells, no*. She shifted sadness straight to rage.

V'kyrri's eyes narrowed, and his chest heaved like a drowning man gasping for air. He swayed, eyes hazing.

"You want off this world?" she snapped, plucking her handheld from his fingers. "Let me do my job."

"We need a minute before you…"

Anger died.

"We need a minute."

She slumped. "Right. Your call. We don't want anyone finding the wreck. Or the people still…" She pressed her lips tight.

He drew himself upright and cast a glance over his shoulder. Parqe blanched. He faced Edie. "Do it."

Edie had to stiffen her spine as the boulder of his unvoiced grief landed on her shoulders.

"You're going to see a bunch of activity on the handheld." She sidled a step away from the emotion in him. She didn't want to explain herself. Not to a khaki uniform. No matter how discolored by the blood of the dead. Yet the anguish represented by all that gore wouldn't let her stay silent. "Activating and testing my trigger charges. Secondary all-ready testing only."

The pressure of his emotion eased. She'd become accustomed to the SEM translating intonation into nerve signals that lit up her brain in a way that let her grasp how people said what they said. Had come to count on it. How twisted was it that she didn't want to understand the Claugh. Yet she'd gotten tangled up with a group overflowing with excess pain at the point that she'd hit max capacity on SEM usage. She was dangerously close to addiction again.

She shook the concern away.

Voices fell silent.

Her nerves arced as the captain closed in beside her.

She pinged each charge. All but one answered. She made certain he could read her screen. Given that it was the last mortal remains of his crew and ship, Edie figured he deserved to know how this was going to go.

"I'm clear for final arm," she said for his ears only.

"Even with one charge negative?"

"It's in the decompressed part of the ship. No one there. It isn't ideal, but it'll blow. Just a second after the destruct triggers go."

The warning she'd been waiting for flashed in her visual field and shot a hot rush of adrenaline into her system. UMOPG closing with the wreck. Finally.

"Captain." Parqe rushed to V'kyrri's other side, his handheld in her grasp. "Life signs south of the *Rhapsody*."

Utter stillness from him. "It's time."

Parqe sucked in a ragged breath.

Rapid-fire, Edie executed final arm. She even spent the useless effort sending the command to the nonresponsive unit. No go.

When everything else read green across the board, she lit the red 'fire' button on screen. Very old fashioned. Very hard to misunderstand.

Thumb poised, she braced and drew breath to say, 'on your mark, Captain.'

She couldn't.

Edie looked into the eyes of a man who'd lost his command, most of his crew, and who now had to authorize the murder of survivors he had no hope of rescuing.

Sure. She was the expert. She was Firestorm, the Claugh killer.

He was the man who'd taken responsibility for the people and equipment he'd asked her to destroy. He'd ridden his ship to ground, survived against all odds, and, as her bruised throat attested, stopped at nothing to save his people.

She didn't have to like it, or him, but she could respect both.

He deserved to finish the job.

She met his eye. Every fiber of her being screamed against handing a fire trigger to a Claugh madman. She did it anyway. "Your crew, your ship, your show."

The corners of his eyes creased. Lines dug deep around his frown. Hands shaking, he clutched the handheld.

Edie looked away from Parqe's wide eyes. Not what she'd expected from someone like Edie. Not what Edie had expected, either.

V'kyrri muttered under his breath.

The SEM presented her with an unfamiliar blessing for the dying. Her fingers twitched, craving the heft of her handheld so she could capture and preserve the prayer for later study. In her line of work, one could never have too many send-offs.

He pressed the button.

Air currents shifted a split second before sound and pressure waves arrived.

Detonation of her kicker charges thumped her

chest, then vanished into the larger, full-body concussion of the ship's self-destruct triggers exploding. It swallowed even the signature of metal rending.

Imagination supplied the final agonized expressions of the people her explosives killed. It suspended her breath. They hadn't deserved to die this way, battered and helpless.

The blast wave swept the canyon, flattening what scraggly vegetation clung to life, and raising a growing cloud of blue-gray rock powder.

Edie stepped behind the shelter of the cavern wall.

The two senior officers stood fast, facing the wrath of their starship's final death throes.

She shouldn't let them. It was unlikely, but not impossible, for shards of debris to be carried by the expanding energy wave.

They'd already survived the unimaginable. If they got themselves killed at this point, Edie could hardly be blamed. She regretted that her handheld was being scoured by dust particles while they stood there, though.

Another sonic signature lit her data field. Rock-fall. Big one. Swift, merciful death for the trapped, destroy the ship, kill whoever had been trying to run them down, and provide burial, all in one go.

The data cascade settled.

A mote of dust falling caught the wan light, glinting as it drifted past her face. Edie allowed herself a moment of satisfaction.

Despite having to kill victims who couldn't be rescued, it had been a precision job. At least those poor souls hadn't suffered at her hands. She'd provided the perfect application of force. Any bigger explosion and she'd have risked bringing the caves down. Based on SEM data, the rock fall her detonation had triggered happened exactly the way she'd planned.

A glimmer of pride warmed her.

V'kyrri stumbled into her, blinking, eyes tearing. From the blowing grit or from something else, she wouldn't hazard to guess.

He stared hard into her face. Rage shuttered his expression. In a flash, V'kyrri caught her tight against his chest. Nerves fired all over her body.

He stared through her SEM lenses, something most people never did. Another reason she hadn't taken the unit off since getting caught by a bunch of injured Claugh. Anything to keep them from looking too deep.

"Admiring your handiwork?" he snapped.

"There's no joy in destroying the helpless. Have you ever heard of professional pride? Maybe you can't comprehend what I accomplished out there with what amounted to a spark stone and Hell powder. No one but my father would have. Had he survived being tortured to death by you people."

Tension ran out of him. His grip loosened.

Caught by the deepening lines at the corners of his mouth and eyes, Edie hesitated. The pair of them kept hitting her old pain off his fresh anguish.

And maybe, being an explosives expert and everything, she ought to have recognized how dangerous that was before now.

She plucked her handheld from his grasp and jerked away from that uniform.

He refused to free her. "Drop off."

He turned them, and she peered into a hole with no

visible bottom. Edie dug her fingers into his sleeve. "Thanks."

He released her a piece at a time as if reluctant to let go.

Discomfited by the glow unfurling in her belly, Edie slid out of his grasp and opted to smother her awareness of him with work. Eying the cave opening, she fished a pale filament out of the inside breast pocket of her environmental suit.

The Claugh watched, furrows in their brows.

"Everyone in," she said. Just inside the deep shade line, Edie poked one end of the filament at the rock forty-five cm from the floor. A faint flash and it fused into the molecular structure of the stone.

V'kyrri's crew, eyes red-rimmed, leaped to follow Edie's order.

Chavolgen, blinking as if waking, glanced around. " 'A cave is a grave to a well-prepared adversary.' "

Fuller and Chavolgen passed Edie. Edie switched on her light bar and handed it to the lieutenant.

"They aren't prepared," Edie said. "Not for me."

V'kyrri moved his stretchers into the deeper shadow, halting near enough to awaken her nerves.

Parqe pushed past.

All survivors present and accounted for. Until they started dying.

"Pher-Kailin wire?" V'kyrri asked.

Surprise drew her eye to his for a split second. Not many people knew Pher-Kailin wire from any other wire.

He stared out the cavern opening, features tightening.

Once she put up the wire, there'd be no retreat. No

one would be able to follow them, either. Which was the whole point.

Something about the twist of his lips told her he was doing the mental math. She shouldn't know that about him. Didn't want to know that.

Edie forced herself to concentrate on stretching the filament across the opening.

"Hold," he commanded.

For a split-second, she froze, then gritted her teeth and shoved the wire at rock. *Oh no, you don't. Not taking Claugh orders*. The wire fused into the opposite wall.

She rose, eyeing her handiwork.

Invisible. Unless someone spotted the thumbnail-sized places on either wall where stone had momentarily melted before solidifying again.

"Damn it, Edie."

"What are you worried about? It's a very final ending to anyone tailing you, Mr. All-About-Revenge."

"The ship exploding could have been written off as an accident," he snapped. "For them, this confirms that we're here. That's what you're doing, isn't it? Leaving a tag, like some arrogant teenager. If anyone is tailing, Edie, they aren't just tailing me. They're tailing *us*." He gestured between the two of them.

"And now I can pay attention to who's ahead of me. Not behind me. If you don't like my methods, I'd be happy to take my toys and go back to a paying job."

"Don't endanger my crew again," he said, his tone flat as an assassin's blade.

She sneered. Wasted effort.

He'd turned to the stretchers.

Uneasiness a clenching pain in her breastbone,

Edie picked up her wounded. Why the hell was she challenging a Claugh officer in extremity?

Sure, he'd seemed to have gained sanity over time, but here she was. Shoving hard against it was as if she wanted him to slip into madness again. Why?

Frowning, Edie led them into the tunnels.

Before the first corridor junction, Edie held up a hand, fist closed. The visual signature of shuffling footsteps behind her dwindled. She unhooked her stretchers and whispered, "Tunnel intersection."

V'kyrri's expression cleared. He drew his gun and offered it to her over the body of one of his wounded.

Edie blinked.

A Claugh offering Firestorm a gun?

Her hand trembled when she accepted the weapon. She picked her way to the junction and studied sensor data. The last time she'd scouted this route, there'd been guards posted. She'd detected their bio-signs long before they'd sensed her.

No indications of life this time.

Her chest tightened.

She eased into the junction, weapon at the ready, and drew up short. Her breath went high and tight in her chest. Edie spun on her heel.

Hands grabbed her, pulled her into contact with a body. Motes of heat shot through her.

"Edie?" V'kyrri had put down his wounded and come after her. "What is it?"

She tried to moisten her lips with a sandpaper tongue. "Blood."

His grip tightened before he freed her arms in favor of fumbling for her hand.

"Light," he said.

"Another in my pack," she said. With her path laid out in SEM data, Edie led him back to the other survivors.

Parqe surveyed the pair.

"Complication," he said.

Edie yanked another light bar from her pack.

"Hunker down," V'kyrri ordered his crew. "Light out."

The whites of Fuller's eyes flashed.

"Safer that way," Edie said. "Anyone else moving around out here will have lights. You'll see them coming."

Chavolgen offered a jerky nod. Fuller's shoulders settled lower.

"Edie." V'kyrri released the neural cuff.

She swallowed the idiotic impulse to thank him by shoving the light bar into his grasp.

He accepted his gun when she offered it.

As if by silent mutual accord, they jogged to the blood-soaked corridor junction.

"Should have been two guards here," she whispered between gusts of overheated breath.

Back against the stone, V'kyrri edged into the open circle of the intersection. Edie followed, watching for any indication of approaching trouble, bomb in hand.

V'kyrri played the light along the floor, walls, and ceiling. Dark sprays of blood spattered the ceiling and stone walls. On the floor, congealing puddles of blood marooned pale drifts of sand like islands in a grotesque ocean.

Edie tasted metal in the grit between her teeth. Metal and over-ripe orxaxi fruit—sacred to Orxacal, the god of death and the dead. Sacred because legend said the fruiting vine had sprung from Orxacal's dismembered, disemboweled body. At its best, the fruit carried a hint of musky rot. Past its prime, the fruit smelled and tasted like a pile of bodies that had been left in the sun for three days.

She'd never had the courage to ask how anyone knew that, but after the inside of the downed Claugh battlecruiser, and now, this cave painted in blood, she could guess.

"Dry on the ceiling and walls," she whispered. "Still wet on the ground."

"Recent." The knuckles of his gun hand went white. "Where are the bodies?"

She shook her head. She did not want to know. "We have to come through here. It's the only way."

He shot a look at her, then examined the floor. "We'll leave tracks. What are our options?"

She breathed a laugh. "None."

He adjusted his grip on his weapon. "Bring them."

Chapter Seven

While he guarded the junction. Edie double-timed it. Fuller and Chavolgen took V'kyrri's stretchers for the transit.

Parqe gasped as Edie directed the group into the junction and through to another tunnel. Chavolgen and Fuller blanched. Fuller swallowed, the motion patently visible. The three of them began glancing over their shoulders. The commander, voice trembling, said, "We need a plan."

"We're headed for a spot where you can hole up with the wounded," Edie said. "Once you're secure, I'm going for a hangar and a bigger boat."

"That's suicide," Parqe hissed. "You don't have any intention…"

"As you were," V'k interrupted from Edie's side, his gaze busy on her face.

She pressed her expression flat.

His fingers twitched. Illuminated by the light bar he carried, V'kyrri's green eyes lit. Interest. Avidity. Anticipation. "Her Majesty needs to know what's happening here. If we can make it to a ship, we have food, water, medical. We don't have to leave anyone behind."

He cast a glance at the bloody footprints his crew had tracked into the tunnel. Edie followed the line of his gaze to those ghost footprints.

She shivered.

"If these people were all at a hundred percent, we might stand a chance," Parqe protested. "How can we justify engagement?"

"We have her." V'kyrri tipped his head at Edie.

Adrenaline burned her pulse higher.

He studied Edie again, in that seeing-more-than-she-had-to-show way he did. "You didn't say 'try'. No hesitation. No doubt. You've done this before."

Never let it be said she didn't learn from her mistakes. Edie smiled to keep her mouth shut and made a mental note to put a lid on cocky. She hoped she was listening.

"Location?" he asked.

"I have a blip where the UMOPG ships descended for landing."

"Meaning you know more than you've told us," he noted. No accusation. No anger. At least, not that the SEM could pipe into her brain for interpretation. "You knew this tunnel was here. Do you already know the layout of the base, too?"

"As much as we're all enjoying this party," she said, "you aren't the reason I'm here. I did some scouting before you crashed."

"What have you got?" Hope burned in his voice.

A tendril of old fear slid cold and heavy down her chest into her stomach.

She was fourteen and running for her life. Three monsters disguised as Claugh soldiers trailing her. Mouths open, laughing whenever she flung a glance over her shoulder. Firing weapons that scorched her whenever she slowed or had to cross an open field. "What have you got, little girl?" the lead monster, his eyes glittering with insanity had whispered, his nails digging into her skin, drawing blood when he'd grabbed her leaving Tollan Qa. She'd bitten him and run. She'd run until her chest ached and her vision swam.

Edie closed her eyes and stopped dead. Her fists clenched. No more trips into memory. She wasn't a frightened child. Not anymore.

She sucked in a shallow breath. Funny. Her chest ached the same way it had all those years ago.

A hand closed gently around her bicep. She opened her eyes.

"You okay?" V'kyrri asked.

"No." She brought up data on the handheld.

His shoulder brushing hers, V'kyrri took hold of one side of the handheld. His fingers overlapped hers.

Awareness expanded within her, a slow-motion explosion. The shower of sparks falling upon her internal landscape weren't fire per se, though they burned as if they were. They were something far more treacherous. Attraction. Something Edie hadn't had to deal with in a decade. Maybe more.

Guilt and mortification stamped out the smolder. Was this what she got for ignoring biology for so long? Her penance was being attracted to the enemy that had murdered her parents and destroyed her home?

Edie tried to extricate her hand.

He didn't give any indication that he noticed. He didn't rearrange his fingers, just left them resting lightly against hers. "Heat vents?"

"Yes. Air circulation units in this one."

"A sizeable installation, then," he murmured.

She called up the next set of data. "Lots of access

points, too, but this should interest you."

He swayed. "The ships that attacked us."

"Six took off. They haven't returned. A few hours before your ship came down, three more took off. Only two followed you down. Landed in this vicinity as I knocked on your door."

"We got one."

That gave her pause. Regret that she hadn't gotten a closer look at his ship before she'd destroyed it crushed the starch from her spine. The Claugh ships she'd known couldn't have looked like his had and still have taken down one of the attackers. The empire had developed a new weapons system, it seemed. With a handheld full of specs pulled from the ruined computers on that ship, she could have lived like a queen on Batella. Instead, she'd blown it to the lowest level of the Three Hells.

Edie swallowed a surge of nausea at the credits she'd turned into slag.

He lifted the light bar and studied her face. "Edie? You're a little green."

She shut down the handheld and her line of thought. What was done, was done. No use regretting a precision explosion like the one that had dispatched the wounded trapped in that ship and destroyed data that could have paved her way to a life of ease. There'd be a bucketful of nightmares and recriminations to wallow in the next time she tried to get some shut eye.

"That's all I have," she said. "Intel on a military base no one knows exists."

"Except us."

Silence while the Claugh eyed the bloody corridor junction behind them.

"And whoever or whatever did this."

"The UMOPG are Autken," Chavolgen essayed.

"Doesn't look like any Autken hunt I've ever seen," Edie hedged. "They usually stand over the dead bodies roaring to let everyone know who made the kill."

V'kyrri stared at her while Parqe and Chavolgen attached his stretchers. His expression hardened until she looked at a face that might have been chiseled from Isarrite.

Chavolgen gave her regen unit to Fuller's broken arm.

V'kyrri started walking. "How visible are we?"

"We're not. The caves scatter energy, too."

V'kyrri drew the first full breath that didn't hurt since they'd started taking fire. How long ago? Same day that felt like a lifetime ago. Two hundred and nine lifetimes. "They can't scan for us. We can't scan for them."

"You can," she countered. "Sort of."

"Sensor scan will travel the line of open tunnel," Chavolgen said. "We'll be blind at corners and other obstructions."

V'kyrri's morale lifted a millimeter. His lieutenant had started thinking like a science officer, again.

Rock walls opened out.

The survivors hugged one smooth wall as the path sloped down. He frowned. "This isn't a cave. It's too neat. Too tidy."

"We're in the access tunnels burned out for the base," Edie said.

"Can't be," Chavolgen said.

"Yeah?" Edie prompted when the young woman

fell silent.

V'kyrri nodded appreciation for the encouragement rather than challenge in her tone. She reserved her testiest tone for him and for Parqe.

"The scale is wrong," his lieutenant said. "Burn outs are inefficient. The UMOPG usually just blow stuff up."

Edie snorted. "They are invested in brute force."

"Your data indicated multiple access points. Why? It would be impossible to secure," Chavolgen said.

"You think this was a pre-existing… What? Warren? Something the UMOPG retrofitted? That makes sense. But it does beg a question." Edie peered up at the stone.

"Who put it here in the first place?" V'kyrri finished for her. *And were they murdering miners in the dark?*

She tossed him a look unsettled enough that she might have heard his thought.

He sucked in a deep breath and frowned. "Is that moisture?"

"Yep."

"In this heat?" Parqe said.

"It'll finish burning off in the next few decades as the star expands, but for now, there's an underground lake we'll need if I can't hotwire one of their rides," Edie said.

"They'll know we need water," Parqe said.

"Yep."

"They'll know that's where we're headed."

"Probably."

"You said they'll kill us."

"Enough," V'kyrri ordered, irritation grumbling

through his chest. "Edie. I'd be obliged if you'd stop baiting my officer."

"But not you? Deal."

"What's the hydration packet status?"

"Dozen packs from my suit. Whatever you salvaged minus what we've used."

"A few hours' worth."

"Fewer than can cover getting to my ship or the span of time it might take your people to wing to your rescue. If they're coming at all."

"You don't think they are," he said.

"I suspect the only people who saw your locator beacon were the miners and me."

Saw, V'kyrri noted. Not heard. So much he took for granted. He rubbed a hand down his face, forcing his brain to remember what she'd said. '*Planetary crust scattering energy.*' Including his locator beacon. "Damn."

POOM.

V'kyrri ducked. Pure instinct. The noise scraping through the tunnels had come from behind them.

Edie tipped her head in a gesture of satisfaction. "That's it for our back trail."

"That back trail," he corrected. He wouldn't mention that bloody crossroads if she wouldn't. "I don't understand why we aren't up to our armpits in Autken."

He cast a glance back along the line of his people. Chavolgen and Fuller met his eye. Parqe lifted her chin. Everyone was as okay as the situation would allow. "I do regret not knowing how many of them you killed."

Edie shot a conspiratorial smile his way, but whatever reflected in his face wiped the humor from hers. She picked up the pace. "When I landed, I couldn't move for tripping over Autken. Then those six ships bailed off world. You and I found what we found. I don't know. That we've gotten this far without having to shoot someone in the face invalidates every known parameter for how the UMOPG works."

He grimaced. "You think they have a problem bigger than us."

"Yeah," Edie said, stretching the word into a long arc of dread. "It was one thing to plan for miners. We have no idea what else is out here."

His chest clenched.

"Watch your step," she said.

The tunnel opened on a cavern.

Edie paused. Her light bars cast a tiny puddle of illumination no farther than a meter before them. Beyond the light's reach, velvety, weighted darkness loomed.

His crew spread out, staring into the gloom. Their footsteps echoed into whispers in the cavern. In the silence, water dripped and impacted stone with a musical *ping*. The sound waves painted an ephemeral work of art on her SEM.

"Water," Chavolgen breathed.

"Hold," V'kyrri and Parqe commanded in unison when Fuller and Chavolgen each took a step. They froze.

"This is not the source," Edie said in an undertone, "but we're close. Our hidey hole is on a ledge against the wall that way." She lifted her right arm, quartered from her body.

"Third of a kilometer. Rubble on the floor makes for tough going. Single file. Keep to the footprints of the person in front of you. One light in the middle and one at the end of the column. Who wants 'em?"

Chavolgen and Parqe took them.

Edie stepped into the dark, her eyes and cheekbones illuminated by ghostly red light. They strung out, V'kyrri at her back, Fuller behind him, Chavolgen, and finally Parqe at the rear. The light Chavolgen carried barely reached the stretcher Edie pulled. As they wound through stalagmites, he had to concentrate to keep Edie in sight.

Rock gave way to a jumble of loose stone that sloped up. Reduced to scrambling, they slowed further. His pulse thudded. His breath wheezed.

Edie vanished into the dark.

Muscles burning, V'kyrri plodded in her wake. Three steps. Four. Above him, light and motion caught his eye. Edie. Waiting. Scarlet ghosts floated before her face, painting her features.

She grabbed his lead stretcher and guided him to the ledge she'd promised was there. He swayed when she released him. Fuller scrambled up, Edie pulling his wounded over the lip. When she hauled Chavolgen up, the light bar lit a smooth rock ledge wide enough that they could deposit the stretchers side by side and still have room to walk between them.

V'kyrri put down his burdens and unhooked Fuller and Chavolgen from theirs. Both sank to the stone.

Edie ventured downslope, hands visibly shaking until she turned her back. V'kyrri frowned. Awareness struck through exhaustion. Parqe and the wounded.

Nudging Edie aside, he took the stretcher carrying the burn victim from her. Edie stumbled, gave up her grip, and stood, shoulders hunched while he unhooked Parqe, and settled the stretchers in line with the rest.

His commander slumped to the stone. V'kyrri ached to collapse in kind. Instead, he put a hand on Parqe's shoulder. "Assessment."

Shuddering as she labored for breath, Parqe nodded.

He glanced at Edie as she settled her pack against the rough rock wall at the back of the ledge.

"What further miracles can you conjure?" he asked as she stuck a hand into the bag.

"You'll want silence," she said in an undertone that brought him down beside her in order to hear. "Noise is your friend when you hear someone moving out there. It's your enemy if you're heard first."

Bobbing as someone walked, light came closer.

"And no light," he surmised.

"Yes." She extracted a pair of packages from her supplies and tucked them into one of her thigh pockets.

"This looks like a nest," Parqe said. "You know the Halkyron?"

"Predatory flying reptile native to your home world, isn't it?" V'k said, glancing at his second.

"They favor hollowed out rock ledges like this." Her gaze moved past him to Edie and hardened. "It's the perfect trap. One exit down an exposed slope."

He scanned the ledge. Stalagmites like jagged teeth lined the edges.

Edie said nothing. She stood, the picture of studied neutrality. Save for the flicker of data dripping down the ballistic lenses of her SEM tracing fingers of light over her shadowed eyes.

V'kyrri forced his shoulders down.

Firestorm could have left them to the dead ship.

"It's also perfectly defensible," he countered. "One

access point up an exposed slope."

Edie's spine straightened. If he hadn't been studying her, he'd have missed the tightening of her lips before she stalked into the midst of the wounded and crouched to whisper to Chavolgen and Fuller. She put a packet in Fuller's hand.

The ensign tore it open and offered the contents to Chavolgen. The lieutenant picked up a piece of thick, pale nutritional wafer. V'kyrri slumped. Rations.

His Claugh-killer, the one he'd bruised, threatened, and badgered, was feeding his crew.

"Commander, do you aspire to a command seat?" He glanced at his officer.

Parqe rocked on her heel, but she shrugged. "In due course, Captain."

"We'll have to work on those prejudices, then, Commander. A few of them border on xenophobia."

Anger colored her face, turning the burn livid. "You expect me to follow a SEM addict?"

"Can you think of no other reason for someone to use a SEM?" V'k prodded.

Parqe sneered. "No one needs a SEM. She's an addict, nothing more."

"Edie's from Nol Jakze."

Distaste wrinkled the woman's nose. "Fringe world under Claugh jurisdiction. Site of the Nol Jakze Separatist movement. My father died on that pathetic backwater."

"I'm sorry," V'k said. "But now you know why Edie uses a SEM."

Parqe blinked. "I don't—ah. Native. Deaf. If she wasn't going to stay on world with the rest of them, why isn't that fixed?"

"Because nothing's broken," Edie said. "Secure this camp. Get some rest."

"We don't need a SEM-addicted—"

"Commander," V'kyrri snapped. "Unless you possess a medical or psychological degree of which I am unaware, you will stow that opinion, and that is an order."

"Hey, Captain." Edie shoved a ration pack into his hands and clapped him on the back.

He winced.

"I appreciate the gallantry, but you don't have to defend my honor. Monsters don't have any." She walked off the ledge.

The pad of Edie's boots on rock stopped. Relief blew through him. She hadn't gone far. "If you have a plan for getting us off planet without any more bloodshed, Commander, I'll let Edie know she's free to go."

"I do not trust that woman," Parqe said. "Why do you?"

"I have my reasons." He flicked a glance at Fuller and Chavolgen. His junior officers watched, wide-eyed, the ration packet forgotten in Fuller's shaking grasp.

"The Nol Jakzians hate the hearing. They exile their own children if they're not born deaf. You're not being rational," Parqe accused. "You were injured in the crash. Unconscious. You aren't thinking straight. Don't make me relieve you."

Chapter Eight

Rage roared through his blood, threatening to blow the top off his skull. "As you were, Commander. You are compromising a tactical situation. If you cannot grasp that the appearance of trust is a strategic advantage, join the Murbaasch Tu. We'll teach you. You had better have a damned good reason for threatening me over a woman who saved your life."

Parqe's weight shifted forward. Her hands curled to fists.

V'kyrri drew himself upright, hands loose at his sides.

She met him glare for glare for several tense seconds. Then Parqe's gaze faltered. "My brother was a surgeon until he put on a SEM to get through a particularly delicate, pioneering neuro-surgery."

Anger settled out of V'kyrri's system. "He became addicted."

"He wouldn't attempt the simplest procedure without enhancement. Then he couldn't function at home without it. He stopped sleeping. Started dialing up the enhancement, buying newer, more expensive, custom-tuned units. Patients began dying."

"I'm sorry."

"The hospital fired him and tried to commit him," Parqe said, her voice raw. "He killed himself and destroyed our mother."

V'kyrri rubbed his aching forehead. "You have reason to hate everything about Edie."

Parqe frowned. "You called her a tactical situation. Are you reading her? Influencing—"

"No." V'k breathed deep before continuing. "The crash burned me out."

"What?" Parqe gaped at him. "Then no one knows where we are? That we need—"

"No one knows." He handed Parqe the ration packet. "I've lost everything. The ship. The crew. My ability. There's nothing left but revenge."

Parqe flinched.

"Eat. Get everyone settled. No talking. I'll need the light for a minute."

"Damage control?" Parqe asked, putting the light bar into his hand and accepting the food in return. She hesitated, then said, "I regret it's necessary."

V'kyrri pressed his lips tight. Maybe there was hope for his exec after all.

He followed Edie. He slid into liquid dark and found her leaning against one broad stalagmite, her SEM field deactivated. The glasses dangled from her belt.

Relief blew through him. Maybe she hadn't been privy to the episode with Parqe.

Eyes closed, she rubbed her temples. Weariness etched lines into the corners of her mouth.

She wouldn't hear him approach, wouldn't see him.

He frowned. She'd gated reconciliation. Anyone else, he could talk. Whether or not they listened, they'd hear, and that could be made to be enough.

Not Edie. She had the means to shut out everyone

and everything. And without telepathy, he couldn't even force the issue.

Should it annoy him so much?

"I'm not running off." She opened her eyes and looked right at him.

"How did you..." He broke off. She wouldn't register what he'd said without the SEM.

"Air currents," she said. "And your clothes smell like electrical fire."

And sweat and death and fear. It did nothing to explain how she could answer questions without her SEM.

Her generous lips twitched, and her expression went smooth the way it did when she was resisting the urge to assuage his concern. He forced himself to relax, to tamp down tension. Let Parqe distrust enough for them both. Every instinct whispered that Edie, while maybe not entirely trustworthy, was salvageable. Even when she patently didn't want to believe she was.

Twice now, she'd called herself a monster.

Actions counted. His Claugh-killing former-revolutionary hadn't walked away from saving people she considered enemies. She'd made the hard choice. Kept making it.

It occurred to him to wonder why.

"You understand me without your SEM," he noted. Her gaze moved to his lips.

His body tightened. They'd been here before. She was watching his mouth as he spoke. Not just that, however. For whatever reason, this time, when her gaze turned to watch him speak, her expression softened, and her brown eyes lit with appreciation.

Reaction shot through his blood. He sucked in a

sharp breath. How was this even possible after the trauma of losing ship and crew?

"I don't need the SEM to understand you," Edie confirmed. Her voice trembled. She looked away.

V'kyrri squared his shoulders. Attraction was a tool. He either used it to shape her or it would shape him. He put a hand on her arm. The contact rippled through her, spilling awareness of her into his blood. It had nothing to do with telepathy. Motes of fire traced his nerves. Funny that it would take the death of his ship and of his telepathy to discover the many modes of communication he'd automatically assigned to his one known talent.

She stared at him, eyes wide.

"I'm sorry," he said, refusing to snatch his hand away as if he'd committed some sin. But he had to steel himself for his body's reaction when her gaze went to his mouth. "I'm sorry we're draining your resources."

She shrugged and averted her gaze again. Her cheeks flushed.

Encouraged when she glanced at him again, he said, "The Claugh will compensate—"

Her toneless bark of laughter cut him off. "You can't afford my price."

Frustration twisted fingers in his ribs. "What? What is it you want?"

"My parents," she snapped. "Barring that? My world's freedom."

Pain shot through him. He closed his eyes.

Guilt flushed Edie's system at the furrows digging into his forehead. Against her better judgement, she'd come to respect the man. When he wasn't trying to order her around. He'd had nothing to do with her parents' murders. Had he?

"I'm sorry," he said, again. He opened his eyes.

"Why?" she grumbled, so afraid he'd say yes that she turned to read the answer in his face before he could speak it. "Were you there?"

"No."

Grim distaste, conveyed by the way he shaped the word, made her wonder what he'd responded to. What the Claugh had done to her people, or what the resistance—what *she*—had done to the Claugh?

Edie turned her gaze to the darkness. Clarification wasn't always a good thing. She wouldn't accept condemnation, and she couldn't accept sympathy. Maybe she'd grown. Or gone soft. Fine line. She could save their lives, but she hadn't grown to the point that she could bear their pity.

"Look." Edie lifted the hand, palm up. A ball of plant material rested there. It would have been fluffy save for the waxy coating. She closed her fingers and shrugged her sleeve lower to flick fingernails against the spark strip embedded there.

V'kyrri jumped.

She opened her fingers. Dim flame danced in her palm. "Hand out. Flat. Palm up."

An intrigued twist to his lips, he obeyed She tipped the burning ball onto his skin. He flinched, then paused, his gaze flicking to her face.

"It's soaked in flammable liquid that burns cool enough to handle. The heat rises, but you'll be happier if you move it around a bit. Leave it in one spot long enough and it'll raise a blister."

He shifted. The little fireball rolled across his palm. "What is it for?"

"Surprise," she said. "Lighting off stuff. Convincing little kids that not all fire is bad."

The muscles around his mouth softened. "Really?"

She lifted one shoulder. "Original use was among jugglers delighting young audiences."

"Is that what you do?"

She sighed and looked away. Ignoring the cold sweat gathering on her skin, urging her to turn the SEM back on, she shifted her shoulders and rolled her neck, trying to break up the ache gathering behind her eyes.

"What's wrong? Headache?" V'kyrri asked. The light of the fireball faltered and winked out. He shook the singed wad of plant material out of his hand.

"Turn around. Hold still." His fingers closed on her wrist. Tugged.

He pulled until her back rested against his chest. He hooked the light bar to her belt. His voice vibrating from his chest into her back urged her to surrender to the lure of his touch. His breath puffed past her ear.

She shivered. "What are you…"

He set warm fingertips to her temples, pressed, and began tracing the muscles, working against spasms of pain. He uttered more words she couldn't read.

The ache in her skull receded and, even though she'd clamped her lips shut, Edie couldn't suppress a groan.

From the methodical way he worked from one painful pressure point to another, massaging the tenderness away, she gathered he'd been trained in a specific technique. Undoubtedly something the Claugh had developed to return soldiers to fighting form.

Even as she sagged, taking her shields offline for the few moments they lingered in the dark, she tried to tell herself he only needed to restore her to peak operating efficiency. Tactics. Not consideration.

The heat quivering at her core didn't seem to hear. Or care. How long had it been since—

Gasping, Edie bolted upright. Out of the Claugh captain's grasp. Spinning to face him, she backed off, a smile pasted to her features. "Amazing stuff. Thanks."

His hands returned to his sides, his gaze busy on her face. "What's wrong?"

"Wrong?" she echoed. She planted her feet. Another step backward and she'd tumble down slope.

He looked at her hands. "If that's a language, Edie, I'm sorry I don't understand it."

Shock detonated. Edie froze, her hands stuck in mid-sign. *Signing*. By the grace of the Twelve Gods. She'd reverted to her native language. In the presence of…because of a *Claugh*. Her knees tried to fold.

Alarm rocketed into his frown. V'kyrri bolted for her, grabbed her biceps, supporting her.

"Sorry," she gasped, quaking. "Sorry. Let me…" She grabbed the SEM, fumbled it into place, and tapped her handheld.

The unit powered up. A split second of agony raked overstimulated nerves. Nausea swelled, then settled into an uneasy slosh in her empty stomach. She swallowed hard. Locked her knees. No more weakness. Not in front of, or for, a Claugh. No matter how compelling.

V'kyrri clenched his teeth on the impulse to turn his mental ability to prying Edie open. He'd come so close to breaking through to her soft underbelly. He craved another taste of her pliable in his hands, her body surrendering to his as if starved for contact. He shifted his hold on her and couldn't tell whether the resulting tremor ran from her to him or the other way around. "I'm…"

"Claugh," she whispered. "You're Claugh. Let go." Edie ripped free of his grasp and vaulted onto the ledge, taking the light bar with her.

V'kyrri shut his eyes. Could he fall asleep standing up? He forced his eyes open. It would take more than a couple of hours of sleep to erase the internal damage he'd suffered. If even that would do. Though his head no longer seemed to be as pieced together by torturous lasers.

Which meant he should take a few seconds to find out whether he'd fried his neural circuits permanently or not. Who to contact?

Not his best friend, Major Damen Sindrivik. V'kyrri had no idea whether Damen still lived, given that he'd been on a mission to rescue the major and gotten shot down en route. It was entirely possible that Damen and Jayleia were gone. Just like his crew and his ship.

He shunted aside the stab accompanying the thought. Later. He'd find a way to entertain and process emotion later.

He'd get a message out now if he could.

That meant Ari, then.

She'd been altered by the Chekydran. They'd made her telepathic. Since she'd joined the Claugh, V'k had been working with her, teaching her to control her power.

If anyone would hear him, it would be Captain Ari Idylle, even after he'd severed their mental connection in the worst way possible during the crash.

He pulled her face from memory. White hair. Silver eyes. Strong jaw. Generous lips she pressed a little too tightly as if perpetually braced for bad news. Since she'd survived being a Chekydran prisoner of war, the caution made complete sense.

He said her name, not really inside his own head. The impression of speaking out across some kind of extra-cranial pathway rolled his friend's name out into what? Space? Time? A kind of mental warp space?

It bounced right back, echoing around within the confines of his brittle skull. V'kyrri flinched.

Gods, he needed to get a message out. He swallowed an icy lump that refused to thaw on the way down. The damage to his telepathy couldn't be permanent. He wouldn't let it be.

The fingers he dug into his aching temples shook.

"Captain," Parqe whisper-shouted.

Startled, he sucked in a gulp of air and opened his eyes. Useless. No dawn in the underground. You'd think he'd remember that. Maybe he did. It would explain the tremble in his nerves. Swallowing a curse, he edged through the stalagmites by feel.

Edie had one light bar on the ground casting illumination and shadows upward. She knelt beside a stretcher, quaking handheld in one hand, the other outstretched to Chavolgen and Fuller. "Hydration."

Parqe—eyes huge with dark smears underneath—the burn on her face glaring angry red, slashed temple to chin when she faced Edie from the opposite side of the stretcher. Holding the only Claugh handheld out and scanning, her gaze found him as he slid between the rocks.

"Sir."

He couldn't breathe. The entire weight of a dead starship and crew settled on his chest. *No*. Not here. Not now. He braced and blew out a steadying breath.

"Give me the damn—" Edie snapped.

"Edie." V'kyrri strode to Edie's side, took her outstretched hand. "You were right. We can't win this battle. I should have listened."

Edie subsided and turned away, but not before a single, red-lit line of moisture slipped beneath the edge of her SEM glasses.

"We can help ease her way. Sedation, Lieutenant," he said.

Not that it was necessary. Not anymore.

Edie slid from his grasp.

V'kyrri crouched beside the stretcher. His joints creaked. How was it fair to find out he'd retained enough of a base level of telepathy to be a captive audience to the last glimmer of light and life going out of his crewwoman?

Her death registered as a dull knife burrowing into his chest. Folding the stretcher cover over the dead woman's face flooded heat into his eyes.

His exec bowed her head over the handheld. "Confirmed. Permission to institute reduction?"

"Objections?" V'kyrri glanced around the circle of faces.

He caught Fuller's red, swollen eyes. At V'kyrri's side, Edie, her face illuminated by scarlet data traces, stared at the dead woman, her fists clenching and unclenching.

Parqe put the handheld before him again.

Life signs. Not in the cavern, but close. He triggered his mental housecleaning routine to clear away emotion he couldn't afford. He activated the process that would reduce his dead crewwoman to a container of remains weighing less than a kilo.

The stench of burned flesh intensified.

An incoherent whimper and the too swift rhythm of Edie's harsh breathing shook him. She rose and backed away. Another line of red-lit moisture slid down one cheek.

His heart bumped. He stood.

Her attention jerked to him. No. To his uniform. Edie's lip curled.

"Edie," he murmured. "Don't. We're not…"

She bolted.

V'kyrri lunged in pursuit. He caught her on the rocky slope and snagged her arm.

Behind them, the light on the ledge winked out.

Edie's breath caught on a sob. She growled.

V'kyrri ducked.

Her fist went over his head, ruffling his hair. Instinct? Or the way her muscles had bunched in his grip? He certainly couldn't see.

Trusting her SEM to pick it up, he whispered, "Edie. Stop."

She ripped free of his grasp.

"Damn it." He pounced as she spun away, something he could track by the glow of her SEM. He caught her to his chest, pinning her.

She fought. An elbow jabbed him in the gut.

"Oof. Edie," he whispered at her ear as if she could hear him. "Edie, stop. Listen. Someone's out there. Look at your data. You can't get us killed without getting yourself killed, too. Look at your data. Stop."

Something reached her. She sagged, trembling, in

his grasp.

He couldn't wait for her recovery. He lifted her, turned, and by the light of her SEM, hauled her into the cover of the ledge.

She twisted free, fled to the far end of the ledge, and based on how the faint gleam of her SEM sank to the floor, she sat. Another line of moisture tracked her cheek, so like blood, his gut clenched.

Her lenses winked out. Clothing rustled beside him.

"What if they have sensors?" Parqe whispered.

He shook his head as much to clear it as to answer his exec's concern. "Then we fight."

Tension dug claws into him, swarming up his body.

Whoever approached came on alert with dim light and echoing footsteps but no other noise. As the light weaving through the boulders brightened, V'kyrri and Parqe took position on either side of the ramp.

A pair of miners slipped in and out of view amid the stalactites and stalagmites below. Muted gray uniforms fitted with tactical ballistic armor replaced the usual bright-colored, loose-fitting coveralls the rest of the UMOPG favored.

They passed directly below V'kyrri. Their light lit the mid-reaches of the slope he and his people had climbed. His pulse tripped into double time. Why wouldn't the soldiers climb the slope and search the ledge? Autken were scent hunters. How could they miss the reek of fear and burned flesh?

His nerves pinged and sang.

Edie crouched beside him in the dark.

"Don't like this," the Autken woman whispered

from down slope.

V'kyrri had to strain to make sense of the thin slip of sound.

"A ship down. Survivors. Something hunting us in the tunnels, and us short-handed. The Guild Mistress took too many troops."

"She's hunting that spy that attacked Silver City," the man whispered in response. "We'll find them survivors."

V'kyrri stiffened. *Damen.* He edged out from behind the stone teeth, listening.

Edie grabbed his wrist. Her grip pinched.

"Everyone on this rock needs the same thing," the man whispered.

The woman grunted. "Water."

"We only got to wait for them."

"We're stuck guarding water like cubs," the female groused.

"Yeah. But we'll live longer," the male said.

The woman snickered.

Edie tugged.

Pressing a fist against the ache in his chest, V'kyrri frowned.

The UMOPG soldiers didn't live longer.

Chapter Nine

Two giant Chekydran, forelegs and tentacles waving, galloped out of the dark.

V'kyrri froze, not even breathing.

Shrieking, the soldiers backpedaled. Laser fire sprayed, singeing the flailing tentacles of the lead Chekydran. It screamed. The creatures fell upon the soldiers and ripped the female limb from limb. They used her bloody, twitching corpse to beat the male into a smear on the cavern floor.

The mystery of what had happened at the corridor junction was solved, at least. He swallowed hard. The stink of blood and hot entrails coated his tongue.

The Chekydran skittered out of the cavern, back the way they'd come.

As if turned to stone, Edie stood, her grip too tight on his wrist. She gasped and hauled him onto the ledge where she sank to the ground.

V'k tried to convince his diaphragm it was safe to breathe again. He glanced at Edie. He couldn't see her in the dark. It didn't matter. Since she'd taken hold of his wrist, he had an unexpected, tenuous mental bead on her. He still couldn't read her, not enough to get at her core. But it was enough for him to have a sense of where she was and what she focused on.

She'd crawled to her spot beside her pack, forehead resting on her knees, arms wrapped around her legs,

SEM lenses tucked atop her bright, fiery hair.

What he knew about Firestorm juxtaposed with the woman who'd somehow known and tried to warn him about the Chekydran made his head spin.

She was counting. Strict, focused discipline to suppress emotion already sinking out of reach, but not before he caught a bitter sip. Horror. Sickness. Shame. Intense desire to flee. Deep, habitual sadness. Fear.

He hadn't needed to rifle her surface thoughts. They swarmed him, wild hiztaps digging needle sharp claws into his skin.

V'kyrri straightened, relief cooling him. He wasn't braindead. Not entirely.

Game changed in his favor.

With a mote of his telepathic power returning, Edie wasn't the only one with dozens of weapons anymore.

"Chekydran," Parqe grumbled in an undertone. "Where the Three Hells did they come from? Permission to scan?"

"Cover that screen," he said.

Parqe activated her handheld. He winced and squinted. His light deprived eyes took a few seconds to recognize that the device barely lit Parqe's face and hands.

"Leaving sensor range," Parqe said. "Which down here is meaningless. I have no idea what that limit is."

A shallow sip of sound—air drawn in and immediately sighed back out—preceded the rustle of Edie shifting. Her SEM lit.

V'kyrri's gaze, hungry for visual simulation, locked on the faint trace of light. It lit her face as if it were a Sunsarramian death mask. From upper lip to hairline. The edges remained lost as if her face floated in the dark.

He shook off the superstitious impression.

She rose, dug into her pack, and then approached, the visible portion of her features ironed flat. Placid water with a deadly rip current running beneath.

V'kyrri snorted at the mental image.

She opened another ration packet, took one of the wafers, and thrust the rest at him. "Eat. You're going to need it. Bugs change everything. You have to get off this hell-hole."

The crunchy hard exterior was back. Fine.

He accepted the ration pack. Back to the business of rescuing his survivors. With the added complication of dodging Chekydran as well as UMOPG. "I need a tactical on the water."

"And coordinates." She worked her handheld. "Link up. I'll give you my maps. Such as they are."

"This is defensible," V'kyrri said, surveying the cavern. "If the Chekydran swarm the ledge, don't waste shots. No one gets captured."

Chavolgen's expression hardened. Fuller wouldn't meet his gaze.

"You can't leave us," Parqe protested. "We stick together."

"This is a scouting mission," Edie said. "I'll be moving fast, staying out of sight, avoiding contact."

"We'll be moving fast," V'kyrri corrected.

Shaking her head, Edie said, "I need you…"

"I know," he said.

Her nose wrinkled and her lips twisted, but the corners of her eyes crinkled.

"Sir," Parqe said.

"We need a bead on the viper's den. Something I

can only get if I know you're here, guarding the injured."

Parqe, Chavolgen, and Fuller drew breath to argue.

He lifted a hand. "Stay here. Guard your shipmates. That's an order."

The faces around him fell.

Edie shifted, her gaze surveying Parqe, Chavolgen, and Fuller before meeting his eye, her mouth pulled down.

She went to Chavolgen's side and canted her handheld screen. Parqe crowded in on Chavolgen's other side.

"Consider working out a fast evac plan. You have my maps. They aren't complete, but the hangar is this way. I tracked ships landing right here." She traced a route on her handheld. Parqe and Chavolgen bent over the Claugh device, syncing the path. "Once I close the gaps, things are going to happen fast."

Parqe's chin came up. A glimmer of light returned to the woman's eyes.

He kicked himself. He'd sentenced them to a long stretch of boredom with nothing to do but replay the deaths of everyone and everything they'd known. And maybe wait for either the UMOPG or the Chekydran to discover them.

Edie'd given his crew something to do, a challenge to focus on, to occupy their minds. Something they needed. He'd missed that.

"We'll have to be ready to march at a moment's notice," Parqe said.

"It's why I'm going to argue your captain into staying," Edie said, swinging to stare at him.

"No."

"They can't carry the stretchers between the three of them," she shot. "You want them to leave someone behind?"

"No."

Her lip curled. "You're a real jerk, you know that?"

"That's what this commendation is for." He tapped one of the stars adorning his collar. His crew snorted. "Too much rides on this. You need me at your back."

"You're injured, exhausted, and hopped up on stim," she pressed.

"Revenge is perfect fuel," he countered.

That set her back. Briefly. She drew a breath and leaned in again.

"Stay here. Stay silent," he ordered, cutting off whatever Edie had in mind to say. He focused on Parqe. "No light. Keep your heads down. Edie. Mission parameters?"

Silence.

He glanced at her.

She stared at him, fists clenched.

He lifted an eyebrow, his own muscles tightening in anticipation.

"Three objectives," Edie bit out. "A spot where we can stow the wounded during action, rapid access to a ship, and a way to keep the other ships from taking off. This is the fallback position."

"I suggest adding an objective," Parqe muttered. "Stay away from Chekydran."

Edie huffed a laugh at the wry, almost conciliatory note to Parqe's gallows humor. "Noted."

Ignoring the annoyance rumbling through her, she transferred explosives from her pack to her tool belt.

"Leave your handheld," she said to V'kyrri. "We'll

take mine."

"Good. Dramind sequence on the light bar when we come back," V'kyrri said to his exec. "But please don't shoot me if I screw up the second cadence."

Parqe snorted. "Since you always do, I'd shoot if you got it right."

"Good luck, sir," Fuller said from the dark. "Ma'am."

Edie gave V'kyrri the light bar and led the way off the ledge.

He followed on her heels.

The stink of cooling blood sharpened.

V'kyrri trailed her in silence, moving in the boneless way trained hunters mastered. He put a meter between them, trading the lead and cover with her as if they'd been casing enemy territory together for decades.

Longing stabbed her. He'd make a stellar mercenary. In another time and place.

Edie boosted signal processing to the SEM until her screens and her gray matter lit up with three-dimensional energy signatures bounced back from the rock.

Readings piled up, vibrating at a frequency she wasn't familiar with. It acted like a kind of sonar, building an echolocation image of the tunnels around them. Maybe that's what Chekydran sound waves did for them. The pulse seduced hers into sympathetic rhythm until her whole body thrummed in heightened awareness.

It did nothing to erase the impression of V'kyrri pressing the edges of her, as if his unspoken trust in her as a fellow warrior pried up one of her corners to reveal what lay underneath.

She shuddered and scrubbed her shirt against the sweat trickling down her chest. Her hand shook. Spent already, and they hadn't even made a kilometer. Breathing hard, Edie took shelter at the base of a huge boulder.

He settled next to her, his own breath gusting and surveyed her. "Why are you doing this?"

Freezing mid-swipe of a sleeve across her damp forehead, Edie said, "What? Resting?"

"Helping us."

She rubbed tendrils of damp hair off her face and stilled. "What do you want? Protestation of what a nice gal I am? I am helping. Isn't that enough?"

He closed a hand around her bicep. Innocent, pay-attention touch.

Her nerves sparked, nevertheless. Edie sucked a breath between clenched teeth.

"You hate us, Firestorm."

"Nothing personal. And everyone will live longer and happier if you never say that name again."

He faced her, the light bar between them. "Why didn't you leave us to die?"

"Almost did. Saw the Claugh insignia and started walking away."

He eyed her, suspicion in his frown. "What stopped you?"

She hunched her shoulders. "It's not important."

He spread his fingers wide. "Whatever it was changed your mind about leaving us to die, Edie. It's important."

"Not to me." She had no intention of telling him. The weapons he had arrayed against her were potent enough. He didn't need that one, too.

"Edie."

"Plaguing a demo gal is bad for your health."

"You'd blow me up?"

"Straight to Hell."

"Edie."

"What?"

"We're on Hell."

His dry as dust tone reached through the SEM and wrested a laugh from her.

His eyes darkened. She stared, fascinated. Maybe it reflected what storms did to the waters of his home world. His fingers smoothed the skin of her cheek.

Electricity sparked her veins. She started.

"Tell me what made you save us," he murmured.

"No," she said, damning the readings telling her the impact of his touch registered in her vocal quality.

His lips twitched, and his gaze shifted to her mouth.

Heat suffused her.

He shifted closer.

"Crying," Edie blurted.

He blinked his gaze back to hers.

She let go the breath she'd been holding and swallowed a curse. He'd considered kissing her, and she'd folded like an amateur. That was mortifying enough without the realization that she'd turned into an idiot because, as she crouched in the Chekydran-infested dark, hot, sweaty, and unspeakably grimy, she wondered what V'kyrri's kiss would feel and taste like.

She straightened her spine and concentrated on her SEM display. Adrenaline kicked her upright. She grabbed V'kyrri by the collar, rocketed to her feet, and dragged him three steps before he got his footing.

Either he, too, registered the pressure of Chekydran soundwaves, or he heard the creatures coming at a loud, disjointed canter.

She dove into a crevice in the rock, V'kyrri on her heels.

The bugs scurried past, tentacles waving an excited pattern, and scuttled into another tunnel.

"They glow in the dark," V'kyrri noted. "I had no idea."

"Would you look at that?" Edie breathed.

"What?"

She gestured at the Chekydran. They slid into the tunnel, their tentacles folding back to protect their eye-ridges. "Perfect fit."

Frowning, he sucked in a breath. "The shape. The height. Width. An exact match. This was built for them."

"Or by them," she whispered.

"Why?"

"Why do Chekydran do anything?" she retorted.

They sank farther into the crack in the rock. It opened into another, smaller cavern.

"We're off route," he said.

"We're not." She slanted her handheld for him. "I mean, we are, but look. Position fix against where I watched ships land."

"We're running parallel. One level down?"

"Looks like. We either backtrack to the main tunnel structures—"

"And Chekydran."

"Or we scout this cave to the hangar."

"Odds it goes through?"

"Beats all the Hells out of me."

He grimaced. "Two unknown tunnels."

"One infested with Chekydran beating UMOPG into the stone and one… Wait." Edie swung deeper into the crevice. "Data."

"What?"

She shrugged. "I'm getting a read."

He crowded against her. His hand on hers tilted her handheld for his gaze. Her screen didn't automatically reflect the data hitting her SEM, but disarmed by the sparks hissing along her nerves, she synced the screen with trembling fingers.

His diaphragm bounced against her back. "There's an energy source in this tunnel."

Edie edged away from the disconcerting impulse to sag into him. "Yes."

"Go," he said, releasing her.

Breathing down the heat trembling at her center, she followed the digital trail.

Rocks and boulders obscured their path. The data didn't wane even as the walls closed in.

"Energy signatures increasing," she whispered, pausing to mop her face. "It's either the hangar or the base proper. Either way, we're on the wrong cavern level. There's a branch here." She traced a line on her handheld, well off the limits of the map she'd made scouting before the Claugh had crashed.

"Maintenance access point, maybe," he said.

"Mm. Main door here, if the number of sensor emplacements is any indication," she said, tapping the screen.

"We're still in line with the hangar," he murmured. "It's a scouting expedition, right?"

"No need for both of us—"

"No getting into a squeeze you can't get out of," he said.

He had a point, and it wasn't *I can't trust you.* Foolish man.

The ceiling sloped down and the walls rapidly closed in. She turned sideways, then went to her knees.

"Hold," she said. Her breath came in gasps.

As did his.

"Okay. You were prescient about the squeeze."

"How tight?"

She blew out a sharp breath. "I have to take off the SEM and my tool belt to get through." *If* she could get through.

"You're smaller than I am," he warned. "If you get stuck, I might not be able to reach you."

"We're right under the hangar. If this goes through, we have the perfect back door for an assault."

"Or the perfect grave if it doesn't and you get jammed," he countered.

Her nerves twisted. She shucked her tool belt and shoved it down her body. "Tie that around my ankle."

"It might not be enough."

"Better than nothing."

He didn't say anything. That meant he was frowning, didn't it? Should she know that? Feel it weighing on her?

He put the light bar into her hand.

She glanced at him.

Greenish lines pressed the corners of his mouth. It might be easier to go without the encumbrance, but faced with V'kyrri's queasy look, she shoved the light into the crevice, then crawled in after it. Stone pressed her to her belly. The air grew thick and difficult to pull into aching lungs. She could only progress by pushing with her toes. Resistance on her right ankle communicated V'kyrri's discomfort.

She shoved the light ahead of her and caught it on a thin, ropey object. The thing rolled under her questing touch. Frowning, she edged forward. Memory hinted she ought to know what it was. Curiosity tugged her.

V'kyrri's grip held her back.

"Let go," she said. Not that she'd know if he answered. Or even heard her. The pressure on her leg abated. She propelled herself another few centimeters. The crushing pressure of rock lifted, opening into a tunnel. V'kyrri could probably get through, though he'd sacrifice a few layers of skin.

She fingered the thing that had drawn her. Triumph shoved air into her chest. Wire. Archaic, physical wire.

Chapter Ten

Edie crawled over the wire, sat up, and unhooked the tool belt with shaking fingers. Ignoring the burgeoning withdrawal headache and the cold sweat trickling down her spine, she stuck her head into the crevice and said, “Push the gear in. Squeeze at your third meter. I’ll get the stuff and bring you the tool belt. Grab hold. I’ll pull you through.”

She wormed into the tight spot. Her questing fingers hit the familiar shape of her handheld, then her SEM. Her fingers brushed his.

Motes of chemical fire traveled the pathway of her nerves. For a split second, it canceled out withdrawal symptoms. Bad. Craving personal contact got a mercenary as dead as being addicted to a SEM. Just faster.

Laboring for breath, she pushed her equipment into the larger tunnel, then groped for his hands. Another shower of internal sparks. She gave him the end of the tool belt and retreated. She switched her SEM on.

Her pulse and respiration rate eased.

V’kyrri’s didn’t.

“Get a good grip,” she said. The slack went out of the ballistic material. Edie pulled. Slow. Steady. For a bad moment, he stuck, and she feared pulling him into a wedge that would suffocate him. His pulse climbed. Respiration fell to zero.

Bracing, she pulled harder.

He didn't move. Then the lifeline shifted a few bare millimeters. A centimeter. Two.

One of his signals bounced. Respiration.

She hauled until his hands appeared. Dropping the tool belt, she grabbed his wrists.

He wrapped his fingers around hers, sending another flood of superheated chemicals into the pit of her belly. She held her breath to both smother the unwelcome fire and bend her will to extracting the Claugh captain from the jaws of the planet.

Sweat beaded his skin. The too rapid flutter of his heart didn't ease. Even though she'd pulled him into the open, he didn't release her or roll to sitting.

"You okay?"

"No."

She stabbed him with a hydration dose. Too early. Waste of crucial water.

He groaned and rolled to his back. "I couldn't breathe."

"I know."

He stuck a trembling hand into his right pocket and activated another dosing unit. His vitals raced as the drugs swept his system, then his pulse settled into something resembling normal.

Edie frowned. Second stim in the past few hours. And him, trying to hide his use. Maybe she wasn't the only addict.

"Got stuck in a spot like that when I was a kid," he said.

"You're claustrophobic?"

"Getting the breath-crushed-out-of-me-phobic."

"Yet you followed me? You're crazier than I am."

He huffed a laugh. "Best news I've had all day."

"No," she said, fingering the wire. "This is."

His brows drew together. "What the Hells?" Studying the wire, he sat up. His eyes widened. "This is ancient tech."

"Unreliable tech. Susceptible to mercenaries like me." She pulled a cutter from her belt and sliced into the black material covering a bundle of filaments. "Never occurred to me that they'd do a physical wire job on the base. But it makes sense."

She spread the filaments inside.

"On a world where the planetary crust scatters energy, directing signals through physical channels is the only option," he said, sitting cross-legged across from her, his knees within millimeters of hers.

Even in the smothering heat, his warmth reached her, alluring as one of the sweet, summer days of her charmed childhood.

Before the Claugh.

She shook off the memory. *Focus, Edie.* She offered him a tool and her handheld. "Get me in there?"

Stim burning his blood, V'kyrri met Edie's eye. She'd *asked* for help. From him. From a Claugh. He closed his fingers on her gear, fighting an unauthorized smile. Stim side-effect. No way would he have been smiling in the normal course of post traumatic experience while sitting beneath uncountable tons of planetary crust with one of his people's most notorious boogeywomen.

"Done," he said, spinning the extractor before applying it to her handheld.

Edie's gaze focused past her SEM lenses, studying him. The assessing look sped his blood.

"Engineer until they promoted me," he said. The back came off the little computer in his hands. He gestured at the wires she stripped. "I know the theory of wired systems like this. I'd never seen one."

"Me, either," she said. Her avid grin touched her eyes before vanishing. It slammed his senses. He couldn't hear for the pulse thundering in his ears.

She indicated the handheld, a resigned light in her eyes. "Pull the datacom protocol hardware. Don't cut the field connections."

He hesitated. "You're going to splice into the wire and what?"

"Download everything I can get my grubby mitts on."

"Your handheld will be seriously limited after."

"Don't I know it." The derisive smile on her face tugged free a mote of sympathy. She was sacrificing precious, expensive equipment on his behalf.

"Here," he said.

Without looking, she accepted the pieces of her handheld. Pulling tools from her belt, she wired her device into the UMOPG communications flow with a sure hand.

Admiration fired through him. She'd done this before, despite what she'd said.

"Trust me with the hack?" he queried.

She hesitated.

He held her gaze, urging her from within the damnably locked and silent confines of his skull to commit.

She passed the unit to him, a faint pucker between her brows.

Warmth, not related to planetary heat, expanded in

his chest. After so much loss in a short time, he'd take victory where he could get it.

They worked, Edie handing him tools from her belt before he could ask for them. She put away what he returned with the blind ease of someone long practiced in mechanical work.

"Were you an engineer? Or a flight mechanic?" he asked as he returned the final tool and powered up their makeshift spy station.

"Mechanically inclined enough that mother begged my father to put me to work before I'd disassembled the house. Done."

"Fragmented security protocols on this line," he said. "Looks like they weren't expecting anyone to come knocking from inside their own system."

She shifted to study the screen. Her thigh brushed his.

Heat and awareness rippled through him.

She tensed.

Every nerve in his body tightened in response. Pulling a slow, deliberate breath, he finished a final command.

File structures and com channels blossomed before him.

"There," she said, reaching to freeze the screen on a data stream.

He captured it. "What else?"

Her fingers closed as if she longed to rip her unit from his grasp. He'd decline. Their hands brushed as she identified files, maps, and communication streams she wanted to intercept. Sparks shot through him at each semi-accidental touch. He needed it, needed to use physical contact and her reaction, to coax her into trust.

As if he could tame Firestorm into trusting him, if it was remotely wise.

"That's enough," she said. "Pull the plug. Don't want anyone deciding to look back at me."

"Got any malicious code in here?" he asked.

"Lots. But unless you want my seek-and-destroy programs embedded in your ride off this rock, you'll get your hands off my file store," she said.

"Damn." He cut the connection.

Edie plucked the handheld from his grasp and reversed out her wire job. Once it was free, she reassembled the device and then activated it. "Charts. Charts. Where are the charts?"

Light flared in her SEM glasses. She grunted. "We're in business. This is an access tunnel for the com lines. Empties into the hangar. Twelve Gods bless calculated risks."

She brought a map up on her handheld display and shoved it at him. "Take it. Go back. Bring them."

She tapped the screen.

"The front door." He frowned over the map. His people were no more than half a kilometer from the hangar via that route. Adrenaline laced his bloodstream. Exultation, too. Side-effect of the stims, sure, but he reveled in the temporary morale boost, even if there was no way for Edie's plan to work.

"By the time you get the wounded to the hangar," she said with a malicious grin, "there will be no opposition."

"This is recon, Edie. We're not prepared for action. Stick to plan. You can't do this alone," he said.

"We're not going to get a better shot. I said I'd get you a ship. That's what I'm going to do. Right now, we seem to have only a few Chekydran running around murdering miners. You and I both know there'll be more, sooner rather than later. We have to get you off world."

"Then we stick together." He put the handheld back in her hands.

"You—"

"Edie," he interrupted. The razor-edge even he heard in his voice deflated her protest. He had to scrub damp palms on the filthy fabric covering his thighs. "No going back through that squeeze. Without you, or someone else, to pull me through—" His ribcage creaked, and he had to force breath into his aching lungs.

Edie rubbed her forehead. "Right. We'll improvise." She rolled to her feet.

V'k tried to rise and groaned.

She quirked an eyebrow at him.

"Twelve Gods," he complained. "Even my blood hurts."

His complaint won a grin. She offered him a hand before the humor in her face evaporated. Her gaze darted to his collar. Her fingers twitched.

She did not retract her hand.

"Be gentle with me?" he begged as he clapped his hand into hers, savoring the rush of hormones. As he'd hoped, her grin reappeared for a split second. She hauled him to his feet.

Attracted to and flirting with a Claugh-killer. Brilliant. Especially right after losing his ship and most of his crew. Unless that was why he responded to her. He'd expected to die. Had counted on it. Yet here he was warming himself by the fire of someone else living.

Anyone. *No*, his biology whispered. *Her*.

Pick someone who doesn't hate everything you value. He pulled free. "Let's do this."

They edged through the tunnel.

"Ladder," she said. "Hatch above. Hangar on the other side."

"We need a plan."

"Get a ship. Don't die." She started up the ladder, the clang of her boots on the metal ladder loud in the tight space.

"Insufficiently specific," he shot.

"What is it with you people wanting plans based on no information?" she groused. "I won't know what we're up against until I'm up there looking at it. I'm winging this. It's what I do."

"It's what you did," he corrected.

A *pop* hit him. A blinding shower of sparks arced. He threw himself to one side to avoid the embers. "Or I shoot you in the back for not warning me you were breaching the hatch."

A crack of light above. She advanced a rung.

He followed three, bringing his chest even with her calves. Her muscles twitched at the contact.

"Save the weapon charge," she said. "We're going to need it."

"Assessment."

She stilled, then, based on the squeak of fabric and the wink of her SEM, twisted to cast him a look. "Four explosives should do the job."

Words dry as the dust trickling down his back. Words that didn't do what he'd ordered. Which was the problem, wasn't it? The Claugh captain had tossed an order at Firestorm.

"Edie. I've got your back whether you want me there or not. I need a picture."

She jerked upright. "Fifteen marks in a one-hundred-meter square cavern. Three ships clustered in the far-left corner. Eight marks with the ships. Four stationary at what looks like the hangar entrance. Three in transit across the hangar."

"Give me the guards at the door," he said. "You and your explosives will—"

"Reverse it," she countered. "First pop has to take out those guards. They're the most dangerous and the most likely to get a call out if we miss. I make the rest as techs. Armed, of course. High alert. No Chekydran. Yet."

"Don't bring down the doorway. We're going to need it."

"Picky." She climbed and rolled through the hatch.

He shut off the light bar, swarmed up the ladder, and followed. He spilled into the open. Not even the high-powered alloy lamps blazing in a circle around the ships could eliminate the shadows. He rolled behind a tower of cargo crates where Edie sheltered.

She concentrated on what he assumed were explosives. They had legs. Many of them. She stroked the body of one. The metal legs splayed flat. Edie set the construct on the ground. The legs jerked, then arched at a creepy, wrong-way joint. The six foot-tips contacted the rock.

He glanced at a crate on the floor beside him. Standard UMOPG ore crate, half a meter high and deep. Half again as long. Electricity zinged up his arms. Frowning, he glanced at one hand. The fine grit embedded there glinted. Suspicion rolled him to his knees. He tried the lid. It wasn't locked. Were the UMOPG really that careless? Or that arrogant?

He rummaged until his fingers hit something solid that zapped a charge straight through his bones. He drew forth a pillar of clear crystal tainted with a smear of yellow climbing the matrix like a clinging vine. He shut the lid and turned to Edie.

The crystal in his hand hummed.

Edie's SEM lenses flared. She reeled, squinting.

Light ignited inside the crystal, following the coloration to the terminal point. V'kyrri spun to stuff the thing back in the box.

"Wait," Edie croaked. "What the Three Hells? It breathes."

"What?"

"Watch."

Her SEM field brightened, wavered slightly, then dimmed. A pause and the light grew again.

His palm buzzed. "It's *alive*?"

"Not unless it bites you," she said. "No. And yes. I suppose in a way it is. But not *alive* alive. I think you've discovered the reason we can't get a signal more than a few meters on world."

"If I'm right, every single box in this hangar is full of this stuff and that means the UMOPG are mining it here."

"Why?"

"That is the question. Along with where they're sending it. I assume it's the reason I lost two hundred and ten people."

"When we have a ship, you can take the whole container to your R&D people.

"Right." He put the crystal away.

Edie flipped one of her life-like machines over and worked a set of delicate controls.

"What are those things?"

"High maintenance friends," she whispered in return.

One of the mechanical monsters started walking. Two more trailed it. They marched around the crates, into the gloom, angling for the cluster of ships.

"What about this one?" He lifted a finger. The legs supported a disk the size of his palm. Another atop the first gave the impression of a head, and maybe that wasn't far from the truth. V'kyrri assumed the smaller disk housed an onboard computer.

"Time delay."

One of the legs jerked.

V'kyrri started. He scowled at her grin even as the sight of it trailed heat down the front of his body. "Do all your tricks give your friends heart attacks?"

"Mostly."

The last device cantered past his toes, headed for the main hangar door. He glanced at Edie. She crouched beside him, a gun in hand. It wasn't the one she'd loaned Chavolgen.

"I distinctly recall searching you," he said, drawing his own weapon.

"Highlight of my day. Five seconds."

He tightened his grip on his pistol, encouraged that she'd bothered to warn him.

Pop. Pop. POP. BANG.

The cargo containers groaned.

Edie heaved to her feet.

He stumbled into the open at Edie's side, scanning for opposition. Smoke rolled along the cavern floor, swallowing the lights, equipment, cargo boxes, and whoever wandered amongst them.

Edie fired into the billows of smoke that smelled faintly of sweet ob tree spice.

V'kyrri angled for the spot memory told him there should be guards.

"Dead," Edie said.

Someone fired at them. A too-fast-to-follow bolt of plasma tore a hole in the haze, illuminating a man in a brown uniform. V'kyrri fired.

The man collapsed.

"This way," she said.

V'kyrri grabbed her wrist. "Can't see."

"Neither can they," she said, leading him into the thinning smoke at a jog.

As they ran, the haze lifted.

The trio of squat ships loomed. Bodies slumped beneath them. The vessels sat in a rough triangle, ramps facing into the center.

Edie circled the outside of the formation, stepping over the blood and, in one case, body parts, littering the smooth floor.

Someone groaned, audible above the noise of their boots. Adrenaline burned V'kyrri's system.

Edie dodged a row of barrel-shaped calibration robots.

V'kyrri cleared the row. A technician had taken position behind the robots. The man huddled on his hands and knees, shaking his head. V'k brought his gun to bear.

Edie pounced. She yanked the man upright. In a flash, she had one arm twisted behind his back and her forearm braced against the back of his neck.

The man's back arched. His in-drawn breath hissed.

"Move." She marched the glassy-eyed prisoner between the ships, up the nearest ramp, and in the open hatch.

Alert to the slightest threat, V'kyrri trod Edie's heels into the cockpit.

Edie shoved her captive at a control panel bristling with crystals.

V'k frowned, studying the familiar, utilitarian navigation panel rendered surreal, crystal-studded sculpture. The crystals pulsed with light. His head throbbed in time. He glanced at Edie.

Her SEM field hadn't been affected. Data ran in unreadable scribbles down the lens field. Though, it looked to him like the script pulsed in time with his head. She appeared too focused on her prisoner to notice.

"Unlock the ship," Edie commanded.

The miner growled.

"Unlock it and live," she said. Hard. Cold as ice.

He sneered.

"Captain," she said.

A thrill jolted V'kyrri. Firestorm had addressed a Claugh officer by rank. And he wasn't in her line of fire.

"My handheld?"

"Allow me," V'kyrri said.

Chapter Eleven

Surprise lifted Edie's eyebrows. Instead of retrieving her handheld from her belt, V'kyrri took the captive with a grip on the man's neck that made her throat ache.

The miner wheezed.

Edie surveyed the panels. She had no idea how the crystal-encrusted controls worked. Nothing she'd learned about system cracking would apply. No choice but to strong arm the captive.

"He'll unlock the ship, now," V'kyrri said.

The SEM communicated the pattern change in cadence and tonality of V'kyrri's words. She glanced at his out of focus gaze.

"These panels. The crystal," he said. "According to our new-found friend, this is how the miners militarized."

His grip on the miner's throat loosened.

The miner's face had gone slack. He blinked and leaned over the ship's controls.

Ice dripped down Edie's spine before her brain had a conscious chance to do the math. Her gaze twitched to V'kyrri.

Concentration lined the corners of his eyes and furrowed his forehead. As the captive hesitated, fingers on the panel, V'kyrri's expression tightened. He tipped his head and leaned forward as if compelling the man by sheer force of will.

Awful awareness expanded in her chest. The absolute zero of cold terror circled the inescapable black hole of a single word.

Telepath.

Edie shuddered. All the times he'd stared at her and she'd felt pried apart. Each time he'd touched her and her head had creaked. It all added up.

V'kyrri was a telepath.

She backed up a step. As if that would help loosen the terror tightening around her throat.

V'kyrri winced.

The captive gasped and jerked upright.

V'kyrri grabbed the miner. Sweat beaded the captain's upper lip. His respiration rate sped.

"Edie," he rasped. "Put a cap on the fear. You're slicing me up, and I can't keep a grip on him. I'm a telepath. I should have warned you. I'm sorry. Like you said. Maybe I should wear a sign."

The desolation in the lines at the corners of his eyes punched through spiraling panic. Edie grappled with emotion.

Obvious solution here.

Use him long enough to get him and his people off world. Do that and her concern about having her every secret exposed would be moot. If the Claugh captain could control the prisoner into unlocking the ship, it made her job easier. Not to mention that it kept him and his talents busy.

Shifting her shoulders, she forced reflexive fear out of sight. She'd cope with that later. Right now, she'd steal a ship for a bunch of beat up Claugh.

The miner stiffened. His fingers returned to the

control panel.

Despite the sheen of perspiration on V'kyrri's face, Edie trusted the fact he had his gun trained on the man and appeared to have regained a mental grip on him, too.

Ship's systems lit.

"Stellar," Edie said, pleased by the steady signal of her voice on the SEM. She grabbed the miner. "Let go, Captain, and go get your crew."

His sea-green eyes zeroed in on her face. For a moment, Edie's skull creaked. Chilly adrenaline splashed her insides. She shivered.

V'kyrri blinked. The sensation faded.

The man in her grasp sagged, gasping.

"You?" V'kyrri asked.

"Disabling the other ships," she said. "Don't bring anything online until everyone's aboard, and then when you do, burn out. Fast. Dirty. Powering up this ship will bring the vermin running."

"I'm not leaving," he said. "This base owes me two hundred and ten lives."

"You're stealing this ship. I'll disable the other two. Chekydran are painting the rocks with Autken blood. And you're going to tell me it isn't enough?" she snapped.

"It isn't," he snarled. Rage and grief boiled up in his expression like storm clouds, obscuring every ounce of sanity she'd imagined he possessed. "It never will be."

She tensed as the knife of old terror and new sympathy twisted in her gut. She'd been where he was. Many times. Because angry Claugh hurt people.

V'kyrri gripped her arm.

She flinched, blood thundering at her temples.

"I want them dead," he rasped. "Every last one."

"I know a little about that," she breathed. "It's how you become a monster."

He focused on her. Whatever he saw in her expression broke through the haze of anguish and fury. His gaze turned inward. "I wonder if it isn't already too late for me."

The bottom fell out of her stomach.

He drew himself upright. "Come with us. We'll replace your ship. With the assistance you've—"

The captive in Edie's grasp snarled.

"Put a plug in it, or I'll give you back to the telepath," she said. "You'll come-to making out with this ship's reactor core."

V'kyrri eyed her. "You've done that."

Edie permitted herself a tiny smile. "Neural locked a traitor to the reactor. Took him two days to die. Go get your crew. I have a better idea for this one."

"Don't make a mess of Her Majesty's newest asset." Appreciation glittered in his eyes. It sped her blood.

"You won't even need a mop."

V'kyrri walked away.

Her captive's muscles twitched. Preparing for attack.

Edie stabbed him with the sole knockout dose she'd pulled from her envirosuit.

He tumbled to the deck plates.

She neural-locked him to a chair. Assured that he'd snooze for the next three hours, even with his metabolism, she slipped out of the ship and moved on to the other two.

The fastest way to prevent them from taking off in pursuit of V'kyrri and his survivors was to sever fuel feed lines. Of course, they'd be shielded. And built from alloy impervious to just about everything.

Just about.

She rushed to engineering and got to work. SQ-9 explosive. Inert until triggered. Blinking sweat out of stinging eyes, she fixed the SQ-9 to the conduit beneath the fuel feed valve and then bedded her trigger. Her favorite thing about SQ-9 was how it responded to energy fields—like a force field protecting a fuel line. The explosive underwent a chemical change, sticking fast and hardening.

Even if the UMOPG found her bomb, they wouldn't be able to pry it free.

As Edie finished placing her surprise package aboard the last shuttle, shuffling footsteps, and laboring respiration rates registered on her SEM.

"Edie?" V'kyrri's voice.

Based on the bio-signs, either Parqe had disobeyed and brought the remaining crew without orders, or V'kyrri had hunters on his tail. Possibly both.

Edie slipped out of the ship not certain she could endure another round of V'kyrri trying to convince her to evac with them. Especially if he turned his talent on her the way he had the UMOPG soldier. Part of her insisted he wouldn't. Old habit countered that she and her murdered family were all too familiar with Claugh ruthlessness. Did she want to stick around long enough for him to prove she wouldn't like telepath ethics into the bargain?

When V'kyrri edged into the hangar and gestured for those behind him to move up, Edie went to meet him. “Clear. Single stasis unit aboard. Board and get out of here.”

Parqe sucked in a sharp breath and stuffed her gun in its holster. “Double time it,” she said over her shoulder.

“Thank you, ma’am,” Fuller whispered as he rushed past.

“Go with the Gods.”

Lt. Chavolgen, burdened with three stretchers rather than two, brought up the rear. She paused before Edie. “Your pack.”

“You’re a mind reader,” Edie said as she grabbed her gear from the stretcher holding the body condensers.

A tremulous smile on her lips, Chavolgen shook her head. “No, ma’am, only the captain.”

Grinning, Edie clapped the woman on the back, then strode to the hangar door where V’kyrri crouched, covering his crew. Footsteps on the ramp dwindled.

“They’re aboard.” She hunkered beside him.

“Edie—”

“Left you a present,” she went on. “You’ll take a ship and a prisoner to interrogate. The other two ships are disabled. Or will be in the next few minutes. The explosions will be contained within the engine compartments. No danger to you, but if you can lift before the explosives go off, it’ll be better. If there’s not another hangar, you’re in the clear. If there’re more ships, these things are fast.”

“Yes.”

“Use it.”

“Get aboard.” He wrapped a hand around her bicep. “Come with us.”

Savoring the internal fireworks his touch set off, she met his gaze and shook her head. "You know what I am, and you haven't shot me. Thank you. But no one on your side of the zone needs confirmation that Firestorm escaped the war."

His frown shadowed his eyes. He let go and rubbed a hand down his face. "I have no way to repay you. But you're right. I can't take who you used to be where we're going. Damn it, Edie."

"Without asking which version of me you'd introduce to your queen, what would she do with someone like me, anyway—besides a firing squad? All I have to offer are explosives, a dislike for Claugh uniforms, and a pathologically bad attitude. How could that possibly go wrong?"

He laughed.

It fizzed her blood. She grinned around the catch in her breath. Stupid. The man was Claugh. And a telepath. He'd tried to strangle her and had kept her from scavenging parts from the wreck of his ship.

Here he was, finally about to get on a ship and fly away. Exactly what she wanted. Needed.

Yet her chest ached.

Light fired in his eyes. Stress lines eased in his face. He brushed fingertips along her cheekbone.

Sparks cascaded across her nerves setting her senses afire. Belated alarms shrilled in her head. *Telepath. Danger*. She flinched.

His hand fell away. His expression smoothed over, a trackless expanse, empty of emotional landmarks. Only his fingers, curling into a fist—one meant to preserve something within it rather than tightening in anger—communicated hurt.

Guilt clawed Edie's ribcage.

Wearing an *it's all right* upward twist of lips that in no way qualified as a smile, he nodded.

She couldn't say what bubbled up within to drive her. Pressure built, a faint buzz, like a distant hive of slug wasps. Since leaving her world, she'd lived being pitied for being deaf. He lived being feared for being a telepath. As much as she hated pity, she detested the fear in her that added to his injury.

"Sorry," she murmured and leaned in to touch her lips to his. Nothing more than a fleeting peck, a clumsy apology.

His lips parted, and he drew a ragged breath, urging her closer. He wrapped fingers around the base of her skull, working his mouth on hers. Even though they were both grimy, beneath the salt and dust on their lips, he tasted clean and faintly sweet, like the haschera berry candy that was a delicacy on her world.

Fluid heat burned in her lower abdomen. Unfair. She broke free and rasped, "Get clear, Captain. Warn your queen. I'll cover your escape, then I'm out in my ship once the sun sets. I'll be a few hours behind. I swear."

Behind but not following.

He stared at her. Biting out that curse her SEM couldn't translate, he rose. "I'll find you."

The promise should have scared her the way the mounting pressure inside her chest did. She'd eluded the Claugh for a very long time. Until this one.

She covered discomfort with a smile. She hoped. "If I don't find you first. Clear skies."

"Clear skies." He grabbed a crate of crystal and sprinted aboard the ship.

Every instinct in V'kyrri raged at him to drag Edie aboard. Duty drove him up the ramp alone.

Parqe slapped the hatch release before V'kyrri cleared it. The door shut, taking a uniform sample with it. He thumped the crate to the deck plating. "Stow that for Her Majesty."

"Our mercenary?" Parqe asked.

"Other priorities," he said. Regret twisted his gut. Wrong place, wrong time. Story of his life. He headed for the cockpit.

Chavolgen sat at weapons, Fuller at navigation.

"First. I'm grateful you disobeyed a direct order to stay put."

"We heard the explosions and took a vote," Parqe said. "You lost."

"You gambled with Chekydran and won. Once. No court martials this time, but don't make a habit of it. Now. Turn out your pockets, people. Hydration packs," V'kyrri ordered. "Any and all of Edie's supplies, save for pain doses. We're going to need those. She's going to need the rest."

His crew scrambled to dump a paltry supply of first aid kit, regen unit, and hydration packs into his waiting hands.

"Ensign Fuller, how's your sensor rating?" he asked as he shoved everything inside the larger first aid kit and accepting the light bar from Chavolgen.

"Still working on it, sir," Fuller said, flushing. "Missed the test by two last time."

"Good enough. Take sensors. We need to see what's out there. Lieutenant, I need you at navigation. We'll be going out hot."

"Yes, sir."

"Fire it up. Commander? If you'd stand by the hatch?" V'k said, striding to the door with Parqe on his heels. "I need this boat ready to burn out the second my boots hit this deck again."

"Yes, sir."

He forced weary, aching muscles into a shuffling jog.

Edie was trudging back the way he'd brought his survivors.

"Edie," he called. Reflex. Long-standing habit of taking hearing for granted. He kicked himself and pressed his pace.

She stopped. Turned. She strode toward him, flinging her arms wide, astonishment and annoyance in the set of her jaw.

"What the Three Hells are you doing?" she demanded. "You're supposed to be on that ship."

He pressed the first aid kit into her hands. "Your hydration doses."

She blew out an unsteady breath and sagged.

"What kind of captain am I if I don't take care of my crew? All my crew?" he asked.

Edie braced against softening her ire, especially when his fingers closed around her hands.

"A live one. I'm not your crew." Weak. And the longer she let him touch her, the weaker she became. *Come on, Edie. Cope*.

"Can you not accept help from anyone, or is it just me?"

Her breath caught. She'd been trying to resist him, failing, and been transparent enough that he'd detected it. Why had she been captured by the singularity of one Claugh officer? She had to escape, even if she tore herself apart doing it.

"Thanks, but if there's one thing I know, it's how to take care of myself. It's what I'm best at," she said, backing out of contact with him and then stuffing the first aid kit into a thigh pocket.

He snorted.

Edie straightened and pressed the heel of her hand against her achy sternum. "Back to your ride. Get off this rock so I can finally put the lot of you down."

Grim lines around his mouth eased. "We care what happens to you, too."

She frowned. Vibration settled deep inside her body, intensifying by the second, mounting pressure upon pressure. Enough to make her bones ache. "Do you feel that?"

His smile died. Eyes pinched half closed in discomfort, he flinched. "What is it?"

Recognition and dread hit at the same instant. "Chekydran troop carrier."

Teeth bared in a snarl, he spun and sprinted for the hangar.

Edie trailed him. She could barely breathe around the buzz inside her chest ripping at her breastbone. Through watering eyes, she studied the data trying to tell her something important. Vitally important. But the harmonic rattled her. Her eyes registered data. Her brain could wrest no meaning from it.

V'kyrri's head tilted. Clenching his fists, he bolted three steps into the hangar and slashed his arms through the air. A shooing motion.

Confusion leaked past the grip of Chekydran engine rumble. He was sending his crew away. Telling them to take off.

Gasping, she stumbled after him. "Get aboard."

"They're landing. Right here." He pointed.

A bulbous ship hung above the break in the hangar ceiling. Coming down fast. Her brain had no problem processing that.

V'kyrri brought her arm up around his shoulder and drew her tight to his side. Nerves sparked and burned. Energy flooded her system.

He urged her into a run.

Vibration shifted. Still painful, but no longer trying to burst or cook her brain. She could breathe. Think.

The Chekydran ramped engines to slow descent. The ragged, high pitch of another engine powering up fed into her visual field. Parqe and the kids. Anxiety squeezed Edie. They had to escape. They had to. She shrugged out of her pack and dumped it to the floor.

V'kyrri yanked her around a corner and into the shelter of a massive rock column. She curled around her equipment.

The stone beneath her shook. The planet itself trembled in dread at the arrival of the Chekydran.

Heat rolled down the wide corridor, eddies of engine wash licking exposed skin. She hunched, face to the cooler stone, arms wrapped around her head, hands shoved into her sleeves. She squinched her eyes shut.

V'kyrri huddled beside her.

The buzz deep in her chest eased. Stopped. Heat dissipated.

She opened bleary eyes and willed them to focus. Data confirmed sensation. The Chekydran had landed.

Chapter Twelve

The UMOPG ship holding V'kyrri's survivors still sat on the ground, engines warmed, but not throttled for lift off.

Edie straightened, the skin of her back and neck stinging. "They aren't taking off." Pressing a hand to the hollow at the base of her ribcage, she sidled around the column, trying for a glimpse of the inside of the hangar.

No Chekydran. Yet.

V'kyrri pasted himself to the rock outside of the hangar doorway and peered around the edge.

She joined him, leaving him a line of unreliable sight while she trusted data to paint the picture for her.

It made her catch her breath and yank her gun free. "Incoming."

Miners bounded up the corridor at them.

Edie grimaced. Caught between the Chekydran and the UMOPG with nowhere to hide.

V'kyrri wavered between the two threats, a snarl on his face.

"Hunt!" One of the miners roared above the rest. "Protect the crystal."

Edie risked a glance into the hangar.

The Chekydran ship opened. The bugs didn't bother with a ramp. Six Chekydran jumped from the underbelly of their vessel to the hangar floor. The monsters landed, skittering on oddly segmented legs. A pair of tentacles protruding from their shoulders waved weaponry. Their brown-striped throat pouches vibrated as the bugs hummed, filling the cavern, and Edie's data field, with sound waves. Chitin armor covered the creatures in shades of orangey-yellow.

She started firing, missing because her hands shook.

V'kyrri's shots hit, spinning screeching, ravening bugs toward the doorway.

Damn, the things moved fast. En masse, they swarmed for the ship holding the survivors.

She gasped.

Roaring, miners sprinted past, ignoring Edie and V'kyrri, likely counting them allies since they'd turned on the Chekydran, too. The miners fixated on the Chekydran and engaged.

V'kyrri started around the massive stone door jamb to join them.

She snagged him by the collar and hauled him back. "Are you insane?"

Stupid question.

He snarled in her face. Claugh. The definition of madness. "They're attacking the ship."

"No," she said. "They're after the crates."

For a moment, he froze.

A sonic signature lit her SEM. Adrenaline took hold. She threw V'kyrri, then herself to the ground out of the way of the hangar door.

"Edie. What…Oof."

Someone aboard the UMOPG ship fired the amidships gun. Impact communicated through rock to her body. She clenched her eyes shut. Even though she didn't see Chekydran and miner life signs wink out on her glasses, she had no doubt they had.

A split second later, the hangar roof came down. Rock smashed rock. Beside her. Around her. Atop her, crushing her against the unforgiving stone.

Edie screamed.

Still, stone cascaded down. Every shard squashing consciousness beneath the avalanche of SEM amplified sensory input.

Rock shifted, settling on her ribs, pressing the breath out of her. Immovable. No matter how she labored. The planetary crust gave not a millimeter. Panic set her clawing at rock, shrieking. Until another shift of the stone smashed her face to the ground.

Stillness took her.

****

V'kyrri roused, gasping. He groaned and tasted bitter, gritty dust. He struggled to roll to his back. Couldn't. Rock weighed down his legs and one hip.

"Edie?" he rasped.

She'd been right beside him. He couldn't touch her, physically, but she was still there, inside his awareness. Life trickling away like sand.

"Edie." Twisting, he hefted stones off his legs and pulled free of the rock fall. He climbed to his hands and knees, sucking in great gulps of air, expanding his chest again and again, driving out the chill of old fear and inhaling the new-found terror of losing… What exactly? His only ally since his crew had escaped? Someone he'd kissed? Someone who'd destroyed countless Claugh?

From a tactical standpoint, he ought to leave her. End an old threat to the empire right here, right now.

His soul twisted.

"No," he growled, heaved to his feet, found her bloody, twitching, outstretched hand, and began tossing rock off her in time with the growing pulse of Chekydran hum.

The monsters were in the base.

He and Edie were running out of time in more ways than one.

****

She ached. Every breath drove pain through her body and her brain, but at least she *could* breathe.

A cloth, smelling of antiseptic, smoothed sweat from her forehead and temples. Arms enfolded her. The last hands to do this had been her father's. When she'd caught Neffa flu and been miserable.

She shuddered. That's what this was. Flu. And everything—every terrible thing about what she and her life had become had been nothing but a fever dream, a warning sent from the Gods. Relief melted tension from her muscles.

She'd get better, and then her father would teach her to make Churkem flower fireworks. They were the pinnacle of his artistry. He'd said she might be ready.

All your hard work has paid off, Altheas, he'd said.

She smiled.

A hand smoothed her hair from her forehead. A tingle followed. Momentary relief curled and crisped. The sensual motes dancing in her blood meant this was not her father. He'd curled and crisped, too, along with his top-secret technique for Churkem flower fireworks.

She'd pulled people who should have been dead from a wrecked, enemy starship. Another tingle traced her cheekbone.

V'kyrri. It was V'kyrri tending her.

Gasping, she forced her eyes open.

He was alive.

She was alive.

She was still twisted and tainted by what the Claugh had made of her.

Through watering eyes, she sought the familiar, calming flow of data, the telltale pressure at her temples to ease the shudders beginning in her body. To drown out the persistent pressure of self-loathing.

Nothing. She frowned.

"Rocks." There'd been rocks, hadn't there? Sharp, insistent stabs ran up her arms. Her head throbbed. Her chest ached. She'd been buried. Crushed.

Confusion gripped her.

V'kyrri shifted from supporting her to kneeling at her side where she could see him. Speaking. His lips moved. His eyes were red-rimmed and swollen.

She couldn't drag the pieces of herself together enough to wrest comprehension from it. She shook her head. Lost. Sick. Aching. Eyes watering. Cold. She brought her hands up to say so, to make him understand.

Her fingers were raw and bloody.

V'kyrri enclosed her hands in his.

Startled, she met his gaze.

He offered her a tight smile, shadowed by discomfort and uncertainty. "*With your permission, I can help.*"

She drew a sharp breath. His lips hadn't moved, yet she'd understood him.

"*Your SEM was crushed. How you weren't, I will never know,*" he whispered into her head, his remembered fear bleeding into her brain. "*I may even be able to hear for you. You have my solemn vow to respect your privacy. Whatever it is that you're afraid I'll find out.*"

Fear stormed her system, and in that instant, he was gone. He blanched and rocked, eyes narrowed.

Shaken, she grappled with emotion. *Enough.* She wanted to understand. She needed to. Because even without her SEM, vibration rattled the rocks, beating at her. That meant Chekydran. Neither she nor V'kyrri had time for her fears.

She grabbed hold of his wrists, clutched hard. "Yes. Hurry. We have to go."

Leaning closer, he shook with a disbelieving laugh she could read without the SEM. He peeled her hands from his wrists and folded them together, his clasped around hers.

"*The ship took off without us. Parqe fired at and destroyed the Chekydran. The roof came down. It crushed the Chekydran and the miners.*"

"And very nearly us," Edie said.

"*Probably looked like it had. I'd like to think that's the only reason we were abandoned. You okay?*"

Motion behind him caught her eye and tripped her still-stumbling pulse. *Bug.* Edie snatched his weapon from its holster.

He twisted aside.

Edie fired.

The Chekydran went down, one eye stalk severed and twitching on the ground. The creature's tentacles writhed before going slack.

Edie pressed the heel of her free hand against her sternum. V'kyrri had registered her alert without her having to speak. Convenient. Her breath caught. *Terrifying.*

V'kyrri picked himself up and, staring at the dead thing, reached a shaking hand for his weapon. "Thanks."

Even from the side, she could read that word on his lips. She huffed a trembling laugh and gave him the gun.

"My pack," she said, shifting her knees beneath her before climbing to her feet. She'd lost a light bar. They were down to the one he carried, and it was cracked. The light blinked at random intervals.

She tottered down the dim corridor, disoriented and dizzy, because her gaze kept searching for the missing flow of data.

She sidled past the Chekydran leaking yellow-green fluid into the rock flour. Tremors wracked her muscles. Pain stabbed from her temples inward with every step she took. Nausea sloshed her gut. SEM withdrawal. *Great.*

Edie bent to sling her gear to a shoulder. Headache blinded her. She fell to her knees and gagged.

Hands gathered her hair. Fire traced her veins. It soothed the dry heaves wringing her stomach. She straightened, mortified. What was it about the man that let him straight into the worst parts of her life?

At least she didn't have to read the disgust and distrust in his face. *SEM addict.* Edie sighed. Parqe had been right. That rankled.

V'kyrri offered her a cloth streaked with mud.

A hint of antiseptic suggested it was a first aid wipe from her kit. The one he'd used when he'd hauled her from beneath the rock fall. She swiped her face, wishing for actual water to clean her mouth. Instead, she carefully wiped her quaking hands before discarding the dry cloth.

She threaded one arm through the strap of her pack.

V'kyrri assisted as she stumbled to her feet.

Edie raided her tiny store of hard candy. One for her. One for V'kyrri.

He stared at the orange-wrapped sweet laying in her palm. When she scraped hers out of the wrapper with her teeth, he set his hand on hers as if sealing a deal. The curl of his fingers against her skin sent heated tremors through her, while sweet, slightly astringent grebnol fruit-flavor lit up her taste buds.

"You're stuck with me," he said when she met his gaze. His smile took a secretive, sexy turn that shook her to the core. He unwrapped the candy and popped it in his mouth.

Despite the headache hammering her skull, her nerves tingled, trailing sensual promise along her gritty, perspiration-damp skin. *Stuck with him.* His idiotic smile, his weight tipped toward her, and his prying gaze struck flame to her awareness of him. Electricity sparked every nerve. The madman looked *pleased* with himself

"You did this on purpose," she gasped.

"Getting left for dead? Sure. Because it's such a holiday being stranded on this burning ash-heap crawling with Chekydran." He drew and lobbed a shot into the darkness to his right. Her left. Flailing tentacles fluoresced a weird, vibrating indigo, then collapsed.

He said something.

"Slow down and look at me," she said.

"I get another shot at these bastards. So what? You'd have died without your supplies," he said.

"Had you gotten on that ship and taken off like you were supposed to, I'd have stolen what I needed."

"While—"

"Slow down and look at me," she snapped.

His features tightened. He sucked in a measured breath, damped down expression and very deliberately said, "While dodging miners and bugs?"

She snorted. "Do you really imagine I wouldn't recognize a deep need for vengeance when it stares me in the face?"

"You would," he muttered. "And you, resistance soldier. With your vast experience in revenge against my people. Are you suggesting I should get over it?"

"Good money in revenge," she said. Then she pinned him with a stare she hoped got her message across. "But the way I see it, you don't have a plan for getting out. At all."

He met her eye, his expression bleak.

"Survivor's guilt, much?"

He said nothing. His expression darkened.

"Yeah. I know a lot about that, too, Claugh. Get past it. You're worth more to your queen alive."

"Not anymore."

She gaped at him. "You can't be serious."

"Edie, I burned out. I told you I'm a telepath. And you've had some experience with it."

"Slow down or get in my head. I can't understand when you go that fast."

He grabbed her wrist. "*This is touch telepathy. The lowest form of the talent. It's what I'm reduced to since the wreck. Touch telepaths are common among my people. It wasn't why Her Majesty brought me into the ranks.*"

"You've suffered injury and trauma. You'll heal."

He shook his head. "*As a natural consequence of working in close contact with a high-powered telepath, connections develop. Pathways into one another's brains. No matter where I was, no matter where my friends were, I had a constant sense of them. I knew where they were and whether they were alive. If need be, I could get messages to them, or they to me via that link.*"

Frowning, she eyed him when he paused. Furrows marred his forehead.

"*Useful, but there's a price. If I die, that link can kill. Even if doesn't, it does serious injury.*" His forehead crease hardened, and his gaze slid away from her. Shadows hollowed his cheeks. "*The Rhapsody was in pieces and already going down. I'm not telekinetic, but I did my best to hold her together. Mentally. I couldn't.*"

"You expected to die, and you didn't want to take your friends with you," she whispered, the ache in him infecting her. "V'kyrri, what did you do?"

He shrugged. "*Cut the connections.*"

Such a bland trio of words. "You're in my head, trying to block me out of that memory. You have no idea how it's hemorrhaging all over me. You didn't 'cut' anything."

"*Ripped,*" he allowed. His eyes closed. "*Ripped the connections out by the roots.*"

Desperate measures…because no one survived the kind of wreck she pulled him from. He hadn't taken the time to be neat or tidy.

"You did damage," she said.

"*Permanent*."

There was more. How she felt it trembling just out of her reach, she couldn't know. They'd long since passed her limited understanding of how her own brain worked, much less any knowledge she might have about a telepathic brain.

"You believe that's the only use your commanders had for you? That they'd put you in command of a brand-new class of starship simply because you're a telepath?"

His eyes opened. He released her. "I appreciate what you're trying to do—"

"You're afraid. I get that."

"Afraid?" He jerked back a step.

"Totally rational," she said. "I'm afraid, too. Cause if I take you into Claugh space, there's a good chance I'll get shot on sight. You're afraid your commanders won't want you back. But they need what you know."

"The others got away," he snapped. "No one needs me."

"They took off," she countered. "There were Chekydran inbound on the planet and likely a carrier in orbit."

He paled.

"We hope to all Twelve Gods they got away," she said. "If the well-being of your empire rests on knowing what's going on out here, they need you. And if I want your empire to stop the Chekydran—and I very much do—it's in my best interest to get you to them. If you're still bent on revenge here, just so happens I'm looking for work."

"You'd work for the Claugh?"

"No. But I'd work with you on this job."

"Edie. I'm touched."

She balled up a fist. "Not yet."

He grabbed her arm and yanked. "Run."

Sick-making dizziness doubled her over, and he dragged her several steps.

"Run."

Her skull creaked at the volume of his shout inside her head. Dizziness vanished, and Edie found her footing.

V'kyrri lobbed a trio of shots over her shoulder.

Laser fire scorched the stone beside her. Rock shards exploded outward. Edie flinched at the gravel peppering her cheek.

They pelted into the gloom. The light bar on V'kyrri's belt flung illumination and crazed shadows across tunnel and misshapen stone alike.

Head buzzing, pins prickling her scalp, Edie dug into her belt with shaking fingers. She yanked free of V'kyrri's grip, losing a layer of skin in the process, and spun to face an oncoming tidal wave of Chekydran.

"Catch, you baxt'kal freaks." She threw a tiny, glowing marble at the lead bug. V'kyrri caught her by the scruff of the neck and jerked her off her feet.

She yelped, fell shoulder-first into a bed of scree, and half tumbled, half slid down a slope.

A green-cast flash from above lit the cavern for a split second. The blast wave shook her.

Gasping, counting cuts and bruises, Edie skidded to a stop, spread-eagled on her back. Sharp-edged rock dug into her skin. Her right arm and leg dangled in open air. Terror coated her insides. Another few centimeters and she'd go over that edge into who knew what. Edie tried to ease her too-fast gulps of air and realized she could see. A little bit, at least.

Sand trickled to her chest from the impenetrable dark above. Grains jumped on her coverall driven by the thud of her heart.

She turned her head to look up-slope, gasping when she slipped another millimeter. She couldn't go on lying there, waiting for more Chekydran to rush toward the racket she'd undoubtedly made blowing up their friends. Did bugs have friends? Not to mention that if there was light, it meant V'kyrri had tumbled down slope with her. Maybe. He could be hurt. Or suspended over the void, clinging to the edge for dear life. He might even be calling for help in a voice she'd never hear.

That sent a pang through her. Some time when she wasn't caught between Chekydran and falling to her death, it might be interesting to unpack her newfound wish to *hear* his voice.

She sucked in a long breath and gathered determination to save herself.

Chapter Thirteen

A hand clamped over her mouth.

Edie slid.

An arm circled her ribs and scraped her backward along the edge of the precipice. A belated shower of internal sparks whispered *V'kyrri*.

"*More bugs*," he said into her head. "*And miners*."

Edie sagged. They couldn't catch a break.

The spill of light from the light bar V'kyrri carried illuminated the slope they'd come down and the hole that had nearly consumed her.

V'kyrri hauled her upright, and took her hand, but said nothing. Unfamiliar data trickled into her head, tracing her nerves, setting them alight, and then settled into an uncomfortable itch behind her ears. Edie flinched.

"*What is that?*" Her head spun. Nausea clawed her esophagus.

He set her down on what looked like another trail.

She swayed. If this was what he called hearing, her brain had no means of translating it.

He jumped to the ground beside her and yanked her off the other side of the path into the deep shadow beneath a massive structure. The stone folded and draped like petrified cloth. He drew her behind one of the folds and shut off the light.

"*Listen,*" he commanded.

The cascade of meaningless information scraping her nerves redoubled. Edie jerked out of his grasp. Peace. Emptiness. The intolerable, unfathomable itch behind her ears quieted. Edie breathed a sigh of relief and caught a glimpse of bobbing, swaying light. At least one set of incoming.

V'kyrri took her arm. "*What's wr—*"

Pins stabbed through her skull. She scuttled away and held up a hand to forestall him when he reached for her again.

"No."

He pulled her close and cupped a palm over her lips, his own pursed to shush.

Wishing she could dismiss the flare of heat in her blood as easily, she batted his hand away.

He grabbed her wrist. Things crawling her nerves and stinging above and behind her ears came back. "*What is wrong with you*?"

She sucked in a breath between clenched teeth and flinched out of his grip. She gave him the crooked finger sign for pain. His frown deepened. Of course he couldn't know what it meant. Who'd have taught it to him?

"Hurts," she whispered.

He reared back, eyebrows high. Scowling, he set fingers to her skin once more. Edie shivered. Good-shivered. Except for him being Claugh.

"*Don't try to talk. Think at me. I'll catch it.*"

She pressed fingertips into her skull above and behind her ears. It did nothing to assuage the discomfort crawling like bugs inside her skull.

"*I don't understand. Stop,*" she begged. "*Make it stop.*"

Silence.

Edie sagged.

V'kyrri caught her.

"*Is this painful*?" V'kyrri whispered into her head as he craned his neck to survey the approaching light.

Edie shook her head.

"*But this is*?"

Nerves fired the itch inside her head to life. Edie stiffened. Gasped, "Yes."

It died.

"*I should have known it wouldn't be that easy. I can't hear for you.*"

"*Fine.*" She'd cope. Anything was better than feeling like her head had been turned into a star drive overflow valve. Overflow valves were tough. Had to be. They vented radiation overboard in an emergency. But she'd never seen one that had survived being used. At the moment, her head felt pretty pocked full of dings and holes.

She shook off the impression and focused on reaching V'kyrri via his instruction to think at him. "*Miners and bugs. Run or fight*?"

He wiped his expression clear as if he'd been chiseled from Isarrite. The light in his eyes hardened. He smiled.

Her blood ran cold.

"*I want this base turned into a pile of smoldering rubble.*" V'kyrri drew his weapon and brushed past. "*My ship, my crew, my show.*"

By all means. Edie breathed anticipation into her bloodstream. Marvelous anodyne for the withdrawal headache stretching the bones of her skull.

A dozen UMOPG soldiers, silent, and bristling

with weapons, rounded a stone formation that looked like a waterfall turned to stone.

V'kyrri picked his way through a dried-up ripple dam bed, looking for a better sighting picture on his approaching slice of revenge. He welcomed the burn of his body's own stimulants. Adrenaline heightened his senses, sharpening his vision and steadying his hand.

Edie took cover behind the shattered teeth of stalagmites.

The miners rounded into view.

V'kyrri brought his pistol up, supported by both hands. Braced against a broken off stalagmite, he pulled the trigger, hard.

Soldiers shouted and fell. At least two of them had the discipline to return fire that struck and melted stone before V'kyrri burned them down.

Silence, except for the drumming of his pulse in his ears.

Edie set two fingers against the back of his hand. A palpable tremor moved through her.

His pulse changed tempo in response. Sensual anticipation proved as good as a stim shot. He shifted to loosen the tight seams of his trousers. Side-effects nearly as uncomfortable.

"*Who the Three Hells taught you to shoot*?" She flung a gesture at the scene, then turned a look at him that sped his blood. Admiration lit her face. "*Not a single melt mark on the rocks. Are you sure you want to go back to a life of rules and regulations? Think of the credits we could make with your aim and my bang.*"

"Oh, I'm going to want to hear more about that," he whispered, making certain he faced her, and that she was looking at him.

Her grin lit his system.

Chekydran hum sobered him. Even the stone beneath his feet resonated with the damnable, unending vibration.

Edie winced.

V'kyrri held his breath, listened, and scanned the darkness beyond what the light bar cast. The distant thunder of rock cascading over rock caught his attention. It moved. Came closer.

Beside him, Edie's breath rasped. "They're coming."

He frowned. His brain rearranged noise.

Chekydran. Not rocks falling. He was hearing countless chitin legs on stone.

Adrenalin thumped his heart to a gallop. V'kyrri spun.

Edie grabbed his wrist.

The first glimmer of weird indigo fluorescence poured into the cavern above them.

V'kyrri and Edie ran.

Chekydran swarmed after them. Hum, and the weird, scratch and clatter of insect legs on rock reverberated off the walls.

A rock turned beneath his boot. His ankle twisted. Biting off a cry of pain, he wrenched sideways.

Chekydran spilled into the path behind them.

"Baxt'kal hells," Edie barked and pulled him into a jumble of shattered rock.

Limping in her wake, he bent double to keep stone between him and the bugs firing at them.

Gun fire and screams, Autken and Chekydran both, echoed from the deep dark before them. V'k reached for Edie.

She set her fingers against her bare temple, wavered, and stepped in a hole. Edie vanished without a sound.

V'kyrri gasped and dove to catch her. Her grip on his wrist twisted away, leaving friction burn on his skin.

Heart clamoring against his ribs, he stared into the opening in the floor.

"Jump!" she ordered.

He rolled headfirst into the pit. A tentacle wrapped around his injured ankle. Pain stabbed his leg. He wheezed.

Like a goddess materializing in the depths of the lowest Hell, Edie's upturned face swam out of the gloom. She stared past him, eyes narrowed, and lips twisted.

She lifted a tiny gun. Fired.

Nothing happened.

Suspended head down in the gloom, V'kyrri kicked at the tentacle.

A flash. A noise like a child's balloon popping.

He fell and hit water. Surprise sucked it straight into his lungs. He floundered. Something caught him by the scruff of the neck and heaved. He broke the surface, choking.

His knees touched bottom. V'k crawled slippery rock out of the water and collapsed to his side, coughing.

Edie moved into his line of sight and shot a leery glance at the ceiling. "We gotta go."

"Stim," he croaked, praying she could read the words. "Hip pocket."

Lips pressed to vanishing, she shook her head, then seemed to catch herself. Her expression didn't change.

She knelt close. Her body heat entwined with his. She set one hand to his shoulder, giving him access to the tremor rattling her and shoved her hand in his pocket.

Edie gave him the dose.

His blood turned to fire. Gasping for breath, he curled into a fetal position while the approaching pressure of Chekydran hum lashed him. He forced his hands and knees under him.

Edie left off casting surreptitious glances at her handheld screen. She shook her head, hooked an arm through his, and levered him upright. Their run deteriorated to a shuffle.

He glanced over his shoulder.

A writhing mass of glowing indigo monsters swarmed the dark at the far end of the cave.

In the miserable heat, cold gripped his chest. They couldn't outrun the bugs. *Edie*. He shoved what he'd seen into her brain.

She snarled.

His own lips curled in response. Fear exploded to rage within her. Images flickered through his head. Edie, flashing through options and scenarios. Coming up empty.

Light rushed up from behind his right shoulder. It exploded against an exquisite chunk of white stone hanging in folds beside him. The light seared an image into his head. A fissure. He lurched off the path for it.

Edie pressed close. Another shot struck rock above them, sizzling.

V'kyrri shoved Edie into the break between stones. She shucked her pack. It splashed when it hit the ground. She turned sideways and sidled deeper, dragging her pack. He followed, his boots sliding in the thin trickle of water tracing the stone.

V'kyrri lost the individual thumps of his pulse to the erratic crackle of pain pounding through his chest. Air weighed heavy.

On his fifth hurried step, the floor shattered beneath their feet. He fell.

"Oof." He hit a smooth surface and slid. He clawed for purchase. Found none.

CRUNCH.

Edie groaned.

V'kyrri landed on a bed of thorny stones. It hurt to breathe. It hurt to not breathe. He forced himself to move, to put aside cataloging new cuts and bruises. He had to find Edie.

Distant thunder rumbled into the chamber. He had no means of identifying the source. It went on and on.

He frowned and set aside trying to make sense of it. He tapped the light bar.

Nothing.

The fall had killed it. With shaking hands, he fumbled for his pistol. With a minor adjustment, the energy chamber could be repurposed as a wan, blueish emergency light. Dangerous. The weapon couldn't be fired without being switched back, and they had a swarm of enraged Chekydran hunting them.

A tiny flush of light from his gun. The weak glow grew, flashing, reflected from shining crystal facets gathering and amplifying the light until he squinted, dazzled by the shifting play. He gasped.

They'd fallen into a massive crystal deposit. Translucent crystal bristled, glittering. Mammoth specimens as thick as his personal command shuttle crisscrossed the chamber. A thin fall of water tumbled from the hole they'd fallen through.

It heightened sweltering heat by introducing humidity into the equation, but at least they had water.

V'kyrri spun, looking for Edie.

She stood, staring up the broad slide of the crystal between them. V'kyrri detected fresh blood tracking the side of her face. Edie shivered and wavered on her feet, her face gray, and her lips blue-white in the ghost light.

SEM withdrawal.

Parqe had been right, after all.

"V'kyrri." The tremor in her over-loud voice jerked him to attention. He followed the line of her gaze. Shards of dark stone pattered from the ceiling. His breath caught on a glimmer of indigo.

Chekydran. The source of the sound rolling through the caves. Chekydran tentacles flailing the stone. Chipping it away. Carving a new, Chekydran-shaped tunnel.

"They're breaking through," she said.

He slumped against crystal. His pistol-turned-flashlight came into contact. With a sound like a forest of string instruments all striking a single note, light exploded into the cavern.

V'kyrri reeled and stumbled, eyes shut tight. His hands slipped free of the crystal. Darkness settled. He cracked an eyelid, then blinked his eyes open on deep dark marred by round after-images of his seared retinas.

The pounding of Chekydran tentacles on rock had stopped.

"Three Hells," Edie croaked.

Thud. Chekydran attempts to reach them resumed.

He blinked his eyesight clear. Light flickered in the matrix of the crystal in front of him. His brain buzzed.

It hurt. More distinct noises of tentacles on stone overhead. Chips of rock cascaded down.

He gritted his teeth.

"Light the place up again," Edie said, "so we can look for a way out of here."

In the spirit of experimentation and hope that he wouldn't blind them, he touched the supposed-to-be-sealed energy chamber of his gun against a smaller crystal.

Light suffused the crystal and bloomed down the base and across the matrix to spill around the chamber, setting the walls, floor, and ceiling aglow. Where the crystal bed had fractured or broken, the spread of light stopped.

"Wild," she said and spun, presumably searching for an exit. "Energy amplification."

"Usual thing for crystal," he said. Not that she'd hear him or read what he'd said. Not while she was busy looking for an escape route and unable to see him. He scanned his side of the cave. Gleaming crystalline structures glinted.

"No good," he said. "Cravuul dung. We have to get you a heads-up display at the very least."

"Why?" She'd faced him and stalked closer to the center broad slab. "To assuage your discomfort over being stuck with a deaf SEM addict?"

"You're Firestorm," he snapped. "If we want to rank discomforts, that, combined with the color of my uniform, goes right to the top of the list."

To his surprise, she grinned.

A bigger chunk of rock fell between them. Edie ducked, smile dying.

"No exit," she said. "You?"

"No exit."

She paled and clambered across the massive crystal dividing the chamber. She cased his side of the cave.

"Baxt'kal Hells," she breathed.

More rock bounced down.

Edie plopped her backpack at his feet, crouched, and began digging in it.

"Edie."

He scowled and crouched, careful to keep his gun in contact with crystal. With his free hand, he gripped her wrist.

"Edie. Energy amplification. You said it yourself. We can't risk explosives in here."

"Dead is better than captured by Chekydran," she replied, voice wavering.

He shot a glance at the ceiling. The hole was visible now, both because of the light in the chamber and because of the glowing Chekydran steadily carving out access. "*Capture isn't in the cards.*"

She froze, gaze searching his face. Pulling out of his grasp, she rocketed to her feet. He opted for contact with her booted foot.

"*There has to be a way out of here,*" he said.

"Through them," she said, jerking her head to indicate the bugs. "You're using up the only weapons charge left between us."

A tentacle unfurled from above. It slammed into her, knocking her off her feet.

V'kyrri growled and instinctively jerked his gun up, trigger pressed. Light died in the room and the gun, notably, did not fire. He slammed it back to the crystal which blossomed back to life.

Edie yelped.

The tentacle grabbed her ankle and jerked her airborne. Her pack slid. Things—he could only assume explosive things—rained from her tool belt.

Another tentacle whipped around her throat.

A dam burst within him. Rage. Grief. A clawing, biting, wild impulse to rend and tear exploded through him. Two bugs jockeyed for position in the opening they'd beaten out of the stone. They held Edie between them. Her eyes bulged. Her lips were tinged blue. Her mouth was open on a shriek he couldn't hear above the roar inside his head.

Snarling, he released the useless pistol, clenched his fists, and reached for his most familiar, innate weapon. He advanced two steps and bumped against the massive crystal slide.

Water dribbled down his face. He ignored it.

It had been years, decades, since he'd turned his ability to harm. Memory lingered, though, as did the know-how. He flung out a trembling tendril of awareness, speared in through an eye stalk of the first monster. Then it was a matter of feeding a bubble of power into the creature's brain stem before detonating it.

One brutal *click*, and it would be permanent lights out.

But he couldn't muster the mental steam. Power flickered and dribbled like the water falling from above.

V'kyrri's knuckles brushed crystal. Agony and power burst into him. Maybe burst his skin. Heat consumed him. Light, too, as if he'd become the path a bolt of lightning took. Lightning he turned straight at the pair of Chekydran strangling Edie.

More of the monsters crowded in behind the two he

could see. Lit up the way he was, he *felt* them, the endless roil and scrabble of ravening Chekydran touching the matrix of the planet, as if the world was tuned to them. Their hatred and rage beat at him.

Mutual.

He jabbed every ounce of frustrated vengeance at the aliens killing Edie.

Let. Her. Go.

They screamed.

V'kyrri welcomed their pain, became it, and, finally, lost himself to it.

Chapter Fourteen

Edie groaned. Every part of her ached. Her throat. Her body where she lay against pointy crystal. Her head. All Twelve Gods, her head. She was in the middle of a thunderstorm named V'kyrri. Full-body percussion rattled her creaking skeleton the way spring storms had rattled her childhood home. She'd been afraid of them and of the pressure that had always felt like it might crack her bones.

This one threatened to explode her skull. She shifted, opened bleary eyes, and squeaked.

Blazing light rippled in waves through the crystal room. It threw knife-edged shadows and illuminated a pair of Chekydran reaching from a hole in the ceiling. Light and power pierced her brain. Her eyes watered.

The bugs slumped.

Adrenaline all but levitated Edie upright, and she scrambled out of the way. The Chekydran fell, first one, then the other—an obscene cascade of awful. Yellowish fluid sprayed in all directions. Hot spatters hit her skin. Edie flinched and threw her forearm in front of her face too late to shield her from bug blood, but the move offered her a glimpse of V'kyrri.

He stood rigid, one hand planted on the big crystal slicing through the room.

Weird, visible energy pulsated from him in waves that rang against her skull and breastbone. The massive crystal gleamed like a cold sun, engulfing him in the glare.

Motion at the hole in the ceiling caught her eye. She gasped and recoiled.

Another Chekydran swung grasping tentacles at V'kyrri. The tips curled and quivered. The bug writhed and strained as if reaching for the Claugh captain. Pleading. Begging, maybe.

It, too, slumped and fell.

Edie trembled at the raw power pulsing from V'kyrri.

Bloody shadows streamed off his face, his arms, his legs, and his torso, as if the light pounding in the crystals were blasting bits of him away. He twitched.

Her headache built. Nausea pressed the back of her throat. She staggered, desperate to haul him to safety. There wasn't any to be had.

Not to mention that with the telepath radiating menace and pain, she couldn't bear to get within a meter of him.

He swayed, pulsing rage, fear, and cutting hatred. It hacked at her bones. Edie clutched her aching head.

As far as she could tell, he was slicing the Chekydran to ribbons with his thoughts. A pair of Chekydran swarmed through the hole in the ceiling, rushing to attack.

Edie dove for the gun V'kyrri had abandoned. Crystal cut into her skin as her fingers closed on the weapon. She pulled the trigger.

Nothing happened.

Despair clogged her throat. Breathing hard, smearing moisture from her face with an impatient swipe of her sleeve, Edie flung the gun into one bug's eye stalks.

It reared back, tentacles swiping its eyes.

"V'kyrri. What's it going to take to get you to stop crushing my skull?" she yelled.

He blanched. The flow of blinding light beating around the room eased but didn't die. "Edie?" His knees gave. V'kyrri crawled to her side. "*We aren't going to make this*."

He didn't need to touch her to be heard. Edie swallowed hard. "I know. I'm sorry."

"*Me, too*."

He dialed up power. His eyes clouded over, the pupils expanding.

Edie shuddered.

The Chekydran, two in the chamber with them, and the ones pressing into the hole in the ceiling all froze. One by one, they collapsed.

Edie wrapped her arms around her throbbing head and swallowed hard. Beside her, V'kyrri jerked and gasped.

Light and color in the chamber winked to black.

"V'kyrri?" Edie shrilled. Quaking with adrenaline, she sat up, but couldn't see a godsdamned thing.

"*S'okay. I'm okay*." Faint words inside her skull.

Sea green glimmers, as if the room had found V'kyrri's eye color as attractive as she did, ran through the crystals, shedding enough light to see. She cast a glance at the ceiling.

No bugs. No living ones, anyway.

V'kyrri planted a shaking hand on her ankle. The knuckles paled. "*Something's happened*."

Besides finding out he could murder with his mind?

"*The Chekydran are* scared. *They're running away.*"

Edie climbed to her feet a centimeter at a time. She gathered resolve along with her scattered gear. "Then we have a hole. Time to get out of this death trap."

She glanced at him. Shadows like dark bruises beneath V'kyrri's eyes rocked her. Apprehension snagged in her ribs. She couldn't draw a full breath. "Are you okay?"

The corners of his eyes crinkled. The laugh he uttered twisted his expression in a way that made her glad she couldn't hear him. He didn't answer, just levered himself upright to stand swaying for several long seconds while he watched her pluck up belongings and hook them into her belt. Her morale recovered with every familiar piece she put in place.

She abandoned several explosives and tools trapped beneath the dead bugs. At least she still had her pack. For all the good it would do. Grinding resignation between her teeth along with gritty rock flour, Edie flung her Skeppanda line tied to a hook. It caught in the body of a dead Chekydran.

"Can you climb?" she demanded of the Claugh telepath.

"I'll climb," he replied. "Go. I've got your back."

She distinctly recalled lobbing his useless gun at a bug. He had her back without a weapon of any kind. Her gaze caught on broken, dead Chekydran bodies. Right.

Her dreams would be so pleasant if she ever got to sleep again.

Edie tried to moisten cracked lips with a dust-dry tongue. Grabbing her line, she climbed slick crystal with green light flaring beneath her every step. She scaled the bug corpse and turned back.

V'kyrri climbed. Light and shadow swarmed up the crystal room in his wake, as if begging him not to go. Whether he was infected by the odd pleading impression filling Edie's chest with the mad impulse to jump back into the chamber, or whether it was injury and exhaustion, V'kyrri's climb took longer. She finally hauled him free.

They hobbled into the pool chamber.

Edie spent precious seconds filling water containers and treating the contents. Then they climbed a wending path toward the main base corridors. She kept scanning the empty air, searching for data that would tell her where the UMOPG and Chekydran were.

The ground beneath her feet rolled.

Edie sprawled to the rock. Debris pelted her. She covered her head with her arms and curled into a tight, quaking ball. She couldn't get her breath. Couldn't separate memory from the present. Terror shrilled, cold and sharp into her body, crushing her.

"*Edie. Open your eyes. Look at me.*" V'kyrri had hold of her.

Gasping, she obeyed. She wasn't buried. Could see light, in fact, bright, burning daylight. Perspiration popped on her forehead. Frowning, she struggled upright. Confusion flushed her system. "Daylight."

He pointed.

Someone had blown a hole in the rock fifteen meters above them.

Edie gasped. "A way out."

"*The base is gutted. You took down a third of their ships. The Chekydran are busy slaughtering miners while running for their lives.*"

"What the hell makes Chekydran run in fear?"

"*Don't know. Don't want to find out.*"

Amen.

"If the Chekydran left any of the UMOPG alive, the miners will be bailing in the ships that do remain," she said between gulps for breath. "If they're smart."

"*No ship for us to steal?*"

"No. We're stuck making the run to my boat."

"*In daylight.*"

"Yeah. Here." She dug into the dwindling contents inside her pack and handed him a package. "Open that?"

Edie extracted her Skeppanda silk line.

"What is this?" V'kyrri asked when she glanced at him. He hefted an open box containing a little flier and remote control in his hands.

"Our way out," she answered, taking them. "You'd be surprised how much can be accomplished with a child's toy when you pull the battery pack and replace it with a miniature fusion core."

He rubbed his palms down the seams of his pants.

She grinned and secured an anchor system to her line. "Want to do a wire job on the anti-gravs from your ship?"

"Got another power supply?" he countered, pulling a pair of the units from his belt.

"Last one." She handed him the spare mini reactor core she kept for emergencies. To her mind, a base full of Chekydran running scared and fighting miners for control of deadly weapons counted as an emergency.

V'kyrri pulled tools from her belt, lighting off her system with every innocent brush of his hand.

She attached her line to the flier and, using her handheld, sent the tiny toy to the surface. "This'll be a gamble."

"*That the Chekydran and UMOPG are too busy to pay attention to us*?"

"Exactly." Using the flier's sensors, she found a boulder on the surface and fired an anchor into the stone as V'kyrri finished powering up the anti-gravs.

"Fix them to my harness," she said.

"*Good. That'll put us well inside the field.*"

"Let's go before we find out what scares Chekydran."

He grabbed her pack.

She stepped into the main part of the harness and held his open. Hand on her shoulder for balance, he stepped in. They straightened and Edie pulled the harness into position. A perfectly innocent excuse for her hands on his backside. Taut muscles twitched.

She clipped the anti-grav to the line. "Going up." She switched them on.

Their feet left the floor. Their bodies came together, supporting one another as they hung in the harness. He set a hand to the ascender and looked at her. Looked hard, willing her to meet his eyes, to process and accept what she'd begun to believe she'd find there.

Edie couldn't. She shivered. Want and anticipation coated her insides. Totally rational while waiting to get shot down.

She turned on the ascender and left her stomach behind.

V'kyrri craned his neck, a grin on his face.

They made it out of the caves in seconds, then rose

past a thin layer of bedrock. Heat rose with them.

Squinting in the over-bright sunlight, she stopped shy of her anchor and let V'kyrri climb out of the harness. Edie grabbed V'kyrri's hand to haul herself up. She retrieved her gear.

Surveying the sweltering landscape for new threats, V'kyrri stuck a hand in his pocket and fingered his last stim dose. Rise to one side. Hole in the rock to the other. Nothing but battered stone casting knife-edged shadow as far as he could see. He triggered the stim dose.

Crushing pain took his breath. His knees buckled. The distinctive shriek of a ship launching gave him adequate excuse to pretend he'd been taking cover rather than falling. He shifted into the dubious cover of the rocks.

Edie seemed to register the vibrational shift and dove to join him.

Two bulbous shuttles crested the slash in a hangar roof.

One slowed. The other angled for the blue-sky boundary. It climbed, abandoning its partner which dipped, spun, and fired at them. Plasma blew rock and soil into the thin air, working steadily closer.

V'kyrri bolted to his feet, pulling Edie with him.

They ran into the sunlight. Scorching heat slammed him. He couldn't get his breath. Every sip of air burned.

The Chekydran ship dogged them, not firing. It drove them, shooting when they approached the least bit of shade, playing hiztap and tezwoul. Laughing, if the bugs laughed, while he and Edie baked alive.

Edie broke free and squinting, spun to face the ship.

V'kyrri stumbled.

She rocked back and forth in her quest for oxygen. Every trace of moisture had evaporated from her skin. Bad. Wasn't it? Not being able to sweat anymore.

She threw her pack to the ground and withdrew the tiny pistol she'd used in the caves.

The Chekydran ship hovered, sliding back and forth in the sky. A grinning bully dancing in glee at having cornered its prey. The forward atmospheric gun glowed hot. Ready to destroy them.

V'k straightened.

Fine. Killed by Chekydran was better than captured by Chekydran.

Edie sighted, feet planted wide, one hand supporting the other.

V'kyrri snorted. His fire-haired goddess, spitting in the face of death.

She fired.

A tiny projectile arced out of the weapon. No way could it hit. A laser rifle might have. Her little gun shooting antique physical bullets didn't stand a chance.

The projectile reached the apex of its arc, far short of the shuttle.

V'kyrri grabbed her arm.

Edie tossed a vicious grin over her shoulder.

He froze.

The projectile sprouted wings and launched at the Chekydran ship.

Edie cackled.

"What the Three Hells is that?" he breathed.

The shuttle darted sideways and fired.

He yanked Edie out of the way. They tumbled to the dirt and into the shade of an overhang. Clasping

Edie to his chest, he rolled her to protect her for a split second with his own body.

The Chekydrans' shots never came.

Edie lifted her head, hand braced against his chest, lighting his nerves with an avid smile, anticipation in her wide, brown eyes.

The Chekydran ship exploded.

V'kyrri ducked.

Edie laughed. Debris and sparks showered out of the sky.

V'krryi wrapped his arms around her, ignoring the sharp-edged stones digging into his bones. He planted a quick kiss on her nose. "You scare me."

"Why, Captain, that's the nicest thing anyone has ever said to me," she chirped, her face waxen.

"Your bar is too low," he countered, digging into her pocket for hydration. He medicated her and took one himself.

Some of the tension ran out of Edie's muscles, and she softened against him as the color returned to her face. Within seconds, moisture appeared on her skin. As his own misery faded, heat that had nothing to do with solar radiation and everything to do with Edie dove straight to his gonads.

Even as the seam on his trousers tightened, he rolled Edie away and struggled to his feet. How could he be attracted to someone who'd killed thousands of Claugh?

He shook off recrimination and glanced at her a she rose. He waited until she looked at him. "Got another one of those things?"

"Nope."

Great. "We'd better get moving."

"The only way to survive this is to go from shadow to shadow," Edie said. She pointed. "That's our next stop."

He led the way into the sun. They made maybe ten meters, possibly fifteen. He collapsed into the shade, weak and shaking.

Edie sank to the sand beside him and tipped her head back, eyes closed, gulping for air.

He checked his fingernails. Blue. Hypoxia *and* heat. He shoved himself to his feet and led the next charge. And the next. He lost count of how many times they forced themselves into motion.

Lips white, blue tinging her pale cheeks, Edie finally pointed.

A glint of metal caught his eye.

A ship.

Gray enough to blend into the stone and shadow of a rock wall.

Edie shoved a water container at him. She took the other. Her throat worked exactly three swallows. She capped the container.

He followed suit. Hot, stale water, tasting of antiseptic hit his tongue. He forced down a trio of gulps and frowned as a weird buzzing *chur* sang in his ears.

Edie started down slope, skidding and sliding. He followed, the noise in his ears pressing deep into his bones.

The sound burst from inside his head to palpably audible. A swarm of massive, iridescent insects flew into the sky, rising from the opposite rim of the crater.

V'kyrri grabbed her arm.

Edie blanched.

They ran.

The massive insects swung to follow.

Their wings. It was the sound of their wings in the thin air driving into his skull. For a split second, the noise resolved into whispery, pleading voices.

"*Save us. Save you.*"

He shook away dizziness. Panting for oxygen the world didn't have to give, he locked his gaze on Edie's ship.

Edie stumbled. "*What the Three Hells are they*?"

He hooked arms with her but couldn't say who supported whom. Much less identify where the shivers of dread originated. With him or with her. A glance over his shoulder showed the massive insects dipping into the crater, wings a blur.

His pulse tripped and his throat closed before his brain registered how slowly they moved despite their frenetic wing motion. A trill brushed him.

It said *save*.

He slowed.

Edie yanked.

He fell and hit deck plating.

The hatch closed. A cool breeze touched him. Sweat coalesced on his skin, soaking his hair and his clothes.

V'kyrri looked at Edie.

Relief swept her, leaving her weak and shaking. She swiped a sleeve across her stinging eyes, then her damp forehead. She met V'kyrri's gaze. The bottom dropped out of her stomach. Gasping, Edie scrambled backward until she came up hard against her hull.

His pupils shrank to pin pricks. Sea green expanded until it took over the entirety of his eyes, obscuring even the whites.

Though his gaze lined up with her face, she detected no hint of V'kyrri in it. His mouth moved. "Out," it said. "Emerge." V'kyrri's green gaze turned to the hatch. He went on repeating "out" and "emerge" over and over.

"Out of what? What is wrong with you?" she demanded.

The chant didn't stop. It struck her that he wasn't blinking. Edie shuddered.

"V'kyrri," she snapped.

He crawled to the hatch, began striking it with the heel of his hand.

"Stop it." She couldn't get a full breath. This wasn't run-of-the-mill Mad Claugh. It was as if someone or something had hold of him.

The ship trembled. Overhead lights flashed a ship-under-attack sequence. Edie clenched her fists.

The massive flying things. Imagination supplied a mental image of the creatures prying her and V'kyrri out of the ship.

She clambered to her feet and stumbled for the cockpit. She needed weapons. Shields. She needed off this thrice-damned rock.

"V'kyrri. Snap out of it." She climbed into her command sling, the biomechanical mesh that allowed her to control her vessel from one place. It folded around her, providing data via tactile and visual feedback. The mesh popped her with a double dose of hydration therapy, one in each leg. The treatment spread through her system. Atmospheric controls lowered ambient temperature. Cool air brushed her sweating skin. She shivered.

V'kyrri's core temperature had to be as high as

hers. Not good and nothing she could do about it while he was possessed.

She flipped on the cabin mic.

Data flowed down her screen. V'kyrri, still pounding on her sealed hatch like he couldn't figure out the control, repeated "out" and "emerge" over and over.

Affording a cursory glance at the vital stuff, containment and life support both doing their jobs without a hitch, Edie fired engines and popped the shields.

The tremble in the ship ceased. She probably hadn't hurt the creatures with the energy fields. Probably.

"Edie?"

The cabin mic picked up the word and pasted it on her heads-up display.

"I'm in the cockpit," she said. "We're getting out of here."

"Open the door."

Gritting her teeth, Edie lifted in answer. The ship shuddered off the surface. Irrationally, she hoped the big *things* out there had cleared off before she'd sprayed superheated exhaust all over.

"No. No." Flashed on her screen, punctuated by what she guessed were fists on hull plating. It was the only logical translation of the sound data her system fed her. Edie sucked in a half-breath. Hell of a thing, finding out she needed shields for the inside of her hull. If she made a career out of hauling crazy Claugh, she'd look into it.

The ship thundered into the sky.

Chapter Fifteen

"Save us," V'kyrri shouted. The pounding on her hatch finally stopped.

Edie glanced at her internal sensor readings.

V'kyyri's heart beat an erratic rhythm in the corner of her screen. Okay. He lived still. She canted the ship sideways. The planet tilted and slipped in an arc past the view screen.

"Grab a handhold," she hollered.

Whether he was aware enough to respond, she couldn't know. He didn't answer. She eyed sensor data. Nothing on her tail. She didn't relax. She still had to evade who-knew-how-many Chekydran cruisers in orbit and deal with the medical emergency V'kyrri represented.

Alarms fired warning buzzes against her left shoulder. Data crowded her screen. Sensors pinged off a slew of debris in orbit. She frowned.

First things first. Find out whether the Claugh was going to live and whether he was going to have to be neural cuffed to keep him from tearing her ship apart.

Urgency plucked at her ability to draw a full breath, but Edie routed through a set of delicate calculations. Within minutes, she had *t'Achreides-myn* in low orbit, close enough to the debris field to be mistaken for trash, far enough away to keep from being hit by trash.

She disliked abandoning the cocoon while in tight flight quarters, but she had to get V'kyrri and her shields sorted before she'd be able to get through the debris field orbiting the planet. Edie stuck her left arm into the bio-mesh. It closed, then opened again, leaving a band that would act as a remote control around her wrist.

V'kyrri slumped against the hull beside her hatch, his face the same gray-green as the alloy supporting him. Misery dragged his slack features and clouded the glance he lifted to her face. Edie ripped open the first aid kit strapped beside the door. Hoping it was safe to treat him, based on the ship's assessment of her medical condition, she grabbed a pair of hydration doses and shot him with both.

The rise and fall of his chest slowed and deepened. Color returned to his face. He sat straighter.

"C'mon," she said, hauling him to his feet. She led him into the onboard shower, propped him against the back wall, and sidled out from beneath his arm to close the door, with both of them inside.

"Close your eyes."

The unit cycled on.

Icy spray wrenched V'kyrri wide awake, gasping in the frigid water. He rasped a protest. Edie wrapped her arms around herself, laughing as the water soaked them.

The water ran muddy with dust and old blood. The cleansing cycle ran down.

V'kyrri shivered. Was it a measure of misery that he couldn't care that he'd gotten to share a shower with Edie? Even though they were both still fully clothed.

She aborted the dry sequence.

"No," V'kyrri said as she ordered the water temperature lower and activated the unit again. "Dammit."

A blast of icy, soapy water caught him in the mouth.

Three cycles later, he acknowledged that if Edie had detected his attraction to her, the increasingly cold shower hadn't been intended to cool his ardor. She'd been bringing his core body temperature out of the red zone.

"What happened out there?" she demanded while the drying cycle pulled moisture from their clothes and bodies.

Studying the crinkles between her brows, he frowned. "Out where?"

"You have no idea, do you?" The crinkles deepened. New ones formed at the corners of her eyes.

Caution cut a path down his windpipe and lodged in his lungs.

"I can't prove it," she said, "but I think those things that chased us into *t'Achreides-myn*—"

"What?"

She swept a hand wide. "The name of my ship."

The drying cycle spun down.

V'kyrri straightened and ran a hand over his tattered uniform. Some of the terrible stains had come out, the remains of his crew washed down the drain to the water recycling unit. Anything not H2O would be reduced to dust and ejected into space. His breath stumbled on the mental image.

"Those things *had* you. They were controlling you," Edie said. The door slid open. She exited.

He followed, refreshed in a way he hadn't thought

would be possible without a day of sleep. Possibly a week on Batella. Retirement, maybe. In one of the temperate regions.

"You were demanding to be let out," she said, "beating your fists against the hatch, like you'd forgotten how to open one."

Staggered, he stopped dead. He curled his hands into fists that throbbed confirmation. Exhaustion buzzed in his brain, spreading outward to muscle and bone. He slumped. "What the Three Hells?"

She looked over her shoulder. "You don't remember."

"No." He combed his memory. "Nothing past falling into the ship. The door closed. Cool air. Then, I don't know, waking in a heap on the deck plates with the engine rumbling."

Her brows lowered. "And now? Do you want to go back to the planet?"

"Twelve Gods, no." Except, deep, deep inside, an impulse tickled. *Come back*. "No."

Doubt shadowing her frown, Edie strode forward, angling out of sight.

He spotted the first aid kit she'd opened on the amidships bulkhead and hesitated.

Forward, Edie rustled something and then closed what sounded like a drawer. A servo activated.

Fine. He took the single stim dose from the kit and injected it. He bent double, gasping for breath. Once he managed to wrest free of the hurt, V'k tottered forward, marveling at the silence.

Edie's boat made not a sound, save for the engine. Lights flashed varying colors and patterns. He had no idea whether the trio of indicators he examined meant 'all clear' or 'reactor core breach.' They flashed amber-green-red in staccato, as if the lights were a code.

He shook his head. Claugh ships were symphonies of sound built to communicate via tone. Edie's ship did the same thing with light.

He emerged into the cockpit and whistled in frank admiration.

She didn't have a cockpit. She had a cocoon. She hung half a meter in the air in an anti-grav-assisted mesh embedded with biomechanical controls. He could barely make her out. Webbing and rigid panels enfolded her, clasping her ribs and waist. A heads-up display folded before her face. She'd customized the layout of the vessel to the point that she controlled every station from within the sling. She'd dismissed her blocky vessel as a useless one and half man, but he knew an Iskant when he saw one. Tagreth Federated Intelligence Command favored them for spy missions. Something V'kyrri's fellow Murbaasch Tu agents knew from decades spent chasing the little ships.

Her view screen offered a debris and star-studded panorama that made his head swim.

"Water rations in the bin at your left knee," Edie said. "Get started and don't stop until you've had four."

V'kyrri smiled. His rogue mercenary, who didn't want to be a team player, affording a Claugh consideration. He opened the bin and extracted a pair of water packs. Resisting the urge to tear one open and down it in a single gulp, he forced himself to take the second one to her.

"*Right hand,*" he said into her head. "*Follow your own orders.*"

She snorted but accepted the water.

He tore into his packet. By the time he'd taken position beside the ration bin, he'd drained the contents. He fished out another.

"Did you use the stim from my aft kit?" she inquired, her tone bland. "Talk. Cabin mic is on. I'll see."

"Had to," he said. "We've got to get out of here."

"One man, remember? We're in low orbit paralleling the debris field while I wait for the Chekydran to clear off. You have to stop taking stims."

Shaking, he stared at the view screen. He'd never been so torn about leaving a hellhole of a planet before. Glad on one hand to be free of the suffocating heat, the Chekydran, and the UMOPG. Miserable on the other, because he'd buried his people down there. And maybe a part of himself.

"The stims are eating you alive," she accused.

V'kyrri planted his feet, leaned against a panel, and swallowed hard as a piece of hull plating cartwheeled past her view screen. "Yes. I'm using dangerous medication on top of brain injury and who knows what else. I am aware there's a price to pay. It can't matter."

"Brain injury?" she squawked.

"I am no use to anyone unconscious," he snapped. "If I die protecting the empire and its citizens, that's what I signed on for."

Edie swung in her command cradle, only her glorious red hair and her generous lips pinched into a thin disapproving line showed past the equipment.

"Your survivors are away," she said, "and as safe as they can be. You did your job. Can't you be happy with that?"

"You did my job."

She laughed, a warm, rich sound that enfolded him the way her sling did her.

"We did your job," she allowed. "No shame in needing a hand from time to time."

"Especially after a reactor core explosion?"

"Especially. All you have to do, Hells, all you *can* do is sit back, relax, and hope the bugs don't spot us. You're killing yourself for nothing."

"No. We have to follow them."

Silence. Then she leaned out to stare at him.

He faced her. "They were stealing crystal, Edie."

"Spawn of a Myallki bitch." She jerked upright into her bio-mesh.

"If they integrate it into their ships the way the UMOPG did—"

"I get it. I get it," she snapped. "End of war. End of everything. What the Three Hells are you suggesting we do? I can't put a dent—"

"No," he said. "No shooting. We need to know where they're going and what they're doing."

"And find out if they already have crystal somewhere," she finished for him. "My point is that if you want to end the bugs before they build crystal into their boats, we'll have to call for help."

"I can call for bigger guns. Let me give you a recall signal to broadcast. Doesn't hit voice channels," he said.

"No."

"The Chekydran haven't worked it out. We don't know if the pattern hits a frequency they can't register or if it's one they assign no meaning to."

Edie catalogued the lift of her courage at V'kyrri's assurance. Look at her, taking the word of a Claugh.

Worse. *Wanting* to be able to.

"Look. To survive, we must be invisible. I get eyes on the bugs, orbit into position, and then act like debris caught in their slipstream as they power out of system. If your recording gets picked up, we're done, the bugs get a superweapon, and your queen gets no warning."

"They won't pick it up. They never have. It's a series of pulses in a particular pattern," he said.

"The one Parqe said you never got right?" she ducked out of her sling to eye him.

His lips curved. "I'll get it right."

She routed com access to a panel in the corridor. "Panel lit, port. Direct access to the com protocols. When it's done, I'll bundle it up for broadcast."

He spent several minutes. "Ready," he said. "With your permission, I'll put the channel specifics into your head."

"Sure," she said aloud and braced, expecting it to worsen her headache.

It didn't. One moment, she had no notion how he needed his program sent, the next she had frequency data, timing, and the knowledge that the signal needed to go out in a particular burst pattern.

"That is a damned useful talent," she made herself say.

"*One of many.*" He managed to tuck an impression of a leer into the words.

Her body warmed. Edie went to work sending his distress call.

He raided her first aid kit again, because once more, he gripped her ankle to get her attention. "*Pain killers.*"

Breathing a laugh, she accepted the packet and

drank the contents. Though her hands still shook, the band of withdrawal headache loosened.

"How'd you get on world without being spotted?" he asked.

"Same way we're going to sneak up on Chekydran. Small enough to be mistaken for space junk."

"Which this ship patently is not. You have amazing, bleeding-edge tech," he said. "These customizations cost a pile of credits I could swim in. What were you doing chasing a bounty?"

"Dodging the TFC government's extravagant offers to bring me back into the fold."

"The despot ruling Tagreth Federated finally worked out that exiling people puts them out of his reach. Took him long enough. President Durgot froze your assets?" he surmised.

"Yep. Plenty of cash. Just can't get at it without painting a target on my ass." She stared at the whirl of detritus on her view screen.

A jagged bit of metal whizzed past *t'Achreides-myn.* She shook her head. "My shield config doesn't have the power for this."

"Help me route reactor output to the shields."

"Those feed lines aren't rated for that kind of plasma temperature," she protested.

"Don't fire it up all the way."

"I don't think that's how that works."

"The fuel feeds are shielded," he argued. "It'll be a short-term thing, then we'll flush the conduits to space and bleed lower power fuel into them again. An hour maybe. Just until we zero in on the Chekydran. We'll dump shields before powering out of system, anyway."

"You've done this before?"

He met her eye. "No. Can you trust me to make it work?"

The question shook her. At least he was sharing the risk with her. She swallowed hard. Let him try or breathe vacuum when a piece of space junk punched through her existing shields and hull. Some choice.

"Okay." Edie let herself out of her sling. Brow furrowed, she took off her tool belt and passed it to him.

V'kyrri's brows came together. He accepted the belt with a solemn expression and with both hands. A formal gesture. As if she'd given him far more than a set of tools.

Maybe she had.

He swung into the belt, turned away from her, and went aft, tossing open panels she'd customized with quick release locks.

"*Your shield generator gives me palpitations,*" he said from the back of the vessel.

"Stim side-effect," she countered.

"*The generator is three sizes too big for this ship class.*"

"Yes, it is." Of course she'd over-sized the reactor core. Bio-mesh drew lots of power. He hadn't gotten a look at her environmental set up yet.

Edie returned to her controls and programmed the autopilot to hold course parallel to the debris field. At least until she got shields online. The nav computer vibrated acknowledgement beneath her fingers. Course set, autopilot engaged.

She sprinted to the engine compartment and snagged a tool from her belt wrapped around V'kyrri's waist. She began rerouting power from one end while he worked the other.

If his tools slipped, if he swore, Edie had no way of knowing. He'd left her head. Still, she felt him inside the workings of her boat, inside her private, personal sanctuary. Inside *her*. They were her ribs he shifted aside, her organs he snipped bits of and then grafted to other parts.

Their mutual digging into her extended sense of self filled the corridor and by extension her. Complex enjoyment opened within her—a blend of frustration, being intrigued and challenged, and a sense of competence—emotions not her own.

They had to be from V'kyrri.

He leaned against his engineering skill as something he could rely on and relax into. Maybe his emotional state had easy access to her because she understood. Working on her ship allowed her to use an instinctual sense that had never steered her wrong, and that wired directly into the reward centers of her brain. It was as addictive as a well-tuned SEM.

None of it changed the fact that she had a Claugh officer taking her ship and, by extension, her apart.

Edie shut down power and manually blew the fuel lines clean. Lights died. Air circulation stilled.

"*Ready?*"

"Ready."

"*Last bolt out—now.*"

"Switching over."

"*Switching over.*"

She kept her brain busy counting the turns of the bolts. "Secure. Ready for shielding."

"*Me, too. Restarting power.*"

Lights winked to life.

A breeze cooled Edie's damp face. "Fuel feed shielding online. Field integrity confirmed." She handed him the field tester.

He applied it. "*Field integrity confirmed. Get up there. I'll start the switchover. I need you at the controls shunting the flow.*"

Edie scowled. He was right, of course. She was just accustomed to doing everything herself, to giving and receiving orders from no one. And she'd hesitated too long.

He crouched in the corridor, haloed by the glow of plasma lighting up her shield generator, listening in. Whatever he saw in her face or overheard in her head, his expression softened.

"You want to handle the switch over?" he said aloud.

She shook her head. Not so much in answer to him, as in ruefulness at being self-absorbed. Like it or not, she had him in the middle of her corridor. *Adapt, Edie.*

"Nope." She ran to the command console. Didn't bother strapping in. Not when the construct had been built to fit her every curve. Until V'kyrri, it hadn't occurred to her how womb-like she'd made the thing. How SEM-like.

The panels closed, coming to life with sensory input that soothed ragged nerves and eased the SEM withdrawal shakes. She couldn't plug the data straight into her brain the way the SEM did, but the touch of sensation provided anodyne for the worst symptoms.

"*Switch over on your mark.*" Giving her the illusion of control.

t'Achriedes-myn shuddered.

First collision with a chunk of debris.

Edie keyed up the data for the reactor temp and for the shields.

"Go," she said. No marks. No more playing around.

"*Switching.*"

Data flowed down her screen, red-lit rain that couldn't touch her thirsty-for-contact skin. Controls pulsed and vibrated at her touch.

Warnings buzzed at her back. Conduits not meant for reactor plasma complained. She glanced at proximity data. It renewed her headache. Too many pieces. Several shouting in blinking amber. Collision courses and all of them big enough to punch a hole in the ride, and she hadn't even turned into the debris field yet.

Edie amped power to the shields.

Conduit alarms calmed. Status updates returned to normal. Collision alerts still rattled her teeth, but with so much power pouring through the shield generator, her usually invisible shields took on a greenish glow as the field interacted with random oxygen molecules.

"We're good," she said, turning them to cross the orbiting trash patch. "We've got enough energy out there to vaporize a few of the smaller bits, and I've got a Chekydran mother in high orbit. Night side. Outside the debris field."

She set a course to ease them closer, as if *t'Achriedes-myn* were also drifting junk, and not a tiny cockpit stuck atop a fired-up reactor core. That done, she stepped out of the sling to watch the shields zapping space junk.

"*Closing up.*"

She glanced over her shoulder.

V'kyrri swiped his forehead with a shaking hand. He wrestled a hatch cover into place.

She scowled and turned eyes front. He'd blown through that last stim. It disconcerted her to have him in her boat, yes. Inside her sense of safety.

He was Claugh. It shouldn't matter what he did to himself.

Yet, it did. How was she supposed to handle that?

Contemplating her limited options, she sighed and scanned space. A disembodied humanoid hand brushed her view screen. Slack. Puffy. Pallid as something that might live in the caverns on the doomed world below.

Edie started and clamped her teeth shut before any hint of sound could emerge. Blood pounding in her skull, she forced her gaze past the hand. Primed, her eyes began picking out corpses among the twisted, heat-marred metal. By some perverse eddy in the slow dance of space, one of the corpses drifted closer.

Female.

Blue-black hair drifting in a halo around the woman's head caught the sunshine. Eyes and mouth open. Arms spread as if treading water. The woman's dark brown skin had partially bleached as her tissues had swollen. That would end. The water would evaporate and the sun baking the planet would mummify the remains until the star expanded and swallowed her.

Edie dragged her attention back inside. She stood there staring, not breathing. She shot a horrified glance over her shoulder.

Chapter Sixteen

V'kyrri admired Edie's set up. Rubbing knuckles along his jaw, he levered himself to standing. The job should have taken three times as long. She'd clearly rewired the ship for quick, efficient swaps like they'd performed.

Save you, buzzed inside his head. He scowled and glanced at Edie. She hadn't been speaking. She stood before her view screen. Tension knotted the muscles of her back and shoulders.

V'kyrri peered around her to catch a glimpse of what had her transfixed.

Edie gasped, darted to the command sling, and blanked the view screen. Something clanked against the hull before the shields sent it rebounding away.

He scowled. "What was that?"

The look she shot him iced his insides. Distress pressed white lines into the corners of her eyes. Sympathy reflected in the pinched downturn of her mouth.

"Why'd you—"

"Bodies," she breathed. "I didn't think you needed to see the bodies."

His crew.

So much of the *Rhapsody* had decompressed. Most of his dead were out there in orbit. If the corpses didn't get pulled down by planetary gravity and incinerated by reentry, they'd desiccate and orbit until the end of time.

Save you. He slumped. "I need a stim."

"No."

"Edie…"

"Without a reason, you get nothing. You lied to your people to get them clear. You will not lie to me."

"I'm not lying to you." He clenched his fists. "I need that stim. We're chasing Chekydran."

"Hadn't noticed."

"Then you have a plan that doesn't involve the two of us piloting to stay inside their exhaust stream for who knows how many hours?" he snapped.

Her brows lowered. Her jaw set in a mutinous line.

"You need me to spell you," he said. "In fact, you should sleep first. You'll need fewer hours than I will."

"You're injured."

"So are you."

She barked a derisive laugh. "Not even a nice try, Mr. Went-Down-With-the-Ship."

Save.

He scrubbed a hand down his face. "Those things from the planet."

"The overgrown slug wasps?"

He breathed a wry laugh at her description. "They're trying to get at me. Until we get out of here, I need the stim. I can't block them without it."

"Then we just get out of here."

"Edie."

"My boat," she said. "You don't get to tell me what to do."

He closed the distance and took her hand, savoring the sparks tracing his veins. "I'm not interested in taking command. I'm here. I've got your back. Give me the stim."

"Damn it." She sighed. "Do the Claugh þreed true for weaponized charm?"

He couldn't help himself. He laughed.

Her lips twitched and her ribs expanded as if she breathed his amusement.

Lust fired his system. Could be a stim side effect. Or it could be Edie. She'd gotten under his skin. Something about her shattered decades of hard-won mental discipline. That she hadn't exploited the fact suggested she had no idea.

And he'd never suspected that having his shields broken would be this much fun. He squeezed her hand.

She pulled free, ducked into the command sling, and swore, "Cravuul dung. Another Chekydran mothership coming around the planet. Going slow."

"Sweeping?" he asked, his chest tightening.

"Maybe? How—"

"It's them. They're looking for us." *Me*. No saying that out loud. Not with the buzz strengthening inside his head.

Brows bunched, Edie handed him a dosing unit.

Tension eased. He forced his shoulders lower. Meeting her eye, he said, "Last one, I swear."

"Famous last words," she replied, crossing her arms.

"I'm not an addict, Edie." He set the unit against the skin of his forearm. "Extenuating circumstances."

Her brown eyes clouded.

Bracing for the chemical fire, he pressed the button.

No fire. No pain.

The drug traced velvet fingers through his veins on

the way to his brain. Muscle fibers unknitted. He sagged. Awareness beat the drugs to his head.

She'd tricked him.

Rage fired strength into his body.

"You…" he grunted.

And crashed to the deck plates.

****

Edie picked up the dosing unit. *So trusting.*

"Why yes. I am a devious, conniving Carozziel slime-bat." His fault for not checking which drug she'd offered him. "We're getting the Three Hells out of here."

Edie ripped a rescue blanket from her first aid kit and tossed it over him. She returned to her command center and shut down her shields. The Chekydran ship in front of her had already fired thrusters. Irrational to want to see the Chekydran ship with her own eyes rather than via data. Still, she turned the view screen back on.

Data lit her panel. Vibration like bugs on skin walked her spine. She frowned. Thumps and vibrations assaulted her. Edie stared at her readout.

The ship rounding the planet raised shields and altered course. The Chekydran in front of Edie also put up shields.

She scowled, her pulse slamming inside her temples. They couldn't transition to supralight with shields. They'd only pop defenses this way if they'd detected a threat.

She was the only thing between the pair of bulbous boats. Her bio-mesh bruised her ribs with alarms. She flinched. Weapons fired from the Chekydran in front of her. They hadn't shot at her, or she'd be dead already.

The burst of plasma impacted the second Chekydran ship's shields.

Edie sucked in a startled breath. "What the Three Hells?" The Chekydran didn't fight amongst themselves. Not ever that she'd seen in the copious reports about the creatures.

The massive ships traded a volley.

Shaking, Edie nudged her engines. Her choices were limited. Make a run for the closest mothership and hitch a ride into supralight. Or she drifted, until the squabble played out, and she lost her shot at figuring out what the bugs were doing with crystal.

Before her, silent bursts of energy lit up each ship's shields.

Edie dared a short burn. It would look like trash impacting other trash, and it would boost her into the gravity well of the nearer Chekydran. Assuming the two big boats didn't destroy one another.

Other bits of detritus, grappled by the big ship's mass, spun out of the debris field with her. Good.

Navigating by the shield flares, she risked another burn. Distance numbers ticked down. The trick with trying to look like trash captured by another ship's mass was that she couldn't get up too much speed. She didn't have to point her nose at her target. Orbiting trash didn't do that. She had to sync her orbital position to the ship she wanted and work steadily higher and closer without looking like she was steadily working higher and closer. If the Chekydran ship's mass overcame *t'Achreides-myn's* inertia, she'd get sucked in.

Internal sensor data vibrated at her back. Her shield conduits. They were carrying all that plasma V'kyrri had routed through for shields. With the shields up, the system ran at tolerance. With the shields down, she shook her head. She couldn't raise shields. Space trash didn't glow as it arced through space. She had to reverse out the shield hack.

Damn.

She studied the data on the two ships. Neither had suffered any meaningful damage other than depleting shield generators. Her sling vibrated, drawing her attention.

The ship she wanted to shadow had started accelerating. No time to contemplate the evidence of intraspecies hostility.

Edie banked her core to reduce her heat signature. Then she, too, would look like a piece of trash captured by the massive Chekydran vessel.

She coded up an alert for a distance window so she didn't get too close. Or left behind. That done, she sprinted aft, glancing at V'kyrri as she passed.

Weird. She'd expected him to shut off in sleep, but the telepath unconscious didn't get him out of her head.

He was everywhere. All around her. Part of her. She was breathing him while he touched everything she was. She'd always had the impression of sinking into sleep.

V'kyrri relaxed *out* in sleep.

She couldn't escape him even when he was unconscious.

With a sigh, she rerouted power and flushed the fuel feed lines. Harder than it sounded. Especially when V'kyrri started dreaming.

She could ignore it at first.

He grew restless, tossing in his sleep.

Edie worked, flicking glances at him when he

thrashed. The sense of him in the ship—Hells—in her head and in her damned bones—sat on her. Slowly, steadily, pressure built inside her ribs.

Her vision hazed. Frowning, she swiped a sleeve across her eyes. There was nothing to wipe away.

Pain lanced from instep, up the right side of her spine, and straight into her skull.

"Ow. What the Hells?" she yelped. The hurt drained away leaving not even a ghost of soreness behind. Edie groaned. This wasn't her pain. It *was*...but it hadn't originated in her blood and bones.

It had to be V'kyrri entering dream state.

Blinking watery eyes, she forced her focus back to rerouting fuel flow.

Another burst of pain and the ghosts of crew members Edie didn't have floated past her eyes. She glared at V'kyrri's sleeping form.

Damned telepath.

She returned to confirming field integrity before turning on final, normal fuel flow. She hoped.

Field integrity reads flashed *all clear*.

In the ghost sight haunting her, an explosion blasted through the phantom crew. In the cockpit, V'kyrri writhed, his motion violent enough to kick the ship into sympathetic motion.

Edie glanced at him and threw the fuel feed switch. Green across the board. Chewing her lip, she fought to keep focused outward rather than at the nightmare she got to experience by virtue of sharing close quarters with a telepath. She sealed the line and closed the access hatch.

No explosion. No temperature change alerts on her bracelet. Good. She returned to her controls and eyed the readouts.

V'kyrri's nightmare pasted Edie back with a vision of a station manned by a trio of young men and women blown to bits. Body parts splattered outward. The phantom of a bloody, headless and armless torso, ribs exposed and shattered on one side, hit and knocked the breath right out of her.

Gasping, Edie rushed to V'kyrri's side. She had a telepath killing her with his nightmares from inside her own head.

She resisted the urge to kick him awake and shook him instead. Maybe not as gently as she could have. She'd imagined a telepath in control was the worst thing that could happen to her. His pain prying her skull mocked the notion.

"Wake up," she said. "C'mon. You're having a nightmare. Wake up."

She didn't want to touch him.

Edie rolled her eyes. She did want to. That was the problem. Crouching beside him felt like she'd routed reactor core plasma into her veins.

Another ghost explosion. Blood spatter this time. She jerked under the lash of memories not her own.

His face twisted. His mouth opened. Yelling. Screaming maybe.

Not waking.

Edie flinched. He'd tried to warn her. She hadn't listened, and here she was. Staring at a man suffering terrors he couldn't wake from because she'd tranqed him. Her fault. And she had no clue how to fix it. No idea if she even could.

All she had was a vague and distant memory of her mother at her bedside, soothing her bad dreams. She blew out a trembling breath.

Commit, Edie, or blow your own fool head off to end the torture.

No help for it then. She wrapped her arms around him.

He fought.

Setting her teeth, she held on. "Calm down. C'mon. You're okay. You're on my ship. You're safe. Unless you keep this cravuul dung up. Relax. V'kyrri. Stop it and relax."

As if her voice was a trigger of some kind, he subsided. Didn't wake. But his respiration slowed. His muscles let go a piece at a time.

The ghosts of his dreams dwindled.

Edie sagged. The surges of pain drained off. Weariness set in. She sighed.

He stirred.

"Rest easy," she said.

He stirred again.

Edie touched his cheek.

He sighed and subsided. Great. Skin. He needed touch, the only thing that cured the icy dreams of dead friends.

She relieved him of his boots, tucked the blanket around him, and secured him in a set of gravity straps.

In sleep, the stern lines of stress and injury fell away. V'kyrri looked too young to be the captain of a prototype starship. Too young to have had most of his crew killed. Too young to be addicted to stimulants.

Edie sighed. *Me, too, right*?

Without the conscious decision to do so, she smoothed his hair from his forehead, clenching her fist when a tingle walked her nerves.

She left him long enough to glance at acceleration data and to cut gravity.

V'kyrri floated.

Under normal circumstances she'd haul him snug against the hull where he could sleep weightless. Hanging over her head both literally and figuratively. Not an option with the nightmares.

He needed touch to keep from killing her. She needed to be in her sling to manage the transition to supralight. Since she'd been awake for two days under some really messed up circumstances, she'd risk a sip of V'kyrri's poison.

The last stim shot on the boat called to her.

Edie launched for the first aid kit before V'kyrri could tumble back into REM sleep. Fortified by the chemicals burning through her body, Edie reconfigured her bio-mesh cocoon into a chair and maneuvered V'kyrri to where she sat. Supported by the straps, his back rested on her lap as if she meant to use his chest as a work surface.

She couldn't quite close the front of her cocoon, but she'd cope. She'd have to. The Chekydran and the Claugh telepath were running neck and neck for most clear and present danger.

He stirred and her vision hazed.

Edie tripped the seal on his uniform jacket and tucked one hand beneath the fabric. Her vision cleared.

He sighed and settled.

Smooth skin and crisp hair met her touch. She was rendering aid. Not taking advantage. No exploring. No matter the temptation.

Still. She might as well hold a lit firecracker. The charge went up her arm and settled into a fizzing pulse between her thighs. Embarrassing.

At least he was sound asleep.

Look at her. Defusing an enemy forced to relive the terrors of having his ship destroyed. At least, she wasn't a part of those nightmares.

Not yet.

Every time the ghost crew appeared before her eyes, she set her palm to V'kyrri's chest and let the rhythm of his breath fire awareness through her system. Good as a stim shot at keeping her uncomfortable and awake.

The Chekydran ship overwhelmed her view screen. She'd left all but one other bit of space junk behind. Either the bugs weren't paying attention, or they rightly believed there wasn't a damned thing she could do to them in such a puny ship.

Except cling like a Deaccolo tree thorn jabbed into the seat of their pants. She frowned at the mental picture of Chekydran in pants.

The bigger vessel led her across the paths of the moons, brushing close to the outer moon. The maneuver sheared off two pieces of debris that had been sucked in by the big ship's gravity.

The Chekydran fired their star drive.

Any concerns Edie had about being detected vanished. She lifted the lid on reactor output and brought her own drive online. Her energy signature would vanish in the Chekydran exhaust.

The big ship flashed to supralight, sucking *t'Achreides-myn* straight into the groove with it.

No!

Blinking back tears inspired by the wail of protest in her head, Edie cut power and got a hand on V'kyrri again. She had no idea how he'd managed to yell at her while asleep, but she'd be happy to have it never happen again. Especially not shadowing a bug ship through supralight.

The move was illegal, dangerous, and a dead bore.

Even with the stim burning her awake, she'd need something to occupy her mind. Just so happened, she needed a new SEM. Might as well get started. She walled off a secure location in the shipboard computer, plugged in her crippled handheld, and began the process of offloading the data she and V'kyrri had stolen.

Looming death in the form of the aft section of a Chekydran ship inspired Edie to rapt attention to every bit of sensory detail her sling had to offer regarding their status.

Which left her captive to the pervasive, all-encompassing presence of one Claugh officer who required her touch on his bare skin to keep from killing them both with his nightmares.

Chapter Seventeen

A breeze smoothed V'kyrri's face. Light bubbled inside him. Cool air caressed his face again. Recognition flashed. Shipboard. State of the art scrubbers and O2 generators. The breeze lacked the stale, flat smell of air circulated through nothing but machinery.

He drew a deep breath. Pain. It was missing. At his right side, a warm, soft surface moved. Breathed. Scent enfolded him as if he'd napped in a field of sunshine and flowers.

It threw him back to the first time he'd seen daylight with his own eyes. One glorious spring day, he'd emerged from the underground where he'd been born and raised. He'd stood, dazed, in a stand of pale pink Cullal flowers. Their subtle sweet and musk fragrance wrapped forever around his brain.

Awareness jolted.

Edie.

Her hand nestled against the bare skin of his chest. Even though she'd moved not a millimeter, his body rushed to instant attention.

Before he realized what he was doing, he'd eased into her mind.

She was awake. Relaxed, but on alert.

And here he was, a telepath with a set of ethics he'd violated because he'd awakened relaxed, wrapped in sanctuary.

He opened his eyes. Red light dripped down a panel, coming straight for him. His nerves tingled, anticipating a touch that never came. Boneless and heavy, he rested on his back, tucked against Edie, content to linger before she realized he'd awakened and allowed old habit to turn him into an enemy.

Before he had to summon the anger to convince her the price of betraying his trust was too high. A rush of desire followed.

She'd let him into her ship, into her space, and into her head. Granted, she'd done it because she'd had no choice. It didn't equate to letting him into her bed. Despite their current physical location.

But damn he wanted her. Despite, Hells, maybe because of her treachery swapping a tranquilizer for a stim. More to the point, he wanted her to break pattern. For him. Because of him. He wanted her trust.

No.

If he could be honest with himself in the silence of her little ship while she held him, he could admit he wanted to crack her open to get a glimpse of her heart. Because he wanted it, too.

He suppressed a rueful smile. The Claugh officer wanted to seduce Firestorm. Why not ask for a winged Batellen wraith for his birthday, as well?

He covered her hand with his, fingering the metal band encircling her wrist.

Edie twitched. Her hand beneath his curled.

She froze.

"*How long have I been asleep*?" he asked.

A wild swarm of thoughts, fears, confusion, and dread clawed her.

"Three days," she said. "During which you sleep-walked to the head four times and made me use up every last hydration and emergency ration dose on board."

The steady timbre of her voice gave no hint of her turmoil. He admired her control. "*Status*?"

Her diaphragm bounced on a laugh she didn't voice. She tried to pull away.

He canted his head to meet her eye. "*Thank you.*"

"What for?"

"*You know I half took the stims to avoid the dreams?*"

"You did not, you addicted liar," she retorted.

V'kyrri smiled. Life at last. "*How bad were they?*"

She shifted as if the question burned. "Bad."

Bad enough that she'd overcome her reluctance to touch him to get them to ease. "*I was broadcasting. Wasn't I?*"

"Yeah."

"*That's what you get for tranqing a telepath. Sorry.*"

Edie didn't answer. Didn't even breathe.

V'kyrri shifted, tried to sit up and failed. "*You tied me up?*"

That won him a laugh. "No gravity. Hold on."

Keeping one eye on her readouts, Edie released the straps binding V'kyrri into his blankets and turned gravity back on.

He pulled himself upright.

Edie tensed. She wouldn't meet his eye. Her lips trembled.

He frowned. "*Edie? What?*" He lifted a hand.

She flinched, turning her face slightly, as if bracing

for a blow. V'kyrri couldn't get his breath. His people had conditioned her to this while she'd still been a child.

Before or after she started blowing up Claugh soldiers?

Before. Because once she'd become Firestorm, the only way she'd have been struck would have been with a laser bolt.

His gut tightened. Drawn by her heat, he cupped her cheek, thumb brushing cheekbone. She jumped, her pulse racing beneath his fingers.

"*What's wrong?*"

"Nothing," she said. It came out a whisper.

"*Not even a nice try.*"

"If you're going to muck around in my head, figure it out for yourself."

She avoided his gaze by making a show of studying her data. Her knuckles were white on her controls.

"*I'd rather you tell me,*" he said. "*What happened? Why are you afraid?*"

"Nothing personal."

"*So you've said.*"

Edie shook her head, determined not to do this. Not here. Not now. She couldn't. Not even with the soft, sweet stroke of his thumb on her face. It shook her, rattling free words and memories. They piled up on her tongue. Waiting to spill into the silence.

"*I'll apologize again for making you help—*"

"That has nothing to do with anything," she snapped. "You asked for status. Let me—"

"*No. Why have you cast me as the Orythy?*"

The mythical two headed monster of Claugh

legend. One head was benevolent, wise, and kind. In all the heroic tales, its counsel was sought before a hero embarked upon a quest. The other head vomited acid on anyone or anything that approached. The heads were identical. Many a hero had his or her legend cut short because they never knew which head they'd asked for help.

"*Have I hurt you in any way I could reasonably avoid?*"

"Besides trying to strangle me and shred a kidney?" she muttered. "No. I have been very careful not to give you a reason." *Until now*.

She shouldn't have bothered keeping that to herself. Not with a thrice-damned telepath in her brain.

"*You're afraid I'm angry?*"

"You were," she said.

"*You betrayed my trust,*" he acknowledged.

"I kept you from killing yourself," she flared.

"*Yes. You did.*" He lowered his hand from her face and smoothed a curl of her hair against her collarbone.

The caress smashed her senses. She sucked in a long, slow breath.

"You still are," she managed. "When a Claugh is pissed there's a price tag. Always."

He stilled. His features tightened. "*Go on.*" When she didn't, his gaze focused on her lips. Then the creases in his forehead smoothed and a sly smile overtook his expression. "*Will I have my revenge? Absolutely. I look forward to it. Maybe I'll demand access to ship's systems and engines.*"

Her jaw went slack. "Why don't you just cut me open and rummage around in my guts?"

"*Your heart,*" he corrected, setting his palm to her

chest where the organ in question leaped to meet the touch. "*I assure you I won't be 'rummaging around' in such a fine, delicate instrument*."

Her brows drew together. Were they talking about her heart or her engine? Either way, she could barely breathe.

"*I'll ease in. You'll never know I'm there. And when you look around for something to stem the bleeding, I'll be there. I'll be so good at it, you'll want me there before you know you want me that deep into your inner workings.*"

"The ship's," she breathed, while every sensuous word resonated straight through her core.

"*That, too*." He traced her lips with a feather light touch that left her weak and trembling. "*I look forward to it. And the first bit is you telling me what happened to poison you against the Claugh.*"

The sensual haze burned off.

"War wasn't enough?" she snapped, batting his hand away. Manipulation. Again. When would she learn? "War. With Claugh bent on torture and murder. What more would you need?"

Shaking, she closed her mouth and longed for a shield between them. She didn't even have her SEM to give her a layer of defense. She'd lost. Again. She closed burning eyes.

"*I'm sorry, Edie. How do I convince you I am not that Claugh?*"

She shook her head.

Silence. He even vacated her head. Funny being able to tell the difference and to miss his presence someplace she'd never wanted him in the first place.

"*Come in,*" he said. "*Look around. I can say I'm*

not angry about the tranq. I can't think of any way to make you believe me. Except this. I'm wide open. Shields offline. Come look."

Edie opened her eyes to scowl at him. "I'm not a telepath. How am I supposed to…"

An impression—as if he'd taken her by the hand and led her—invited her to walk through him, through maze-like museum displays. She waded in emotion not her own. Peered at thoughts she'd never had.

He'd lied.

She froze even though she wasn't actually walking, brought up short by anger swirling around her. Too late, it occurred to her that this had been an elaborate trap. One she had no means of fighting. Fear shuddered through her.

V'kyrri groaned.

Blood tinged the anger washing up over her knees. She gasped. What had he said? *Her fear sliced him up.* That made no sense. She grappled it, nevertheless, stuffing it into the box where she stowed all her terrors and regrets and sorrows.

Relief and gratitude washed away the impression of blood in the flow of his emotions. Something more caught her leg and twined up to nestle at the base of her throat. Pride. Admiration. In her. For her.

Her knees buckled, and she landed on her butt—save that her physical body already sat in her cockpit.

Concern, followed rapid-fire by sympathy, wrapped around her. The tendrils of anger she'd encountered had vanished, and she caught a glimpse of the rational, disciplined man observing, and analyzing everything he felt, everything he experienced. His anger had been transitory because he'd examined and dismissed it.

The new perspective gave her access to the undercurrents of V'kyrri. A vast whirlpool swirled, sucking life and light out of him. Sorrow. The wound of a lost ship and crew was fresh and still weeping.

Edie climbed to her mental feet. Did he have a similar physical construct when he went rifling through her head?

"*I don't see you as a museum, if that's what you're asking. More a temple.*"

She snorted. The fire-haired goddess thing. Of course he did. And it appeared she didn't have to speak while inside his head. How much of her could he see while she traipsed through his internal works?

"*Surface thoughts,*" he said. "*An experience like this can be disorienting, I'm monitoring your equilibrium.*"

Fair enough. She thought a question at him. "*May I?*"

Pleasure rippled around her, impact waves rolling outward. She'd caused that? She had to catch her breath.

"*Please,*" he said.

A heated, hungry hand caught her ankle. The river of emotion erupted to a boil of mortification around her. V'kyrri fought that hand. Shrouded it, trying to hide it.

Her pulse stuttered, and she couldn't get her breath. From the instant the hand that he didn't want her to notice had brushed her ankle, she'd been shaken by the sparks it showered through her veins and the fire it set smoldering in her blood and belly.

Desire.

He wanted her?

He was Claugh. No. He was first and foremost and uniquely V'kyrri, who happened to wear a Claugh uniform because he loved the empire. Friends who'd become his family paraded past, each plunging Edie into his regard for them.

Devotion. Adoration in one case. Love. Laughter. Fear for them.

She'd felt something like it before. Remembered, recognized emotion landed Edie smack in the center of her last happy memory of her parents and home.

The ghost of her mother grinned at her and jerked her chin at a bowl on the kitchen counter. Her dead father patted her shoulder. "Excellent work today," he signed for her to see. "You're becoming an artist."

He swept Edie's mother into his arms. He kissed her. Long. Hard. She rose on her toes to meet him.

Edie stood, basking in the glow of her father's praise while her favorite cookies sat in a bowl on the counter waiting for her to stir them together.

Edie wrenched free of the sunshine of the past and forced out a shaking breath. Out. She needed out.

Her tiny, non-telepathic skull shrank. Compressing her brain. Constricting. Strangling her ability to breathe. To think. To process.

She clutched her aching head.

V'kyrri shut a door.

Edie slammed into her own body. Her head pounded. Nausea sloshed her stomach. Worst of the miseries, though, her eyes were wet, and her breath hitched as she drew it.

V'kyrri's brows lowered. He reached for her.

Instinct finally came to her rescue. She scrambled to her feet and out of range. If he touched her now, she'd shatter. All because he'd lumped her in with his friends. His family. Did he know? Why? Why do that for a mercenary who'd shuttle him to his fleet and then run like a scared tezwoul back into the shadows?

He wouldn't hurt her. Not physically. Not knowingly. He'd destroy her instead, unless she got her shields online and did it now. Swiping a sleeve across her face, she straightened her spine. "Never do that again."

A smile came and went on his face. He got to his feet. "Edie. I can't help what I catch from you," he said aloud so she could read it. Respecting her need for privacy. "I've spent decades training to shield, to block it all out. You burn my shields straight to the ground. I can't escape you. I know you didn't invite me in. You didn't give me permission to eavesdrop. That memory grabbed me by the throat…"

She shut her eyes and shook her head, backing away.

He grabbed her arms.

She'd been wrong.

He would hurt her. Physically.

She gasped and opened her eyes.

Lines creased the corners of his mouth and eyes. "Don't shut me out. Edie. I am not one of the monsters who destroyed your family."

"They tortured them," she said. She wanted to swallow the words, to deny them access to the open air. She couldn't. "Claugh soldiers. They laughed while my parents begged for death. I hate every one of you. I always have. If I could destroy the empire, I'd give my life to do it."

He pressed his lips tight. The color bleached from

them. Not rage. No hint of madness. Only pain. Sympathy. Impotent outrage directed at the past.

He gathered her into his arms.

Edie shrieked.

It mattered not at all. He locked her against his chest and backed her against the bulkhead.

Denying her leverage to hurt him. Forcing her to accept what she least wanted from a Claugh captain—his concern and sympathy.

At least he hadn't bothered to close his uniform. Her cheek rested against bare skin rather than khaki fabric. He tucked her head beneath his chin and stood. Holding her. Waiting her out. Poking holes in rage and hatred with his insistence on offering what no one since her parents had. Acceptance.

A decades-long frozen section of her soul thawed. That defrosting process hurt. Her chest ached. At the same time, warmth seeped into her bones.

Breathing like she'd run for days, she sagged, spent.

"*We weren't what you expected*," he noted.

"Yeah," she countered. "You were."

"*Can you allow that I had reason for acting like a madman*?"

In his shoes, Edie would have been a hell of a lot madder than he had been. She sighed. "If the Chekydran decide to transition out of supralight in the next few seconds, we're going to die."

He didn't move.

She shoved against his chest. To no effect. "Let go before I scorch that uniform right off your body."

His muscles tightened, but the silent line of communication his skin had established to hers, spoke a thrill of desire through the fabric separating them. Her system arched in active interest.

His arms tightened. Then his diaphragm bounced in a laugh, as did his mental voice. "*That eager to have me out of my clothes? I'm flattered.*"

She snorted in derision, but her face flamed at the mental picture he'd painted. "Get off. I'll find my lighter."

He'd turned to humor. A peace offering. Giving her the time and tools to put her defenses back online.

It was a measure of how much damage she'd taken that she'd accept.

He exited her mind, then loosed his hold. Physically, he peeled away, hovering as if convinced she needed physical support.

He touched her shoulder.

She lifted a brow.

"That my crew and I don't fit your previous experience with Claugh soldiers in no way invalidates what you suffered."

His statement plunked and vanished into the bloody depths of her past. Weary in a way she suspected sleep couldn't assuage, she waved off his observation.

"Help yourself to the shower," she said, trudging to the command panel. "I'm going to validate position and speed."

His brows lowered. He glanced at the view screen. "Where are we?"

"All roads lead home," she muttered.

He rocked. "Nol Jakze? We're on approach to Nol Jakze?"

"Another hour to the point of no return."

"Be right back."

Redlined as she was on psychoanalyzing herself, she climbed into the cocoon without affording him another glance.

From the alert that vibrated behind her left calf, V'kyrri did, indeed, cycle through the shower. She wished for a change of clothes that would fit him. She'd give anything to get him out of that uniform. She grinned, savoring every permutation of that admission for a minute. How long had it been since anyone responded to her as a woman, much less seemed to want her?

She squeezed her eyes closed on the question. No seemed about it. Heat rushed through her body. Edie lingered, savoring the burn. If there were any justice at all in the dark, cold universe, she'd find a way to seduce him into her bed and…

The electric shock of the thought jolted her. And then what? She'd live happily ever after with a *Claugh*? Was that what she'd been thinking? What the Three Hells?

Edie opened her eyes, powered up the medi-system, and grabbed a fold of bio-mech mesh. It closed on her arm. She forced herself to work on slowing the boat, leaving the Chekydran ship's slipstream with one hand while her medi-system sampled out blood and ran diagnostics. Because visions of playing house with the enemy qualified as the craziest thing she'd ever entertained.

Her medi-system spit out a bunch of data that stopped short of *hopelessly insane*, shot her full of nutritional supplements, and finally another pain killer she hadn't realized she'd needed. The mesh released her.

Her nerves lit, arching against the inside of her skin like a hiztap looking for pets.

V'kyrri put a hand on her shoulder.

"Okay." She pushed away the forward half of her controls and looked her nemesis in the eye. Shadows lingered beneath his eyes and hollowed out his cheeks. She frowned.

"I'm bringing us out of supralight. The Chekydran are slowing. I acknowledge it might be a ruse, and I'll lose them if it's just a course change, but if they're about to skip out of the groove…"

"We do not want to be in sensor range," he finished for her.

"Grab a seat." She ordered up a structure change in the mesh beneath her. Another chair unfolded beside hers.

He flopped into it, scowling at her screen.

She concentrated on the steady trickle of calculations and conditions. Emotion and speculation vanished in a cascade of systems checks, position fixing, and automatic sensor scans.

The ship transitioned with a weird sideways slip. Sensors flashed the all clear. No ship traffic. No immovable objects in her path.

Edie opened the engines.

Chapter Eighteen

Riding the extra speed from supralight, *t'Achreides-myn* arced into system, far exceeding posted limits set for the navigation lanes. Her panel never lit with security warnings.

"Security and navigation beacons are offline," she said.

He met her eye, frowning. "Then no one knows the Chekydran are coming."

"Bugs blasting into an inhabited system means they're going in for a kill. The only inhabited planet is Nol Jakze," Edie said. "What the Three Hells is going on?"

The set of V'kyrri's lips made it plain that his calculus matched hers. Not reassuring.

"We should link up to a beacon," she said, "get an SOS broadcast going—"

"Stay on the mothership. We can't let them—"

She shot him a glance. "I can't go to Nol Jakze."

"What are you talking about?" he demanded, flinging a hand at her view screen. "The crystal—"

"It's like you said in the hangar," she interrupted. "You couldn't take me where you were going. I can't go home—"

"You are going to have to get over your past."

"They tried to kill me," she snapped. "Nol Jakze does not want my help. If they ever did. They're a

Claugh protectorate. Let the Claugh protect them."

"I am Claugh," he countered.

"You're going to protect an entire populace all by yourself?"

"If I have to," he retorted. "I'd rather do it with you at my side. You can't condemn a planet full of mostly innocent people to death by Chekydran."

She slumped. No. She couldn't. Because there'd be children out there. Running. Terrified. Pursued. And she knew about that. She wouldn't be able to save them all. No one could. For the weeping, frightened fourteen-year-old she'd once been, she had to try.

She straightened her spine. No one deserved the Chekydran.

"I'm an impediment to you helping people," Edie said. "Replace the relay on my teleporter. Let me put you down in the capitol where you can meet up—"

"We're a team, Edie. You aren't vanishing into the underbrush to hunt Chekydran alone."

Stubborn man. She paid attention to piloting.

They achieved orbit without a single ping from security beacons. She tagged the Chekydran mothership on sensors. "There they are. Entering orbit."

Palms damp, temples beating in time with her pulse, she forced her focus to the Chekydran ship. Bay doors opened. Small craft poured off the larger vessel.

"What are they doing?" she muttered, leaning closer to her readout as if that would force the symbols to make sense.

V'kyrri shook his head. "How do you read that?"

Edie swapped out the symbol-based system she preferred. The direction of information flow changed to accommodate the left to right orientation of Tagrethian.

When she glanced at him, V'kyrri scanned the panel, his expression tightening.

The swarm of little Chekydran ships broke apart into clusters of three as they entered atmosphere. They spread out across the blue-green globe.

"That's not an attack formation," she said. "Unless they—"

"Bombing," he said. "They're bombing."

She grabbed hold of her panel to keep from falling, then dove for the nearest group, her main gun already warming. "Going for the nearest."

"Where are planetary security forces?" V'kyrri snapped. He wrestled free of the bio-mesh and bolted for the com panel. "Give me a line."

"Open."

She brought shields up.

The Chekydran bombers skimmed the layers of upper atmosphere.

She dropped into position behind them. A short buzz of vibration beneath her right ring finger. She had a shooting solution.

One of the ships broke formation, circling to target her, guns hot.

Edie blew the ship into tiny glowing particles.

"Scramble your fighters, now." According to the data on her screen, V'kyrri was shouting at her com panel. "I am Captain V'kyrri of Her Majesty's Destroyer *Queen's Rhapsody*."

Edie flinched. Had to be tough to get the name of his dead ship out of his mouth.

The remaining pair of Chekydran ignored her. Bombs rained from their holds.

Confusion grabbed her ribs. She shot another one

out of the sky. "They're too high. Why are they letting bombs go? They aren't even in position—"

"No. I do not have a destroyer in orbit," V'kyrri snapped. "I'm on an adjunct mission for Her Majesty. We didn't anticipate a Chekydran invasion, much less that your beacons would be offline. Get those fighters off the damn ground. You have bombers incoming. You're Planetary Security. Get out there and protect your people. And while you're at it, get your com arrays—"

Alarms fired off all over Edie's bio-mesh, grating her nerves and rattling her teeth. "Planet-wide alerts firing."

"*Baxt'kal finally*," V'kyrri muttered inside her skull. "*Idiots*."

"V'kyrri," she said aloud, hoping she still had his attention. She took out the third ship and opened her throttle in pursuit of another bomber group. "What are they doing? They aren't fighting back. They're dumping payload too high. None of this…"

As if he'd teleported to her side, V'kyrri gripped her shoulder, his fingers too tight. *Show me.*

Edie replayed the data for him.

He let her hear the breath he sucked in through his teeth. "*Break off. Do not engage*." He sprinted away.

"What?" she shrilled. "I can't just…"

"All channels, all channels, all channels," V'kyrri said. "It's plague. The Chekydran are seeding plague. Do not engage. Destroying the bombers disperses the disease. Take shelter. Institute quarantine immediately."

Edie gaped and twisted to stare at him. "They'll spread disease whether I blow them up or not?"

Misery weighted the shadows of his face. "*Yes. Get*

us out of here. Nearest beacon you can hack and repurpose to broadcast a quarantine notice and distress call."

Edie sheered out of atmosphere. Look at her. Obeying orders from a Claugh without question.

She snuck a glance at him, hunched over the com panel. His shoulders rode high. Tension stood out in the taut muscles of his back. He cared about her people. He'd earned the right to act as equal partner aboard her boat.

If it was a beacon he wanted, a beacon she'd get him.

After several minutes, her bio-mesh buzzed. "Lunar beacon."

Edie slowed, eased close, and brought her ship to station keeping beside the buoy. "If it's been powered down, it'll take a spacewalk to get the thing online and a connection made."

"*Why wouldn't you just code them on or off?*"

She met his eye. "They aren't supposed to be off at all. If they need major maintenance, they send someone in an exo-atmospheric suit and three branches of government have to agree."

"*Just the regional governor has to approve,*" V'kyrri corrected. "*The empire streamlined a little red-tape.*"

A thump against her left thumb brought her attention back. She blew out a shaky breath. "We're in business. Hard connect in 3, 2, 1, mark. Going fishing for who shut these off."

"*Could have been the bugs.*"

"Would have fired alerts on world. This shut down had to come from someone with the government codes.

The governor or someone close. Unless the Claugh streamlined that, too."

"*Not to my knowledge. Messages going in.*"

Vibration like bugs on her skin walked her spine. "Ship incoming. Not Chekydran."

"*Almost done*," V'kyrri said.

"Edie. There you are," her display read. "I knew you'd come. Do you have any idea how many credits your death is worth?"

"Baxt'k."

"*What?*"

"Assassin," she snapped.

"*Weapons?*"

"Oh sure. I can fire at him and rip away half the beacon while I do. Damn it. The governor's code shut down the beacon. Are you clear, yet?"

"*Almost.*"

"Eeeeeediee. I know you see me."

"Spawn of a Myallki bitch." She switched on the com. "Immin? How the Three Hells did you find me?"

"Poor Edie. You were always a sucker for a hard luck case. First a pathetic bounty for miners turned rapists. Only you'd work for so few credits. And look. The Chekydran are attacking home sweet home. Still trying to right all the wrongs of the known galaxy?"

Her breath froze. How had he known anything at all about her home? "Damn, Immin. Got any Rylleian firewater on board? I owe you a drink for alerting me to that tell."

"Not how that works, sweetheart. I could use a drink, but I'm fresh out, and TFC cut the purse strings."

"*You know this assassin?*"

She closed the com. "Former coworker. Contractor.

Brought in on rare occasions for specialty work. Stable as a three-legged Orhait."

"*Can you trust him?*"

"To start shooting the instant he's done gloating? Absolutely. If you're done with the beacon, I can defend us."

"*Yes.*"

She issued the disconnect command and turned her audio back on. "Durgot's gunning for you, too, you know."

"His isn't the only, or even the best, offer on the table," Immin said. "You do know how to make enemies. I'm considering an auction."

"Who?"

"Isn't it delicious when your past reaches out to swallow you?"

A chill walked her gut. Which past? Working for Intcom? Or her past as Firestorm? "Who, Immin?"

"I see you're running with weapons hot. Tough day at the office, Edie, or out for a pleasure cruise in Chekydran-infested space? You get there's nothing personal, right? I mean. I have needs and no credits. I like you, Edie. I really do, but—"

"You have Ykktyryk collections agents to pay," she finished for him. Unpleasant vibration tickled up her spine again. "Sad song, Immin. Oh, hey. Speaking of someone who might want your hide mounted on his bulkhead after the Perrutan Cloud Base incident…"

Immin swore in his native language. Her display panel fed her a series of nonsense bytes.

An enormous blade of a ship arced over the top of *t'Achreides-myn*. Identifiers she didn't need blinked on Edie's screen. She blanked it.

"This is bad," she muttered.

Immin turned tail and ran.

As if magnetically attracted, V'kyrri walked to the view screen, canting his head to follow the arc of the much bigger Erillian Aggressor.

"*I know that ship*," V'kyrri said.

Yes. He did. She knew he knew because she'd been on that ship the last time he'd encountered it.

"*A friend and I diverted to handle an emergency,*" he said by way of explanation. "*We were not the only responders*."

Edie chewed a bitter laugh she didn't dare voice. He and she had come close to having to kill one another during the race to pick up Jayleia Durante after her father had disappeared a few short weeks ago.

V'kyrri and his *friend* had beaten them to Jayleia.

She'd lay odds that his friend had been Damen Sindrivik, the man she'd later found in Jayleia's company on Silver City. Edie shook away speculation and focused on the Erillian.

Rhydian Trente, captain of the ship, had no good reason to ride to her rescue. Which could only mean he hadn't. He'd come for the bounty, too.

"*Another friend of yours*?" V'kyrri asked.

"Remains to be seen," she said.

"Immin's headed out of system. You're clear. Prepare for incoming teleport." The words appeared on her screen. Trente. Telling her to lower her shields. Must have tagged her without audio. V'kyrri didn't tense or shift an iota. Trente wasn't taking the chance that her passenger would overhear.

Great. He was hyped up on full-blown paranoia and asking her to give up her defenses. She glanced at the too-thin man in a khaki uniform standing at her view screen. Maybe he had reason.

"It's not the best time for a visit," Edie wrote back.

"Especially when you're hacking a distress call into a beacon because the Chekydran are trying to wipe out your home world, Firestorm. I'm guessing you'll want a pair of Ioccal IX boosters before you head dirt-side. We both know you're going down there. You won't be able to help yourself."

She bared her teeth at his use of the name he wasn't supposed to know while relief blew through her at the same time. "You stole extra doses when Intcom vaxxed us? Damn, you're good. You're assuming that's what they seeded."

"They haven't changed pattern yet," he replied. "They hit a troop depot last month. Confirmed Ioccal IX. You know, I'd expected Firestorm to be a diva. You weren't. That's the only reason I'm not really pissed off that I hadn't figured it out before Durgot outed you."

Edie frowned. He hadn't had to tell her who'd exposed her. But he had, and Trente did nothing without reason. For a man after a bounty, he sure was collecting favors-owed from her.

Calculated risk, then. He'd either vaporize *t'Achreides-myn,* or he'd teleport in meds. Nothing she could do, either way. He'd dice her to atoms before she'd have her main gun at fifty percent. She killed her shields.

At least she wouldn't have to tell Trente to watch where he put the goods. He'd obviously read everything about her ship. He'd know how many people were aboard before he'd ever considered messaging her. He probably knew before they did where they were going to be standing.

From the way V'kyrri whirled to stare at the center of the cockpit, Edie gathered that incoming teleportation made noise.

A palm-sized box materialized in the middle of her deck plating.

"Cargo arrived intact. What's it going to cost me?"

"We're even."

There it was.

Because Edie had helped him when she hadn't had to, Trente owed her. He couldn't hunt her. Mercenary code of honor. Now that he'd returned the favor in the shape of vaccinations that would let her and V'kyrri get on world and not die from a hemorrhagic disease, all bets would be off.

The next time they met, he wouldn't have to hesitate.

She sucked in a deep breath and let it go. "Message received and understood. We're even. What brings you to this system in time to save my ass?"

"Looking after my interests."

"What interests?"

"None of your business."

She rolled her eyes. "Then you'll want to know the bugs got tentacles on a new weapon."

No answer. Not that he owed her one. But she'd thought maybe Trente had seen the same things she had over the past decade and come to the same conclusion—that no matter their personal issues with the Claugh, until the Chekydran were neutralized, humanoids the known galaxy over were targets.

Including her and Trente.

The Claugh were their best hope of fighting back.

"Good luck getting it back now that there's plague on world. Immin will come after you until you kill him. Either pop him or stay clear so the Ykktyryk can find him and snap him in half. Stop leading him on. S'long, Edie." Trente flashed out.

"*Is this what I think it is?*" V'kyrri had the little case open. He stared at a pair of dosing units.

Edie blanked her screen and climbed out of the cocoon. "Ioccal IX boosters."

"Meaning you've already been vaccinated." He canted a penetrating look her way. "You weren't just a mercenary for Intcom."

"You're not just a pretty face."

A feral grin lit his expression. "Let's go find that crystal."

"You'll do better without me. Leave me here to coordinate."

He gave her a look and popped the vaccine into her arm. "Chekydran," he said, staring her in the eye. "Can you forget the past and lock on right now?"

"The past that was just out there gunning for me? Or the one that teleported over a pair of Ioccal IX boosters?" she flicked a finger at the view screen.

"Edie."

"This isn't about carrying a grudge," she said. "No one on planet will be happy to see me, and if you're in my company—"

"You've changed in ten years," he pointed out. "You're treating Nol Jakze as if it hasn't."

That jolted her.

He was right.

In her head, her home world had gotten stuck in time the moment she'd left it. Intellectually, she could acknowledge things had changed in a decade, but when she pictured any aspect of Nol Jakze, it was exactly as she'd left it. Old arguments and disagreements never shifted or evaporated, maybe because she'd kept them alive when they should have been allowed to pass on in peace.

Who was to say that once she'd left world she hadn't been forgotten? If her people had embraced peace at any cost, then she'd wasted a decade of emotional space believing she was hated.

Edie sighed. Had she always been self-absorbed?

Pressing her lips tight, she returned to her sling and aimed her nose for a home that had nothing for her but suffering and death. Just like when she'd left it.

Who said you couldn't go home again?

Chapter Nineteen

"Chekydran mother in geosync," she said, looking through sensor data. "No shuttle activity. Bombers returning to dock."

"Time is on their side," V'kyrri said aloud. Her panel picked up his words.

Right. The bugs could wait a week until seventy to ninety percent of the population had been infected. Edie swallowed hard.

V'kyrri sat and shoved a hydration pack into her line of sight.

She took it, glad for the distraction and said, "Food in the—"

"Found it." He passed a ration packet.

"Mm. Pureed veggie protein. My least favorite."

"Shut up and eat, soldier," he quipped, then took a pull on his packet. His eyes watered.

She'd have laughed if she hadn't been holding her own tasteless future. Edie choked down the ration packet in a rush. "Until the bugs flinch, I need to build a SEM. Got started while you slept."

"*Got it.*" He took the location of her project pieces from her head and retrieved them. He examined the lenses and frame, frowning. "*Have you run the nano-filaments for the inputs?*"

"Not yet."

"*On it.*"

"Thanks."

She began replacing damaged hardware components on her handheld. "There ought to be a way to build an integral system."

V'kyrri shook his head. "*There is. The developers who created sensory enhancement experimented with building directly into the brain, effectively making themselves cyborgs. They even had a clever data feed filament injecting data straight to the optical nerve. Really inventive hacks.*"

She lifted an eyebrow at him. "But?"

He met her eye and said, "They overloaded their nervous systems and fried their brains. From what I understand the entire team are quietly occupying medical support units somewhere."

"Okay," she said, drawing out the word. "Bad plan."

"Now a holo-projection display rather than ballistic glass…" He hefted the frames and peered at her through the glass.

"Holo-fields are fussy," she protested. "The field generators will work anywhere, but if, say, I'm underwater, sabotaging a rival government's listening station, a holo-field wouldn't resolve."

"You're what happened to that remote spy station on Ginnait IV."

Edie flushed. "Holo-fields let things through, windborne dust, debris, rocks, you name it. Ballistic grade alloy is rough and tumble. Shoot me in the face, and they'll melt a split-second before my brain does, but other than that…"

"*Didn't need that visual, Edie.*"

She grinned.

He shifted. His left thigh rested against her right. Her senses lit. Like his touch was her own personalized enhancement.

She cut a glance at him.

He didn't meet her eye, but he wore a self-satisfied smile and an I-dare-you quirk to one brow.

The mad captain meant to engineer more than her SEM.

A tickle at her right ribs. She sat bolt upright, staring at the partially visible data panel. "What are they doing?"

V'kyrri went to the view screen. Frowning, he bent his head. "*They're on the move*."

"I see that," she said, waving her handheld parts at the display panel. "Are they breaking orbit?"

"*Settling lower. Off-loading shuttles*?"

She tilted the screen into better position and shook her head at the data spike. "They're overpowered for a position shift. It can't be right. Look at that nose pitch. Shields are up. All front. They're landing."

"What? No."

"Then you tell me, Starship Captain," she argued. "What would that power profile, attitude, and shield config mean on your boat?"

"*Those big carriers can't land. They never land.*"

Shields sparking and flaring, the enormous Chekydran ship entered atmosphere.

"Looks to me like someone decided the carriers couldn't land simply because they hadn't."

"I'll be damned. Can you keep a lock on them?"

"Yes."

He came back, grabbed the SEM lenses, and sat down before taking the handheld from her lap.

"Giving you a dose of pain meds. I cured my headache, you're giving me another," she said. She gave him a second to protest before she ordered up the medical processor for him. Mesh closed around his right arm. Since the tightness at her temples eased, she assumed it dosed him.

"Thanks. Didn't realize."

Edie pulled her display panel closed.

"Reverting translation on the screen," she said. Words dribbling across her screen in slow motion vanished. Symbols conveying many nuanced concepts at once rained down. A knock of anxiety she hadn't noticed before that point unknotted behind her breastbone.

At her command, the bio-mesh reconfigured. It wrapped around hips and chest, locking them to their seats.

It afforded Edie full sensory immersion. Vibration, gentle thumps of 'hey, pay attention,' and harder kicks of alarm offered direct tactile access to the status of *t'Achreides-myn*. Her chest expanded without her command in echo of V'kyrri's gasp that sounded inside her head.

Damn. She'd enclosed a claustrophobe. "You okay?"

"*This is amazing. What does it all mean?*"

She huffed a laugh. "Little busy looking like a meteor entering atmosphere. Come in and get it if you can do it without distracting me."

A long pause. "*Tempting, but we can't take the chance. I intend to be maximally distracting the next time you invite me in.*"

He managed to trace his mental voice along her

cheek in place of physical touch. A tingle followed.

Her body heated, and all she could do was concentrate on not actually burning them up in atmosphere while trying to make it look to the ground as if that's exactly what was happening. That was her. Space junk burning up on re-entry.

He slanted a glance at her and asked aloud, maybe to assure her he wasn't eavesdropping on the arousal he'd deliberately stirred. "Not going to burden Planetary Security with clearing us in?"

Edie shrugged. "If the Chekydran don't already know we're here, I am not tipping them off."

"Good plan."

"Reactor banked. Atmospherics online," she said.

It hadn't occurred to Edie to disable alerts for V'kyrri. Maybe the rush of tactile sensation that gave her data distracted him from being closed in. A gentle knock at the base of her spine echoed data on her screen.

"The Chekydran mother is on the ground. Northern hemisphere. Sparsely populated. Wilderness homesteaders and one tiny farming community."

"Planetary capital and most major settlements are in the southern hemisphere in the temperate zone," V'kyrri said. "At least it doesn't seem to be a direct attack."

"Not yet." She leveled off and looped toward the mothership's landing site.

Proximity alarms fired rapid-pulse buzzes into her left bicep.

"Ow," V'kyrri yelped.

"Incoming." Shields popped into place. "The Chekydran set watchdogs."

"Watch bugs," he corrected.

"Hilarious."

Four fighters picked them up. She ached to blow them out of her home world's sky, but she had much larger Chekydran to fry. Turning tail, she poured on speed. "We won't be doing aerial recon of the landing site."

They bounced.

In-atmosphere weapons' fire streaked past her port side.

"Damn it, I hate flying blind," V'kyrri muttered.

Edie loathed having to get her data from slow-poke words and letters. But she could. He couldn't translate her symbol-based system. Not unless he invested the time to learn her native language, which wasn't likely.

In the middle of running from bugs with guns hot on her exhaust port, she switched the screen to Tagrethian.

V'kyrri jolted. His motion translated through the mesh. "*Edie. I'm sorry. I didn't—*"

"You didn't think I'd hear you," she said. V'kyrri had used the fact to say aloud what he wouldn't say to her directly. He hadn't intended for her to know about it at all.

A hard knot wrapped around her sternum as she dove lower and spun *t'Achreides-myn* through the jagged spikes of a mountain range.

The Chekydran followed.

One of them brushed too close, hit and bounced off stone, rolling into its neighbor. Formation flying had uses. Tight spaces weren't among them. Her smile grim, she shook her head.

Shame, not her own, crawled her windpipe. V'kyrri

said, "*I swear I did not mean to take unfair advantage of you. Not consciously. You're the only person I've ever met who doesn't talk to herself.*"

A light clicked on in the dim recesses of her brain. "You're a hearing person aboard a deaf person's ship. Unless I speak to you, you have next to no auditory input, and you're as addicted to the sensory stimulation as I am to my SEM."

"*That makes me feel even better.*"

That made her laugh at the same time she slid sideways in the sky, dodging another shot fired by the pair of remaining bugs.

"*They're breaking off,*" V'kyrri said.

Edie slowed, but didn't take shields offline. "We're a couple thousand kilometers from their landing site. I can sneak back and get us on the ground, but we'll be a couple hundred kilometers out, at best."

"*Several day's hike.*"

"While dodging ground patrols," she said. "I doubt they'd chase us off in the sky and not have soldiers on perimeter."

He looked at her. As well as he could while held in place by mesh. "*We don't have the time. Nol Jakze doesn't have the time.*"

"Juice the shields the way we did getting through the debris field. Then we fly..." she broke off. "No. That won't work."

"*We'd be flying blind because the shields would ionize atmosphere?*" he finished for her.

"We'll have to scan from orbit."

"*No.*" His mental voice lit the same way his face did when an idea he liked struck him. He waggled a finger at her. "*You've been alone too long. Never do yourself what a team can do for you."*

The barb cleaved deep, sticking in her ribs after he'd relied on her inability to hear what he'd had to say. What he hadn't wanted her to know he'd said. She slid him a sideways glance.

He bared his teeth in a fierce, humorless grin. "*When you left world there were few satellites. Your people didn't need them, but the empire did. We put them up. I'll commandeer them.*"

Edie tucked away the odd sensation of being dissected by a scalpel of deliberate isolation. This was too important.

"You can point their eyes right at the Chekydran," she finished for him.

"*If you'll get me a com line.*"

She woke the panels beneath V'kyrri's fingers. "Chest restraints released. Stay put. I'll route it to you here. Line open."

The comforting support of bio-mesh around her ribs vanished. "Your controls are in Tagrethian."

"*Got it.*" His code cut straight through governmental computer routing systems. When someone answered his hail, it was a military officer. V'kyrri and the officer entered a rapid-fire exchange of request, protest, orders, refusal, rank pulling, and, on the part of the other officer, capitulation.

Edie put *t'Achreides-myn* down in the Suvallin Wilderness. Nothing else to do. Until V'kyrri had data, they had nothing—except memories Edie didn't want and regrets over a life she couldn't have.

The mountains she picked had once been a vast plateau. Eons of erosion had washed away softer stone and left needles of hard rock behind. A watery, mysterious landscape painting had captivated her as a child, and she'd vowed to one day see the landscape with her own eyes.

She hadn't imagined it being while she was dodging Chekydran.

She shut off shields, set down atop the bare dome of one of the needles, and fired a couple of tethers into rock. Then, leaving V'kyrri watching data pour into ship's computers, Edie did what she'd ached to do for the past several days, dug out clean clothes and ran through a long, relaxing cleansing cycle. Time to kill, right? Before she got herself killed, because Immin had been right—she was still trying to right all the wrongs of the known galaxy.

Dressed in dark gray trousers, a matching thermal tank, and an old-fashioned cream-colored shirt with actual buttons, Edie emerged refreshed. Manual clothing fasteners were her first concession to her world's religious restrictions. She'd even used the last of a stupidly expensive potion on her hair to tame the unruly mass.

Second concession and a reluctant one at that. She'd left her hair down. It made no sense. Observing local custom wouldn't make people accept her.

Frowning, Edie shoved a fistful of hair ties in a pocket. The instant she had actionable data, the hair went up. Cultural mores be damned. She had a job to do.

She wrapped her gear belt around the outside of the blouse and then opened the hatch. Dangling her legs over the doorjamb, she sat with nothing but air beneath her boots, and drank in the scenery.

Bonus. She sat on a precipice literally and

metaphorically. The literal ledge perched above ghostly blue clouds wreathing the stone needles. The metaphorical one sat in her command cocoon, gathering intel on Chekydran.

Here she was, about to be crushed between the Claugh, the Chekydran, and her own people.

Her insides twisted.

Memory opened a door on her mother's fond smile, her gently curling brown hair pulled back, the tender light in her brown eyes as she sat on Edie's bedside, reciting the nightly liturgy—a tiny ritual Edie had taken for granted, had assigned no meaning to until it had been taken from her.

"Forgiveness is freedom. Service is sacred."

Smile wobbling, Edie blew out a slow breath. She couldn't quite manage forgiveness. She righted a few wrongs here and there. Maybe it could balance out her sins. A little.

Problem was, in order to right the overwhelming wrong of the Chekydran on Nol Jakze, she had to go all in with the Claugh. Not just pretend. She had to drain her wounds and commit.

Her nerves tingled. She looked over her shoulder. V'kyrri. A smile rose unbidden.

He skimmed her with a heated look. "Wow."

She flushed. "You have data?"

"We have data."

At the warmth expanding in her chest, she rose. Points for inclusion. She took one last, deep breath of air sweetened by growing things and shut the hatch.

"With as much data as you're bringing in," she said, leading the way to the command sling, "you're going to need the tricks I stole from Intcom."

Gratified, V'kyrri laughed, took his seat, and pulled her into his lap.

She shrieked as she fell.

Uncertainty clouded her face before he wrapped his arms around her and cradled her against his chest. His heart tore. Damned war. He'd never regret his uniform. But what someone else wearing and tarnishing it had cost her? He'd regret that forever.

"I have what I need," he said and kissed her. Smoke and sweet citrus filled his head like the finest Noc Gallon Whiskey.

Her lips twitched beneath his—another brief smile—and she relaxed into him. "About that data…"

"In a minute," he murmured.

Edie arched into the kiss. Intoxication boiled his blood. Not whiskey. She was incendiary. Edie had his entire body alight.

At least she seemed to be having as much trouble catching her breath as he did. He shifted to ease the tightening seam of his trousers.

He released her, stroking an admiring hand down her hair, then watched fascinated as she shivered. She shifted into her seat, her cheeks flushed. He let her go, content with his small victory.

"What did you do?" he marveled as Edie piled a load of virtual tools against his growing stockpile of data, "steal every data aggregation and analysis tool Intcom built?"

"Yes."

He laughed and brought up the real-time orbital cams. In concert, they leaned forward, staring at a raw scar in a vast plain.

"What the Three Hells is that?" she said.

"Are those standing stones?" V'kyrri asked. The sun glinted on them. He grunted. "Crystal."

The Chekydran mothership sat outside the perimeter of whatever they were building. Bugs lined up at what he took for a cargo door. They marched away carrying UMOPG cargo crates between them.

"They're offloading. They aren't building the crystal into their ships," V'kyrri said.

"No," she said. "They're building them into the planet. Sensors register hum from the bugs. But look at this." She waved at her data ticking on the left side of her panel. "Massive signal I assume is coming from those crystals."

"I'd love to call in an airstrike," he muttered, "and destroy enough crystal to interrupt whatever it is they're doing. Or calling."

She stared at him, blanching. "This can't be good."

"We have to destroy it."

She scowled at her readouts. "Sure would like to know…"

Motion caught his attention. Adrenaline burned his systems. He switched the satellite view. "Fighters leaving the mothership en masse."

"Headed northeast." Edie called up planetary settlement maps. "There's a village."

She ramped her idling engines and blew the tethers.

"We won't make it in time," he warned.

"Not to warn the villagers, no," she said. They lifted, and she put them on course. "But I can shoot a few bugs down."

"Get me a line."

"Done. What are you—"

"Pulling rank. The military can evacuate every

village within a thousand kilometers of this installation." He shunted satellite data out of the way, save for the feed following the fighters.

Edie's hands shook as she redlined the atmospherics and primed her guns at the same time. He swallowed the urge to comfort her, to assure her it would be all right. He couldn't.

Chapter Twenty

Holding her breath, Edie slotted into a break in the trees.

Via satellite, she watched the bugs strafe scattered houses. Wood and sod flew. Smoke rose, yanking Edie's breath from her chest.

At least the residents—even the children—would be in the fields, working the northern hemisphere harvest. She hoped.

"*Look*," V'kyrri's command rang in her skull.

"Just because you don't have to touch me to talk to me anymore doesn't mean you have to yell," she snapped.

"*Sorry*." He'd muted his mental presence, but triumph bounced from him to her.

This was a promising development for him.

Yay. Now maybe she could concentrate on saving some lives.

A stream of people poured from the fields, running for the tree line. For protection. The Chekydran ships, intent on destroying the village, hadn't noticed them.

Edie altered course to intercept.

Two Chekydran fighters broke off the main formation, heading for the fleeing villagers. And Edie.

The Chekydran ships spat plasma; one at *t'Achreides-myn*, the other at the villagers. Good for Edie. The fighters weren't strong enough to damage her. Bad for the villagers. They didn't have shields.

They did have Edie.

Peeling her lips back in a nasty grin, she sighted, and fired.

The ship strafing the villagers bucked and rolled. The nose pitched. It crashed into a kashtef tuber field and exploded.

The villagers didn't look back. Someone had drilled them.

Suspicion tickled her spine. She rolled *t'Achreides-myn* back on course.

Chekydran plasma burst against her forward shields.

"Nice shot," she muttered aloud for V'kyrri's sake. "A dozen more of those might make it through my screens. Be a pity if someone vaporized you before you could get another shot off."

She blew the fighter apart in midair.

V'kyrri's grin turned blood thirsty.

Edie circled the villagers once as they reached the tree line. It wasn't much protection, but it was protection. The leader of the group paused, waiting for her charges to clear into the forest. She lifted a hand high above her head in a sign that confirmed Edie's suspicion.

Resistance.

Proper response? Waggling wings her boat did not have. Rolling a few times would have to serve.

Message received and returned: *You're not alone*.

She headed for the village.

"What are you doing?" V'kyrri demanded.

"Picking off Chekydran."

"Let it go. We have to take out that installation."

"The Chekydran," she corrected.

He put a hand on her wrist. Heat ran up her arm and straight to her core. *t'Achreides-myn* swept into the smoldering remains of town. Not a single bug remained. "Cowards."

"Edie."

"You think installation all you want," she said. "I'm going for massive overkill."

"Good. We're going to need help," he said. "Competent help."

She left the burning village. "Then you don't want military."

Circles, dark and bruised-looking under his eyes, V'kyrri stared at her, expression neutral. "Resistance? You want me to bring in former resistance fighters."

"You specified competent help," she said. "Fighters who know what it means to sacrifice lives in pursuit of a cause. Not a bunch of teenagers with laser pistols trying to figure out what they want to be when they grow up."

"What you're talking about doesn't exist," he said.

"You cannot believe the Claugh wiped out the resistance," she countered.

"It's been ten years. If you could dig up more than two or three people, the only thing they'll be invested in are their farms and families. They'll have moved on. Developed limps, put on weight. The ones who remain will be like you were. They won't agree to work with me."

"You don't want to do this. I get that. I don't want to do this. Hells, *they* don't want me to do this—to remind them and everyone else what they'd once been," she said, "but they *will* remember. Whether they want to or not. They fought for this world once. I have to give them the opportunity to do it again."

"You have to?" he echoed.

Edie clamped her teeth. Looked away. Funny. Pacts had been made at the end of the war, when the resistance had seen the inevitable staring them in the eye. Pacts that included never giving up one another or the nature of their agreements—not to the rest of Nol Jakze and certainly not to the Claugh. Yet here she was. Breaking that vow in the interests of saving the people the pact had been struck to protect in the first place. "Promises were made. I may be refused, but my former comrades-in-arms should have the choice to rise again in defense of their people."

His brow furrowed.

"What?"

"A Claugh officer going into combat with a cadre of former resistance fighters? All carrying old grudges. What could possibly go wrong?"

Edie laughed and flew from northern hemisphere fall into southern hemisphere spring.

****

They put down in the wilderness in the middle of a rainstorm. One of the benefits of the Iskant class ship, besides being modular enough to accommodate customization, was in-atmosphere maneuvering. Edie could hover a meter off the ground and slide sideways into the cover of a mature stand of native honey-fern trees. Enormous canopy spread. Favored nesting trees for hives of slug wasps.

She maneuvered carefully to avoid hitting a tree trunk. Fresh scars on trees and swarms of angry slug wasps would give away her position in a blink. She shut down everything but coms and the incoming satellite streams. Edie switched to atmosphere for air supply.

V'kyrri's chest expanded as he lifted his face and drew a deep breath of rain-sweetened air. He smiled.

She rose. "I'll be back. Two hours. Maybe three."

"No going out there alone." He levered himself out of the chair.

His uniform had grown larger since she'd met him. That's right. He'd been injured, abused stim, and then slept forever without getting nutrition onboard. No wonder his uniform flapped when he rose.

She frowned. "You need another ration packet. Maybe two or three. I have to go alone. Find something better to eat than pureed veggie protein. Get some rest."

"Edie."

She put on her newly built SEM. *Not this time, mister*. She switched on the unit. Sensory information caressed her nerves while V'kyrri glared.

They compromised.

He went with her.

But only after she'd forced another pair of high calorie ration packs on him. Edie led the way into the sullen drizzle and deepening dark of late afternoon.

It took an hour to reach cultivated land. In the last vestiges of daylight, she counted fields and prayed that the people she'd made promises to still lived there after all these years. When she and her former companions had made arrangements and clandestine signaling promises, they hadn't expected ten years to pass before needing them.

A cold finger of adrenaline slid into her chest. She hunkered into a stand of fruity-smelling flowering shrubs.

V'kyrri settled beside her.

She glanced at her SEM field. It picked up an audio signal incoming from the north.

V'kyrri cocked his head.

"Ships," they said in unison.

"Coming in on our flight path," she noted.

"Following?"

"Can't be. No trail left to follow."

The ships swept overhead. Chekydran midrange fighters made up the bulk of the ghostly flight illuminated solely by their exhaust ports. Four were sleek, aerodynamic ships clearly meant for maneuverability in atmosphere. Edie hadn't seen their like before.

The audio signal pitched down.

"Leaving," V'kyrri said. "A patrol, maybe. Or a scouting mission."

"I'll be happy when every last one of them is dead," she said and slipped out of her pack. "Stay here."

He gripped her bicep. "No."

Concern for her communicated through his touch. She drew a sharp breath. Then, a piece at a time, she relaxed.

"It's a signal," she said. "I activate the perimeter alarm and stand there for a minute. Long enough to be seen. I turn around, come back, and then we march to a prearranged meet point."

"You're going into the open where anyone could take a shot at you," he said, "and then we'll be walking straight into what could be an ambush."

"None of this was my idea," she said. "Wasn't made to be easy. Or pleasant. By the time the war ended, none of us wanted to see one another again."

Sympathy caught in V'kyrri's ribs. He released her.

Edie shut down her SEM, rose, and slipped through the brush. The light of the two tiny moons rendered her in grayscale as she stepped into the waist-high grass.

He shouldered her pack and followed, keeping to the edge of the field. She jerked to a halt. Her shoulders twitched as if she'd taken a shock.

Maybe she had. His version of perimeters alarms wouldn't work on a world where most of the population were deaf.

V'kyrri took cover. He couldn't go any closer without brushing that perimeter alarm, too. He settled into the grass, gun out, to keep Edie covered. In the dark. Heart slamming his ribs, he counted down the minute.

A tiny green light flashed. It lit up a fingertip-sized dot right left of center on her chest.

Before he could think, he tackled her into the grass. Out of the line of fire.

The shot never came.

Instead, through the racket of rage and adrenaline storming his blood, he swore laughter drifted on the night breeze.

Edie tapped his shoulder.

V'kyrri shifted off her.

"They know we're here, I guess. That was the point. We can go. They'll either come find me or they won't." She rose. Water cascaded from her clothing.

Only then did V'kyrri realize the field held several inches of standing water. He climbed to his feet, the music of water draining from his clothing loud to his ears.

She switched on her SEM field. Red light fed nonsense-to-him symbols down her eyes and upper cheekbones.

She retrieved her pack, slung it to her back, and the pair trudged back the way they'd come.

Behind them, someone screamed.

He looked over his shoulder. V'kyrri's breath caught.

Weapons' fire.

He jerked around, staring at the dark hulks of buildings clustered at the other end of the fields.

More screams. Children crying.

Edie spun into a dead run, heading for the village. V'kyrri paced her, splashing through the field.

Laser fire flashed between buildings, illuminating the bodies that flew, spread-eagle to the ground. Fire flickered, faint at first, then grew to cast the village in nightmare light.

Blobs on too many legs scurried among the buildings, bodies throwing grotesque shadows as they pulled down houses and smashed barns.

Animal shrieks joined the clamor.

Sobbing audibly, Edie waded into the village. She began shooting Chekydran.

Aching for a plasma rifle, V'kyrri aimed at the bug Edie peppered with laser fire. Their combined firepower blew bug parts into the conflagration consuming a farmhouse.

They advanced into the track between the houses. A child's doll, white dress smeared dark, lay face down in a mud puddle. He shuddered. Pressure landed on his chest as implacable as the rock vise that he and Edie had navigated on the last planet.

It wasn't a doll.

Rage clenched him in a fist. He didn't need air. Killing Chekydran would sustain him.

A trio of bugs emerged from the dark, misshapen monsters bent on ripping apart lives.

Edie tossed something into the soil at their feet. She backed away.

V'kyrri followed.

POP.

Legs, tentacles, and ichor splattered the street and nearest building.

Chekydran hum rose above the noise of battle and hungry flames. The monsters poured into the street, zeroing in on them. Or maybe just Edie. Did Chekydran have angels of destruction? Edie fit the bill. Except…the bugs angled for him. He backpedaled.

Edie held up a hand. He tapped her surface thoughts when he couldn't read the signal she gave.

'Retreat,' the gesture said. She gestured again, her body arching. 'Evacuate.'

Spraying the oncoming surge of Chekydran with suppression fire, V'k drew Edie into the dubious shelter to be found between buildings.

"Run," she said aloud. She sprinted for the fields.

V'kyrri rummaged in her head and nabbed her still forming plan. He paused, turned, and blew away one of the Chekydran cantering in their wake.

First step: Draw fire. They'd done that.

Second step: Lead the bugs away from the village. Laser fire hit the ground beside him. Mud and soil sprayed into the air. That part of the plan seemed to be working, too.

They veered into a field flooded ankle-deep.

Humanoid shapes appeared from the brush along one side of the field. Weapons strobed laser fire across the field, past Edie and him. Villagers, he deduced, covering their retreat.

Edie reached the edge of the field and turned, already firing.

A single expletive arrowed through her head. He caught a mental glimpse through her eyes.

Super soldiers. Massive, misshapen humanoids modified and mind-controlled by the Chekydran. Six of them. They'd joined the tumble of bugs, forming up with them, something that seemed to impose order on the ravening Chekydran. They marched for Edie and him, guns down, ignoring the villagers.

Villagers sprayed the misshapen super soldiers with gunfire. To no effect.

Cold rage spilled from Edie into V'kyrri's brain and down his spine.

She was out of explosives.

The blood drained from V'kyrri's head. He changed focus from bugs to soldier faces. It was their only dimming hope.

Caught between physical chill and the blast furnace of internal fury, Edie studied the bugs and soldiers splashing through the field. She'd distracted them from the village, right enough. Now to wipe the abominations from the face of her peoples' sacred land with nothing but the useless dregs in her pack, which amounted to little more than one tiny mini core attached to a flying toy.

Water lapped into her boots, cold and unpleasant. An electric charge ran up her spine. Edie smiled as her synapses lit up with an idea. Hers? V'kyrri's?

He grabbed open the fastening on her pack and dug in.

"Out of the water," Edie sign-shouted. "Now."

In the dark, hardly anyone would see her, much less understand the retreat order. One woman did. She whirled and holding the "retreat up" sign over head, she ran through the villagers. They picked up the order, passing it. They scattered for higher ground.

V'kyrri hauled Edie out of the water by the scruff of her neck. He set her on her feet, then ripped free the electrical leads on the mini core before he slapped it into her palm along with a sense of relish.

"*Set. Ten seconds.*" Pride in her resonated in his mental voice.

Savoring the rush of V'kyrri's admiration, Edie opened her fingers. The mini core rolled out of her hand.

Splash.

"Oopsie," she said aloud.

V'kyrri snorted.

5, 4,

The soldiers lifted weapons on her. No. On V'kyrri. *Interesting*. Bugs fired at fleeing villagers. 3, 2…

Edie nodded. *This* was why she'd become what she had. It had taken Chekydran, super soldiers, and one shipwrecked Claugh captain to get her to see.

1…

Blue-white lightning lit the night, crackling through the water, confined to the tidy rectangle of flooded marsh grain. Electricity climbed the organic structures of the plants until the water-logged leaves caught fire.

Bugs and misshapen soldiers thrashed, screaming.

Her SEM drove their agony into her brain. It wiped the smile from her face. She couldn't celebrate taking life, but spite and vindication refused to die along with the things that had destroyed Nakuri village.

The creatures fell, limp and silent, several seconds before the electricity ripping through their corpses released the bodies into the mud.

Edie turned away.

A man, broad shouldered and thick waisted, trudged to meet her and V'kyrri. A stripling boy at his side lit a lantern to compete with the blue-white lightning still arcing behind her.

The man had dark hair silvering at the temples, brown skin weathered by time and sun, and dark eyes shadowed by rage, sorrow, and the angle of the lantern light. But he wore a familiar, lopsided twist to his lips.

Recognition shoved air into Edie's chest. Her hands moved of their own accord. "Jonas."

Her former cell leader, wet, muddy, possibly bloody, said, "You just couldn't stay away."

Like a finger laid against her skull, the faint pressure of V'kyrri tapping into her head increased. Right. Translation. She hadn't had time to teach him her native language.

Jonas's gaze flicked to V'kyrri in a long, hard look before he returned his attention to her and jerked a finger at her SEM. "Take off that insult."

"Now that the attack is over, sure," Edie replied. She shut down the SEM, removed the glasses, and put them in her belt.

Villagers gathered behind Jonas. He looked between Edie and V'kyrri, lifted his hands to speak, sighed, and shook his head.

"Get off my property," he finally said aloud. "Let us bury our dead and sift through what remains of the lives we built after you left."

"You don't get to make that an accusation, Jonas. I left because no one wanted me," she snapped, her motion short. Sharp.

"Still don't," one of the women said at Jonas's shoulder.

Jonas slapped the woman's hands down and rounded on Edie. "You could have had your pick of families, girl. Families who would have sheltered and protected you, if only you'd let go of that monumental rage and thirst for revenge."

Edie's gut twisted. Everything she'd ever wanted, and she hadn't been able to see it. Much less accept it. She couldn't get her breath. "I would have endangered anyone who would have had me, and you know it. It doesn't matter anymore. I couldn't let go."

"It made you a monster." His hands fell to his side, slack.

Chapter Twenty-One

"Like the monsters that tried to murder you?" V'kyrri demanded, rage in every sharp word. "The ones she dispatched in your defense. Like those?"

Edie translated.

Jonas stared at V'kyrri for several seconds, then turned and walked away. The villagers followed, giving the electrified and still-sparking field wide berth.

Edie set a hand to V'kyrri's shoulder. He vibrated. Indignation, seething fury, towering impatience. All on her behalf.

She drew a deep breath and allowed herself to nestle into the warm shelter of his outrage. Sighing, Edie straightened and put on her SEM.

"Let's move."

"*They're out of their minds. You saved their lives.*"

"*We* did."

The ire grumbling in his mental presence quieted. "*Thank you, but you—*"

"You don't have to patch me up," she said as they trudged into the deepening evening. Awareness blossomed in her chest.

She'd believed V'kyrri had forced her to change her view of the Claugh. He had. But he'd somehow forced her to look at herself from a new perspective, too. Self-acceptance hadn't settled in yet, but she could almost taste the smooth sweetness of it on her tongue.

"If I became a monster, it was to protect something I believe is worth protecting. I won't ignore that anymore."

He stopped her, his palms cupping her shoulders. His delighted grin stretched her own lips. "You know I have to recruit you now."

"Maybe we should survive this invasion first."

He laughed, froze, and looked up.

Ship signatures flashed in her data field.

"*Searching for us*," he said.

"You," she corrected in a hush. "Those soldiers. What were those things? The soldiers and bugs were focused on *you*."

They ran out of the fields into a line of foothills that turned rocky and steep. Nothing looked the way she remembered. Ten years of plant growth and the sweet line of little trees that had once bowed their heads to the rain squalls had turned into a forest. Tracks and paths had vanished, which had been part of the plan. But trying to remember how to get from point A to point B when the goal had been to prevent anyone from finding point B turned into more guesswork than Edie wanted.

She finally found her point B. A supply cache the last surviving resistance fighters had set up when it became clear the war had been lost.

Edie edged behind a decade of foliage growth.

"*More caves*?" V'kyrri's plaintive question drew a laugh from her. She stooped to climb into the deep dark of a tunnel.

"Shelter. Food. Water. Medical supplies. Weapons." Six steps in, half the number of gods. Straighten. Face left and demonstrate trust. Reach into the darkness. Grab the light.

Religious colonies and their liturgical metaphors.

She switched on a lantern.

V'kyrri, blinking in the light, raised his eyebrows. "The resistance has a stockpile. After all these years? I don't think my commanding officers knew what kind of danger they were in on this world."

"Always have a plan," she said. "Not that ours mattered. No one ever rose against the occupation."

For the first time in her life, it occurred to Edie to wonder why. Standing amidst the neatly stacked cargo containers holding everything from food to explosives and decade old weapons, she met a Claugh captain's eye without reservation and accepted that the resistance had died because it hadn't been needed.

Until now.

"You'd better learn the language," she said, tapping her forehead. "You're going to need it."

He took her hand. V'kyrri crept into her brain and poked whatever part stored symbol and meaning. She caught glimpses of herself as a child learning not just the language but forming emotional and contextual associations.

She frowned. He'd forever walk around knee deep in her reflexive, unexamined emotions surrounding words and concepts. He wouldn't have the opportunity to forge his own.

"*Limits of the ability*," he said.

Her frown deepened as she contemplated the value difference between knowing something and learning something.

"Done. Thank you," he said with his hands. His first signs were slow and clumsy, but readable.

"Okay." She scanned the symbols on the cargo containers. "Help me get at this one?"

They shifted containers until Edie could break the seal.

"Dry clothes? You guys thought of everything."

"Not entirely," she said. "The ones I put in here are the size I was as a hungry nineteen-year-old."

He laughed and his mental presence expanded, suffusing her with good humor.

She dug out clothes, shut the lid, and led him deeper into the cave. "Let me show you the best part."

"*A shower? A real water shower*?" he marveled.

"Spring fed," she said. "It's cold. But we'd dealt with chemical attacks…"

Comforting good humor iced over, chilling her. His brows lowered. "*What the Three Hells went wrong on this world? The Claugh brought all kinds of worlds into the empire before and after Nol Jakze, without the kinds of brutality your slips of memory slice into my brain. What you're describing goes against everything the empire stands for.*"

She lifted a shoulder and let it fall. "I can only speak our experience."

"It should never have been your experience," he bit out. His shoulders fell and he scrubbed a hand over his face. "Sorry. I am aching to be clean and dry and in clothes not stained with the blood of my crew."

Edie set clean clothes and drying cloths to one side, shut down her SEM, tucked the glasses into a pouch on her belt, took it off, and set it with the clothing. She wrestled free of her sodden boots. "Go right ahead. I'll find food while you—"

"*What's your hurry? You've been dying to have me*

out of this uniform you hate. Here's your chance."

He grabbed hold of her and ducked them both, fully clothed under the frigid fall of water, laughing and yelping at the icy shock.

Edie shrieked and gasp-laughed, captive both to his arms wrapped around her waist and to his contagious laughter. Teeth chattering, she retrieved a single cleansing strip from a canister standing beside the little waterfall serving as their shower.

They flung away filthy, torn clothing. Any lingering amorous intent shriveled in the chilly water. They washed and rinsed as fast as shivering allowed.

Edie stepped out of the water and shook out a pair of drying cloths. She hugged one to her chest and offered the other just out of V'kyrri's reach both in retribution for dunking her and so she could get her fill of admiring the long, lean—still too lean—lines of his body. Her face, and anatomy much lower, warmed.

Grinning, he snatched the cloth from her, dried swiftly, and pulled on clean clothes that weren't khaki. He pulled his insignia from his uniform, curled his fingers around it, then tucked it into a pocket.

"You're the demolition expert," he said as she yanked on clothes and tucked her glasses into place. "How do we warm up?"

"This is a religious settlement, Captain," she informed him with mock severity. "If you're cold, you aren't working hard enough."

His smile shifted. "Challenge accepted."

She laughed while he pressed, frowning, at the buttons on his shirt.

"That's not how those work. Stop pushing them. Here." She sidled close, batted his hands away from his shirt, and buttoned it for him.

He settled his hands on her hips.

Sparks traced her nerves.

He tugged her into contact with him. “Sorry. Did I fail to specify my preference for the two of us undressing one another?”

“We did. In the shower.”

“Stripping while numb with cold?” he mused. “I don’t think it’ll sell.”

She patted the final button on his shirt with one hand and tapped her SEM to life with the other. “Hold still.”

Edie rose to her toes and kissed him. Every fiber of her lit. A little like Sensory Enhancement. Infinitely better. Her entire body stirred, focused and intent upon V’kyrri and the contact of his lips on hers. He’d wanted warmth? Between them, they’d kindled a fire.

She drew back and opened her eyes to meet his gaze. Normal SEM data flow to focus past. One heartbeat. Two. Three.

Edie’s chest constricted. She froze.

V’kyrri was instantly in her head. No questions. Only his gaze staring through hers at a third heartbeat that should not be in the cave with them.

She slipped into the labyrinth of cargo containers that had been arranged long ago to provide exactly the cover she needed.

A light switched on in the front of the cave. Seated atop one of the boxes, lounging against the stone wall, boots propped on top of a second crate, Rhydian Trente met Edie’s gaze. His thick, black hair fell across indigo eyes. His face was set and cold as the glacial fields on Chemmoxin.

Edie stared.

"You going to tell me where the tracker is, or do I dump everything and start over?"

"Are you that naïve you think IntCom only vaccinated for disease?" Trente asked.

"Spawn of a Myallki bitch." She rounded crates and sat across from him. "You aren't here for the bounty or I'd be dead already."

At the faint curve of his lips, Edie shrugged. "It didn't escape me that you teaching me to spot assassins also taught you how to get at me. I'd tell you to take a number and stand in line for your shot, but the whole of my people seems to be ahead of you."

"How dare you remind them of what they once were," Trente said, flashing a mean grin. His dark gaze moved past Edie to V'kyrri. His brows lowered. "Eilod Saoyrse's life is in danger."

V'kyrri sat beside Edie, relaxed. Unmoved. The muscles in his leg against hers didn't even flinch. A faint smile appeared on his face, and his presence in the room increased. "Tell me something I don't know."

Edie sat back. Trente had something in play, something that affected the Claugh, apparently the queen, herself. He'd sworn vengeance against Eilod Saoyrse long before Edie had met him. Whatever his ultimate plan, Edie wasn't a part of it.

"Her political opponents are gaining ground," Trente said.

"Assessment?" V'kyrri asked, an officer recognizing a spy and cutting straight to risk.

"Assassination."

V'kyrri straightened. "Any specifics?"

"Only that it's someone close. Someone trusted."

She lifted her chin in question. "Who's running you?"

Trente met her gaze for several seconds, his own unreadable. And that meant no one had sent him on a mission. He'd come to warn V'kyrri about the Claugh queen's safety—a Claugh queen he professed to loath. Suddenly, the meaning of every time Edie'd caught him monitoring anything and everything to do with Eilod Saoyrse shifted. Maybe he'd started out plotting revenge, but somewhere along the line, he'd softened. He wanted her alive. Maybe, so deep down he couldn't even admit it to himself…he just wanted her.

His brows lowered.

She smiled.

"Have you seen the TFC pipeline?" he demanded. "Such a nicely worded invitation for the valued mercs to c'mon home to the bosom of the people who understand and love them."

She snorted. "A bosom that looks an awful lot like a black box?"

"Yeah." Trente rolled to standing. "Clear skies, Edie. I'm getting off this baxt'kal planet. It's making me insane. If either of you has a brain, you'll do the same."

Edie lifted her chin.

"Commit or hit the lanes," Trente said, strolling out of the cave. "They'll eat you alive otherwise."

"What the Three Hells was that?" V'kyrri demanded. "Who'll eat you alive?"

"You. The Claugh. The Chekydran. Nol Jakze." She hunched her shoulders. "The monster wasn't supposed to come home."

"Stop calling yourself that," he ordered. "Monsters

don't save the lives of their enemies."

"You aren't my enemy."

"I know. How long will it take you to realize it?"

"Dammit, V'kyrri. I'm Firestorm. How can you trust me?"

"Because you're more than worthy of trust, and you certainly aren't going to do the job for yourself."

His gaze went past her to the cave entrance. His expression tightened.

Footsteps on the trail up the hill.

A sensation like he'd put a finger against the back of her hand though he hadn't actually touched her. "*May I?*" sounded in her head.

She didn't particularly want him inside her brain, but it made tactical sense. Counting heartbeats in her data feed, she nodded, and ignored the warmth spilling down her breastbone simply because he'd asked.

"*Villagers,*" she said inside her head. Couldn't be bugs. No hum. Not Trente returning. Too many of them.

"*Going to need a brief on your friend,*" V'kyrri noted, tucking Trente's image into her gray matter.

Right. The one obsessed with his queen.

She crept behind a cargo container and drew. V'kyrri's shoulder contacted hers. He held his pistol at the ready, as well.

The lantern sat where they'd left it, illuminating a yellow circle.

The first person emerged into the circle of light, squinting, one hand half lifted to shield his eyes. Broad shoulders, dark hair silvering at the temples, and work clothes stained with blood.

"Jonas." Edie rose and rounded into the open.

More villagers filtered into the cave.

Jonas caught her by the shoulder and yanked her into a bear hug.

She laughed. When he released her, she slipped off her SEM lenses and concentrated on his hands as he said, "I've waited a damned long time to welcome you home, Altheas."

"Edie," she corrected. "I've buried a lot of past. It's the name least likely to get me shot on sight."

He chuckled.

She looked past him to the woman standing behind his left shoulder, arms crossed, a scowl on her lovely face. She'd thickened with the years. Her shoulders and hips had broadened, as if her body had decided she belonged to the rocks and soil of Nol Jakze rather than the air and clouds. In youth, she'd been slight. Her clan had liked to say you could see the wind blow through her. That was gone. Her eyes were still ethereal blue—one of the impossible shades Edie passed through on her way out of atmosphere.

"Gallena," Edie said. "Not happy I'm still alive?"

"No." She glowered.

Jonas grimaced.

"It was too much to hope you'd made your peace somewhere, and if you hadn't that you'd died the way everyone said you must have done," she said. "Cause the thing about you, little girl, is that you expect everyone to give their lives for your causes."

Causes? Edie shifted her shoulders to unseat the word. "I only ever had one."

"Yet, here you are," she accused. "Activating a cell like we don't have families. And farms. At least, we did. Until you."

"You didn't have to come," Edie said.

"You didn't have to start killing civilians after the war."

Chapter Twenty-Two

"What?" Edie gaped at the villagers. She slid a glance at V'kyrri, lounging with his feet on the cargo crates beside her.

He nodded.

"I did not." Indignation boiled up from her gut. She kicked his boots off the crate and demanded, "You knew and didn't mention it?"

Rocking forward, holding her gaze, he rose. "I knew."

"I. Never," she bit out aloud and in sign at the same time, glaring at each villager in turn. "I wouldn't when you wanted me to. What makes you think—"

"If it wasn't you," Jonas said, "then someone went to a lot of trouble to make it look like you."

Edie's brow crinkled. "When?"

"Four days after the surrender."

"Wasn't me." Edie dug in a pocket. Skeppanda silk spilled over her splayed fingers.

Villagers leaned in.

"You were on Skeppanda," Jonas said.

"Wasn't staying to watch cowards capitulate," she confirmed aloud, trusting he could still read her. She shoved the silk away so she could use her hands to finish saying, "Had a few too many people trying to kill me."

"That's right," Gallena said. "You ran instead of

rescuing that worthless boyfriend of yours."

Edie flinched. She ought to ask where they'd buried him after she'd left him for dead.

"Not that I blame you for dodging that set up," Gallena said, rolling her eyes. "Problem is there were too many bombs, Al—Edie. Exact match to your work."

Edie jerked at that blow. "Impossible. No one had my formulations. No one."

V'kyrri stirred. All eyes, including hers, turned to him. "We don't have time for this."

He met her eye, his own intent. "You refused to harm civilians during the war, at tactical cost to the resistance. There's no reason to expect you'd suddenly recalibrate your moral compass post-treaty."

Edie's shoulders lowered. At least someone believed her.

V'kyrri swept the villagers with a glance. "We can't resolve this until after we've survived the Chekydran."

"If we can survive them," Gallena said. She flickered a finger at Edie. "And her."

"You can either work with me or you can't," Edie said. "No one's holding a gun to your head."

The woman waved away the dig. "You do realize that the rest of us lost people we loved, too, right? Not just tonight. But all those years ago about the same time you did? Had the same survivor's guilt. The difference is we grew up. We built lives and new families. You didn't just live in the past, Altheas. You were consumed by it.

"You were so wrapped up in *you* that you couldn't notice that everyone else around you was bleeding, too.

If none of us were quick enough to feel sorry for you, you've always been more than willing to do it for us."

Edie sucked in a slow breath. Had she? Had she so fixated on her story that she'd ignored anyone else's? She'd spent a lot of time lately having her nose rubbed in her past. Maybe, considering she'd made revenge her motive for all that time, it was her own damned fault. Maybe living in the past was the price tag of revenge.

Thanks to a wounded Claugh captain, it occurred to her that she didn't have to go on paying it. She pressed the heel of one hand against her achy sternum.

"Okay. I've been self-absorbed for a long time. I'm trying to learn—be better," she signed. "I'm sorry, if it makes any difference. I'm—We're here because the Chekydran are here. They mean to wipe us out."

"Us, who?" Gallena challenged.

"Anyone on world," V'kyrri said. "We expect conventional attack once the plague hits."

"You're proposing a humanitarian mission?" Jonas asked, his brows twisted together.

"Do you know me?" Edie retorted. "A single Chekydran mothership put down on world."

Gallena nodded. "Northern hemisphere. Near Antasin Village."

"They've got a weapon," Edie said.

Jonas straightened, his brows lowering. "What weapon?"

She glanced at V'kyrri. This was Claugh intel as much as hers. That intel shot his starship out from under him.

"Crystal," V'kyrri signed for them. "I'm guessing it's a massive power focus."

A ripple went through Edie's former companions.

"You taught this unbeliever our language?" Jonas demanded.

"He taught himself," she replied. "Which, as I recall, has never been an issue before. Is it a new, xenophobic rule added to the litany since I left?"

"Stop," Gallena demanded. "You don't actually know what this weapon is?"

"No," V'kyrri said. "I haven't had the time or bandwidth to reverse engineer the ship Edie stole for me. Weapons enhanced with those crystals shot down my starship. We've been a little busy surviving, since."

"And shadowing Chekydran into supralight," Edie volunteered.

Jonas started laughing, amusement that bowed his head and shook his shoulders.

"I have enough satellites pointed at them to tell you what they ate for breakfast," V'kyrri said. "But not what they're building."

Povora, another of Edie's old resistance team, grinned and slapped Jonas on the back. Pale scars crisscrossed the deep brown skin of her face and scalp. Claugh torture lasers had traced the labyrinth pattern into the tight glossy curls she kept cropped short enough that no one could miss what had been done to her.

Maybe Edie wasn't the only one who'd clung to the past longer than she should. Not that she'd ever say so. She'd sat with Povora after they'd recovered her in a brutal, bloody raid. They'd left nothing alive in their wake. She'd laid rags soaked in pain killers across Povora's face and head. When someone had relieved her, Edie'd run away to be sick in private.

Povora got to handle her memories her way.

"Are you happy, Gallena?" Povora asked. "You got to vent the poison you clung to for a decade. Can you close the wound now and decide whether you're going to rise to the defense of Nol Jakze again?"

Gallena flushed. Her lips pressed thin.

"We're taking out that weapon," V'kyrri said.

Jonas, Povora, Gallena and the rest of the villagers straightened, their shoulders tightening, their expressions going blank.

It brought a bitter smile to Edie's face. They'd faced V'kyrri in the fields, a Claugh captain in a blood-soaked uniform they hadn't registered. Now that V'kyrri had washed and changed clothes, they'd finally worked it out, even without his insignia on his collar.

"Captain V'kyrri of Her Majesty's Starship *Queen's Rhapsody*," Edie said, gesturing between them all. "Captain. Jonas. Gallena. Povora. Among the rest, you see before you the great bulk of the empire's twenty most wanted list."

"I'd appreciate living to suggest to Her Majesty that the list needs to be retired," he said into the frozen stillness that followed her sardonic introduction. "We have three concerns. First, the plague. People will begin falling ill within the week. Second, the Chekydran are on world deploying crystal. Whatever they're building, to whatever purpose, we can be sure it won't be to our benefit. Third, Nol Jakze is quarantined. We've put out a call for help. Until Claugh ships arrive, we'll have to make do with what's available on world.

"The Chekydran that attacked your village had ships," V'kyrri said.

"Had," Povora replied. "They sent another flight and blew them up before we could recover them."

V'kyrri groaned. "Spawn of a Myallki bitch. Tell me you didn't lose anyone."

Edie warmed.

Povora arched an eyebrow. "Not for want of trying."

"You've been chasing those bugs?" Gallena demanded. She stabbed a finger at Edie. "You brought them. Our lives, our village, our dead—all your fault."

"This is bigger than you or me, Gallena," Edie said. "The Chekydran are on the ground. Planetary alerts never fired because they were offline. The first villages the bugs hit are old resistance strongholds. If my suspicions are correct, they'd have come for you anyway."

Stone-faced, Gallena arced her hand through the air, from collarbone to hip, swearing.

"The captain wants the weapon destroyed. I want that mothership and most of the bugs into the bargain. I'm going to need some things that aren't in this cache," Edie said.

"You're going to the farm?" Jonas's brow lowered. He curled his hands into fists and wouldn't meet her eye.

"Is that a problem?" Edie arched a brow.

No one answered. Gallena sorted through her pack with sharp, jerky moves. Povora sat with her chin propped in one hand, a faraway look in her eyes.

Edie glanced at V'kyrri.

He frowned and shoved gear into her pack.

Great. She'd been such a pain in the ass no one wanted to tell her that they didn't want to deal with her angst over treading the ground of her long-lost home. Fine.

Edie strode for the exit. At the door, she drew up short.

A teenager stood to one side wearing the coat Edie had worn during the resistance. Some people kept count of their kills with notches on their guns. Edie'd known one young man who'd cut himself, etching his sins into his skin. Edie had opted for a jacket patched together with uniform fragments from every job she'd done where Claugh had died.

In a fit of ego, she'd put the jacket in the cache. Because of course, the thirty-something-year-old woman she'd become would always fit the nineteen-year-old's jacket.

Yet here was the coat, worn by a young woman no more than fifteen.

"I'm Bennura," the girl said.

"Nia's daughter?" Edie guessed. "Your eyes are the same. Where is she?"

The girl's expression crumpled, then hardened into a brave mask. Edie's hope fell. Gods. Had she ever been this young and transparent?

"She died. The chemical burns. My tenth year."

"I'm sorry."

Bennura shrugged. The gesture of a teenager who'd grown accustomed to her mother's absence but who hadn't figured out how to handle the pain.

"Where'd you find this?" Edie asked, plucking the jacket fabric.

"Ma told stories. About you. You lost your parents. You know. In the war. When she died, I needed—" She didn't quite look Edie in the face. "Sorry. It's yours." She made to shrug out of it.

Edie put up a hand. "Keep it."

Had she just given up a hard-won piece of her past? Someone ought to be proud. She wasn't sure who.

Bennura's shoulders settled lower. A tiny smile lit her face. "I saw the call. I came because Nia couldn't. She'd want—"

"You to be safe and well and happy. Not out here with a bunch of idiots about to go up against Chekydran." Edie's nerves sparked. Her insides warmed.

V'kyrri set his fingers to the back of Edie's wrist.

She frowned. Where the Three Hells had he learned that? She couldn't imagine he'd pulled how to be polite on Nol Jakze from her head along with language lessons. Though why not? He'd gotten everything else about her.

"We need your help," V'kyrri said to Bennura.

"You're going to give me some meaningless, keep-her-safe, make-her-feel-important job, aren't you?" Bennura said.

"I wish I could," he replied. "We don't have the personnel for it. We need someone to babysit *t'Achreides-myn* and patch through communications and coordinate data."

Holy hells. Such a good idea. Edie's morale perked up. Not only had they reprogrammed a beacon, they'd made her ship a distress call. It was still broadcasting V'kyrri's signal. The Claugh would come knocking eventually.

The teen blinked.

"Claugh ships will begin arriving," he said. "I need someone we can trust making initial contact and routing them to me. Normal communications protocols are going to break down as the plague takes hold."

"I don't know anything about ships," Bennura signed.

"I can fix it," V'kyrri assured her. "With your permission."

Her eyes wide, she glanced between Edie and V'kyrri, indecision in her parted lips and in her short, gusty breaths.

"Tell your family what you're doing," Edie said, "where you'll be. But once you enter the boat, you can't leave, and no one can come in. Your greatest safety will be in no one knowing where *t'Achreides-myn* is hidden. People coming and going will—"

"Lead the enemy straight to me," she finished in a slack-fingered series of signs.

Jonas stepped past Edie and clapped the girl's shoulder. "You answered a call never meant for you, Bennura. You've made your mother proud. This is a volunteer fighting force. The choice is yours."

"Yes." The girl jerked her head in assent. "I will help. I will fight."

"*Not if I can help it*," V'kyrri said into Edie's brain in echo of the vow she'd made to herself. They traded a look, passing the promise between them.

It caught in the ragged edges of her heart because, for a split second, his promise encompassed her, too. Wishful thinking.

Edie returned her gaze to the teenager watching, gauging. She met Edie's eye and offered a tiny crook of a knowing smile.

Great.

With Bennura's okay, V'kyrri transferred a how-to for *t'Achreides-myn*'s com systems straight into her head.

Edie gave Jonas and Gallena coordinates.

"Three hours," Jonas said. "We can take my freight sled until we hit the tree line."

"If anyone is looking, they'll see us checking fields," Gallena agreed.

Edie handed Bennura the gun she'd loaned to Chavolgen. So recently. So very long ago.

Jonas, Gallena, and Bennura marched into the night forest.

Povora clapped Edie's shoulder. "Get some rest, Firestorm. Let us rummage through these supplies. I, for one, never thought I'd be doomed to eat hundred-year-old war rations again."

V'kyrri laughed.

Edie put on the SEM, grabbed a pack of sensors, and synced her handheld to them.

V'kyrri slung a lightweight bag of bedding over one shoulder.

They left the cave and descended through the brambles. It was probably silly. The cave was well hidden and fine shelter, but Edie'd had enough of being enclosed. Since he made no protest, she assumed V'kyrri had, too.

They set up camp beneath the leafy umbrella of an ancient cotweth tree. The arch of branches would shelter them from all but the most violent of spring storms.

Edie set up perimeter alarms in the knee-high grasses, sedges, and rushes. In a pinch, she could dig edible roots. In the fall, the plants would be hip-high, and they'd provide a meal from their tough grains. For now, she'd hide her sensors among the blades.

When she slipped into the shelter of the tree

branches, arms went around her waist, pulling her against V'kyrri's warm chest. A charge went up her spine, exploding in a shower of sparks. She gasped at the chemical fire tracing her nerves. Her body arched in greeting. She'd known him for a few days. This neediness was not okay.

He pressed his lips to her neck, smiling against her skin when the caress took her breath. He knew who and what she was, yet he hadn't shot her. Or left her to die. He'd known and it hadn't mattered.

"*It did. You matter more.*"

Her breath caught. She stared at the hope that had fluttered up out of the forest of her thoughts like a vittero startled out of picking bugs from tree bark. Chest aching, she sucked in a slip of air, as if by holding perfectly still she could avoid being seen and attacked by it. Except. Why did it already feel like a whole nest of the winged furry bastards were chewing on her guts with their blunt, poisoned teeth?

"*I'm sorry. We should have talked about this.*"

She huffed a laugh. " 'This' being what exactly? And when? While we were running for our lives? Or after I drugged you?"

His laughter enfolded her, blossoming inside her head as well as communicating from his body to hers via contact.

She closed her eyes and savored the sensation of his amusement resonating within her. She'd found him overwhelming when he'd had her throat in his hands—now that he'd been at least partially healed mentally and physically, the man was an impending supernova. He didn't just speak inside her head, his presence enveloped her, permeating her boundaries. Leashed power seethed. It wasn't just his power. He *was* the power. As if they'd somehow overcome the laws of physics, and he and she occupied the same space at the same time.

Edie choked on the mental image while his lips traced the line of muscle up the side of her neck to her ear.

She couldn't breathe. "Are you finally getting your revenge over the tranq?"

"*Consider this several ghur, one stun charge.*"

Picturing herself as one of the delicate herbivores from the marshy grasslands of Gharvan III, she smiled. Warmth and pain blossomed in her chest. Not a day or two ago, his revenge jest would have sent her scrambling for cover like a ghur who'd spotted an Azym. What was happening to her? Her knees tried to buckle as her brain replayed the conversation detailing his notion of revenge.

Within the confines of her head, he paused and highlighted a piece of her memory. He repeated the words for her, "*I'll ease in. You'll never know I'm there. And when you look around for something to stem the bleeding, I'll be there. I'll be so good at it, you'll want me there before you know you want me that deep in your inner workings.*"

"Check the revenge thing," she breathed. The burn at her core heightened. "You don't get to go rummaging around in my head."

"*No rummaging,*" he countered, turning her in his arms.

By the faint glow of her SEM, she registered the self-satisfied smile on his face.

"*We covered that,*" he said.

Right. Easing. Stroking. Stroking had been mentioned, hadn't it? Her body buzzed with interest and biting hunger.

His smile fell. Gently, he took the SEM glasses from her face.

She blinked and realized she could still see.

Light glittered above them, hanging on pale strands from the canopy of branches overhead.

V'kyrri followed her gaze. "*Beautiful. What is it*?"

"Flashing Gharrus," she said. "At least that what they're called in Tagrethian."

"*What do you call them*?"

"*t'Achreides-myn*."

He started as if it hadn't occurred to him that the name of her ship might mean anything beyond the words themselves. "*What does it mean? What are those things*?"

She grinned. They were little flying reptiles with needles for teeth and a keen appetite for bugs. They painstakingly lowered a long tendril of sticky saliva that bio-luminesced upon contact with the air. One ancient avopon tree right outside her bedroom window had lit up with murderous blue and green fairy light hanging from the branches by the hundreds every spring and summer. She'd spent long summer evenings watching them angling for fluttering insects.

He seemed to pick it all right out of her memory, too.

"*Hunger Flash*? *Or Death Flash?*"

"Interchangeable names. Watch," she instructed. It didn't take long. An insect fluttered into one of the viscous fairy-lit tendrils. The blue-green string flashed bright, stunning the insect, then the light winked out entirely. "The lizard will reel up supper."

"*Because its light is out, competitors can't steal the meal. Very romantic.*"

Chapter Twenty-Three

Edie and V'kyrri had bruised the thick, springy anethum moss. It smelled like the tiny, exotically sweet berries it produced in the fall. Sap, sharp and clean-scented, folded around them on the blanket of warm spring air.

Visible through a gap in the leaves, the first and largest moon hung near the tops of the trees, the crescent barely illuminated. The twins would follow, a pair of tidally locked bodies that couldn't properly be called moons, but her culture did anyway, and planned important events around the rare occasions all three were full and visible in the night sky at the same time.

She sighed. She hadn't let herself miss her world before, and now she stood to lose it to the Chekydran.

V'kyrri brushed her cheekbones with gentle fingertips. The touch resonated through her nerves, lighting up pathways in the darkest parts of her brain, in places the SEM never accessed. He closed the door between their minds. She gasped.

Desire twisted her the way she'd twist ignition wires.

He caught her lips with his.

Every ounce of Edie narrowed to that contact. To the subtle, sweet taste of him. Old scabs came off her wounded heart.

He deepened the kiss, lingering, taking his time,

testing her response, seeming to delight in every gasp and in the quiver running through her muscles.

Lost in the sea of him, she wrapped her arms around V'kyrri. The weight and heat in her lower belly built to an ache. As if she'd been engineered specifically for him, the stroke of his lips and brush of his tongue left her at the edge of her control.

Panting when he drew a breath away, she muttered a protest. He smoothed a palm up her ribs to cup her breast through her clothes.

She arched into the caress, her body starved for tender attention. To her mortification, her eyes prickled. She pushed against him, weak, muscles barely functioning through the haze of seduction.

His lips returned to hers. Moving. Whispering words she couldn't hope to comprehend. He kissed the single trail of moisture that spilled, still breathing words against her cheek as if he believed they could sink through her permeable skin.

Maybe they could. Her nerves settled as he gentled and soothed her. Something no one else had bothered to do after her parents had died.

His tenderness tore at her senses.

He seemed to register that and lingered, giving her the time and space to assimilate the turmoil of her emotions.

Except she couldn't. It was too big a task—the past a minefield of wounds each more mortal than the last. But maybe she could drown them briefly. In him.

Edie directed his mouth to hers and applied herself to learning every nuance of his response to her. How his breath stopped in his chest when she gently closed her teeth on his bottom lip. The way he groaned when she unbuttoned his shirt and worked her hands into contact with his skin. His chest expanded to meet her touch. He broke the kiss and encircled her wrist, stilling her hands. He breathed a laugh against her cheekbone and shook his head.

Impatience kicked her. She didn't deserve his tenderness or his care. The thought jolted her. She reflexively shoved it into shadows.

"We're wearing too many clothes," she rasped, tugging against his grasp.

He put a finger to her lips.

She looked at him.

A teasing, self-satisfied gleam lit his eyes. "So impatient."

Heat rushed to her face. She couldn't hear. How in the hell had he managed to caress those words down her spine with the shapes of the letters on his lips?

"Will you stay with me?" he asked.

"Do I get to strip you?"

He grinned, sending her senses spinning. "Eventually."

"I'm in."

"My line."

She sucked in a heated breath at the sly dig. "Hurry."

He crouched before her and undid her boots.

Edie stepped out of them.

V'kyrri set them aside and swept her into his arms. He carried her the last few steps to the bedding. He sat on the edge, shifting his grasp to cradle her against his chest.

Shaking, she hooked a hand around his neck, drawing his lips to hers.

His kiss consumed her, first stealing her breath. Then her thoughts. With the first brush of his tongue against hers, his kiss stole her will to do anything but dive into him.

He left her lips, kissing her eyes closed, brushing her temples. He buried his face in her hair and breathed deep.

She shivered with need.

He rolled her to her feet, facing him, holding tight when she swayed. His smile made promises that had her body clenching and damp.

She swallowed against the rising sense of not knowing herself and met his eye, not certain what was expected.

He opened her shirt, blocking her attempts to rip the garment off. Her wrists wrapped in his grip and held captive at her waist, she could only stand, locking unsteady knees while he set his lips against the thin line of exposed skin.

Heat piled higher. She could barely breathe. No matter how she protested or strained against him, V'kyrri would not be hurried. His notion of undressing her turned to torture. With every twitch, every gasp, every moan he wrested from her, he smiled against her skin, stealing every vestige of control until she was reduced to pleading even as her body bowed, eager for his hands splayed across her back, and the shock of his teeth on exquisitely sensitive nipples.

He tripped the release for her trousers. They slid from her hips. He removed her underwear.

She might have sobbed in relief. Her body hummed in anticipation.

V'kyrri held her at arms' length and looked. No.

Admired. His face flushed and his eyes stormy with desire. Pulling in an impossibly long breath, he rose.

She reached for him.

Again, he intercepted her, wrapping her hands in his. "Not yet. You destroy my control, and I'm not done with yours."

A disbelieving laugh scraped out of her. "Me begging isn't enough?"

"It's damned flattering." He turned them and backed her onto the bed. His lips in the center of her chest pressed her into the pillows. He came back to claim her lips.

"Invite me in," he murmured against her mouth. Needed no translation. How did he know? Whole new meaning to reading his lips. It took her breath. "Can't otherwise. Ethics."

"Yes. Please. I want you. Now."

As if drawn, he leaned in to press his lips against the center of her forehead.

Via that innocent kiss, V'kyrri slipped into her head, into her sense of self, caressing into her awareness, into what she'd once naively imagined were the private places guarded by the impermeable envelope of her flesh and bone. They'd been here before, when he'd substituted for her SEM. In no way had that felt like this.

She sucked in a ragged breath that did nothing to cool the desire coating every nerve and fiber of her. She'd gotten far more than she'd bargained for. This was entirely sexual. Entirely vulnerable. Him to her. Her to him. She had nowhere to hide. And more, she no longer wanted to. Not from him. Given his tender regard, maybe not even from herself. She wanted to be the woman he seemed to see.

She didn't know if she could be. She did want to try. For him. For herself.

His desire tangled with hers. His trembling breath matched hers. It should have hurt. Should have scared her senseless. Instead, heat and light expanded in her lower belly. Sizzling heat and desire ravaged her.

She moaned.

"It'll settle," he whispered.

She shook her head, pulled back. He opened his eyes, trepidation in his frown. Steeling himself for the pain of anticipated rejection.

She took his face in her hands and gave herself up to drowning in his eyes as if she, too, could enter his psyche the way he had hers.

"I invited you in," she rasped, speaking aloud even though she didn't need to, not when he was buried deep in who and what she was. How could they be together like this, so intimately, and still be separated physically? "You have ten seconds to accommodate me. You won't like my solution for getting you naked."

His flash of a grin knocked her pulse out of regular rhythm. "No rushing. I'm learning to savor the burn."

"You're burning me to the ground," she groaned and levered up to press her lips to the pulse point in his neck. Answering sensation lit her skin, a phantom of the two of them mentally and emotionally entangled.

His pulse tripped, hammering against her caress in answer. His chest expanded in the same instant she drew breath.

She couldn't tell where she ended and he began. Only that he'd taken such careful time setting her afire and prying her open, she badly wanted to do the same to him.

"*Next time*," he whispered into the places they collided. "*This is for you.*" He pulled off his shirt, then shed his pants.

She stared, stunned by the sheer beauty of him, her breath catching at his assurance that there would be a next time for them. The glimmering ghurra light rendered every line of muscle sharp enough to cut her fingers.

Pleasure not her own suffused her. He returned, stretching out against her.

She finally set trembling hands to his skin. He arched into the touch. She gasped at the ghost of it tracing her skin as if it were his. She closed her eyes, savoring shared sensation.

He kissed her, and her head swam.

She utterly lost her mooring. Was she kissing or being kissed? Her system quivered with confusion and delight at being immersed in two sets of experiences. They created a feedback loop, driving one another beyond control. Past reason.

When at last, he set a shield in place that cut him away from her, she gasped and froze. She opened her eyes. "Oh Gods. Please don't stop."

"For you," he said, and pressed into her in slow motion.

She wanted to scream but couldn't find the air.

He teased his way in.

She drew in a sob of relief when he seated himself and rested his weight against her. He claimed her mouth again not moving. He held her, pinned, every fiber of her being crying for release.

Had he not been kissing her, she'd have been

begging. Maybe she was. Mentally. Emotionally. On all the levels that counted.

She flexed her fingers in his backside, silently urging him to move.

His shield fractured. Sensation flooded her. The two of them. Together. Whose weight rested against whose, blurred. Who filled, and who was filled merged into one taut bundle of nerve-endings seeking completion. Wholeness.

They moved. Fire and water. He was a tidal force surging, drowning her in sensation, yet she burned, her body the fuse he'd lit. Each stroke, each shiver and every cry spiraled around them, through them, winding them tighter.

In the surge and roll of all-encompassing mental, emotional, and exquisite physical stimulation, passion ignited, caught and detonated. She went up in flames.

As if her release triggered his, V'kyrri arched and shuddered, groaning, before he draped himself across her sweat-dampened skin.

The thunder of their hearts knocked against her ribs, hers from inside her body, his from outside. They lay still entwined as the substance of who and what they were cooled, coalesced, and fell back to bodies on the bed.

He shifted, rising on one elbow, and kissed her.

She met him, every cell aware of every aspect of him, tuned to his need for the assurance that she wanted him still. That though she was newly his, she'd been made for him, and gifted to him.

Not rational. But then, neither was succumbing to him.

The joy trembling in him scraped her raw inside.

"*You're safe,*" he whispered into her head. "*You can be happy. It's okay.*"

"*It's…*" She forced herself to stare at the thought she'd spent the past fifteen years running from. "*It's just that being happy means everyone I love dies.*"

V'kyrri froze. Still. Silent. His wide eyes reflected gharru light.

Pain knifed her ribs, taking her breath.

His. He pressed a fist against his breastbone and bowed his head. He retreated mentally to the point that only an echo of his pain remained in her.

"*I'm sorry,*" he whispered inside her mind. "*That's…I…Let me hold you? For tonight.*"

Because neither of them could talk about living. Not while planning to whack a Chekydran nest.

Edie tried a sip of air. "I'd like that."

Yet, once Edie nestled against V'kyrri's side, her head on his shoulder, captive to the irregular beat of his pulse, and his arms closed around her, she couldn't sleep.

A sweet, intoxicating sense of safety enshrouded her, lulling her, tempting her to sink into V'kyrri and everything he offered.

Ridiculous. He was Claugh.

She was not.

They were together by necessity. Maybe she'd gotten a little emotional and nostalgic. It didn't change anything. It was just another night. Just biology.

Wasn't it?

Her heart's whispered *no* kept her awake for a very long time.

****

Edie made damned sure to wake at first light.

Before any of her former companions came looking for them.

As she dressed, V'kyrri woke, going from sleep to alert without a single stage in between.

"Got to take down the perimeter," she signed.

"And the bed," he asked in kind, scowling, "so no one knows you slept with the enemy?"

Edie stepped back from the stab of accusation. "I slept with you. Not the uniform."

He rolled to standing and yanked on clothes, brows lowered, and lips tight.

Temper flaring, Edie rounded the bed.

He straightened to face her, muscles in his glorious bare chest tightening, bracing for a fight.

If that's what he wanted… Edie tapped him between the eyes, then tapped her forehead. "Get in here and tell me what the hell is really going on."

V'kyrri opened into her awareness. For a split second, agony dug hot pokers into her skull. Nausea slugged Edie in the stomach.

Squinting, she gasped and swayed.

V'kyrri twitched. The tenor of his frown shifted. The corners of his eyes creased. Meeting her gaze, he blinked confusion.

Pain and queasiness drained away.

"What was that?" she asked aloud. "An attack?"

Lips outlined in white, he squared his shoulders. "*It was. And I have no idea why. I am sorry.*"

No question of that. Not with him speaking inside her head. He turned inward, not shutting her out while he absorbed recrimination, and ran a set of filters through the minutes they'd spent sniping at one another since he'd awakened.

"Want to talk about it?"

He flung his hands wide. "Love to, if I had any clue what had me so out of my head as to overcome decades of training and deep ethical conviction."

"Hey." Edie risked setting a palm to his cheek.

His breath caught, and he leaned into the touch before he'd focused on her. Weird. It was as if she'd awakened a stranger and had just now gotten V'kyrri back. "You could have mentioned you're not a morning person."

Laughing, he took her hand from his face and kissed her palm. The mental weight of him lightened. The creases in his forehead vanished.

"*I don't like not knowing what happened.*"

"Right there with you."

"*I'll break camp while you clear perimeter. Is breakfast a part of the plan? I'm going to need food before I finish plotting the demise of a Chekydran mothership.*"

Edie grinned, her own stomach grumbling.

He released her.

She put on the SEM and ran a quick scan of the grasslands. Bio-signs. None of them humanoid. Or Chekydran. Edie jogged a quick circuit, snatching up sensors as she went.

They trekked to the cave, led by the smell of breakfast cooking. Cargo containers had been lined up, their contents sorted and stacked in a supply line.

From it, Edie managed to half-fill her backpack. Mostly consumables. Food. Water. Simple explosives.

A boy with a black eye and a broken arm motioned them to the cooking fire.

The rest of the farmers-turned-reluctant-revolutionaries tramped into camp, stinking of wood smoke.

Povora sat opposite Edie and accepted a cup of flavorless tea.

Edie took off her SEM glasses and met the woman's eye. "You burned it?"

Povora set her tea down, and said, "If the bugs brought plague, we can no longer walk where they have."

"You'll send everyone into the mines?" Edie asked.

Povora lifted a shoulder and sipped tea. Her nose wrinkled.

"Translate?" V'kyrri murmured, joining them.

"They burned down the village," Edie replied in sign. Internally, she said, "*Cultural thing. It's unforgivably rude to deliberately take advantage of the fact that someone doesn't hear.*"

He glanced at the SEM glasses lying beside her. "*Thank you for telling me.*"

"The village was torched because of the plague?" he signed.

"Lore from planet fall," Edie said. "Our forebearers quickly found out which creatures on world carried disease. Until treatments for Sylga palm tragit, a disfiguring disease, were developed, people habitually burned anything the Sylga palm herdones touched."

He shook his head. "What the hell are herdones?"

"We'll have to find a tourist's guide for your Claugh friend," Povora said, her grin cutting.

"If any of us expect to survive," Edie countered in sharp, short gestures. V'kyrri gave her a headache digging into her skull to comprehend. "Captain V'kyrri is your new best friend."

The malice in Povora's grin deepened. "Sure seems to be yours. You've given up everything we are."

"What is that? Has-beens who've honed our skills and instincts birthing razor-tooth hoppers? Do you imagine I don't still hold a grudge about the war? And if I do, yet I've learned to trust V'kyrri…"

He clapped her shoulder, grinning. "Hey. You don't have to protect my honor."

Edie snort-laughed at her words said back to her.

"What Edie hasn't said is that I'm the second in command of the Murbaasch Tu, reporting to Her Majesty's Aurnach Riorchjan," V'kyrri said, rising to make his hands visible to everyone.

Edie did her damnedest to keep her features smooth. Placid. She hadn't told anyone because it was news to her that she'd slept with a spy.

Chapter Twenty-Four

He shoved a hand into a pocket, drew forth his insignia, and attached it to his collar. "Edie has my complete trust. I am honored to have hers. We're a matched set. You work with us, or you go back to your razor-tooth hoppers."

"There're bugs to stomp," Edie said, rising. "Anyone joining up, standard march rules. No groups. Spread out. Keep moving. Doubly important now because it turns out an old ally can track me. He's the only one, but he is a mercenary."

Povora bared her teeth. "You're only safe until someone finds his break point."

Edie nodded. Matter of time, wasn't it? Because just her luck. Mr. Second-in-Command-of-the-Mubaash-Tu had directed an SOS right at Trente's break point.

Eilod Saoyrse.

Edie shoved a packet of the flavorless tea into her pack, closed it, slung it to her back, and started down the opposite side of the hill, V'kyrri at her side.

"*How far?*"

"We'll be there by lunch time," she said aloud, shooting him a sidelong glance. "I have the SEM. You don't have to translate for me anymore."

He lifted an eyebrow. "*What's wrong? Afraid you'll become addicted?*"

"Afraid I already am."

Staggered, V'kyrri lost his grip on pain suppression. He got out of her head fast. Too fast.

She glanced at him, her expression filled with such uncertainty, misery sank dull teeth into his skull.

"Having issues broadcasting and not killing myself on the terrain at the same time," he joked. He stumbled on a loose rock obscured by the lush grasses reaching to his knees. As intended, her expression lightened.

Weight settled on his chest. He'd lied to her. First to protect his survivors and himself. Then, he'd imagined, he'd lied to protect her. But he hadn't, had he? He'd caught the set-in-Isarrite cast to her features when he'd mentioned the Aurnoch's name.

Maybe the deep, soul-shaking ache in his head and the nausea it inspired were his penance.

Neither would buy back the trust he'd violated by not telling her everything. He should get the rest out into the open, too. Face the consequences. He lived to protect the empire. He'd served at Her Majesty's pleasure for half his life. He'd faced Chekydran, UMOPG, and Tagreth Federated forces without flinching.

Yet he couldn't come up with the courage to tell Edie that the telepathic injury he'd taken during the wreck of the *Rhapsody* was killing him.

Not after her trembling admission—in his arms—that being happy meant everyone she loved died. He closed his eyes, absorbing the knife to his gut.

Did she realize she'd introduced love into the equation? His eyelids scraped his dry eyes when he opened them.

She led him out of the foothills into forest, sliding

between tree trunks, twisting through the underbrush with practiced ease. Based on the buzz of laser focus and memory blocking casual access to her head, V'kyrri suspected she moved on muscle memory alone.

She pressed through the final layer of trees and stopped dead.

V'kyrri swiped a sleeve across his forehead and measured his breaths to slow the uneven thunder of blood in his ears. He kept his gaze on her face, uncertain how she'd take the changes that time and the Claugh had wrought on her family's home.

Edie's eyes widened. Her jaw dropped. Her family home had been turned into a park—a monument to the resistance. She stared at the reconstruction of her parents' house, eyes reddening. Shaking her head, she lifted her hands in question.

He captured one of her hands. "*Her Majesty*," he said in answer to her unasked question. "*Shortly after she came to the throne.*"

Edie swayed. Her memory whirled up and broke against the reality of her rebuilt home. V'kyrri stayed inside her head, absorbed by her sensation that she'd somehow stepped back in time. The pain of swallowed words clogged her throat, creating ghost pain in his.

Eilod had gone to great lengths to reproduce Edie's childhood home perfectly. Too perfectly. Edie flashed on herself as a child. The back corner of the house where her bedroom had been had sagged long before she'd been born. Rainy seasons sent water cascading in sheets from the low corner. The vibration of water hitting the roof, and then running in a torrent to drum the stone her father had placed beneath, had thrummed through her child's body, lulling her to sleep.

Longing for what he hadn't experienced opened an ache in V'kyrri's chest.

Edie put a lid on a surge of tangled emotion before he could dip in to examine it. She started up a deliberate inventory of the ways the reconstruction failed to match memory.

The hole in the foundation where generations of garden snakes had sheltered hadn't been reproduced.

Statues lined the front yard.

"Why?" She signed the question as if she couldn't trust her voice.

"*Her Majesty believes that every culture needs heroes—something to aspire to. Something to be proud of.*"

Jonas stepped out of the trees, then Gallena and Povora. The rest of the villagers who'd come to fight trickled into the open as well.

Her trepidation shook V'kyrri as she crept into the midst of the statues, studying them. Names flared up from her memory and were suppressed in such rapid succession, he doubted she realized how much sorrow she repressed.

"Using us," she blurted aloud. "You co-opted the resistance. The empire is using us. Again?"

"You were missing," he said, fighting the sense that the ground had gone dangerously soft beneath his boots. "Presumed dead. It is only the lost—"

Rage bubbled from her gut into her chest, silencing him. She stared hard at the center of the installation. Faced away from her parents' house, outside the gate to her father's workshop, another monument caught her eye.

V'kyrri released her hand when she pulled, but he

kept his line into her head open. He studied the statue through her eyes.

It had been captured in midstride, face lifted, shoulders back, hands cupped together at her belt. A single, star-shaped explosive rested in those hands.

Edie's frown pulled at the corners of his mouth. That was one of her father's explosives. One of his specialty fireworks. She glanced into the face. A young woman's features, brows lowered, lips set in a stern line, eyes resolute and cold, hard brown Isarrite.

Recognition rocked Edie. V'kyrri leaped to catch her.

It was her.

She shook her head. "Why? Why like this? In front? Like I was leading someone? Anyone?"

V'kyrri didn't answer.

Edie tipped her glance to the tag.

"*In memory of Firestorm who led the resistance by courageous, daring example. Born Altheas Drake in this modest homestead on 3 Hagtlim NJC 417.*" The words echoed inside his skull as she read them. "*Led the resistance.*" Edie snorted. Her bitterness cut.

V'kyrri had to lock his muscles to keep from ducking.

"I didn't lead anything," she muttered. "I did what I wanted. Everyone else whined about insubordination."

"*Then, in your absence, someone got sentimental and built a memorial.*"

"To a Claugh-killer," she snapped. "So the Claugh could manipulate my people while also plastering my face on Claugh wanted notices."

He had no response for that.

Chewing sharp, sour shards of ire that made his

stomach cramp, Edie turned for the replica of her father's shop. They'd gotten that building wrong, too. According to her memory, it shouldn't have been big enough to house the dozen soldiers pouring out the door, weapons drawn and aimed at her.

She swept the park with an assessing glance. Another half dozen soldiers spilled from the house, lining the porch, covering her and the villagers. Edie's sneer caught on V'kyrri's lips, too.

A man in a black suit led a pair of soldiers down the porch stairs, his arms outspread as he spoke aloud. "Home at last."

Shock rolled from Edie to V'kyrri. Tearing pain in her chest clawed through his, taking his breath. He wheezed.

Edie stared. The blood drained from her face.

The cadre of soldiers herded the former resistance fighters in behind Edie and V'kyrri.

Creating one target.

V'kyrri shot a glance at Jonas who met his eye with lowered brows, lips pressed tight, and his hands balled into fists.

Edie sucked in a breath that hissed between her teeth. "You look good for a dead man, Tiimetes."

The bitterness in her spoken comment yanked V'kyrri's attention to the man. He dared a tendril of inquiry. She'd been angry, hurt, and confused by finding out the Claugh Empire had been using her the past decade.

Now, here they were, nascent relationship challenged, and facing someone else from her past. He had dark hair, dark eyes, and a trim but not-quite-cut physique. He wore an expensive black suit and blinding white shirt. The insignia of the planetary governor adorned his breast pocket.

Tiimetes Calamae. Planetary Governor of Nol Jakze.

V'kyrri scowled. He wanted—no—*needed* to know who the man had been to her before he could assess his chances of repairing the damage he'd done by not telling her everything. Hells. All the words they'd said, and in retrospect, he'd told her nothing.

The man smirked.

Edie's hands clenched.

Misgiving fired through V'kyrri. Ice pierced his innards as the information he'd sought slapped him in the face. *Former lover. Her first.*

V'kyrri slammed the door on his impulse to dig for details, or for any reason to murder the man for the outrage ripping through Edie. He had no right to the details of her past. And, idiot that he was, he preferred she offer them.

"You shouldn't have come," Tiimetes said.

V'kyrri lifted an eyebrow. The man did not sign. One of the soldiers, a young lieutenant wearing a slim-line SEM, did the translating.

"You don't belong," Tiimetes said, striding past her statue to face her. "You ran out on me. On all of us. Now you come crawling back wanting to play hero? We can no longer afford you. You'll spread panic and kill civilians. You've done enough damage already. You're all under arrest."

"You tried that once already," she retorted, speaking and signing at the same time. "When luring me to my death didn't work, I'm guessing you cut a deal. The plenkinors are already in the field."

V'kyrri got a confused image of native golden-coated herbivores stripping crops from the soil. He shook his head at the "too late" metaphor.

"I want to know why the planetary governor's code shut down the security and navigation beacons sixteen hours before the Chekydran entered system, Tii." Edie's forced-cheerful statement yanked Jonas, Gallena, Povora, and Tiimetes's translator to attention.

Tiimetes brushed an imaginary speck from his jacket. "I don't answer to you."

Rage boiled over inside Edie. Answering adrenaline accelerated V'kyrri's pulse. Edie rushed the man. Forearm at his throat, she drove him against the base of her monument.

He hit and choked.

"What's the matter, Tii?" she demanded. "You used to like a little rough housing before kissing and making up. Or was that only when you were dishing it out?"

V'kyrri swallowed another urge to murder the man. Instead, he chuckled and sauntered to Edie's side, getting between her and the governor's wide-eyed soldiers.

"If you haven't re-evaluated your stance about answering to Edie, I'll point out that you do answer to me," V'kyrri said, tapping his insignia with relish. "Governor."

Jonas shoved his way forward to stand at Tiimetes's shoulder, his back to the statue. He gazed between them; Edie, Tiimetes, and V'kyrri, and translated.

V'kyrri nodded his thanks.

Telepathy could teach him Edie's native language.

It couldn't give him the ability to speak that language at the same time he spoke aloud the way Edie did.

Except now that she had an ex-lover by the throat, she didn't seem invested in making herself understood by anyone else.

Pique? Or registering legitimate threat? He skimmed the sinister pop and crackle of her surface emotions. His fingers curled on the butt of his pistol. Question answered.

"Have you met Captain V'kyrri, Tii? Officer in her Majesty's service. Second in command of the Murbaasch Tu?" The pride and possessiveness in her voice warmed V'kyrri, especially since he'd sprung the Murbaasch Tu part on her.

"Claugh?" Tiimetes sneered. "You, of all people, colluding, Firestorm?"

"Nice shot. Way too late. He knows who I am. Let's get back to the fact that I accused you of collusion, Mr. My-Code-Let-the-Chekydran-in-to-Commit-Genocide."

"You abandoned Nol Jakze, and everyone on it." He craned his neck to look his lieutenant in the eye. "What is wrong with you? Shoot her."

Edie leaned into her forearm.

Still, Tiimetes choked out, "She killed thousands of innocents."

"I am getting damned tired of hearing that lie," she said. "I wouldn't kill civilians during the war. Which, as I recall, was the single biggest reason you and I argued. What makes you think I'd do a 180 on that? I didn't. Not ever. I can prove it."

Silence. Complete stillness once Jonas's gestures stopped.

V'kyrri cast a glance around.

Baby-faced soldiers exchanged glances.

"Lieutenant?" one of the soldiers questioned.

"Firestorm saved my parents' lives when she liberated Tomiltnor prison. I owe you my life, ma'am." The woman holstered her weapon.

V'kyrri made certain the translation made it into Edie's head. He doubted she could see either the lieutenant's or Jonas's hands. She deserved to know she'd left a positive legacy.

"Tomiltnor. That's in Darmka Saal. You're from Darmka Saal?" Edie's face darkened. Her voice rose in pitch and volume. "You came from the capital."

An Isarrite band clamped V'kyrri's chest. The soldiers glanced at one another as if mystified by the statement.

They'd broken quarantine.

Snarling, she yanked Tiimetes away from the stone, then slammed him into it again.

He winced, eyes squinted, and his face flushing deep red.

"You broke quarantine," she snapped. "Deliberately. You infected us and everyone else in this region. Why? Because it wasn't enough you lied to me about being up against a death sentence ten years ago, you selfish child?"

"You hero types. Righting all the wrongs of the universe. You're easy to lie to," Tiimetes whispered.

'Righting all the wrongs…' the turn of phrase struck V'kyrri. Where had he heard it before?

"Edieeeee," a sing-song voice, riding the breeze at their backs, lased through speculation.

V'kyrri frowned. The call was faint, and he

suspected she hadn't registered it until she sagged.

"Tiimetes had to know what he'd be up against if you ever returned to stir the slug wasp nest, Altheas," Jonas said as if he hadn't heard—V'kyrri mentally kicked himself. Jonas hadn't heard. The man was deaf. Just like Edie.

Jonas spoke in a smooth baritone that wavered as if uncertain of where it wanted to land. "He couldn't murder us over the years, though the Gods know he's tried."

Tiimetes wheezed a laugh. "You can't prove a thing, old man."

"Why not use a Chekydran plague to attack the remnants of the resistance he once loved?" Jonas said.

"Because he's a coward," Povora snapped. "Someone gave or promised him medicine."

Tiimetes's expression twisted. He began shouting, "Shoot her. Shoot her. I'm ordering you."

V'kyrri noted that the lieutenant, the only one wearing a SEM, didn't bother translating.

"Don't kill him yet, Edie," V'k said. "I'd like to extract a little extra intel."

Edie slanted a blood-thirsty grin his way. His body clenched tight and hot, an unauthorized grin stretching his lips in answer to hers.

"Edieeeeee." That high pitched singsong again. Closer. Much closer. On the dirt path that connected the nearest village to the park

V'k's smile died.

Edie lowered her chin to her chest, shoulders sagging. "Godsdammit, Immin. You have the worst timing."

The assassin strode into view on the road. The wiry

mercenary had lavender and pink striped hair, preternaturally long arms, and over-sized hands, both bristling with conspicuous weaponry.

"Did you not get the quarantined world memo?" Edie demanded.

She yanked Tiimetes's gun free, glanced over her shoulder, and lobbed a trio of shots at the assassin. His eyes went wide. Her former coworker took the bolts in the chest. He flew backward half a meter, raising a pall of dust.

The assassin twitched, then sank into slack stillness.

"I don't know what I expected from a guild assassin, but that was not it," V'kyrri said.

Utter and complete stillness from the soldiers and villagers.

The governor surged against Edie's grasp. She slammed him into the stone and poked his gun in his face. "We aren't done."

"You were supposed to come for me," Tiimetes snapped. "You were supposed to love me."

"I did," she said, her tone dull. Weary. "As much as I was capable of loving anyone or anything."

V'kyrri rocked.

Edie tucked the gun into her belt, jerked Tiimetes away from the statue, one arm twisted behind his back, and dug her fingers into his throat in mimic of the hold V'kyrri had used on her.

"You killed that man," one of the soldiers signed.

V'kyrri rubbed a hand down his face.

Jonas settled into shoulder-shaking laughter.

Impending danger tickled V'kyrri's nerves. He straightened, eying the soldiers busy talking amongst themselves. *Murder. Cold-blood.*

"You're soldiers," V'kyrri barked out. The lieutenant translated. "Act like it. Keep your opinions to yourselves until you've investigated."

The lieutenant added a series of sign beyond relaying what V'k had said. Four of her soldiers saluted and jogged to the corpse.

Two bent down. Almost immediately, they straightened and backed away. They raised their hands overhead to spell something out.

"Guild Assassin," Jonas said aloud.

"He had a ship, Tii. How'd a Guild assassin get close to a VIP like you? Did you shut down surface security, too? You didn't want anyone fighting back when the Chekydran started killing people?"

The governor's face turned purple.

V'kyrri pressed his lips tight and allowed himself an admiring smile. A park full of soldiers and weapons, and she'd isolated and immobilized the highest value target without a shot fired, and without a single weapon in her hands.

He had to convince her to switch sides. "Edie…"

Teleport distortion snatched him out of the park. He shouted a curse and materialized into damp twilight. Rainwater wet his face. He blinked confusion and drizzle from his eyelashes.

He spun, head pounding. "Edie?"

Chapter Twenty-Five

She was there, to one side, Tiimetes's throat still in her grasp, her eyes narrow and assessing behind her SEM lenses.

The teleport had grabbed Jonas, too. He sank to his knees, shaking his head.

The governor sagged.

Edie released him and bolted to V'kyrri's side.

His heart swelled.

She'd chosen her alliance.

"Where the Three Hells are we?" He registered the force field fencing them and at least forty other people into a holding pen. Pressure on his ears warned him—another incoming teleport.

The lieutenant and four of Edie's former companions materialized.

"Darmka Saal. Capital," Edie said.

"Captain V'kyrri," a male voice distorted by broadcast said. The words appeared projected on the smooth fence walls as well. "Report to the gate in the southeast wall."

Tagrethian. He scowled. Teleport had him hoping to hear the friendly lilt of Claughwyth. Preferably spoken by a friend. Or friends. He sucked in a breath. Southeast? How the Hells was he supposed to direction find with the sky obscured by a wall of clouds the color of a heat-cured bulkhead?

"There," Edie said. She lifted her chin to indicate a section of force field.

He claimed her hand.

She holstered Tiimetes's gun. They threaded through people hunched, avoiding their gazes.

"*ID on the voice*?" he asked.

A bare shake of her head.

A section of force field wavered and fell. A trio of soldiers in Nol Jakze crimson and gray covered them with shock rifles. A young man wearing double gray slashes above the breast pocket of his uniform jacket stepped into the doorway, no gun in his hands.

"Captain," he both said and signed.

Tiimetes plowed past V'kyrri. "Good work, Corporal. Altheas Drake and her companions are to remain under arrest…"

"Step away from the gate, Governor," the soldier said. "For your safety."

Drawing himself upright, the governor said, "Nonsense. There's work to be done. Stand aside. That's an order, corporal."

"I'm sorry, sir. That's not possible."

"Son, I am the ranking official on this world. You will…"

"No, sir. You aren't. You've been remanded to detention for breaking quarantine, sir. Step away from the gate."

"This is ridiculous," Tiimetes snapped. He made to stride past the corporal.

One of the soldiers fired her weapon.

Hair all over V'kyrri's body stood on end.

Tiimetes yelped and fell back.

Edie sidestepped.

Clutching his right shoulder, the governor stumbled into the detainees.

"I'll have your stripes," Tiimetes growled.

"Captain," the corporal said. "I have orders to escort you to decon, sir."

"Edie's with me," he said.

The corporal held out a hand. "Ma'am. Your weapon."

Behind the soldiers, the squat, ungainly bulk of a ship sat. Adrenaline lit V'kyrri's uneven heartrate.

"*Sen Ekir*," he breathed as Edie passed over Tiimetes's pistol. "That's the *Sen Ekir*."

Edie's head jerked up. Her eyes widened. She'd worked for Intcom. Of course she knew the ship.

The corporal led them through a maze of fences, gates, and checkpoints before gesturing to a decontamination unit. "You may entrust your gear to me. It will be waiting on the other side."

Edie hesitated.

Terror not his own stumbled through V'kyrri, placing him inside Edie's memory of another long-ago holding pen. Force fields. Skeletal, weeping children. Limp, despondent women too weak to wave the insects from their infants' eyes. Corpses. Filth. Blood.

He couldn't breathe.

Hands shaking, Edie divested herself of packs, tool belts, and weapons. She took off her SEM lenses and blinked reddening eyes. When she thinned her lips and stared at the decon door, he backed out of her memory. He bent double, gasping.

He screwed his eyes shut. It couldn't erase the internal picture. During the war, it hadn't been decontamination. It had been a chemical chamber.

"Captain?" the corporal said. "Sir? Do you require assistance?"

V'k opened his eyes. He waved the young man away. Blowing out a breath that did nothing to settle the horror, he forced himself upright, took Edie's arm, and pushed around her. The least he could do would be to go first.

"Sorry," her trembling fingers said.

She'd guessed or known what he'd seen. He took her hands, gathered his courage, established a link, and doing his best to keep nausea at bay while he stood amid her ghosts said, "*You aren't the one who should be sorry. Not ever. Not for anything you did for your people. Never again.*"

She twitched, shoulders stiffening. Brows lowering, she looked away, her entire face reddening. No tears spilled.

"We'll go together," V'kyrri said, drawing Edie in with him.

Her eyes widened when the door slid shut at her back, and she labored for breath.

"*I'm here.*"

Her respiration eased audibly.

Sanitizer-impregnated water cycled on.

Edie flinched. Nothing more. She tugged her fingers free of his.

"*Edie?*"

"*I'm okay.*"

She was weeping under the cover of water. He ached to fold her in his arms, but she didn't seem to want him inside that old sorrow.

The cleansers cycled off. The dry and water recycling units started.

If only decon could sanitize their respective pasts, too.

Several minutes later, he led her out the door opposite the one they'd entered. Another fence towered above their heads.

V'k opened the only door available.

Edie shuddered with every heartbeat. Memory had broken open beneath her feet. The Claugh had rounded up people during the war—separating families, tearing children from parents, spouses from one another's arms—isolating them, treating them as specimens to be sorted, killed, and mounted on cards.

It had been ten years.

She'd imagined she'd banished the nightmares along with those memories. Or at least gotten over it.

Nerves quivering, Edie followed V'kyrri through the door. Solid deck plates beneath her boots. Big space, but one had been chopped in half if she gauged correctly.

To her right, the *Sen Ekir*'s closed cargo bay doors. The rest of the walls and roof were collapsible plates. A single row of equipment lined the wall opposite them. A narrow gap in the row allowed access to the only other door.

V'kyrri glanced at her, his eyes wide, eyebrows raised, and a massive grin splitting his features. Her tool belt, pack, and SEM glasses sat on the floor inside the door. Edie helped herself to her SEM and tool belt. Getting the SEM in place settled her nerves.

Through a door in the right-hand wall, a pair of towering Abyllon monks entered and took station on either side. Edie's brows rose. She knew about Abyllon monks. Everyone did. She'd never seen them, only heard the legends. What the Three Hells had lured them out of the monastery?

V'kyrri's respiration flat-lined on her SEM.

A young woman, fear in her tight shoulders and hope in her wide-open, red-rimmed eyes came through the door. She met Edie's gaze for a split second.

"Eilod," V'kyrri's voice broke.

Edie's nerves pinged. The queen of the entire baxt'kal Claugh Empire.

The woman gasped. Tears spilled over her lashes. "V'kyrri."

V'kyrri strode into the center of the room.

Laughing and weeping at the same time, the queen rushed him. She threw herself into his arms and locked her arms around his neck.

Envy bit down on Edie hard.

Amazing-looking young woman, and Edie couldn't even say why she made that assessment. Brown hair. Green eyes swollen and red. Tall, sure. Slender. Curved in all the right places. She ought to be slightly more than average. The regal bearing might account for some of it. But it didn't. She shone, a beacon in an otherwise unlit night.

She carried herself with the ramrod straight spine of someone shouldering a backbreaking load. Compassion warmed her eyes. Not for Edie, necessarily. It looked habitual. Awareness. Intellect. She wore it all unconsciously—Edie suspected, in place of the crown that didn't sit upon her head.

And here Edie was. A grubby nobody getting every aspect of her world blown out from under her. She couldn't keep from tugging her shirt straight.

Holding the ruler of the Claugh Empire, V'kyrri

opened watery eyes, looked at Edie, and offered her a lopsided grin.

So that's what homecoming looked like.

Edie crossed her arms to fend off the tidal wave of emotion from their reunion while she bled jealousy all over someone else's deck plating.

Wave upon wave of sorrow, joy, pain, elation, and she couldn't identify what else, surged from the pair. Edie couldn't join in their rejoicing, even as it lured her closer.

She forced her feet to stop out of arm's reach, where she stood stiff and unable to process.

How was she even catching their feelings when they weren't speaking? Was V'kyrri piping it directly into her head? Edie shifted at the burn climbing her ribcage. It hurt. Even if it was spill from the telepath, the pain seemed very much her own. Loss. A sort of homesickness she recognized from the years following her parents' death. Longing for something she'd lost, but more than that, a longing for something she could never again have.

The burn in her chest expanded, stinging. She blinked back moisture. Oh Hells, no, she would not cry again and not in front of the Claugh queen.

As if she'd heard the thought, the queen lifted her tear-stained face and glanced at Edie. "You have returned a brother to me," she choked out. "I will never be able to repay you."

V'kyrri's shoulders hunched, and his breath caught. Something Edie registered via a simple data bump on her SEM, but it echoed through her when her own breath caught in response.

It hit her.

These people had brushed the event horizon of the same thing that had destroyed Edie.

V'kyrri's life, and the lives of his survivors, had gotten caught at the edge of death. Edie had been there to yank them back.

Maybe that explained how and why this reunion was doing such a good job of gutting her. She'd invented scenes like this, a fantasy of finding. She'd come across her parents still alive, maybe in one of the refugee camps, where she could walk in and be enveloped by them. By everything good. By everything she'd once been. Sheltered. Happy. Loved.

She'd dreamed that reunion. For years. Over and over. The Reunion-That-Could-Never-Be. She ached for it. She'd spent the past fifteen years recreating family units over and over. Only to have them sundered. Every. Single. Time.

A solitary hot tear slid down Edie's face. She smeared it with her shirt sleeve, settled her glasses in place, and started at an audio signal. Spiking and falling. Growing. Like a roar. Or a scream. From the door the young queen had come through. More audio signals joined the first.

The door burst open and spilled a roiling mass of shouting, gesticulating humanoids into the bay. A man, red-gold hair flying, his face twisted in rage or agony, maybe both, pressing his hands to his ears, led the pack.

Recognition jolted her.

Major Damen Sindrivik. Edie and Trente had accidently rescued him on Silver City. He'd been rational, calm, and calculating then. He wasn't now.

To Edie's relief, Jayleia Durante, the real reason Edie had gone to Silver City, followed in Damen's wake. Determination set Jay's features but did nothing to mask the terror in her too-wide eyes as she cast repeated "what's wrong" demands at Damen.

Eilod and V'kyrri broke apart.

Her Majesty's bodyguards flanked her.

Four men, one with silvering hair and light blue eyes, one dressed in medi blue, who had black hair and black eyes matching Jayleia's. The third had brown hair and an aquiline nose. Last through the door, a Shlovkur in Claugh khaki. Anger twisted the men's faces. Their steps rattled the deck plates while they snarled at one another.

Instinct tripped old alarms. Edie backed away before she could even think.

Damen stumbled a half dozen steps into the room and went down, his face to the deck plates, screaming, "Turn it off. Please, stop. Make it stop."

"Damen," V'kyrri gasped. He bolted for the man cowering on the floor. "Jayleia?"

Black braid flying, Jayleia flung herself into V'kyrri's arms. "You're alive."

"Sedate him," one of the men shouted.

"When you're a doctor, you can give that order," the medi shot. "Get him in my medi bay."

The silver-haired man snarled, "The both of you…"

Audio data spiked again, and the *Sen Ekir*'s cargo bay door opened.

Enormous, black wasp-looking creatures stumbled from the ship into the room. Six legs. Wings. Antennae, huge, rows of jeweled eyes. One of them lunged.

Recognition shocked the breath out of Edie's body. The *things* from the last planet that had tried to get

V'kyrri.

"Damen," V'kyrri yelled.

Edie flinched, squinted, and backpedaled as the smaller of the two creatures yanked the major out of the cluster of people. Jayleia followed Damen and laid a hand against the bug's carapace as it hugged the struggling major to its body.

Edie's blood galloped in her veins, making her head throb. Too many players. Too much danger. She fingered a pouch on her belt.

The enormous, scowling Shlovkur turned a dead, cold gaze upon her. The chill froze Edie to her marrow.

The men who'd killed her parents had had eyes like his.

V'kyrri pursued the creature grappling the major. "Damen. Let him go."

Blowing out a trembling breath, Edie forced herself to evaluate. Bugs, Damen, Jay, and V'kyrri in a tight knot. Eilod and her bodyguards not a quarter of a meter away. The arguing men in one another's faces a half meter from Damen.

The Shlovkur had put his back to the Sen Ekir's hull where he could command an unimpeded view of the bay.

Two bombs, then. Because no question. She had to take him out first. Once a fight broke out, the monster behind those depths-of-Hell cold eyes would snap her in half.

One of the wasp-things swung multi-faceted eyes at V'kyrri. He stopped, mid-step. Stiffened.

V'kyrri.

Clutched against the smaller bug's thorax, Damen sagged and went silent.

The Shlovkur started for Edie.

She threw a stupidly old fashioned tranq pellet at his feet. It hit and burst. Sleeping agent aerosolized.

Snarling, he dove for cover that didn't exist. He was unconscious before he hit the floor.

Holding her breath, Edie spun, intending to throw another. Color, more intense than her father's best work, burst across her field of vision.

"Edie. Don't," V'kyrri shouted.

She checked her throw at the bugs and sucked in a sharp breath. Adrenaline burned her veins. Before she could parse the data her SEM piped into her skull, the larger creature threw something at her.

A yellow ball struck her. Web burst across her torso, engulfing her in sticky tendrils. Edie yelped. The web touched the wall and stuck fast, gluing Edie in place. Panic scraped bone.

Sticky fear burst inside her skull, draining the strength from her bones. She sagged. At least she could still breathe. And she could still see.

V'kyrri, eyes wild, started toward her. Then every mote of expression drained from his face. He halted, eyes oddly flat.

Another glittering cascade of color confused Edie's eyesight. As it cleared, her focus went to V'kyrri's face. He smiled. A twinkle of humor lit his eyes.

He stalked to her, plucked the pellet from her fingers, and whispered, "You were going to tranq me again? Edie, you still owe me for tranqing me aboard your ship. You can't afford the debt."

Heat traced her veins as if their lives didn't hang in the balance.

He touched the web. It loosened and fell away.

Confusion froze Edie as surely as the web had.

V'kyrri turned and motioned to Eilod.

The queen moved away from the trio of men yelling into one another's scarlet faces.

They were insane. It was the most charitable word Edie could assign. The rage, the cold, inhuman set to their faces. She shuddered. Maybe she'd been teleported fifteen years back through time. She had to press a shaking fist against the tearing pain in her sternum.

The small bug laid Damen Sindrivik on the ground. It squatted on its four hind legs and rubbed its forelegs against its face like a hiztap grooming, Jayleia at its side.

V'ykrri threw Edie's pellet at the men's feet.

Bodies collapsed to the deck. Eilod's retreat from the expanding cloud of soporific dust brought her to V'kyrri's side.

"Your Majesty," he said.

The change in the pitch of his frequency data froze Edie's spine. As did the fact that the small bug turned Damen's head and spat a yellowish glob into his ear. Using its forelegs, the creature tapped and patted the substance before turning Damen's head and repeating the process on the other side.

"I have yet to face inquest over the loss of my ship and crew, but—"

"We had it," Eilod interrupted, her tone sharp enough to cleave through the SEM into Edie's skull. "You were dead. Again."

"Parqe and the others made it?" Edie gasped.

Eilod cast a smile at Edie, then at V'kyrri. "Parqe and the others made it and provided testimony to the board of inquiry. We'll need you, both of you, to fill in the gaps, but the council concurs. The loss was unavoidable and unforeseeable. You are at no fault, Captain."

"Easy conclusion when I'm dead," he countered. He sighed and rubbed a hand down his face. "There's more. I had no choice, Eilod. I did my damnedest to hold *Queen's Rhapsody* together. Mentally."

"I didn't know you could," she whispered.

"Me, either."

"Was this before or after you chopped us off?" Eilod's voice trembled. "Ari and I passed out. Seaghdh had to take command. Turrel was blind for more than six hours. If it did that to us, what did it do to you?"

"I'm bleeding out."

Chapter Twenty-Six

Edie and Eilod rocked.

"You knew?" Edie whispered, then bellowed, "You *knew*?"

Pale lines outlined his lips. It smote her silent.

"Denial is a powerful tool," he said and then cast a glance at the insect staring at him. "I don't know how, but these are Chekydran."

Edie started. "From the planet."

"Those were soldiers they'd sent to find me," he said.

"Chekydran-ki," Eilod corrected. "The adult form. The Chekydran-hiin, the Chekydran you're familiar with, are the larval form. You do not get to leave this at you're 'bleeding out.' "

"He knew," V'kyrri said, gesturing at the bug, conferring with its partner, antennae flicking and touching. The small one gave the large one a glob of yellow stuff. They split up. The littler one found the Shlovkur and spat yellow goo into his ears.

The larger went for the trio of men who'd been arguing. It broke off bits of yellow stuff and patted it into their ears.

Shuddering with every breath, Edie frowned. A snippet of a legend played through the reflexive Chekydran-terror fogging her brain.

"Captain Jerna blocked their ears that they would

not hear and no longer fear the assassin seeking Jerna's end. Thus did the assassin's contract turn upon the wielder.

"Noble Jerna and her loyal crew burned the assassin to ash, for who suffers a sonic attack no ear hears?"

Was that what the bugs were doing? Blocking ears? They'd singled out Damen. Then the Shlovkur, and then the angry trio. As if bugs—*bugs*—had assessed and catalogued the same dangers Edie had.

"They're a telepathic species," V'kyrri said. "He recognized the injury in my head when he tried to talk to me. He believes he and his queen can heal me before it kills me, but it must be now. And he doesn't know what I'll be…after. I'm already useless to you. To the Empire. You needed to know. My usefulness to you—"

"What are you trying to say, Captain?"

"I did permanent damage out there, Eilod," he said.

The terror buried beneath layers of frustration in his voice twisted sticky, barbed tendrils through Edie's SEM to wind around her throat.

"I'm nothing but a contact telepath now, and that's assuming I live to go on being that. If you didn't drum me out of the service over the *Rhapsody*, you'll have to now because I cannot do or be what you need."

Laughter filled with razorblades and torture lasers cut through V'kyrri's words and into Edie's chest. She had to back a step away from the Claugh queen.

"Do you think that little of me, after all, that you believe I love you like a brother based solely on what you can do for me?" Eilod demanded.

V'kyrri jolted. He shook his head. "Eilod. All those years ago. Your dreams. That was me."

Eilod frowned. "You."

The smaller bug, the queen, Edie corrected, picked Damen up and carried him into the *Sen Ekir*.

Jayleia roused the medi.

"I influenced you from light years away," V'kyrri said. "You were the only person I knew heard me, and you were a toddler. But it's possible your father heard me, too, and that I sent him out conquering worlds."

Edie's head spun. He was trying to say it had been *his* fault her world had been conquered and her parents killed?

"You don't know that," Eilod said.

The medi woke, scowling, and put his hands to his ears.

Jayleia grabbed his wrists and shook her head. She took his handheld, typed, then handed it to him. He scanned the device. The tension in his facial muscles eased.

His companions began stirring.

"It stands to reason," V'kyrri argued. "But I can't prove it. No."

"You were a child, born a slave to an enslaved mother," Eilod said, setting a palm to V'kyrri's cheek. "You needed help. It is no wonder you cried out for it without ever knowing if it could work and, if it did, what greater danger it might bring."

"Slave?" Edie squeaked.

V'kyrri met her eye, his brows drawn together. "I didn't know what I was doing. Your parents could be my fault."

Staggered, Edie folded to the floor.

V'kyrri paled, but he made no move save to return his gaze to Eilod. "Your father didn't bring any of my fellow telepaths into your family."

Humor sparkled in Eilod's eyes. "Because my mother's culture speaks in terms of soul-matches. My parents had decided that's what my dreams meant."

Edie closed her eyes. More good news. Only she could end up in a love triangle involving the Claugh queen. Might as well face the rest of it. She opened her eyes.

The bug queen returned and stood beside the larger drone.

V'kyrri gaped at his monarch. He breathed a laugh. "Soul-match?"

"Mother told me because she's growing impatient for grandchildren."

"Eilod, I adore you," V'kyrri burst out. "You know that. But…"

Smiling, she lifted a hand. "But we are not mirrored pieces of the same soul? I know. You are brother-of-my-heart because of your heart. Not because you went out of your way to make yourself indispensable. You are. Regardless of telepathy. Speaking strictly as your queen, though, if you think your utility to the Murbaasch Tu is predicated only on your telepathic ability, you need your head more deeply examined."

Edie barked a laugh.

He met her eye.

She had no idea what he saw in her face that the tension ran out of his expression. Color returned to his complexion.

"Your Majesty," Jayleia said as the trio of men sorted themselves. "According to the Ki, Damen and V'kyrri are in active medical trouble. They need Raj and Dr. Idylle. And if V'kyrri won't say it, I will. He is in immediate danger."

Edie's entire being threw itself against the inside of her skin.

Eilod frowned.

"Thanks, Jay," V'kyrri grumbled.

"Go," the queen ordered. "Please."

V'kyrri bowed his head, then went to the bugs.

Antennae quivering, they settled the feathery tendrils across V'kyrri's forehead.

Edie's eyesight dimmed, and she swam in color. It surrounded her, engulfing and supporting her. Edie sucked in a shard of breath and shook off the hallucination.

V'kyrri crumpled.

Based on the bump in respiration data, Edie and Eilod both gasped.

The insects, standing head to head, caught V'kyrri and draped him, limp, pallid, and emaciated, across their forelegs. Their antennae blanketed his face.

Guilt knocked Edie's ribs. How had she failed to notice he'd been dying right before her eyes? Scooting on the floor because she doubted her legs would hold her, Edie crept closer.

"Where is she?" the Shlovkur bellowed. "I'm gonna twist that gal's head from her neck. What the Hells happened to my ears?"

Edie flinched.

The medi and his now-conscious companions closed around the Shlovkur. One of the men shoved his handheld toward the Claugh colonel who scowled but scanned whatever Jay had typed there. His scowl turned to grimace. "Fine."

The Shlovkur rose, glaring at Edie. He followed her line of sight to V'kyrri. When he returned his gaze to her, she met his eye without flinching. Icy irrationality had been replaced with normal, sane ire and even that softened as he scanned her features.

Before Edie could blink, he crossed the bay and hauled her gently upright.

She tensed. Adrenaline sent her pulse skipping in alarm.

Supporting most of her weight, he walked her to within arms' reach of V'kyrri and the big creatures holding him. The colonel propped her against one of the computer banks and met her eye. "I got a bone to pick with you."

"Take a number," Edie said.

Humor sparked in his eyes, suggesting that he'd worked out what she'd said even with his hearing obstructed. He glanced at the queen, bowed his head, and said, "By your leave, Your Majesty." He trailed Jayleia and the three other men into the *Sen Ekir*.

During his nightmares, V'kyrri had forced Edie to live through the brutal moment he'd maimed himself to save his friends. He'd been caught in a trap. Rather than taking his friends down with him, he'd savaged his own limb, if telepathic connection to everyone he cared about could be described in those terms.

She'd had no way of knowing that he'd never stopped the bleeding. Maybe he couldn't. And he'd used stims, knowing full well they'd speed the hemorrhaging, knowing he could do nothing less and still save his crew.

The captain *had* gone down with the ship.

Even after they'd left that ship behind on a burned-out crust of rock.

"What is going on here?" the queen murmured beside her. "Why are people, rational, scientific people I know and trust, so out of their minds that you intervened?"

Edie met the woman's green gaze, her brain circling the phrase *so out of their minds*. It was how V'kyrri had described attacking her that morning. Shutting her eyes, she shook her head. *C'mon, Edie. Adapt*. She opened her eyes and stuck out a hand.

For a split second, a lonely, vulnerable young woman stared at Edie. Then Eilod blinked, straightened, and pulled her regal mask into place.

"Ms. Drake."

"Edie."

She didn't miss a beat. "Edie. We were not formally introduced in the confusion. I am—"

"Eilod Saoyrse, Queen of the Claugh nib Dovyyth Empire," Edie said. "Our reputations, and our identities, precede us."

Eilod smiled. The vulnerable young woman vanished in that flash of cunning and appreciation.

"Sorry about the tranq," Edie offered.

"Should I be reassured that the first bomb you threw in my presence was filled with sleeping powder?"

Edie tried and failed to suppress a grin. She did not want to be charmed by anymore Claugh. "Think of it as evolution. Your captain has tried to convince me that the past might ought to stay in the past."

A smile crinkled the corners of Eilod's eyes.

"A couple of days ago," Edie said, settling comfortably into agent-reporting-mode, "Captain V'kyrri and I watched the Chekydran get their tentacles on weaponized crystal. We traced them here. Twenty-six hours ago, they seeded plague on world. Shortly after, they landed a massive carrier in the northern hemisphere. They're building out the crystal."

"To what purpose?"

"Not enough data. Sixteen hours ago, I activated the aging dregs of the resistance. A bunch are in your holding pen out front. An hour or two ago, the planetary governor broke quarantine to intercept, arrest, and infect the remains of the resistance."

Audio data with no tag lit up Edie's SEM.

Eilod started, glanced at the ship's badge pinned above her right breast, and activated it.

Edie stared at V'kyrri. Her brows came together. The color had come back to his cheeks. The dark shadows smudging his eyes dwindled.

The smaller Chekydran slid antennae from his face and walked into the ship. The larger bug swung iridescent eyes at Edie. It laid V'kyrri within her reach.

Sipping shuddering breaths, she hauled upright, desperate to touch V'kyrri, to assure with contact what her SEM already told her. His heart still beat, and his respiration was slow, deep, and even. She glanced from V'kyrri to the Chekydran.

It *knew* V'kyrri mattered to her.

Edie fell back on her heels, head spinning. *V'kyrri mattered.* Cravuul dung. She shook her head. Was still shaking it when the Shlovkur and the medi, each wearing a SEM unit, emerged with an anti-grav stretcher.

The Chekydran backed into the far corner and subsided as if settling down for a nap.

The medi popped the buttons on V'kyrri's shirt. He

stuck sensors to V'kyrri's skin and scanned the field projected into the SEM glasses he wore.

"What the Three Hells has he been doing to his heart?" he demanded.

"Abusing stim," Edie croaked.

"Heeeey. Raj," V'kyrri slurred. "Turrel. Good to see you."

The Shlovkur grinned.

"Don't you 'Hey, Raj' me," the medi snapped. "You're dying."

Every muscle in Edie's body clamped tight.

Turrel's smile collapsed.

V'kyrri waved a slack hand. "Been a long few days of that." Scowling, he struggled to sit up.

Turrel knelt at V'kyrri's back and levered him upright.

"Edie?" V'kyrri said.

Uncertain of the wisdom, her new-found emotional awareness still raw, she met his eye. The solemn light there and the lowering of his brows looked like an apology. Or regret.

"You don't get to die, you damned Claugh." Barbed hooks caught in her throat. "I didn't haul your ass off that miserable rock so you could die here."

His lips curved, and his gaze warmed.

"They were right," a male voice called. "It's sound." Running footsteps pounded across Edie's data field.

"Interesting," Eilod said at Edie's shoulder as the silver-haired man bounded into the bay. "I have a quartet of Nol Jakze soldiers asking for General Firestorm."

Edie gaped at her.

"Firestorm?" Turrel repeated. "You mean those cravuul dung stories parents tell kids to scare 'em into behaving are for real?"

Edie cupped her hands around her glasses and dug her fingertips into her forehead. V'kyrri laughed.

"Order of precedence, if you don't mind, Dr. Idylle." Eilod's tone rippled across Edie's SEM field. It grabbed Edie by the sternum.

Edie straightened.

The silver-haired man, Dr. Idylle, she presumed, banked his enthusiasm. He rocked on his heels.

"Go ahead," the medi snapped at V'kyrri. "Laugh. Another day, two at the outside, and you'd have been in stasis for a month while I grew you a new heart. As it is, you'll report to me every twelve hours for assessment and extra doses of regen. Mess it up, and I will lock you in stasis."

He injected V'kyrri, then cut a glance at Edie. "Raj Faraheed, *Sen Ekir*'s medical doctor. What's your vaccination status?"

"Initial vax right after you guys came up with the stuff." She gestured between V'kyrri and herself. "He and I were boosted just before we put down."

"With?" Dr. Idylle demanded.

"Ioccal IX lifted from Intcom while it was still Intcom."

Turrel barked a laugh.

"I need blood for verification," Raj said.

Edie hesitated. Sure. She knew of the crew of *Sen Ekir.* Everyone in TFC did. But except for Jayleia, Edie'd never met any of them. These were V'kyrri's friends. Not hers. "Do I get to keep any after knocking you out?"

The question sent V'kyrri and Turrel into a paroxysm of laughter.

"Dr. Idylle?" Eilod said.

The older man shifted from watching the blood sampling to waving his handheld. "The Ki were correct."

"Where are they?" V'kyrri asked.

Edie pointed behind him.

He twisted, craned his neck, and looked at Turrel. "Mind telling me what the Three Hells you've been doing since I left?"

"Making friends and influencing bugs." Turrel shook his head. "It's Sindrivik's fault."

"The Chekydran attacking Nol Jakze are Chekydran-hiin," Raj said. "Intrinsically bad-tempered teenagers. These are their parents, trying to stop them. There. All done."

"Teenagers," Edie echoed.

"Focus, people. The Ki were correct about what, Dr. Idylle?" Eilod prompted.

"The planet hums," he said as if that solved everything. He rocked to his heels and then to his toes.

"Insufficient data, Linnaeus," Raj said.

"Ah. Nol Jakze hums. I have no idea why. I suspect a geologist or planetologist could work it out, but the important point is the planet-wide hum," Dr. Idylle said. "Major Sindrivik, with his Autken senses, could and did hear it. Prompted by that and the Ki, Pietre and I reconfigured our scans and detected it."

"Why would that make everyone so angry?" Edie prodded.

"Were we?"

"I didn't throw sleeping pellets at you because

you'd forgotten to seal your jacket," she said.

"Why isn't V'k affected?" Turrel demanded.

"He may have been," Edie said.

"What are you say—" V'kyrri stopped and spun to stare at her. "You think that's why I attacked you this morning? But why then and not now?"

Edie shrugged. "You were in my head when you snapped out of it, and I still don't know."

"Could telepathy provide some protective benefit?" Eilod asked.

Raj shrugged. "You, your guard, and Jayleia are unaffected, suggesting that if telepathy helps, it isn't the only mechanism at play."

Dr. Idylle shook his head. "We have plumbed the depths of my knowledge on this issue. Pietre is building hearing protection for us. Once I have Major Sindrivik on his feet, lucid, and pulling research for me, I'll have better answers."

Eilod shook her head. "It may have to wait."

He lifted his gaze to the door Edie and V'kyrri had come through. "Plague. Quite. Alexandria should have *The Dagger* in orbit shortly. Raj and I will have the vaccination protocols, priority suggestions, and casualty projections ready for you and your staff." He marched out of the bay.

"General Firestorm," Eilod began, turning on Edie.

Like she'd fallen from a step she hadn't seen, displacement stabbed Edie. She shoved to standing. "Absolutely not. I've never been military. They wanted nothing to do with us during the war, and I want nothing to do with them now. I did not tell those—"

"Your people need you," Eilod interrupted.

Edie threw her arms wide. "You've used me as a

lash to my people's conscience long enough."

"Initial estimates put population loss at greater than fifty percent," the queen said. "Over half your world. Your people need a hero. One of their own. Help. Me."

Chapter Twenty-Seven

Horror knocked the breath right out of Edie's chest. She stared at the grim-faced monarch.

"Edie." V'kyrri said.

Displaced rage, scattered by Eilod's demand for aid, coalesced and landed square on him. She jabbed a finger at him. "Don't you dare try to sweet talk me. Not when you knew you were dying. And especially not when you knew that everyone I give a damn about gets ripped away."

"Hear the soldiers out," he urged, eyes irrationally alight and a smile on his lips. He rose to face her, his shirt open and the lines of his chest taunting her.

Her mouth watered, recalling the taste of his skin. Damn it.

"If these are the soldiers sent to investigate Immin's ship, it means something that they're asking for you and not their commanding officers," he said.

Stiffening her spine, she forced her gaze away. "Fine. I'll help. On this one thing." She strode back the way she and he had come.

"Wait for your attaché," he said, peeling away Raj's sensors and buttoning up his shirt when she glanced over her shoulder. He met her eye. "General."

Turning away, she fumbled the SEM frames from her face, hands shaking. She'd never, throughout the occupation and war, bent her head to the empire. Yet here she was. Marching to their signal because it matched hers. And maybe because she couldn't resist a certain Claugh captain.

Her people needed her.

Except as a means of manipulating her people, the Claugh didn't need her. Neither did V'kyrri. Not anymore.

She'd kept her promise. She'd reunited him with his people. It was time to cut the cords. Before Trente's admonition came true and the Claugh ate her alive.

Her skin tingled. Awareness prickled her nerves.

V'kyrri put a hand beneath her hair and massaged the stony muscles. "*Ever lead a squad?*"

Edie sagged, shook her head. "I'm not qualified to lead a group of kids on a camping trip, much less act as any kind of general."

"*That's where I come in.*" He drew her against his body. "*I've got your back.*"

Relief flushed her. She straightened when she longed to go on leaning and pasted a smile to her face. She put her glasses in place. A twinge of headache suggested she was coloring well outside the addiction lines. Again. On both the SEM and V'kyrri.

Maybe she'd better get a grip on this general-ing business and stand on her own two feet. Even if she wobbled.

V'kyrri needed his people and his family.

She needed—what she couldn't have. Withdrawal would be hell.

"I've got this," she said.

"No officer shall enter any potentially hostile situation without backup."

"Officers of the Claugh nib Dovyyth probably

shouldn't quote regs to resistance fighters." She walked out from beneath the comfort of his touch.

He chuckled.

When they emerged into the holding pen, V'kyrri mapped the lay of the people contained by the pen and tucked it into her head.

Jonas and the rest of the cell clustered to the left of the gate. The quartet of soldiers asking for her stood at the gate, brows lowered, gazes focused dead ahead.

From the far-right hand corner, Tiimetes threw a vicious glare her way.

The sergeant at the gate snapped to attention and made to salute.

"Don't," she signed with a swipe of closed fingers across her body. "No tipping anyone off. I'm unofficial, right?"

Comprehension widened the man's brown eyes. He canted his body to shield what he said, "We investigated the assassin's ship."

A private stepped forward, a handheld in her grip.

"Given the information we recovered," the sergeant went on, "we wanted to give it to someone who all the Nol Jakze can trust. Will you accept the files?"

Jonas and the knot of resistance fighters shifted, a subtle motion of spines straightening, and traded glances.

Edie registered how they'd been privy to the conversation. The fact that these soldiers now trusted old revolutionaries rather than their own commanders made prickles tighten on the skin between her shoulder blades.

"Summary?" she asked. "What's on there that you can't trust to your higher-ups?"

"Proof, ma'am," he said. "Everything you said and worse."

Edie wilted. She accepted the handheld.

"*No.*" V'kyrri whispered into her head when she hesitated with it.

"*Your queen needs this,*" she thought at him.

"*She's your queen, too. And yes. She does, but the last thing you want is for people to see you pass Nol Jakzian military secrets to a Claugh captain.*"

Excellent point. One that drove home how little experience she had playing hero. Or general. She tucked the unit into a shielded pocket of her tool belt.

She couldn't lead these people. Couldn't even begin to know how. They deserved better. Jonas, maybe.

Still. She'd be happy to rub Tiimetes' nose in the mess he'd made. She met Jonas's eye, then the sergeant's. "If we don't arrest the governor, the Claugh will."

"Yes, ma'am. It will be necessary to surrender custody anyway, as the captain can tell you," the sergeant said, looking at V'kyrri. "Ranking Claugh officials have jurisdiction."

"For the duration of the outbreak, Her Majesty is on world to coordinate medical relief efforts. Her Majesty recognizes and encourages the right of the people to police their own," V'kyrri said aloud.

Edie translated, then added, "Will you assist?"

"Yes, ma'am."

Edie moved to the middle of the yard, V'kyrri and the clump of soldiers at her left shoulder, Jonas and the other resistance fighters closed in on her right.

Tiimetes met her gaze, his features impassive.

Detainees clustered into position to see what she had to say.

"Never hire an assassin who'll dig up everything about you to sell to the highest bidder," Edie said. She tapped her tool belt. "I don't understand what you hoped to gain by killing everyone on world."

Onlookers shifted, fingers and hands fluttering as they murmured amongst themselves.

"You've always lacked vision," he replied. "And the will to do what was necessary to achieve freedom."

She gaped. "The occupation benefited you directly. Tii, your own soldiers searched Immin's ship. They found proof that you not only authorized the murder of our people, you actively aided and abetted it."

The people clustered around him eased away.

"How dare you…" he wheezed, his muscles tightening.

"You planned to use the Chekydran to drive out the Claugh and then what?" she demanded. "You'd be beholden to TFC where you wouldn't even get a vote in the council?"

"I'd have freed us. The thing you wanted and failed to do," he shouted. "That's what they promised. Equal recognition under TFC law. We'd have been wholly independent, while I—"

"You what? Pretended to be king? Of a dead planet? You've murdered millions."

He shrugged it off and waved a hand to indicate the holding pen. "They idolize *you* of all people."

Faces around the yard hardened. Shoulders rode high and tight.

"They idolize the resistance," she countered. "Not me. You were included."

"It wasn't enough," he snapped. "All the stories are about you. No one knew my name until I became governor. And now, it doesn't matter, does it? The Chekydran are here. People are dying. And this time, Firestorm, there's not a damned thing you can do about it."

A man in a limp, damp business suit rushed Tiimetes. Tii sidestepped and planted the heel of his hand in the man's lower back, sending him sprawling. Another onlooker planted a fist in Tii's jaw.

The crowd surged.

Pure instinct. Edie darted between Tii and the mob. V'kyrri and the soldiers joined her.

"Stand aside."

"Let us—"

"He deserves to die."

"The same has been said of me," Edie said, making her words big enough to be seen by everyone. "That I killed innocents, and I deserve to die. It's been said of several of us. We don't have a death penalty on Nol Jakze for a reason. Who among us is qualified to judge this man?"

Hands and expressions trembled.

Finally, a woman in mud-smeared trousers asked, "Did you? Kill my father and brother on the train to Jorzance City?"

"No," she said. "I swear on my parents' graves. I've blown up my share of trains, I admit. But they were troop carriers."

"Once the Claugh started forcing our civilians to ride the trains with them, she refused to blow up any more," Jonas said.

"You are such children," Tiimetes slurred. He

uttered an eerie, high-pitched burble of laughter that rode up her SEM's audio display, and then he crumpled to the concrete behind her.

Edie turned.

Blood leaked from Tiimetes's nose. Her stomach lurched. The hit to his jaw. Or the fall. Right? Not plague. Not so soon.

Terror clenched her in a cold fist. "V'kyrri."

"Medical emergency," V'kyrri said into a ship's badge she hadn't registered. "The governor is down. Repeat, planetary governor is down. Active bleed."

****

Edie sat at the makeshift conference table in a tent behind the *Sen Ekir*, her head in her hands.

"We're out of options for Governor Calamae," silver-haired Dr. Idylle said, his hand heavy on her shoulder. "I'm sorry."

Did she have to lift her head for him to see her nod? No. But she did have questions. Lots and lots of questions she didn't want answers to.

"How long?" she forced herself to ask as she sat upright.

The fine lines at the corners of Dr. Idylle's eyes and mouth deepened. "Days and only a few of those."

"He had to have been infected before the bombs," Jayleia said. "One man in detention had a fever. He's in the isolation ward. Everyone else has been vaccinated and released. The soldiers you asked for and their lieutenant are through decon and getting some down time."

"There's a teenager in my ship," Edie said.

Jay nodded. "No problem."

"What evidence do we have that the governor

might have been exposed prior to planetary infection?" the blonde, silver-eyed hologram of Captain Ari Idylle asked.

Edie tapped the handheld the soldiers had given her. "If there's direct evidence, it'll be in here. At the very least, it proves he's a traitor."

"Major?" the captain said.

Damen, newly released from medical, took the handheld, and plugged it into a port.

Edie, V'kyrri, and to her shock, the Chekydran-ki had helped Pietre set up the massive tent, bring in chairs, tables, solid fuel heaters, and then they'd installed com gear. It brought holograms of Admiral Seaghdh, Captain Idylle, and Zain Durante, Edie's former boss, to the chairs at the conference table.

Despite the heaters, Edie shivered. "You think Tii's 'allies' poisoned him at their last meet up."

"Working hypothesis," Captain Idylle said.

Edie shook her head. "Cold. And I say that as someone who knows a few too many ways President Durgot can be a treacherous Orhait's ass."

Admiral Seaghdh, the razorblade of a man wrapped in a uniform so dark green it looked black, met her eye, his own narrowed. Sizing her up. "How do you figure into this situation, Ms. Drake?"

"Name's Edie. I don't. I grew a conscience in the wrong place at the right time."

"You saved enemy soldiers," V'kyrri said, contradicting her. "Your conscience was a pre-existing condition."

"There's a price on your head," Ari said. "Several, as I understand it."

"Suggesting you do figure into this," the admiral

concluded.

"Durgot's a paranoid psychotic, but until he started sending messages pleading for me to 'come home' after the Silver City thing, I had no idea he knew I existed. And now he's trying to fix the 'exist' part," Edie grumbled.

"When you failed to respond to his messages, Durgot released your identity," Durante said. "The prices on your head rapidly followed."

"I want to know how he could give up something only you were supposed to have," Edie replied.

Her former boss studied her. That hazel gaze and the faint downturn of his mouth kept agents and mercenaries alike in line for the entire decade she'd been subject to it.

No one spoke.

Durante taught Edie to play this power game. She'd never won. Not against him. But then, she'd been betrayed before, and this time, she'd be damned before she went down without a fight.

Finally, he spread his fingers wide. "I do not betray my agents' trust, Edie. It was not I."

Sincerity delivered with perfect grammar even. He believed what he said. She believed what he said. Relief stung her eyes. She sighed, pulled her lenses down and pinched the bridge of her nose. She opened her eyes and slid the glasses back into place. "Doesn't explain why Durgot wants me dead."

"You have something on him," Turrel said.

She threw her arms wide. "What? I am—was—an operative with very specific and limited scope. What could I possibly have on him? Director?"

"I'm sorry, Edie. I have no further data on that

front."

"Will you allow us access to *t'Achriedes-myn's* systems?" Ari asked.

"You mean you aren't past my lockouts already?" she sniped.

V'kyrri put a hand on her wrist. "*We're on the same side, Edie*."

Edie slumped. "How fond I am of being reminded I have nothing left to lose. Here."

Damen took her access code.

"We're not after your trade secrets," Ari said. "Just digging for whatever has Durgot interested in tying up the loose end he thinks you represent."

"You're going to take what you want anyway."

"In the interests of fighting Chekydran and, if I have to, TFC? You bet," the woman said. Not a mote of guilt or remorse in her expression. "TFC plays hardball. You should be used to it by now."

She was. "Tell me you can bomb the Chekydran out of existence from your orbital position."

"The Hiin," Ari corrected. "I wish I could. They've erected a defense screen."

V'kyrri and Edie traded a glance.

"The crystal," V'kyrri said.

Edie sucked a breath between clenched teeth. "I need in there before it's impossible to get in there."

"It may not be necessary," V'kyrri began. "We—"

"It is." Dr. Idylle and Jayleia said simultaneously.

Eilod leaned into the table. "New data?"

"The Ki flew over the installation," Jay said. "While the crystal is in place, they cannot influence their Hiin."

"Translate," V'kyrri said.

"The Chekydran-ki sing their Hiin into metamorphosis," Jayleia said. "We developed an endocrine bomb, a chemical that, in combination with parental song, triggers the Hiin to spin cocoons, where they stay until the queen releases them."

"Ship's engines in atmosphere interfered with the song in one case," Dr. Idylle said. "It appears the Hiin noted the aberration and found a way to turn sound to their defense. Our hypothesis is that the crystal is augmenting the planetary hum as a means of blocking their parents' song."

Edie frowned. He wore inserts of some kind in either ear. They all did. Eilod and V'kyrri included. Edie touched her ear. The doctor dipped his chin.

"Pietre customized noise-cancelling com-sets used by in-atmosphere fighter pilots." Dr. Idylle tapped one of the earpieces. "We no longer remove them. The headaches, irritability, sleep disturbances, and irrationality seem to have been cured. The effect appears limited to non-natives."

"Non-hearing," she corrected, the blood draining from her head.

He lifted an eyebrow. "Non-hearing? Can you elaborate?"

"Occasionally hearing children are born," she said. "They don't often survive on world. Tiimetes is one of the very few who did, in fact. Shortly after birth, hearing babies stop sleeping. They stop eating. Nothing our medical people did worked. The only cure was taking them off-world. No one ever knew why."

He shook his head. "Hearing tests became codified procedure, and any child born with hearing is removed from Nol Jakze because the baby's system would be overwhelmed by a sound no one else could perceive."

"When I realized who our esteemed guest was," Ari nodded at Edie, "I remembered the hysteria in the TFC media over the Claugh invasion of Nol Jakze."

Dr. Idylle's head came up. His blue eyes glittered with interest. "Right's violations. If I recall, the Council filed formal protests with the empire over Nol Jakze."

"Many of them," Eilod said.

"Alexandria," Dr. Idylle said, eyes wide, one hand outstretched to the flickering holograph of his daughter.

Ari tipped her head. "I believe I'm thinking what you're thinking. The Claugh forces that occupied Nol Jakze had no way of knowing about the planetary hum. The Autken had no reason to set foot on world before we brought Damen in as an ancillary member of the *Sen Ekir* crew."

"If we could establish a pattern as to how and when incoming troops were driven mad—"

" 'Driven'?" Edie erupted. "There's no 'driven' to it. They just are." She shot a glance around the table. "Present company excepted only when wearing hearing protection."

Dr. Idylle's light blue gaze slid her way, his brows scrunched.

V'kyrri smoothed a hand down her spine. Welcome warmth spread into her body.

Propping her elbows on the table, Edie framed her face as if her hands were blinders. If the Claugh who'd invaded hadn't been mad before they'd arrived on Nol Jakze, then they, too, were victims. Right alongside Edie's parents. So many assumptions from her past, so many self-evident truths, all being ripped apart.

She shoved away from the table.

V'kyrri rose with her, lines at the corners of his eyes and mouth.

She shook her head. "I'm not okay with rewriting who the victims were."

"Nothing will make what happened here okay, Edie," V'kyrri said, the lines on his face deepening.

"No. It won't." Edie tried to shift away the ache in her chest. It didn't work. "Leave it. Time to focus on right now. Tiimetes has information. Someone needs to get it from him. Might as well be me. At least I know when he's lying."

V'kyrri's eyes widened, and his fingers flexed before he forced them ramrod straight. She waited for him to say something. Anything. He'd closed off since they'd brought Tiimetes inside. She'd resorted to her SEM to navigate the nuances of this group of strangers. It left her nauseated and in pain. Not to mention lonely.

Ah, the joys of addiction.

"I'll allow it." Dr. Idylle said. "Provided you follow all sensible precaution."

"Does he know?" Edie met the older man's eye.

Dr. Idylle frowned.

"That he's dying, Linnaeus," Jayleia clarified.

"Yes. We could not ethically withhold that information."

"Good," Edie said.

The man paled, but he summoned Raj.

"Ms. Drake, one does not…" the admiral began, the harsh peaks and valleys of his audio signal reaching through her SEM to give her a splitting headache. He broke off.

Edie glanced at the table. The queen had a hand up. "Captain V'kyrri, be seated."

"Eilod—"

"Dr. Idylle," the monarch went on as if V'kyrri hadn't protested and taken a step closer to Edie. "Is the governor in any condition to present a physical danger to Edie?"

"He is secured," Dr. Idylle said. "Patients in later stages of the disease can become confused and attempt to rise."

"Very well," Eilod said, then met Edie's eye. "May we rely upon a report?"

"You're really going to pretend you won't be listening?" Edie shot. "He hates speaking our native language, but if he does, and it bears repeating in polite company, you bet."

Turrel snickered.

"Edie?" V'kyrri murmured.

She looked at him. Uncertainty hung on the shadows in the hollows of his cheeks and darkened his eyes. Edie's fingers twitched with the impulse to smooth the tension from his jaw. If he'd only get into her head and *talk* to her—with her head aching from emptiness, she offered him a faint smile, the only reassurance she could summon.

His features relaxed. "Be careful."

Chapter Twenty-Eight

Edie followed Raj into a medical bay fronting an isolation ward. “Dr. Faraheed.”

“Raj, please.”

She took off her SEM and put it in her tool belt. Time to break the dependency cycle. On all levels. A frisson walked her nerves, exacerbating the growing thump in her head. “Raj. Edie. Nice to meet you.”

“Thanks for bringing V’kyrri and his people back,” he said. “We owe you. Even if no one else is willing to make that commitment.”

To a monster... She knew how that sentence ended. “Glad to help. That said, Raj, I have torture lasers drilling into my skull.”

His eyes widened.

Edie waved away Raj’s concern. “Pre-existing condition. I-I’m a SEM addict. I’d recovered, but recent circumstances—”

“Of course.” He gestured to the scan bed. “Have a seat.”

He bore a striking resemblance to Jayleia. Maybe that’s why she could read what he said, she’d learned to read Jay while working for her father. Jay and her cousin spoke with the same word formation habits. “I’ll get pain and nausea control onboard, but I need a glimpse of the neural damage. I can’t ignore that you’ve been in close contact with a wounded, and from what I hear, broadcasting telepath. I wouldn't be surprised if some of your symptoms are V'kyrri's fault."

Edie shook her head. "He's cured. Isn't he?"

"He's recovering from what should have been mortal wounds," Raj said, activating equipment. "But he's still carrying an untreated emotional wound. You were trapped in proximity. I have no doubt you've taken damage."

He shot her up with pain and nausea killers. "This will take another few minutes. Relax. Let the meds work. You're still awfully pale and your cortisol levels aren't easing."

"There are some pains no drug can touch," she muttered, glancing at the airlock door for isolation.

Raj followed her gaze. "I'm sorry."

"Me, too. I'd have liked Tiimetes to face the judgement of his people before he died," Edie said. "At this point, it'll just be mine, and that's inadequate."

Raj's brow furrowed. He studied his screens and scowled. "You have active damage being done."

She sat up straight. "How? V'kyrri went radio silent hours ago, when we brought Tii into isolation."

"I—" he broke off, frowning. His gaze turned inward, before focusing on her. "When we thought Captain V'kyrri had died, Major Sindrivik was on my operating table. TFC doesn't have telepathic species among the member worlds. I know next to nothing about how V'kyrri establishes lasting mental connections between himself and someone else, but I have seen firsthand the damage they can do."

Edie slumped. "Long, intensive exposure, maybe? Like a telepath substituting for a crushed SEM unit in the middle of a tactical situation?"

"Looking at this scan," Raj jerked a thumb over his shoulder at his diagnostic screens, "I'd say that's a yes. He's got a line straight into your head."

"How? If he's not talking to me? I knew the difference on that world we escaped. It was obvious when he was here," she tapped her forehead, "even if he was silent."

"I don't know," the doctor said. "I'm sorry. I don't have enough experience with telepathic injury. I can only tell you you're taking damage, probably from his inability and unwillingness to process the loss of ship and crew."

She blew out a shaky breath. "That kind of thing leaves a permanent mark."

"Yes, it does," Raj said. "As a medical professional, I can say the size of the scar is up to V'kyrri. The longer he delays facing and processing his loss, the worse and longer-lasting the trauma. If I'm right about the connection between you, you'll both bear the scars."

"I don't have time for stasis," she said.

"Not necessary," Raj replied. He collected another set of medications. "Regen. A little nutritional boost to ease some of your withdrawal symptoms. I'm going to want to see you tomorrow to assess progress."

"Thanks," Edie said. She gestured at the airlock. "Let's get this over with."

He helped her don a clean suit. Raj switched on her air supply, tapped her shoulder and mouthed, "Fifteen minutes."

He let her into the airlock, pressurized it, and opened the inner door. Rows of beds lined either side of a walkway. Two were occupied. One, in the far corner, held a man huddled beneath his covers. He did not turn. Tiimetes lay flat on his back in the nearest bed, staring at the ceiling, his fists clenched in the blankets. Three different fluids fed into the graying skin of his arms.

"I should have known you'd come to gloat," he said as she pulled a chair into position beside him. It took effort to read what he said.

"Don't have the time or the energy for it," she retorted. "When I look at the recorded explosions of civilian kills post-surrender, I'm going to see your signatures, aren't I?"

He laughed, exposing bloody teeth and gums.

Her gut constricted. "You're the king of Carozziel slime-bats. I look back at you being captured at the end of the war—"

"And you running away?" he snapped. "You were supposed to care enough to save me."

"After you'd made damned sure I couldn't? It took me a decade and a half to figure out you were actively trying to get me killed. Seeing you alive when you were supposed to have died in a Claugh prison did the trick. Why, Tii?"

He rolled his head on the pillow. "Poor little Altheas. Dead mommy, dead daddy. You could do no wrong. Even when you went out of your way to make everything as hard as possible in fighting the Claugh, there was nothing you could do, nothing you could say that would make the resistance see you for what you are."

"What's that?"

"A wanna-be. A pretender. You weren't out there fighting for freedom. You were out for revenge."

"I got the job done."

"You were this sweet, innocent little thing. You came into our midst hemorrhaging pain all over, refusing direct orders, refusing to do your duty. Refusing to fight the Claugh with the same ferocity they fought us. Yet the resistance idolized you. Still do. I tried to convince the Chekydran to bomb your idiotic statue out of existence. They couldn't even do that."

"You wanted to be the one who single-handedly defeated the Claugh and freed our people? And you're pissed off because nobody could accomplish that?"

"I would have," he snapped. "Until… They sing songs about Firestorm." His hands waved to a beat while his fingers spelled her name. "There are fairytales. It's all your name, your red hair, your explosions. All the noble, naïve sentiment about not blowing up civilians, not targeting anyone who didn't have to die. No collateral damage. As if you were better than the rest of us."

"Just you, Tii. No one else sold our entire civilization out to the bugs."

"I was the best. Without you, I'd still be the best."

She shook her head. "You like showing off. You have no line. No conscience. There is nothing you won't do to manipulate circumstances to your benefit. The resistance never fully trusted you. I get that it was easy to assign the blame to me. But the hard truth is Tii, you have no one to blame but yourself."

He turned his face away. She sank into reexamining the lies upon which her past had been built. Finally, he turned back.

"Did they tell you I'm dying?"

"Yeah."

"That's it? No sorry?"

She shrugged, eyes stinging. "The Tiimetes I cared about died a long time ago. I'm just trying to figure out if that charming, smart, funny man was someone I made up in my head. It's not easy admitting I must have been a really stupid kid."

The muscles around his eyes softened. "Charming? You weren't stupid. Young, sure. Gullible. Starving for affection. I took advantage."

She hugged her arms to her chest. It didn't stop the last bandage from being ripped from her dumb, possibly arrogant ego. All this time, she'd wanted to believe that what they'd shared hadn't been a figment of her imagination. She'd been wrong.

"I cared. I did," he mumbled. "And hated you for—"

He sighed. His eyes drifted shut.

Edie tried to swallow past the cold, hard lump in her throat and failed.

"Forgive me," his hands said against the sheet. His hands went slack. His chest still rose and fell, the motion shallow and irregular.

Edie drew a deep breath. "For everything you tried to do to me, I forgive you. For what you've done to countless innocents, may the Gods have mercy, because I can't."

****

Every step Edie took on her way to the isolation ward ripped holes in V'kyrri's resolve. He'd given her space. Privacy. She didn't deserve to have him in the middle of her memories of her dying former lover.

Then the admiral had ordered him to remain silent in a bid to force Edie to either resort to her SEM or rely on translators.

"Leverage," Seaghdh had said.

Even after V'kyrri explained it was a gross violation of the culture and of Edie. He'd lodged a formal protest, but he'd obeyed the order.

It had taken Edie's show of bravado as she'd walked away to drive home what a mistake he'd made.

"Captain," Eilod said.

He returned to the table empty of everyone but the queen.

"We picked up your survivors six hours after they reached orbit…" she began.

He collapsed into the chair beside hers. "I am so sorry." By the end of the sentence, his voice was a croak. Closing his eyes did nothing to hold back the poison of terrible loss, but it saved him from seeing accusation in Eilod's face.

"I thought the worst day of my life was being shot down." He desperately wanted to stop the words, but ragged and maimed, they trickled out. "By far worse was coming home without two-hundred and ten people who'd trusted me with their lives…and facing you, who'd entrusted me with those lives."

"V'kyrri." Eilod grabbed his hands. Her voice broke. "I would do it again. I will do it again. The next ship commissioned will carry the *Rhapsody's* name and her captain."

Already shaking his head, he opened his eyes.

Eilod's eyes were red. Tears weighed against her lashes but did not spill over.

His eyes burned. "No."

Eilod tightened her hold. "V'k. Listen to me. Ari and Cullin have been where you are. On a smaller scale, granted, but both are adamant. Your best hope of surviving that ambush by ships we didn't know existed is predicated on getting back in a command seat. Until your ship is ready, you will meet with Ari and Seaghdh weekly. I beg you. Talk to them."

Talk to someone who'd have some small insight into what had happened to him and to his crew? "On one condition."

His monarch raised her eyebrows.

"There's an endless supply of Noc Gallon Whiskey at those meetings."

Her smile wobbled. "I can promise some, not 'endless'. This won't be easy, and this is selfish of me, but I need you."

"My survivors?" he managed to whisper.

"Aboard the *Dagger*. Recovering. All of them." Eilod released him. "Major Uvoga will be in stasis for some time, but he will recover. I've had their reports regarding your companion."

Edie. Swallowing trepidation, he forced a smile. "How did Commander Parqe take the news?"

"That you were alive? With such heavy guilt, Dr. Annantra increased her intensive psychological therapy."

"That Edie is Firestorm," he clarified.

His sovereign's lips twitched. "That was colorful. The commander believed you knew her identity."

"I recalled the wanted notices," he said. "Before she stole the ship that saved my survivors."

"You knew who she'd been, yet you brought her here."

"She brought me," he corrected, his tone sharp. "To *her* home world."

"Threat assessment."

"She saved our lives, Eilod. She didn't have to. She knew who and what we were before she pulled us from the wreck."

"I've heard. It earned her enough benefit of the doubt that she has neither been arrested nor shot. Can you turn her to our purpose, Captain?"

Not 'V'k' or even 'V'kyrri'. His queen opted for 'captain'. Reminding him of his duty. As if, after everything, he could possibly forget. Weariness weighed the hand he rubbed down his face. "Edie has a personal stake here, Eilod, and a ten-plus year history of teamwork."

"In TFC. Intcom, if I read Edie and the director correctly."

"You did. She was a part of a core team of mercenaries. Edie needs a team at her back to compensate for her deficits."

Eilod propped her chin on one fist. "Her hearing."

" 'Her hearing?' " he echoed, frowning. When had he started thinking of Edie first and deaf dead last? "That has nothing to do with it. Edie's a specialist. Her great strength is her artistry with explosives. She can run a mission and a team, but it's not second nature, not like taking something apart is."

"Can you influence her?"

He stared at the young queen, not at all certain he wanted to know if she meant telepathically. "Ask what you mean, Eilod."

"Have we descended to the point that you're reading me?"

"Of course not. It's taken losing most of my ability to find out how much of what I thought of as telepathy was being able to read people. I don't need telepathy to tell you have an agenda. Perhaps you shouldn't keep your friends quite so close."

She tipped her head back and laughed.

It brought a grin to his face.

"Very well," she said, sobering. "Give me her psychological key."

"Edie needs to belong, to create a family unit like the one that was taken from her."

"What's our exposure?"

"Split loyalties," he said.

"The resistance."

"Before we hit Nol Jakze, I'd have given you good odds that she'd have bonded to an alliance with us."

"With you."

"I should be that lucky," he returned, meeting her gaze without flinching.

She smiled. "Now?"

"I can't tell. The pressures of finding her first love alive, that he'd manipulated, abused and used her, set her up, and then got the plague he'd caused in the first place…" He broke off and shook his head.

"Guess."

"Eilod."

"It's important, V'k."

"I don't know. Fifty-fifty, maybe."

The young queen shifted and drew an audible breath. "You under-estimate yourself."

"We've been using her, Eilod. We thought she was dead and wouldn't come back to find out the empire had turned her into a glorified mascot.

"Edie needs connection. Needs it enough, she's terrified of it and does everything in her power to sabotage it when she gets it. The drive for connection overcame her prejudice when she saved us and drove her to cooperate with me to keep your prototype and its data from the UMOPG. Without Edie, the *Rhapsody* would have fallen to the UMOPG military, and the crew I had no hope of rescuing would have died slow, lingering deaths." Pulling in a deep breath, V'kyrri edged away from that emotional black hole.

Eilod laid a hand on his. "I don't deny we owe Edie a debt of gratitude."

Swallowing the cold weight of sorrow, he shook his head. "I couldn't have gotten anyone off world. We might have escaped the ship, but we'd have died on that rock. She gave up her mission and every resource she had to get us out of there."

Eilod sat back, studying him.

Admiration lit through him. She was reading him. Not the way he might read her, but Eilod was poking and prodding his emotions in as skillful an interrogation as any he'd ever seen Seaghdh conduct. No wonder Eilod and Seaghdh were such a good team.

V'kyrri's boss played a take no prisoners approach to interrogation, and his monarch plied emotional appeals and physical contact.

He'd known Eilod for half his life. He'd still blundered right into her snare. Straightening his spine, he took a second to get his shields online. "You asked for an exposure assessment."

"You gave me one. Are you going to confess your true fear? That Edie will return to the resistance?" Eilod asked.

"No. I'm afraid she'll work out that I fostered connection and attraction as a means of binding her to me, making her do what I wanted the way I wanted."

"You manipulated her."

"I manipulated Edie and discovered she's adaptable and determined and resourceful and—"

"We do have a plague to combat, Captain."

"Fine." He pinned Eilod with a look. "I cut myself with my own knife. I started out using Edie. Now, I don't want to lose her. Tactically, you can't afford to alienate her. Circumstances and our own meddling are pressuring her to become the leader, the legend we made her."

"The price we pay for returning a people's heroes to them."

"She'll be offered the opportunity to resurrect the resistance and overthrow the occupation," he said.

Eilod's eyebrows rose, and she sat up straighter. "Does she have the tactical capacity?"

"We handed it to her by what we made her on this world. She has the flexibility, the drive, the blunt honesty, and the long memory of a girl made an orphan by men wearing these uniforms."

"She also has the Chekydran on world," Eilod pointed out.

"You have them threatening an entire empire. Like you, she's already made the choice to go down fighting, if that's what's necessary, and it strikes me that you're remaking her in your image."

"I'm asking her to fulfill her potential," Eilod countered. "I am asking *you* to analyze the risk that represents. We're out of options and short on allies. I am willing to consider any number of unholy alliances in the service of the empire. But if she turns against us?"

"I will fight with everything I am for her and the

people of this world," he said. "You put her in this position, Eilod, and you want me to declare my allegiance to the empire and to you above all else. I won't let you off that hook. You don't get to write her off. You were born and bred for leadership. She still calls herself a monster inside her own head."

"When I look back over war footage, so do I," Eilod muttered.

The edge in her tone brought V'kyrri bolt upright. "The Councils know about her and are pushing you to prosecute her. What are you fishing for here?"

"The Councils know and want her head on the Royal Seal in the middle of the council chamber floor," Eilod said, but she did not answer his question.

Heat flushed his system. He pressed his expression flat. "I wish them luck."

Finally, the queen shifted and looked away. "Thank you, Captain. Dismissed."

"Eilod, you're intimately familiar with the price and perils of your position." For a split second, Eilod's expression fell, leaving him short of breath. What wasn't she telling him? "Edie needs your help."

She met his eye for several seconds, her breath suspended. Her gaze turned inward, then she smiled the bland, meaningless smile she employed when dealing with her Councils. "We are due in a critical council meeting within the hour to discuss unholy alliances, Captain. I require your presence. I'll trust you to convince Edie and her comrades to join us."

Space broke open behind his sternum, taking his breath. He had to lever himself to standing before he could bow to his monarch. "By your leave, Your Majesty."

"Dismissed, Brother-of-My-Heart."

Chapter Twenty-Nine

When V'kyrri entered the medi-bay, Raj glanced up from sealing himself into a clean suit. "Captain. Good. Eilod summoned the entire command structure of the planet as far as I can tell. Two are symptomatic. You're here for Edie?"

"She still in there?" V'k indicated the isolation unit air lock.

"Three more minutes."

"I've got your systems check." V'kyrri examined the panel on Raj's back.

"Thanks. We'll bring the sick into isolation via the outer door," Raj said. "Once Edie clears the airlock, seal it, and do not look back."

"Understood. Your systems are green. Suit air on standby."

"Good to have you back, V'kyrri." Raj picked up his kit and walked out the door.

V'kyrri peered through the airlock porthole. The door on the other side opened.

Edie slipped in and glanced at the porthole. Her gaze met his.

Even though an airlock and a clean suit stood between them, the faint sweet, musk smell of sun-warmed Cullal flowers tickled his memory. Edie would forever be comingled with his scent memory of his first taste of freedom. He started the decontamination and pressurization routine.

Some trick of the light penetrated both the ballistic glass in the airlock porthole and Edie's faceplate. It gave him a clear view of the pucker between her brows.

He edged close to her surface thoughts, warmed by the glint and flare of sparks rising and falling. Fireworks? Or magma?

The collision of images made him smile until a dull knife shoved into his left eyebrow. Not his headache. Edie's.

The airlock pressurized. Decontamination protocols cycled.

She turned a complete circle in the sterilizing chem spray.

Ice trailed her spine, and by extension, his. She wrestled it away by turning it around, examining it. He squinted, trying to pry meaning from thoughts not his own. A brief, numbing flash of her remembered past and the chambers used to murder people during the war, and then she was cataloguing the differences. Decontamination chemicals smelled sharper. Medicinal. Lacking the underlying stench of death.

The spray shut off. She stood still with eyes twisted shut, her emotions bubbling beneath the surface. Very much a volcanic image.

Guilt seized him. He shouldn't be eavesdropping on the whirl of Edie's mental processes like this. Yet he couldn't pull the plug. He was violating her privacy, breeching every personal and professional ethic he professed to hold sacred. Again. Above all, he couldn't leave her mired in old fear.

"*You're safe,*" he whispered into her head.

Edie flinched. Sharp pain skewered his chest. *Her*

pain. In response to his assurance. It took his breath.

The drying cycle whirred to life.

Images struck from Edie's brain into his. Two caught. One, Edie's memory of a younger Tiimetes Calamae, and the other of V'kyrri, crouched beside her in a Chekydran-infested cave.

Her memory flashed to the rock fall that had nearly crushed her. Only this time, her view of it didn't include tons of stone. It was Tiimetes, her past, and V'kyrri, her present that squashed her.

V'kyrri eased shut the door to Edie's awareness and closed his eyes, absorbing the wound.

The airlock dinged.

Forcing his eyes open, he avoided Edie's gaze by hunching over the controls. Scan data flashed green. No stray pathogens. With shaking hands, he opened the airlock door.

She exited.

Duty first, no matter how he ached to scoop Edie into his arms. V'kyrri tapped his badge. "Isolation is clear. Airlock sealed and set."

"Acknowledged," Raj answered.

V'kyrri closed the channel and turned to assist Edie. She'd already yanked off her faceplate and hood. She didn't have on her SEM. Her gaze lifted from his lips to meet his eye as he finished with Raj.

Behold the almighty telepath. He could summon rescuers from across the galaxy. He could infiltrate interrogation subjects' minds so they never realized he'd been there, and he couldn't think where to begin with the woman who held his heart.

Twelve Gods.

"Are you all right?" he blurted.

"No."

He flushed hot. His breath suspended.

"I don't know what all right looks like anymore," she said, yanking at gloves that wouldn't give.

"Here," he said, circling her to open the seal at her back. "*Much easier to get out this way.*"

"Thanks. Get out of my head. You're hurting me."

"*What*?"

"Knock it off," she yelled, yanking free of the suit and spinning to face him, eyes squinted, and hands held up as if to ward him off. No. Her fingers crooked in front of her forehead. 'Headache' in her language. What the Three Hells?

He stared at her. "What happened?"

Her laugh raised the hair at the back of his neck. She flung her arms wide. "What hasn't? A man I imagined I once loved is dying and decided to confess that he'd seduced me to get close enough to destroy me out of professional jealousy."

Sweet as the grebnol fruit candy she'd once given him, confidence and hope surged into V'kyrri's chest. He took her hands. "What about your second love?"

Her gaze jerked to his. She pulled in a breath like the start of a sob and held it while color rose in her cheeks. She didn't pull free. "I've fallen for someone I can't have."

"Why not?"

"Because it's not real. I was a naïve, gullible kid starving for affection. Tii took advantage of it. You did, too. Even if I am more idiot than kid, now."

"I am not Tiimetes Calamae."

"No, thank the Gods, you are not," she said. "But you are second-in-command of the baxt'kal Murbaasch

Tu. When you crashed, I'd just lost my team, the only analog for family I had, twisted and violent as it may have been. I was vulnerable. You took advantage."

He drew breath.

She cut him off with a wave. "Solid tactics. I'd have done the same. I'd like to think I'd have helped without you turning attraction against me, but I had a good time. I can't complain, can I?"

Her voice caught, and her eyes reddened.

He wrapped his arms around her.

She shrugged. "I'm playing out old trauma. Ulcerating for the family I lost all those years ago. I fell for the first guy I'd stumbled across who offered a modicum of kindness after I'd been orphaned. Just like Tiimetes. And just like him, you had an ulterior motive. At least you weren't out to kill me."

She uttered a desiccated husk of a laugh. "I've made myself sound like a featherless baby gipstal imprinting on the first living thing to feed me slug wasp eggs when I hatched."

"I am the second-in-command of the Murbaasch Tu," he rasped drawing away so she could read what he said. His pulse beat so hard the words would barely sneak past. "I used you. At first. Then, by all the Gods, Edie, I don't know when or how it happened—when you put the control for blowing up my ship in my hand, or when you found out I was a telepath, and it terrified you. But you fought fear because you hated hurting me based on what I was…"

"Have you been listening to every private thought I've had since?" she shrilled.

"No." He rubbed a shaking hand down his burning eyes. "No. I couldn't. My job would have been much easier if I could have."

She snorted. "You have no idea we're connected, do you?"

He jerked back. "That's not—I haven't—Twelve Gods, Edie, I wouldn't do that to anyone, much less you."

She canted her head, brow furrowed as if she couldn't comprehend his anger.

"It's a gross moral violation to force a connection on someone without consent. I'd have known. And that would make me no better than…"

She covered his mouth with her hand.

His system lit brighter than one of Edie's explosions. Her eyes shone. Crinkles appeared at the corners. To his everlasting regret, she removed her hand and asked. "What's it take to establish connection with someone?"

"Consent." He stressed the word. "Conscious effort over time."

"Like you being injured, and us forced to work together while running for our lives? Raj did a brain scan. I'm taking active damage because you're here." She tapped her forehead.

He gaped, shook his head. "I'm healed. The Chekydran-ki healed me."

"Can they heal grief you haven't let yourself process? That's the problem." She shrugged. "Do you know, I'm half-expecting you to tell me you were ordered to install the connection as much to keep tabs on the monster as to have the means to destroy me if necessary?"

The matter-of-fact statement rocked V'kyrri. Some second-in-command spy he made. It's precisely what he *should* have done. Or at least thought of to influence his unpredictable ally. Not that he'd have been capable of forging a connection with anyone or anything. Not when he'd needed it most.

"Don't pretend those hours of mental silence since Tii collapsed weren't a direct effort to drive me to put on a SEM. Addicts are easily controlled, don't you find? It's why Tii addicted me to the SEM in the first place. Do your people really think the resistance and Intcom taught me nothing? Or that I haven't white knuckled my way through withdrawal before?"

"Edie," he growled. "You're—"

His com badge trilled. Eilod's code. He closed his eyes and opened the channel. "V'kyrri."

"We need you."

He needed time no one had. He opened gritty eyes on the challenging light in Edie's eyes. "Acknowledged."

Longing to touch her physically and mentally, he instead curled his fingers into his palms. "I was ordered to let you use the SEM. It occurs to me I was not ordered not to tell you that I was. I swear on my mother's life, Edie. If we're connected, I never meant it, and I will sever it when we have the time and medical facilities for it."

"Six marks on approach to Her Majesty's shuttle." She tapped a finger against his chest. "You'd best ask for consent on that, mister. You call me Edie when you want to play friends and lovers. You call me Firestorm when you want me to act in the interests of the empire. Your commanders call me by my given name when they want to remind me I'm nothing but a little farm girl who turned into someone they want dead unless she can be yoked. Do you know why I'm a monster?"

"You aren't, and we're needed in council."

"I am." Acceptance rang in the words. "Because I am all those things. I am the farm girl who was forced to grow the will and discipline to become one of the most feared and destructive resistance fighters the empire has ever seen. Gods help me, I can't get past being proud of that. Once it became clear it wouldn't save my world, I turned destruction to the protection of the innocent and helpless. At first it was from the Claugh. Now it's Chekydran."

"You are what the invasion of your world made you."

"Yes, I am. You've spent a lot of effort convincing me the Claugh weren't what I remembered," she said. "It's been an effective performance. You might want to manage your commanders, because they are blowing your hard work to the lowest level of all Three Hells."

Headache easing, Edie strode out of the *Sen Ekir* into the big room she and V'kyrri first entered several hours, that felt like a lifetime, ago.

An enormous table occupied one end of the bay. Eilod sat with Turrel to her right. The entire crew of the *Sen Ekir* occupied chairs on the queen's left, as did holograms of Captain Idylle and Admiral Seaghdh. A row of people dressed in gray-and-crimson uniforms filled the seats along the right.

Nol Jakze's military leadership.

Edie's hackles went up. Resistance fighters and the cadre of Nol Jakze soldiers Edie seemed to have acquired after arresting Tii trooped into the bay. There were no chairs for them.

Prickles of sensual awareness informed her V'kyrri

had come in behind her. She clenched her fists, wanting to go on being angry with him, but she couldn't. He hadn't crash-landed on purpose. Yes, he'd used her to help his people. She'd volunteered.

Time to grow up and accept responsibility for her own mess. Edie loosed a slow stream of air.

"Captain V'kyrri, Edie," Eilod said. "Please be seated."

Edie balked. No chairs for her people, no chair for her. No way to understand the room without a SEM. Eying Admiral Seaghdh, she put the lenses into place and switched the unit on.

The pleasant mask he'd made of his expression changed not a whit, but she imagined triumph glittered in his holographic eyes. V'kyrri took position beside Admiral Seaghdh's hologram. Second-in-command. Just in case she'd baxt'kal missed the message.

Eilod eyed the last empty chair at the table, then Edie. Her gaze went past Edie's left shoulder and the crinkles between her brows cleared. She met Edie's eye again and offered a faint, short-lived smile.

Edie blinked. Approval. Had that been approval?

Eilod rose. By way of introduction, she named everyone at the table. The young queen then turned to Edie. "This is Edie. I trust most of us are familiar with her companions."

"Aged farmers pretending they're still resistance fighters, Your Majesty?" one of the generals sneered.

"I see nothing but grizzled white hairs on your fat head, old man," Edie snapped aloud and in sign.

"You…" The old man tried to shove himself to his feet. His paunch snagged on the table.

"General Gliwt, as you were," Seaghdh said. He

glanced at Edie. Face to holographic face with the infamous Aurnoch Riorjchin. She steeled herself, but he merely said, "We're in the same room for reasons surpassing old enmity."

Edie capped her simmering temper.

"Doctors Idylle and Faraheed have a vaccination plan," Eilod said.

Linnaeus Idylle leaned into the table. "Between the *Dagger* and the *Sen Ekir*, we can make a good start at vaccination. Alexandria has requested the assistance of the *Balykkal*. They are en route. They're bringing more vaccine and will begin evacuation."

Edie jolted. "Evacuation? Has no one told you what Nol Jakze means? Promised Land. From the ancient religious texts that sent my ancestors to the stars. It means Promised Land. You aren't going to need that prowler for evac."

Eilod closed her eyes.

"We'll force the issue if we have to," said one of the generals Edie didn't know. "We swore oaths to protect Nol Jakze. Even if that means rounding up—"

"You'd violate the most sacred tenets of the faith you swore to protect," the admiral seated beside the speaker barked. "You've always been a coward, Kartz."

"My troops come home alive," Kartz snarled.

"As you were," Seaghdh thundered. "Doctors?"

Raj shifted. "Vaccination is our first and last defense. Without it, no one can evacuate. Without evacuation, no one will remain to fight Chekydran-hiin. Therefore, we need rapid, world-wide distribution. Models indicate it's the best chance for the greatest number of people. We need a plan and the resources for distributing vaccine to rural and remote communities."

"Lift quarantine," one of the generals said aloud. "We'll direct people to come to the major cities."

Edie translated.

"That leaves farmers to die," Turrel protested.

"He's right," Jayleia said. "We can't afford the travel delays, and it penalizes rural communities. Farmers won't leave their farms until people begin getting sick and it'll be too late for vaccine to help, anyway."

"Does administering vaccine require medical knowledge?" Edie asked aloud and in sign.

Raj and Dr. Idylle shook their heads.

As a group, the generals folded their hands on the table and patently did not turn their gazes to Edie the way everyone else did. She allowed herself a tiny mean smile. *Mutual, you Carozziel slime-bats*. She caught the glance V'kyrri traded with Admiral Seaghdh, who studied the tableau with a neutral eye.

If there was meaning or message in the look, Edie couldn't interpret it. Neat trap she'd walked into after reading V'kyrri the first half of the Tenets of Returning to Communion back in the medical bay. His superior officers deserved to hear their sins called out before them, too. Yet here they were, seemingly in earnest about not leaving anyone to die without at least trying.

She blew out a short, sharp breath.

"*Commit or hit the lanes*," Trente had said.

She angled so both Eilod and her former companions could see her. "Though our hearing guests have been rendered deaf, few of them know our language. Their accommodations are designed for speech. If you can speak aloud what you say in our language, by the laws of all we hold sacred, let no one be left without understanding."

Resistance fighters and soldiers alike steepled and interlaced their fingers, agreeing.

Edie shifted her gaze to the table. Seaghdh and V'kyrri both sat ramrod straight, staring at her. She faltered.

Based on the shake in his shoulders, Turrel was laughing.

Eilod, eyes crinkled at the corners, nodded. "Please go on."

Suspecting she'd committed a grave error of protocol she'd never comprehend, Edie plunged ahead. "Some of us were taught spoken language. Some weren't. Taking deliberate advantage of someone's inability to understand is a grave sin in our culture. If one of my people doesn't speak aloud for you, please understand it is because they can't. We will translate as best we can. Lieutenant, would you translate for Her Majesty?"

The lieutenant saluted Eilod and took up position.

"Thank you, Edie. Lieutenant," the queen said. "First, my apologies for not being able to speak to you in your language. It is a situation I should have remedied long ago. Edie, you asked about vaccination. Do you have suggestions?"

"Call for volunteers to vaccinate everyone around them," Edie said.

En masse, Jonas, Gallena, Povora, and the rest of the resistance stepped forward.

"No." Edie shot them a look. "I need each of you to take a media outlet. Activate every resistance cell around the world that will answer. No travel. No breaking quarantine. We'll use those cells to give vaccinations and to recruit everyone around them to do the same."

"The volunteers should screen for symptoms before vaccinating," Dr. Idylle said. "Once symptoms have set in—"

"Can we agree not to put volunteers in the position of telling neighbors and loved ones they're doomed?" Edie interrupted.

Stillness settled.

"We are a pragmatic people, Altheas," Jonas said.

"Even though vaccine doses are precious, I agree with Edie on this," Eilod said. "Scatter our stores across the planet if we can find a way. Captain Idylle?"

"We'd need an armada of ships with teleport to get vaccine into every town and village."

"Teleport vaccine to the military bases you built," Edie said. "You can port in large cargo rather than melting your hull with thousands of little teleports. Between big freight teleports, dump excess heat while you position for the next teleport."

"Distribution?" Seaghdh rumbled.

"Planetary Defense Forces," Edie said. She ignored the line of generals in favor of the lieutenant. "There's still an Air Force, right? Tell me the bugs didn't destroy our in-atmosphere craft."

"No, ma'am, they didn't," the lieutenant said.

"That is MY command," General Kartz thundered. This time, she both spoke and signed. "You will not—"

"General Kartz." Admiral Seaghdh interrupted. "Go on, Edie."

"I'd need a supply officer. Secure warehouses on the flight lines. Volunteer pilots and ground crews—"

"I've pulled census numbers," Damen said.

Data scrolled down Edie's lenses. Based on that data, they'd ration out vaccine to as many areas as possible. "Fly vaccine into rural areas and establish vaccination centers to mirror the ones you're setting up in the cities."

"The pilots can't leave quarantine," Jayleia protested.

"The whole of the world is quarantine," Edie said.

Heads shook around the table.

"Pilots stay in their ships, then. Vaccines remain isolated in cargo and get dropped along with every field com array we can lay hands on. That will get us eyes across the planet. Pilots land only at bases to refuel and resupply. Base personnel institute clean protocols and maintain them until further notice."

"Your Majesty, this is outrageous. The Chekydran are on world. That they haven't yet attacked does not mean they won't. We cannot scatter our resources. We'll be defenseless," the sole admiral at the table protested.

Eilod, brow furrowed, returned to her seat and folded her hands before her. "The Chekydran-hiin are waiting for the plague to render us defenseless. However. I take your point. We're in an unknown situation with their mothership on the ground."

Edie froze. Hope tripped and fell. She caught the "here it comes" look Jonas shot her and wiped her expression clean. Perhaps these people didn't know or had forgotten how capable the resistance had once been at putting their plans into play despite official disapproval.

Edie suspected covert messages were already going out to other resistance cells. Lives were at stake. The lives of family and friends. The resistance wouldn't hesitate in the saving of those lives, even if it meant eventual civil war.

As if she'd triggered an explosive inside her own head, awareness burst over Edie. She'd said it herself. If the resistance put out a call for volunteers, people planet wide would flock to their cause. It would start with vaccinations. With saving lives.

It wouldn't end there.

The flames of possibility swirled within her, heady and potent. Terrifying.

Chapter Thirty

"Admiral Seaghdh," Eilod said, "build a task force. Get me options. Pull whatever data you and these leaders of Nol Jakze's forces deem necessary. We await your report. Let no one rest until a solution is found."

Seaghdh's hologram rose and bowed. "As you wish, Your Majesty. By your leave. Generals? Admiral? Through this door. We'll have every resource the *Dagger* can offer at our fingertips."

The cluster of uniforms shuffled to their feet. Several of them squared their shoulders and tugged uniform jackets straight. Only one of the generals, a woman who hadn't yet spoken, cast a glance over her shoulder at Edie. Doubt and tension clouded her furrowed brow.

Edie passed a frown to Povora who dipped her chin. She'd seen. The resistance could cultivate doubt. Especially if it meant turning even part of the military to their cause.

The door closed behind the last crimson and charcoal uniform.

Eilod pointed at Damen Sindrivik. "Secure their clearances. We cannot risk any of them having known about or been in cooperation with Governor Calamae's betrayal. Captain Idylle, please relay an encoded message to my Aurnoch Riorchjan. I want those people stripped of their secrets."

"Done," Ari said.

Edie sucked in a breath. Plans and schemes and visions of civil war collapsed. Her companions laughed. Admiration lit through Edie. Maybe V'kyrri was right. Edie suspected Eilod was a queen she could follow. Maybe not trust but follow. "You never intended for them to help."

Eilod settled in her chair. Her smile reached her eyes this time. "No. I didn't. I believe I'm beginning to see the bones of a workable plan. Execute it. Now. This is our window of opportunity. Do not screen for symptoms. That's a level of detail we can't afford. What more do you require?"

"Clearances for my people to begin leveling the kinds of orders they're about to start leveling," Edie said. "And your blessing."

Pride exploded through her, filling her chest to the point of taking her breath. It wasn't hers. She winced and glared at V'kyrri. "Stop it. I learned to play nice over the past ten years, okay?"

A smattering of laughter around the table.

"Major," Eilod said. "Coordinate clearances with Edie. Fit her personnel with adapted com devices and route all files through Captain Idylle."

"By your will," Major Sindrivik and Captain Idylle said in concert.

Eilod met Edie's eye. "Go."

Edie inclined her head and pinned the young lieutenant with a look. "Commandeer warehouses. Let's get the vaccine on the ground. As always, we are a volunteer fighting force. That doesn't change, not even for this. Remember that in your recruiting. Start with people you trust and the people they trust. Supply chain. Pilots. Ground crews."

The lieutenant saluted.

Edie's stomach summersaulted.

"Route all coms through the *Dagger*," Captain Idylle said. "Don't use planet-side assets at all. We have concerns about their integrity."

"Acknowledged. General Firestorm. Your Majesty. By your leave." The lieutenant strode out the door.

"Altheas." All eyes turned to Jonas. "Your people need to see you, Firestorm."

"When half of them think I murdered innocents?"

"You said you could prove you didn't," he countered. "Do it."

She frowned. "You want me to get up in front of holo-cameras and what?"

"Lay out the plans," he said. "Tell them the Claugh offer evacuation. Let us at least send the children to safety once they've been vaccinated."

"I'm not—"

"Altheas. Truth is the first obligation you owe the gods…and your people."

Right. Page one, line one of the Tenets of Returning to Communion, as read to her by her former commander. Edie swallowed the boulder of her fears. *Not good enough. Not pious enough. Not Nol Jakzian enough.* She glanced at V'kyrri and lifted an eyebrow. He looked at Eilod, so Edie did, too.

The queen met her eye. "Work with Major Sindrivik to compile the files you need to prove your innocence. Quickly."

Jonas, Gallena, and Povora trailed Edie to the table as if dragged in her wake. They sat, clustered around Pietre and Damen Sindrivik. Edie detected no disgust or contempt in their faces while she laid out the challenge of breaking into ten-year-old file stores, if they still existed. Instead, as she talked, a faint, intrigued smile grew on Damen's face.

"You don't know the passcode," he surmised.

"Still cute and smart," she said.

The grin he flashed lifted her spirit. He remembered the help she'd given him and Jayleia on Silver City.

She sighed. "All I have is where this stuff got stashed after the takeover. It's possible someone wised up and deleted everything."

"Here," he said, rolling out files on her handheld. "The jobs attributed to you after the treaty."

If he wasn't going to say *surrender*, neither would she. She watched the files while Damen combed data stores. In every single one, Tiimetes not only destroyed a target, he'd blown out surrounding structures. So not her style. Was this kind of sloppy work what people thought of her?

"Is this what you're looking for?" Damen asked.

She cleared her SEM screen.

Data streamed before her, all encoded with old Nol Jakze resistance encryptions. It startled her to find she could still read them after a decade or more. More. Definitely more.

She stabbed a finger at the scrolling data, stopping the flow. "That's the stuff."

Uneasiness made her hesitate. Stupid. It wasn't as if these people didn't already think the worst of her. Why should she feel bad for confirming their suspicions? Her gaze slid to V'kyrri.

She'd killed men and women wearing the same

uniform he did.

He covered her hand with his own. "What?"

She met his gaze and saw acceptance in his sea green eyes. Something sharp lodged in her breastbone.

"Nothing you can show us will change the fact that you saved my life and the lives of my crew when you didn't have to," he said. "Let's get on with saving your people. And let's get you off that SEM unless it's necessary. Damen?"

Sindrivik fiddled with his panel. The table before her lit with a replica of his panel. Tagrethian. A holo-field screen flicked to life before her.

Warmed, Edie shut down enhancement, but kept the lenses in place. She still needed to read what everyone said. She opened the files with the code reserved for Firestorm. Hitting play on the first one turned out to be the hardest. As soon as the surveillance footage rolled, it sucked her in.

The first showed a job she'd done on a cargo landing pad. Open air. Bad angle. Not at all comparable to the files claiming she'd blown up buildings, and transports with civilians inside.

She went fishing for jobs she'd done on Claugh barracks and weapons caches, reviewing a string of five, looking for the markers she remembered.

V'kyrri watched the holos opposite her, his face illuminated by the orange-red light of her flames. The sight had cold sweat breaking out on her body. She shut down the files and resisted the urge to swear in sign. Especially since she'd been foolish enough to teach V'kyrri what it meant. Instead, she created an aggregate of her explosions, then of the ones that weren't hers. She split the holo-screen and put the results side by side.

Frowning, she glanced at Eilod. Caring what the Claugh thought of her at this late date? She couldn't count many more ways to be ridiculous. Edie squared her shoulders and lifted her chin. "A bunch of explosions someone tried to lay at my feet aren't mine, but in the coming footage, they are. We were at war. Your soldiers died in the commission of their duty."

Eilod clasped her hands. The knuckles went white. "I understand."

"I wonder," Edie muttered. She hit play. "Zero point. Before detonation. Detonation." She stepped through the expanding fireballs a second at a time. "Maximum for mine. Advancing through to maximum for my imposter."

"Altheas…" Jonas rasped.

"I know."

The queen looked between them, one eyebrow lifted.

"He was showing off, using too much power to get the job done," Edie said. "Wasting resources and doing incredible collateral damage."

"Did he confess?" Jonas demanded.

"I don't give a damn about the redemption of his soul, but yes," Edie said.

Eilod's shoulders slumped. "Governor Calamae."

"I do seem to bring out the worst in people," Edie said.

Gallena snorted.

"We need the rest of your files," Pietre said to Edie.

Damen met her eye. "We'll run chemical analysis on the fireballs. It should have been done long ago."

"My work will fall within a certain chemical profile," Edie said. "These will fall into another. Yes."

"It is enough, both for your people and for my councils," Eilod said.

"Your Majesty." Jonas pushed to his feet. "If you'll excuse us. We're off to set up a circus." He clapped Edie on the back. "Thirty minutes. General. Bring the pretty sight bytes."

The rest of the resistance pinned eyes to Jonas. "Drum up a crowd. Gallena. Povora. I don't care if you have to threaten the news people. Get them there. I'm on equipment."

They filtered out of the bay. Edie marveled. Save for the graying hair, old habits clicked into place as if the decade hadn't passed. The only difference was she'd inexplicably graduated from being one of the youngest and least experienced faces in the crowd.

The queen straightened. "Captain Idylle?"

"Princess Len af Baan in seat five. Director Durante in seat two, Your Majesty," Ari Idylle said. "Admiral Seaghdh—"

"Is otherwise occupied," the queen said, her tone forbidding. "Everything my beloved cousin and heir-apparent has to say on the coming subjects has already been said in private. At volume."

Edie turned sensory enhancement back on. Chances were good she'd need more information than what was being said.

A flicker of light and Director Durante sat in Admiral Seaghdh's empty seat at Eilod's left hand. A couple of chairs left of Ari, the hologram of a sharp-faced woman encased in intricate golden robes appeared.

"Your Majesty," the princess in gold robes said.

"Aunt Len. Thank you for coming." Eilod rose. "In response to action initiated within this company, Tagreth Federated declared martial law some days ago. Despite our petition for aid against the Chekydran-hiin incursion, they are withdrawing troops from the front."

"We assume the Balykrat Accords are no more," the princess said, naming the treaty of mutual cooperation and protection TFC and the Claugh had signed a century ago.

It shouldn't have surprised Edie. Not after the group baxt'k the spawn of Myallki bitches within TFC had created with their purges and power grabs. But it did. "They really think the Chekydran won't steamroll them? I'm glad I'm out. Saves me the trouble of having to quit. I can't work for stupid."

"Durgot is a petty tyrant burdened by delusions of competence." Eilod bit out as she sat.

"I don't care how Durgot came to power or why he's still there merrily leading TFC down a suicidal path," Edie said. "How do we take him out, and would it benefit us anything if we did?"

"I like her," Turrel said.

"As uncomfortable as I am with Edie's blunt assessment," Durante said, "we had a similar goal when we triggered the action that dismantled a significant portion of Durgot's network."

"It missed him," Turrel rumbled.

"Yes," the director said. "Though he declared martial law in response, he's vulnerable. Exposed. You and Edie want him dead, Colonel, understandably. Would you settle for him remanded to an Intcom black box?"

"You could do this?" Eilod's sharp question sliced everyone to stillness.

"I have resources still in place," Durante said, "but no ability to get assets close to Durgot."

"Even though the empire would benefit by Durgot's ouster," the princess said, "the Claugh nib Dovyyth cannot afford to commit forces. Nor, politically speaking, can Her Majesty authorize the use of Murbaasch Tu agents to get close to the madman. The weight of regime change falls to the citizens of Tagreth Federated."

Because a Claugh led coup would look like the power grab to justify Durgot's worst, most erroneous points.

"Co-opt someone already close to Durgot," Edie said.

"We've covered the president's former advisor, Ildri Bynovan, Edie," Durante said. "Assuming she's who you had in mind. She's unreachable. I've bent considerable influence on her."

"She is the leverage you need," Edie pressed. "Before I bailed, I got word he'd accused her of being in on the coup attempt. He's shipped her to the front lines. Without back-up, pulling her out of that kind of no-win might be enough to turn her."

"You transport?" Turrel demanded.

"Nope," Edie said. "She wouldn't have been hung out to dry had it been me. I can no longer do any good inside the mess Durgot has made of TFC."

"I can," Turrel interrupted.

Silence fell on the room.

Edie wrinkled her brow. "One of the last surviving Shlovkur natives is going to mount a one-man op inside

TFC lines? Can I paint the target on your admittedly nice ass?"

"Hey, now," V'kyrri protested.

"Yours is nicer," she crooned, patting his hand.

Laughter danced fractals down her SEM. V'kyrri met her gaze. She fell into the ocean of his eyes, only this ocean had been heated to boiling. Fluid heat scorched her core. She couldn't get her breath.

"Any clue what Durgot's holding over her?" Turrel asked.

Forcing her attention back to the conversation, Edie shook her head. "Nope."

"Kirthin—" Eilod began.

"I want him," Turrel said. "We've got him dead to rights on genocide."

Edie pulled data from her stores aboard *t'Achreides-myn.*

"You'll be a target the minute you hit the buffer," Ari warned.

"It's a simple extraction," Turrel countered. "I want Durgot, but I can't walk into the council tower and start shooting. I'll recover Bynovan. Then it's a matter of turning or breaking her. Her choice."

"She's a Priestess of the Twelve. Good luck with that last one." Edie turned her handheld for Turrel to see. "Give me a link. I'll transfer the data I have on her, including the edge of the known systems shithole where he shipped her. You'll have to get there before he gets her killed."

"That's the plan."

"Director. Your Highness," Eilod said. "Assessment."

Durante tipped his head. "Extraction as the first

phase of a long game? Gain outweighs the risk."

"Without assessments of the politicians waiting to fill the power void should the long game succeed," the princess said, "I cannot judge."

"With Her Majesty's and the admiral's permission, Your Highness," V'kyrri said. "I will provide intel to that end."

"Granted," Eilod said.

"Cut the chatter and give me the go," Turrel demanded.

"Not without a link," Ari said.

"We don't have time," Turrel said. "The key to my world's murderer is out there in the middle of a firefight."

"Not without a link." Eilod, Ari, and V'kyrri said in unison.

"Fine," Turrel shouted.

V'kyrri grinned.

"Your Majesty? By your leave?" Turrel asked.

The man's diffident posture and the softer sine wave of his voice set Edie back.

"Send the colonel to a pickup point I will trans to a secure location of your choosing," Director Durante said, working a panel before him. "The CRU will provide transport and a cover team. We can at least get you in, Colonel."

Trouble clouded Eilod's brow, but she nodded at Captain Idylle who went to work securing the information Durante offered.

"Single objective, Kirthin. Find the counsellor and return to us." Eilod rose. "Colonel Turrel."

Turrel went to one knee before her, took her hand in both of his, and then touched his forehead to the back of her hand.

"You are vital to us," Eilod said. "Remember that in all you do."

He looked up at her, his expression the softest Edie had ever seen it. For that split second, Colonel Kirthin Turrel, eyes alight and a fond smile on his lips, was breathtaking. "No unnecessary risks. I got a score to settle."

No give at all in him.

"Ildri Bynovan is a nice gal, and I like her," Edie said before she could weigh the wisdom of saying anything at all. "Whatever your plan, Colonel, factor into it that she's been played by a madman for the past four years. You think you're a hard ass, but you're sane."

He shot her a calculating look and rose. "I'll keep it in mind. Don't get yourself killed, Edie."

V'kyrri met Turrel at the end of the table. He clapped the colonel on the back. The two strode out of the conference room.

Edie massaged the ache gathering at the base of her skull.

"Our alliances have fallen one by one," Eilod said. "Leaving us to stand alone in the face of the storm. It is time we accept the alliance offered by the Chekydran-ki."

"No."

The raw fear in the twisted faces around the table rocked Edie. Though she'd benefited by contact with the Chekydran-ki, even her stomach turned over the notion of allying with them.

"I have been in contact with the newly elected head of the United Mining and Ore Processing Guild,"

Durante said. “We aren’t entirely without allies.”

“The new guild master does not control the military that destroyed the *Queen’s Rhapsody*,” Eilod countered.

“No,” Durante said. “He doesn’t.”

“The UMOPG’s military forces are down,” Edie said, “but not out. We didn’t have the bandwidth to get every ship. Give me a team after we’re sorted here, I’d fix it for you.”

Eilod’s smile overtook her entire countenance.

Chapter Thirty-One

"Your Majesty, you are advocating alliances that go against everything we stand for," Princess Len, clothed in gold, said, "and I fear what we are becoming."

Sobering, Eilod lifted her fingers in invitation for her aunt to continue.

The holographic woman shot Edie a dagger disguised as a glance. "We've been forced to abandon too many of our principles in the name of winning this war. Justice. Rightness. Fairness. We've embraced things we know are evil in the name of defeating an enemy. Such things have compromised us to the point that I fear our enemy has so changed who we are as a people that they have already won."

Edie rolled her eyes.

"I'm to countenance the deaths of millions in the name of what?" Eilod asked. "Some halcyon notion of what the empire is meant to be?"

"In the name of principles upon which the empire was founded. Principles carved into the base of the royal throne," the princess said, tapping a finger against the table before her at each point.

"If we lose this war for want of allies simply because they don't look like we do, there will be no empire. Nor will there be citizens who survive to care," Eilod countered. "We're Claugh. We adapt. We change.

Above all, we grow. It is time we grow beyond our prejudices."

"You cannot do this." The princess's countenance twisted. "The councils—"

"They have a plan." Eilod clenched her fists atop the table. Her face reddened. "The Ki have a plan to end the war. No treaties. No compromises. No more of our people would have to die. It comes days too late for Nol Jakze, but I will accept the alliance. In full."

Captain Idylle sat bolt upright, her eyes wide, and tension in every line of her taut expression.

"You will destroy your rule," the princess protested.

"If it saves even one life, it will have been worth it," Eilod responded. "An empire that cannot put the good of the people before the interests and prejudices of the government doesn't deserve to survive."

"How long will your people survive without the government?" Princess Len demanded. "Eilod. My dear brother's child. Stop. Think. Bring the matter before your councils—"

"Again? To what purpose? With every moment's delay, people die," Eilod said. "I need a location suitable for formalizing the agreements."

"What agreements?" The princess shoved to her feet. "Your Majesty. What agreements?"

"Suggestions for a secure—"

"Lunar ag platform?" Edie ventured. It was where she'd found a buoy for V'kyrri to program. "Deserted. Still in good condition. All systems operational. It won't be pretty, but it's big enough for the kind of party you want to throw."

"This is—" the princess began. Her hologram

winked out.

Damen started and leaned into his panel. "Connection lost. Trying to raise Claughwyth Council Complex."

"Lt. Aklasin," Captain Idylle said over her right shoulder. "Get me a line to the admiralty."

"No response," Damen said.

Captain Idylle's brows lowered. "Seaghdh. Situation."

The admiral winked into the same chair as Director Durante's hologram. The light streams flared. Damen worked his panel and the Director shifted to Ari's right.

"Pull the specs on the lunar platform," Eilod said to Sindrivik. To Ari she said, "Find out what's happened."

"Very convenient loss of communication," Durante noted.

"Very," Ari echoed.

"Edie? A moment?" Eilod gestured away from the table.

Stiffening her spine, Edie followed the younger woman to the other end of the bay. She dialed enhancement way up. Not only had she not yet learned to read Eilod, she suspected she needed access to every nuance of what the queen had to say.

"We'll require guards for the treaty signing," Eilod said as if to the wall. She did not want the contents of their conversation known.

"Guards you can't pull from the *Dagger* without exposing them to plague," Edie murmured, tucking hands behind her back to keep from signing as she spoke.

"Precisely. I can't trust the former governor's military," Eilod said. "I can trust you and the resistance, if not with my life, then with the lives of your people."

"You're here putting your life on the line for our people," Edie said. "You're safe with us. Careful. Next we recruit and convert you."

Eilod laughed. "I'd be honored."

"Volunteer force," Edie said. "I have to ask."

"Understood."

Edie studied Eilod, then, paying strict attention to the audio levels on her SEM so as not to alert anyone else within hearing distance, said, "You know your life is in danger, then."

Eying Edie, Eilod turned to assess the room with a glance before settling a bland smile upon her face as if Edie had commented on the weather.

"My source brought the intel to V'kyrri. Not to me," Edie said. "I left it to your officers to handle. But this conversation over alliance with the Ki makes it stark. Someone you trust is plotting your assassination."

"Do you distrust my captain that you bring this information to me?"

"I trust your captain to sacrifice his life and his sanity to protect you. I trust him to have already worked up everything he could find on the source and has taken it to your Aurnoch Riorchjan."

Eilod's smile twisted her lips but didn't ease the tension around her eyes. "Seaghdh and V'kyrri have protective streaks. I gather they've decided not to burden me with this information. Thank you. When we've settled this situation with the Chekydran-hiin, Nol Jakze will need a governor. I'd like you to consider stepping into the role."

Edie gaped.

"I never expected to find Firestorm alive. When it

became plain you were, I expected you to be a self-aggrandizing, selfish child interested only in yourself. You've proven me, and everyone who believed they had your measure, wrong. No one could have anticipated your commitment to service."

"Does no one read our holy books?" Edie muttered.

Eilod smiled. "You're out of communion."

Edie's chest went hot. She had to clear her throat before saying, "I have a lot of amends to make before I can join my parents in paradise."

" 'The only path to redemption runs through service,' " Eilod said, quoting the Tenets of Returning to Communion. "You'll never regret serving your people." The queen's expression softened.

Old, tangled, thorny sorrow in her voice reached through sensory enhancement, enclosing Edie in such a tight grip she couldn't breathe. Her parents' faces awash in flames filled her internal landscape. She gasped at the hurt and recognized what Gallena had long wanted Edie to acknowledge. Someone else's pain.

"You quote the Tenets of the faith to me while you've strapped a bandage across the gaping hole in your soul?" For no good reason, Rhydian Trente's face filled Edie's internal view. She sucked in a sharp breath. *Of course*. "Sorry, but whatever—or whoever—you gave up for your duty—"

"Thank you, Edie."

"No. I won't let it go. You're bleeding over whoever you gave up for duty. Service hasn't been enough. Now you're driving a wedge between V'kyrri and me and trying to get me to embrace blatant manipulation," Edie said. "I won't."

"Neither will V'kyrri?" Eilod's bitterness cracked straight through Edie's system setting her pulse knocking against her bones.

"I don't presume to speak for him," Edie countered. "He'll choose. It's his right."

Eilod held her eye. Then in a flash, every hint of emotion vanished, swallowed by the competent, astute mask she pulled across the vulnerability.

The hairs at the back of Edie's neck stirred. Which part of what she'd experienced had been real? She'd assumed the pain because who wanted that to show? Or was she guilty of judging another culture from within the mores of her own?

"Time to deliver you to your people," Eilod said, reaching into a pocket.

The phrasing raised Edie's eyebrows.

"Keep this hidden until after your speech," the queen said, presenting Edie with a ship's badge. "If your people decline to guard the treaty site, you may return it to me."

Edie tucked the device away.

Eilod activated the badge of the royal house that adorned the left side of her green and gold jacket. "Captain V'kyrri."

"V'kyrri."

Edie's SEM tagged the reply with his name. Warmth tingled every nerve fiber.

"Report to the bay when you're done there, Captain. I have a new assignment for you to handle a delicate political situation involving a native military leader."

He groaned. "What did I do to deserve that?"

"You handle dignitaries well, Captain," Eilod said.

"I have a general in need of a bodyguard."

Edie's gut kicked. The thought had never crossed her mind. It should have. Plenty of Nol Jakze's erstwhile military personnel were about to have all kinds of reason to want her dead.

"Bodyguard? If I get to handle that general," V'kyrri said, "I'm all in."

Edie flushed hot. "Thanks."

"We're done here," he said. "Raj and Dr. Idylle insisted on a complete medical scan before releasing Turrel to Director Durante. I am en route to your location."

****

V'kyrri wouldn't let her change clothes. When they took the argument to Jonas, the traitor sided with the Claugh.

"I look like—"

"Exactly what you are…a farm girl turned resistance fighter, turned mercenary who returned to the fold," V'kyrri said.

"So to speak," Jonas added, the corners of his eyes crinkled.

"My hair." She'd pulled it into a ponytail at some point. She barely even recalled doing it.

"Leave it," Jonas instructed. "It may not be part of the teaching, but it is a clear message that you're taken."

V'kyrri lit in triumph.

"It says you're devoted to a cause, not to any one person. It's a message the people need to see—that you're devoted to them and to their well-being."

The light of V'kyrri's smile dimmed.

Edie's chest tightened.

"It's time." Tension gathered at the corners of V'kyrri's eyes.

The square teemed with people. Jonas had set up recording equipment, including a prompt screen, pointed at the steps of a church.

Edie's confidence faltered as she scanned the crowd. "I can't do this."

"What is your problem?" Gallena demanded. "You deliberately walk into danger for a living."

"To blow things up," Edie said. "I know how to do that. I have no idea how to do this."

V'kyrri cupped her shoulders. "Edie. Listen. No, sorry. Look. Breathe. You made notes. This doesn't have to be elegant or pretty. These people need to know what's going on. That's it. You're performing a service. They're frightened, and while Her Majesty's teams have made certain there's been no lack of information, we haven't had a solid plan of action until now. Focus on that."

Action. Plan. "Yes. I can do that."

Jonas leaned in. "Want an introduction?"

"No standing on ceremony. Let's get this done." She took off her SEM.

Edie climbed the steps to stand on the x someone had thoughtfully marked. Gallena and Povora stood at either shoulder a step behind. V'kyrri remained off to the side, his gaze scanning the crowd. Reading them? Sweeping for assassins? There was a comforting thought.

The throng stilled. All eyes turned to her.

Edie quelled.

Hands throughout the crowd whispered, "Firestorm."

Her hands shook. She didn't know where to start. Or how. "By now, you've seen the broadcasts. Nol Jakze has come under attack by the Chekydran-hiin. If you don't know that distinction, ask a neighbor who does, or find a media kiosk. The Hiin seeded plague on world. There is a vaccine. If it's given in time, you can survive. We need volunteers to administer it. Anyone can give the vaccination, but time is of the essence. Get vaccinated, then begin vaccinating everyone you can reach. Ask them to vaccinate everyone they can reach.

"We've put out a call for pilots. We're flying vaccine around the world, cargo dropping doses into remote and rural communities. If you are a pilot who would like to volunteer to save the lives of your people, report to the gates there." Edie pointed at the holding pen before the *Sen Ekir*.

"A processing center?" an older man in a business suit asked, his face twisted with scorn underpinned by old terror. "You want us to walk into a processing center?"

"Decontamination," Edie said. "Been through it twice myself, and I'll walk back through again when we're done here."

"They could change it to kill anytime they wanted."

"Yes, they could. Given who and what I am, if anyone here ought to be afraid to die at the hands of the Claugh, it should be me. What have you done that you're afraid to die?"

He pulled himself upright. "I have cleansed my sins in communion with the church. You can't pretend people haven't disappeared into that jail and never emerged."

"It is a holding pen for people who break or attempt to break quarantine. Most of them were vaccinated and released. Those who remain are already sick. They're in medical, being treated. If you are immediate family, you may present yourself to the sergeant at the gate. You'll be allowed to visit."

A blinking message lit her prompt screen. She couldn't afford to glance away. Not when she needed to read the crowd.

Again, hands fluttered. Edie caught snippets of what people said. "Ill." "Visit." "Lie?" "Truth?" "Killed my mother."

"I never killed civilians," Edie said. "I left world after the surrender. Some of you knew me as Altheas Drake. Most of you knew me as Firestorm. I fought the Claugh until the very end of the war. Then I vanished and, in my absence, someone tried to make it look as if I were perpetrating terror attacks against our people. The Claugh are investigating. They've released old security cam footage of my work set against the work of the person trying to frame me. It's been distributed to the media outlets. You can see and judge the differences for yourselves."

She scanned the message blinking on the prompter and faltered. Her shoulders slumped.

"Who?" a woman sign-shouted from mid-crowd. "Who murdered my family in the Gorbayon Concert Hall?"

"I am sorry. That investigation is still underway," Edie said. "I have been informed that it is my sad duty to relay that Governor Tiimetes Calamae has died. May judgement be merciful."

"May judgement be merciful," the crowd

responded in unison.

Edie closed burning eyes. It wasn't sadness or a sense of loss as much as registering at long last what she'd never actually had. She opened her eyes to face the crowd still hovering on the edge of uncertainty. She'd known what a bad idea this had been. She just hadn't been able to get anyone to see sense.

Jonas would have inspired assurance. All Edie could do was make everyone question everything they'd ever believed they'd known.

"You aren't going to lead prayers for his soul?" a young woman in front asked.

Edie snorted. "Of all people here, I think I'm least qualified to lead any kind of prayer. I'm going to opt for saving lives before saving souls. It's vital that you decide whether you trust me. Because once you and your children are vaccinated, you're eligible for evacuation."

Exclamations and denials erupted through the crowd.

"Evacuation? From what?"

"Chekydran," Edie said. "They've destroyed every village and settlement within one hundred kilometers of their position."

"They're building something."

"Yes, they are. Suggesting that they're setting up housekeeping," Edie said. "Or farming. I have no idea what they eat."

People recoiled.

"To them, we're nothing more than slug wasps," she said. "Pests to be poisoned and burned out so they can do whatever it is bugs do."

A man with his eyes red and swollen said, "They

aren't attacking us."

"Tell that to Rukstod Settlement and Nakuri Village," Edie said. "They aren't attacking because they expect us to die in their plague."

"We've been sick before. Besides, I've been vaccinated."

"The more people who survive this plague, the worse the attacks by the bugs will be. I need you to vaccinate everyone you can, and then I need you to evacuate," Edie said.

A rush of protests. "What? No. You're giving up without even trying? We need you. You fought for us once before."

"Yes, I did. When I was full of idealism and naiveté. When I thought I was fighting for freedom."

"You were. Why not now?"

"When the people I thought I'd been fighting for tried to murder me, my priorities shifted."

"Revenge?" an elderly woman with scars crisscrossing one side of her face said. "Is that what this is? You've become a coward."

"I've become a realist. Even if we kill every Chekydran on world right now, how many more will come? We cannot win this. I couldn't see that fifteen years ago. I can now."

"How could you? This is our home. Your home. The bones of your parents are buried here. The Claugh murdered your parents, and you're in bed with them. You're a heretic and a traitor."

Rage seized Edie's chest in a vise. "You throw those words at me when you're the ones who capitulated and surrendered. Do not speak *traitor* to me when you've lived fat and happy and content under

Claugh rule, benefitting from their schools and their indoctrination in customs that aren't ours. Someone reminded me not long ago that truth is the first obligation owed the gods."

Edie's hands shook as she said, "Everyone believes the Claugh killed my parents. They didn't."

Her breath locked hard and high in her chest. Her vision hazed, and she blinked to clear it to no effect. Instead, her mother's face filled Edie's sight, her smiling lips whispered, "*Lying to someone is rarely justified. Lying to yourself never is.*"

Edie sucked in a breath. It ripped open a jagged, burning wound down the inside of her breastbone. Eyes heating, she squared her shoulders, and tried again. "The Claugh didn't kill my parents. I did."

Stillness took the crowd.

V'kyrri reeled.

Edie didn't need to see him to know. Agony and shock sliced into her through the connection he'd sworn couldn't exist.

Hands in the crowd before her moved, all saying the same thing. "Monster."

Chapter Thirty-Two

People at the edges of the crowd began slipping away. As if the entire mass of bodies had taken a collective step back, space opened between the foot of the stairs and the crowd.

"They begged to die," Edie forced her hands to say. "For three days the Claugh tortured them. At first, my mother and father begged them to stop. They'd do anything, say anything, if only they'd stop. They didn't. Then their pleas changed."

Edie gritted her teeth and looked away from the reddening eyes of the onlookers nearest her. She could gauge former resistance and former Claugh victims by the respective pallor of their faces and, in the latter, whether they looked as if they might throw up.

"No more," the woman with the scars said, her hands trembling. It was hard to decipher her plea.

Edie's eyelids prickled. "When I've suffered the magnitude and duration of what my parents endured, then I can give up. Not until then."

She had a long way to go.

"You were there?" a young man four rows deep asked. "Y-you saw?"

The people at the edges had closed into the crowd again. The throng had pressed close to the church steps.

"I was there. I read them until the Claugh captain burned anything like lips from my mother's beautiful face. Then he went to work on my father."

The sea of people before her, no matter their skin color, went ashen. Jonas, facing her from behind the holocam, stared at her, brows lowered, his upper lip puffing out and then back in. Edie pulled in a badly needed deep breath.

"Demented with pain, my parents still pleaded." Edie signed, *help*. It had been seared forever into her mind's eye. "Even with their fingers broken, burned, and bloody, they asked for help while I hid. Like a coward."

She'd huddled in the woods. Terrified. Fourteen. Paralyzed with horror. Not knowing what to do. How to stop the monsters. She was sick to her stomach. Sick to her soul. She'd learned to live with that sickness.

"I'm ashamed to say it took me days to realize they weren't asking the soldiers for death. They were asking me."

She looked straight into V'kyrri's face. Color leeched from his complexion. His stunning eyes stood out, wide and vibrant in his washed-out face.

Her heart tore, but given what she had to say, it hardly mattered. She couldn't lie anymore. He deserved better.

She looked away.

"I wired the last mortal remains of my family with explosives and laid in wait for the Claugh. I will regret to my dying day that I killed my parents and two of the soldiers who'd tortured them, but I missed their leader. That's why Firestorm was born. It's why I joined the resistance. I wanted that captain roasted by my hand. I wanted him to suffer the lowest level of Hell, forever."

Utter stillness. Finally, the woman with the scars

shifted. A cadre of bleak-eyed men and women surrounding her traded glances. Edie closed her right fist and pinned Jonas with a look, willing him to get the message.

He blinked. His gaze went to her fist and his brow smoothed. He turned, taking the camera with him as if picking up a reaction shot. When he turned back, he shielded his hands with his body. “Cell.”

Edie dipped her chin.

“You tell us this,” the young man who’d questioned her said. “Yet you want us to evacuate with the Claugh?”

Murmurs of agreement.

“How can we trust anyone who’d murder her own parents?” hands held above the heads of the crowd demanded. “She abandoned us for a decade.”

Raw with ire and old wounds running hot, Edie snapped, her motion short and sharp, “You forget the teaching of the church. We are the children of the stars. Born and bred from the same molecules and lifeless dust that gave birth to everything in the universe. We are the universe, the same lineage as every living thing known and unknown. Me. You. The Claugh who killed us all those years ago. The Claugh who are now sacrificing their lives for ours and who are trying to ensure our survival. Even the Chekydran. Even this ball of rock.

“My parents aren’t just buried in the soil of this world.” She thumped her breastbone with a closed fist. “They’re buried here, in the fire and water of my blood. In the rock of my bones, in the air of every breath I will ever take. You spit on this blood-soaked dust and call it home. It’s one tiny room of our home. The whole of the universe is meant to be our home. You've been shut in this playpen so long you've forgotten."

She stomped on the stair. "This is not Nol Jakze. It never has been. We are! If any of us survives, every hallowed thing that matters survives with us. So, yes. Evacuate. Take the children and go. If any of us lives, Nol Jakze lives."

Chest burning, Edie spun on her heel and strode away. Tears slipped her control, burning her face. Gallena and Povora, eyes red, expressions haunted, formed up at her shoulders. V'kyrri came to her side. His fingers twitched, "Edie."

Jonas and the rest of her companions circled them, watching what he had to say. Shielding them from casual view.

V'kyrri pulled Edie into his arms.

For a split second, she resisted. He was Claugh. They were using her to manipulate people. She shouldn't want, much less need, comfort offered by a Claugh over pain caused by the Claugh. Her body ignored her and sank into his embrace. Part of her longed for acceptance. But the question haunted her. How could anyone trust someone who'd kill her own parents?

"*You didn't.*" Desperation swarmed from him to her. Pain because of and for her and the child she'd been. "*Edie. I am so sorry.*"

Clumsily, because it was hard to speak while your arms were full of overly emotional resistance fighter, he signed what he said inside her head. He'd opened to her enough that the edges of who did what blurred. "*You didn't kill your parents, Edie. You didn't. Those soldiers did. No matter who pushed the final button that ended their suffering. They murdered your parents. That guilt is not, and never was, yours to carry.*"

For no good reason, Edie's tears ran faster.

He pulled away and activated his badge. It must have been in answer to a hail, because after answering with, "V'kyrri," he said nothing else, only tipped his head. His gaze turned inward and shifted back and forth.

"By your will, Your Majesty," he said.

The wall of resistance fighters parted. The scarred woman entered the circle, her cell at her back. Edie scrubbed moisture from her face.

V'kyrri released her but touched the back of her hand. "Her Majesty asked me to convey a message. The man you sought in the murder of your parents was caught and tried by Claugh military tribunal. He was precisely the monster you describe. Amoral, little more than a ravening animal. We have no death penalty. We could find no means of rehabilitating or containing him. For the safety of the empire, he lies in stasis because no one can think what to do with or for him. Her Majesty deeply regrets that he did not die in the trap you set. This last is private and she will deny it if anyone repeats it, but she feels a quick, clean explosion might have been too merciful a death for the atrocities he committed."

Edie wilted. Weight she hadn't realized she'd carried for the past fifteen years came off her frame. Bone-crushing weariness took its place.

"General Firestorm," the scarred woman said. "I'm Raz. Resistance. I led a Dharmka Sal cell. We came out of Tomiltor. We're volunteering." She shot a glance at V'kyrri, then met Edie's eye. "What do you need?"

V'kyrri said, "General, the *Dagger* has begun teleporting vaccine to your lieutenant and her supply officers. Manifests on your handheld."

Her lieutenant. Her burgeoning cadre of fighters. "Thank you, Captain. Please convey my compliments and appreciation to Her Majesty."

He nodded, a pleased, proud smile on his face.

"Raz. We're glad to have you," Edie said high enough for the people behind the woman to see. "Jonas, Gallena, Povora, Raz. Her Majesty needs to sign a treaty that has a shot at cutting the Chekydran attack off at the knees. I'm looking for volunteers to secure and guard the site."

Eyes going wide, V'kyrri whirled.

Edie grabbed for her SEM lenses and, scanning the crowd and surroundings, shoved the lenses into place.

"Incoming," Jonas and Povora yelled above their heads.

Gallena pointed at the nearest air raid alarm light. It flashed a steady, rapid amber/red sequence. Edie's SEM came online. Alarms sliced pulsing light into her visual field. Vibration rattled her brain. She spun as if she could spot the incoming danger through the mass of buildings and people.

"Report," Eilod snapped over an open com channel.

"Chekydran-hiin fighters," Ari answered. "Coming in hot. Dr. Idylle. It's up to you to protect Her Majesty. Lock down the *Sen Ekir*. Raise shields. We're scrambling fighters. It'll take time to get them into atmosphere and to your location. Someone, activate surface guns."

"Transport the Ki queen and her drone to their ship

in orbit so we can get that treaty signed and end this," Eilod thundered.

"Are the bugs gunning for us? Or for their parents?" V'kyrri asked.

"Attack." Edie sign yelled, hands above her head. "Chekydran. Take command of the guns. Clear the square."

"With me," Jonas commanded, then took off running. Resistance fighters bolted in his wake, passing the alarm. People in the square scattered.

Edie itched to follow the fighters, but she'd accepted responsibilities. That meant sacrificing some of her ability to do what suited her. When and how had that happened? After she'd pulled V'kyrri out of his wreck? Or something indefinable a long time before hand?

She grimaced.

"*Edie. Get to safety,*" V'kyrri commanded. He stood at the open gate into the holding pen, hand reached for her. Whatever he saw in her face made him lower his hand.

"I'm not at my best in safety." Her SEM fed her the first rumblings of approaching engines and the periodic low frequency thumps of shots impacting. The first finger of fear trailed her spine. The queen aboard a science ship. It had shields, but those wouldn't hold forever.

They had to destroy those fighters.

She caught the flash of V'kyrri's teeth. His eyes lit, touching off an answering thrill in her blood. Her seemingly mild-mannered Claugh captain had a bloodthirsty streak. He tapped his badge. "V'kyrri and Edie. Surface. Going after Chekydran-hiin."

Edie regretted not having her pack. She shoved her handheld into its holster and fingered her store of explosives.

Ships spitting fire dove for the *Sen Ekir*. Smoke and flames twisted into the sky above the city. She tracked the strafing pattern, then jogged for the graveyard, V'kyrri at her side.

Edie ducked the twisted metal arch gating the cemetery. Gravestones had fallen over or been broken completely. The bugs had hit even this sacred place. Her parents were buried under the sprawling shelter of a massive tree that blossomed with brilliant yellow-gold flowers each spring. When the flower petals fell, they rained upon her parents' graves as if the Gods, themselves, wept tears of gold.

That would come in another month. Edie doubted she'd see it. Doubted the Chekydran would let any of them see anything to do with their world ever again. In the center of the cemetery, a slender, polished, white stone tower reached into the heavens. She threw herself up the narrow stairs. One hundred-twenty steps to the top. Ten for each of the Twelve Gods.

By the time Edie collapsed at the top, her blood throbbed in her veins. Leaning on the handrail, chest heaving, V'kyrri took in the light and massive lens in the center of the floor. Gasping, Edie crawled to one of the twelve openings in the stone wall as Chekydran ships zipped past, not ten meters from their position.

"*Whoa*," V'kyrri breathed into her head.

She picked up a flash of the view they commanded.

"*Represents the path to heaven*," she thought at him. "*Every cemetery has one, just not as tall. You're in the tallest structure on world. Here.*" She tossed a blocky gun to him. "*Brace. Fire at will.*"

Edie opted for the tiny gun that shot seeker bombs.

Her breath faltered when she peered out an opening, looking for targets. The *Sen Ekir* remained, but everything, including the steps to the church where she'd given her first, and she hoped, last speech, had been destroyed. Where were the Claugh fighters Captain Idylle had promised? As she chewed burgeoning terror for her new-found and unlikely allies, the first stream of anti-aircraft fire lit the clouds gathering above the city.

"*Returning fire*," V'kyrri crowed.

Edie grinned. Clever Jonas. From the looks of things, he'd dragged everyone to the nearest teleport station and 'ported into place.

They had a chance at defending the grounded science vessel and the city.

"First flight, coming around," she yelled aloud.

Chekydran fighters, spitting fire, looped, stopped firing, and came their way. Three flights of three ships each. Edie levered to her feet and took aim.

Whoever had the two nearest anti-aircraft guns were coordinating. Streams of armor-piercing rounds converged for a crucial second. A Chekydran fighter bounced like a rock skipping on water, then it canted sideways and, trailing smoke, slid out of the sky. It went down in an already smoking suburb and exploded.

Edie's gut clenched. The air attack alarms had been lit. The residents would have taken shelter. Wouldn't they? They wouldn't have forgotten. It had only been a decade. They wouldn't have forgotten the cost of ignoring alerts, right?

Enhancement buzzed her nerves. Ships

approaching. She picked her target and pulled the trigger. Her projectile arced into the path of the incoming craft. V'kyrri fired the ugly gun she'd given him.

She swore the air bent, then snapped back into place in response to his weapon. Audio data registered V'kyrri's yelp, "Baxt'k."

The shot missed.

Edie's bomb did not.

The leader of the incoming flight plowed straight into it. The ships streamed past the tower before arcing for another pass.

"*3, 2, 1.*"

Her polymer clay detonated. It blew the lead ship to scrap. Trees beneath the explosion bent double. Several snapped. Branches thrashed and tossed. The two remaining ships flew right through the debris. One of them sucked something dire through an engine intake. The ship slowed. Smoke twined from the exhaust port.

The air in the tower pulsed again.

V'kyrri didn't miss a second time.

The wounded ship expanded, then the structure of the craft collapsed in on itself. It rained ship and bug dust into the streets below.

"*We're a target now*," he warned.

The second flight, all three ships intact, circled for the tower. They didn't stop firing when they cleared the *Sen Ekir*. Message received and understood. If the humanoids fought back, the bugs would destroy everything in their path, not just the *Sen Ekir*.

Edie sneered. How poorly they knew Nol Jakze.

"*Do not look at the light,*" Edie screamed mentally

and shouted aloud at the same time, praying V'kyrri was paying attention. She'd blind him otherwise. Screwing her eyes shut, she turned on the memorial beacon.

A flash stabbed past her closed eyelids, painting them blood red. Edie turned her back on the light. Her eyelids dimmed, and she risked squinting her eyes open.

The Chekydran had ceased fire and peeled up, out of the line of the brilliant beam. Score one for science. The Chekydran-hiin had sight optimized for dim conditions. She hoped she'd permanently blinded one or two of them with the intense glare.

They'd bought the *Sen Ekir* a few precious minutes.

The Chekydran tightened their pattern run. The third flight of two craft, came straight for Edie and V'kyrri, spraying weapons fire. They'd worked out the light pattern and came in from above the twelve fingers of brilliant light.

V'kyrri fired. A ship vaporized.

Edie fired, then shut down the beacon before the heat roasted them alive. She didn't wait to see what happened. Either she'd gotten one or she hadn't.

Laser fire and explosive rounds sprayed the tower.

Edie hit the floor.

The tower rocked.

V'kyrri grabbed her ankle. "*Time to go*."

It absolutely was. She rolled to the stairs and slid down on her backside while the tower rocked. Her SEM fed her ominous data from the structure above them.

"*Unusual exit technique*," V'kyrri said at the bottom. The ground heaved. The tower rocked. "*We can't get out the door without getting shot, and if we stay here, we're going be smashed into jam when this tower comes down.*"

Edie grinned appreciation for that mental image and cast a glance up. She'd been buried alive. She'd take getting shot by Chekydran fire over being crushed any day.

"*Dagger*. Emergency extract. Two to 'port," V'kyrri yelled.

She cast a glance toward the spot her parents rested. She wouldn't even get to see their graves.

"Emergency extract, two to teleport, aye. Where to, V'k?"

She needed to visit them. There were prayers—

Teleport distortion fuzzed Edie's SEM, but she thought she saw V'kyrri's response before they blinked out of the tower. "Batella."

They materialized at her family's farm.

Edie gasped for breath at the implication—either it wasn't safe to send them to the *Sen Ekir*, or there wasn't a *Sen Ekir*, or a Claugh queen, anymore. "Status of the *Sen Ekir*?"

"Toasted, but intact," Captain Idylle said via com. "My forces are engaging the remaining Hiin ships. All personnel accounted for. You and your people made a difference today, General. Thank you."

Edie grabbed her handheld, tabbed into a channel she'd never imagined she'd need again. "Cease fire. Cease fire. Cease fire. Friendlies in the sky. Return to base."

Single ping responses lit up her lenses. She jerked her chin for V'kyrri's benefit. "Let me make your day better."

"I can make my day better right now," he said, folding his arms around her.

Tension ran out of her muscles as she closed her eyes and surrendered to the beat and surge of energy that was V'kyrri.

"*Ari's right*," he thought. "*You and the resistance saved my friends. I owe you. Again.*"

"The only balance sheet that matters is the one between me and the gods," she said, her chest tight. "I don't want anyone beholden to me." Especially not him. That couldn't be all this was. She wouldn't let it be. It made sense, though, didn't it? What would a man like V'kyrri see in someone like her unless his honor and sense of indebtedness brought him around?

"*Edie. You've galvanized the populace. If your people haven't said it yet, they will. You'd have the entire population at your back if you decide to revive the resistance*."

She flinched.

"Hey," he said aloud when she pulled back. "Remember the legend?"

"Red hair and goddess of destruction," Edie said.

"Goddess of destruction or preservation," he corrected. "We don't get to pick which aspect we get. Except, I think you do. You've surpassed the legend. You've balanced both and integrated them into something worthy of the legends about Firestorm. They're making the rounds on Nol Jakze again. Damen is collecting them. Only you can decide how to use that kind of power."

"Gods," she muttered. "C'mon. Help me with a little extra goddess of destruction."

Chapter Thirty-Three

Drizzle spat from gray clouds that sank low to the hills and drooping treetops as she led him past the replica of her father's shop.

Finding the entrance of what she wanted required pulling a forest of ferns that slipped and shredded in her wet hands, staining her palms. V'kyrri watched, his brows furrowed, then he swam into the midst of the growth and started pulling. The sharp green scent took her back in time to her father battling the same stand of ferns when he and she had dug his storage vault. Edie resisted the urge to glance over her shoulder for his ghost.

"*What're we looking for*?"

"Dad and I built a vault," Edie said. It was a root cellar, really, lined with smooth stones she'd gathered and carted from the river in a pair of sacks slung over her shoulders.

V'kyrri stepped out of the way.

Edie cut the mat of grass roots with a knife from her tool belt, peeled it back, and scrubbed her hands clean on rain-wet grass.

V'kyrri's eyes widened. "*Where the Three Hells did you get Rakoran biometric readers on a religious settlement*?"

Grinning, she pressed her palm against the reader still blinking a red and amber lock code. The system pricked a finger for blood and ran palm scans.

The first group of resistance teleported into the clearing in front of her father's rebuilt shop. Raz and part of her crew.

The vault lock recognized Edie's DNA and opened. Content to let Jonas, Gallena, and Povora handle the gathering troops, she climbed into the musty-smelling vault. Root tendrils poked through the rocks lining the walls and water dripped on the rows of air-tight containers she'd stowed here near the end of the war.

She caught his wordless noise of amazement inside her head when he peered into the vault.

"*A stockpile. How old are these*?"

"Ten years or more," Edie said. Mud and slime coated the tops of the boxes. She had to scrub code locks clean to open them. "Sealed with inert gas. Oxygen free environment. Should be no degradation."

" *'Should be.' Great. It's safe to breathe on them, then.*"

"Better. It should be safe to teleport them." She opened the first box and lifted the lid. The inside was as dry as the planet where she'd imagined she could skip close to the Claugh and escape with her illusions intact. Had it been anyone other than V'kyrri, maybe she could have.

Edie rubbed grimy hands together and refilled her tool belt. "Want anything?"

"*Charges for this*." He patted the butt of the pulse gun she'd given him.

"Box four."

He jumped down and inspected the contents of the boxes. "*Other than the broad category of 'explosive',* " he said, "*I have no idea what most of this stuff is.*"

She handed him cartridges.

She messaged Jonas. "In the vault. Come stock up."

She and V'kyrri climbed out. Former farmers, teachers, businesspeople, mothers, fathers, sisters, and brothers swarmed through the vault devouring weapons and ammo like the springtime swarms of insects that emerged with ravenous appetites for sweet, tender new growth.

"Don't know how our people missed this," V'kyrri said.

"Rakoran ground shielding," she muttered.

His gaze jerked down and left. He activated his ship's badge. "V'kyrri."

"Broad channel. All parties standby for Her Majesty," Ari said.

Several resistance members wore SEM units courtesy of the Claugh and the *Sen Ekir*. They jerked upright and began translating. Resistance fighters climbed out of the vault bristling with explosives and weapons.

V'kyrri closed the distance, looped an arm around Edie's waist, and tucked her against his side.

"V'k, we're reading your badge signal. Edie? You're offline," Ari said.

She stepped out of V'kyrri's grasp and fished out the badge Eilod had given her. She clipped it to her jacket and activated it. "Got it."

"Acknowledged. All parties. This channel is to remain open until further notice," Ari said. "Your Majesty. Go ahead."

"That the Chekydran-hiin fear their Ki and possibly

the work of the *Sen Ekir* makes our path clear," Eilod said. "We must embrace that which they fear. Even if we fear it ourselves. I will solemnize the treaty with the Chekydran-ki. We must do so now. Captain Idylle, do we have teleport for General Firestorm and my honor guard?"

"Captain Xiao does," Ari said. "Transmitting badge codes for Captain V'kyrri and General Firestorm."

Both resistance cells closed ranks before Edie. Jonas and Raz nodded. Volunteer honor guards present and accounted for.

"All personnel in our vicinity," V'kyrri said.

"Acknowledged. Where to?" a male voice Edie's SEM couldn't tag, but which she assumed was Captain Xiao, asked.

"Lunar Ag platform," Edie said. "It's got a buoy broadcasting an SOS attached to it."

"I am familiar with the structure," Xiao said. "Initial scans are clean. Atmosphere is good. Environmentals online. We can put you anywhere, General. What's your target?"

"Standby, *Balykkal*." Edie said aloud. Above her head, Edie signed, "Tijan?"

A rail-thin woman, her brown skin weathered and her once dark hair mostly gone to silver, stepped out of the ranks.

"When I was a kid, we camped on a growing pod on the outer ring, sweeping view of Nol Jakze and the moon," Edie said.

"Ag-pod Skyrt-aman," Tijan said. "Amazing views for a pod dedicated to growing humble spice root."

Edie repeated the pod name aloud for the *Balykkal*.

"*Balykkal*, stand by to receive data," Major Sindrivik said. "I have station diagrams."

"Much obliged, Major."

"Copying to your handheld, General."

"We have your location, General Firestorm," Captain Xiao said. "Standing by."

Edie glanced at V'kyrri. He nodded. She traded glances with Jonas, Gallena, Povora, and Raz. "Ready to go, *Balykkal*. Thanks for the assist."

"Teleporting you in groups of eight. Hold position."

Everyone with a SEM flashed the same hand signal. "Hold position."

Edie and Jonas added, "Incoming teleport. Prepare defense."

Expressions tightened. Hands went to weapons.

Teleport distortion swept Edie off world and deposited her in the center of a fallow, weed-strewn plot of land. She stepped out of the teleport incidence field, assessing and fixing their position.

"Wow," V'kyrri breathed.

Edie looked up as resistance fighters teleported in around them. To her left, lush, blue-green, and swirling white Nol Jakze shone bright through the dome. Pride and longing swelled at the sight. On her right, the golden, pocked lunar surface arced a slice out of the deep dark.

Clear domes of force-field-reinforced alloy glass covered each growing pod. On the moon side, dust particles collected against the bottom edge of the dome. Behind them, a central control and living hub sprouted slender arms. They radiated from the central hub, positioned to guarantee each growing pod a specific and exact measure of solar radiation. While the station had been active, the farmers and scientists had cobbled together tunnels between pods. A station built to look like a flower, had developed into a massive web of arms, blobs, and shiny connective filaments.

It smelled of soil, stale compost, and grease.

"Pod's half a kilometer square," V'kyrri said aloud as he studied his handheld. "A hundred fields, paths, water sources, some apparently active, one ancient, rusting robotractor. No biologics. Not even insects. Looks clear."

"Great," she said. "Now we're doomed."

He laughed and slid an approving glance her way. "Nice choice of location."

"Thanks. Are we teleporting in the primary players?" His approval warmed her.

"Negative," Admiral Seaghdh responded on the open channel. "Her Imperial Majesty's transport is en route to her location and will bring her to the docks. The Chekydran-ki queen and her drone will also arrive via shuttle."

"Acknowledged, *Dagger*." Edie signed, "Volunteers to secure the docks and two security details to escort dignitaries."

"*Assign me to engineering*," V'kyrri whispered into her head.

"Captain V'kyrri, would you be good enough to take a team and secure engineering?" she said as if it had been her idea. Teams separated out from the main troop, organized, and scattered for their assignments. Edie watched them go, frowning. The fine hairs at the back of her neck stirred. Everything she'd ever learned about guerrilla tactics said, "Never brew all your spice root flower tea in one pot." Yet here she was, shivering in dread at splitting up her first major command.

"Cheer up, Altheas." Jonas clapped her shoulder. "You did a fine job managing the people out there on the square."

Edie sighed away her ridiculous sense of misgiving as V'kyrri jogged out of view. She met Jonas's eye. "Including losing my temper?"

"It was exactly what they needed," Povora signed. "Truth in passion. You know that."

"You certainly gave them plenty to think about," Jonas added. He, too, reverted to their native language. "I don't know that everyone will agree to evacuate, but some will. You fired them up, reminded them of who and what they are."

"Look how that worked out for us last time." Edie nestled into speaking her first language with them.

Gallena tossed a glance at the assembled troop, stepped out where she could be seen, and said, "Tii was a spawn of a Myallki bitch, and I refuse to mourn the twisted bastard, but he was right about one thing. You *could* rally the populace. With General Firestorm in the lead, we could finally take it all back." She jerked her chin at the shining planet.

Bile burned Edie's gut as the expanding fire ball of civil war played out against her internal visual screen, again.

No one moved.

Tension deepened the lines on Jonas's face. The smattering of kids in uniform stared, terror and hope mingled in the tremble of their lips. Challenge lit Gallena's eyes. She crossed her arms. Raz's barbed gaze darted between faces before coming to rest on

Edie.

Edie examined the thought. The possibilities. “Drive off the Claugh. Is that what you’re suggesting?”

“Take back our world,” Gallena said.

“Does your scenario account for everyone abandoning us, sick and dying, to the bugs?” Edie demanded.

“You’re saying you can’t blow them straight to the deepest Hell?” Gallena challenged.

Edie grinned and waggled her head. “Did you know they’re flying a ship design based on old UMOPG ore haulers?”

Her friends stared at her. Povora’s brow furrowed. “As old as the ore haulers our ancestors hired to bring them here as settlers?”

“As old. From the specs I’ve seen, the core design is the same.”

Gallena’s eyes lit. “That’s anti-matter tech. You could detonate that in your sleep.”

“If I could get into their engine compartments, yes. I could.”

“What would be left if you did?” Jonas asked.

“There’s the problem,” Edie said. “An anti-matter explosion would make Tii’s showoff explosions look like sticking a lit match up a slug wasp nest. And if we managed to destroy the one ship that’s on world, how many would arrive to take its place?”

Gallena shrugged. “What have you done that you’re afraid to die?”

Edie barked a bitter laugh. “Enough that I’m unwilling to be guilty of getting the whole of my people killed. I have many a sin to repent before the scales balance.”

"Is that what you're doing with the Claugh?" Povora asked. "Balancing scales?"

"Isn't that the teaching? 'Today's enemy is tomorrow's ally.' I admit this wasn't what I'd had in mind when I pulled a bunch of traumatized Claugh from a shipwreck. But look at us. The resistance. Honor guard to the queen of the entire baxt'kal empire. We have options we've never had before."

Jonas lifted an eyebrow.

"Diplomacy."

They rocked like she'd tossed a live grenade into the middle of them. Edie shrugged. "Her Majesty mentioned that Nol Jakze would need another governor." If anything like Nol Jakze survived to be governed.

Povora began laughing. Holding her sides, laughing.

"You'd be nothing but a mascot," Gallena protested. Glowering, she thumped Povora's shoulder with a closed fist. It did little to sober the woman.

Edie shrugged. "It is possible that she said it because she believes I can be kept on their leash."

Jonas snorted.

Edie grinned.

"General." The word on her SEM wiped the smile from Edie's face. Her heart clunked to the soul of her boots. Admiral Seaghdh. The open channel. She shook her head.

"Awaiting team reports, Admiral," she said aloud and signed at the same time. "We're secure on this deck."

Eyes widened around her as it seemed to dawn on everyone that they'd been discussing what the Claugh would undoubtedly cast as treason while the Claugh listened in on an open channel. Since the only hearing person in their midst had led a team to engineering, the group of natives had lapsed into their own, silent language and thereby committed the sin of taking advantage of the Claughs' limitation—they couldn't see what had been discussed. They were bound by what they could hear.

"Gods forgive us," went around the crowd, but no one volunteered to disclose what they'd been talking about before the admiral's hail.

"Her Majesty wishes to inform you the Chekydranki shuttle is en route to your location," Seaghdh said. "Her Majesty's transport has arrived on world and will also be en route shortly."

Alarm bumped Edie a step forward. "The docks aren't secure."

Her team scattered across the pod, sweeping the fields, weapons at the ready, though the most dangerous thing the delegates were likely to encounter was a rogue garden tool to trip over.

"We've scanned in enough detail to be able to count the surviving weeds," Captain Idylle replied, "and to give you species and genus on each."

"Nice."

"General, docks secure," one of her team messaged in via handheld.

"Sweeps?"

"On patrol."

"Captain V'kyrri, what's your status?" she asked aloud.

"Engineering is physically secure," he answered. "Still working on locking down systems. Damen,

Pietre, and I are on it."

"Very well, Admiral," Edie said. "We're standing by to receive all parties."

"Acknowledged."

"Heads up, Edie," Captain Idylle said. "Single Chekydran-ki craft approaching your position."

"Thank you, *Dagger*. Dock team. Stand by to receive delegates." Single pings hit her SEM as the dock team acknowledged.

"Admiral Seaghdh, Captain Idylle, Captain Xiao, and General Firestorm. This is the royal shuttle *Dwyr Balen*," an unknown male voice said. "Her Imperial Majesty, Queen Eilod Saoyrse wishes to inform you she is en route."

"Acknowledged."

"Now would be a good time…" Edie began. Dizziness swept her. She frowned. Was that…? A burst of plasma arced past, close enough for the heat to make her clap a protective hand to the sensitive skin of her neck. Someone shrieked behind her, the audio spike high and ragged. Edie dove and rolled. More shots fired. She came to one knee, weapon up. The soil in front of her sprayed.

"Shots fired! Shots fired!" several voices shouted, lighting up Edie's SEM.

"*Edie*."

"Clear the channel," Edie bellowed. "Get me marks and an ident. *Dagger*, we are under attack. Advise all delegations to stand off."

Teams scattered into the pod around her, Edie returned fire, and climbed to her feet. Raz and three others flanked her, laying down suppression fire. A wild shot from the hostiles burst against the dome, lighting up the force field before the energy dissipated, grounded into the soil.

Jonas's team slipped around behind the invaders. With no cover and nowhere to run, the shooters fell in short order.

"Chekydran-ki are on approach, Edie," Captain Idylle said. "They're committed."

"They want to help clear the station," Damen clarified.

A bolt flashed past from behind Edie.

"Well then, they're welcome," Edie said. She spun, already firing. A squad of six, plain clothing, military weapons. The only thing that had saved her had been lingering distortion from the teleport incidence field. Gallena's team wiped them out. Gallena strode into midst of the bodies.

Hurried consultations ensued. Edie could see the motion, but not the concepts.

"Ident on hostiles." Gallena messaged in. "Seems Firestorm stung Gliwt into getting off his well-padded office chair."

"They're 'porting in. Forces loyal to General Gliwt," Edie said aloud for the benefit of the open channel. Loyal to Gliwt and presumably to the late governor. Just Edie's luck Tiimete's grudge would survive his death. "All teams. Hostiles teleporting on station. No uniforms. Carrying military weapons."

"Sensors," Ari barked. "Where are they coming from?"

"They're teleporting in groups of four and six," Edie said. "Unless you see a bunch of Nol Jakze private ships in orbit, they're coming from planet-side teleporters inside the cities. They're all configured in fours and sixes."

In the same instant, Captain Xiao ordered, "Active scans, all decks of the station. I want numbers, locations, and what those bastards had for breakfast."

Another barrage of weapons fire streaked Edie's SEM. More than one shooter, then, taking refuge behind the decrepit robotractor in the middle of one of the fields. Edie sprinted around the tractor, her breath high and tight in her chest. No quarter asked or given. She jammed down her trigger until Raz put a hand on her arm.

Four bodies seeped blood into the dirt.

"Engineering controls secure, General," V'kyrri said aloud via the open channel.

"You are my hero," she quipped, swiping a sleeve up her damp forehead. Pleasure and heat, not her own, swept her body like a wave.

"*On my way*," V'kyrri said. "*Leaving security teams in place to protect environmental controls*."

"Chekydran-ki delegates arrived," the dock team messaged. "Docks secure. Delegation en route."

Another wave of dizziness struck. "Incoming."

Fighters wearing SEMS picked up and relayed her warning. The teleport resolved. Now that the resistance were accustomed to shooters coming in via teleport, they spotted and focused on the shimmer of field distortion. They began firing as the opposition materialized mowing them down, but urgency beat at Edie's chest. Who knew where else the hostiles were teleporting on station? All they had to do was keep Edie and her crew pinned down on deck, and the rest of Gliwt's soldiers would have free run of the station. Not to mention a free shot at Eilod.

Chapter Thirty-Four

"*Balykkal*? *Dagger*? Please tell me you have something useful for me," Edie begged.

"Got 'em," Ari crowed. "They've accessed and overridden planetary teleport platforms. Ops, shut them down and do it now."

"They're teleporting in all over station," Captain Xiao said, confirming Edie's fear. "Main force assembling on the command deck."

"They'll try for environmental control," V'kyrri warned.

"We're on it," Damen Sindrivik replied.

"*Balykkal*, do you have a count?" Edie asked.

"Sixty," Xiao replied, "and counting. Team of ten in the habitat core between the docks and you."

"Dock team, did you get that?"

An anomalous audio-turned-visual signal seared Edie's retinas. It resolved to words on her screen.

"All parties. All parties," Admiral Seaghdh bellowed. "*Dwyr Balen* is taking fire. Repeat. The queen's shuttle is under attack."

Pandemonium erupted on her SEM. Too-fast-to-read symbols of jumbled together concepts flashed past. The system gave up tagging speakers. Edie caught demands for status. Then for ident. Orders to scramble fighters. Get ships into position to return fire. Teleport Her Majesty out. Belays on that order because all the teleport systems in reach were shedding excess heat and couldn't teleport.

Edie craned her neck, scanning the black beyond the dome and caught a distant, brief flash of a weapon impacting shields. She took a single step toward it. What the Three Hells kind of trap had they walked into?

Teleport distortion swept her again. More attackers, teleporting into the middle of the pod. As far as she could tell, they hadn't risked 'porting near the dome where the protective force fields would distort the teleport. *Balykkal* had teleported her troops into the dead center of the pod for that very reason. She passed swift signs to Raz and her team. They picked it up, flashing the "concentrate fire, center" message.

Resistance fighters sprinted for the edges of the pod. Edie ran, one eye on the dim star that was Eilod's shuttle reflecting sunlight. Pulse thumping inside her ears, she fired at the attackers 'porting into the pod.

"Captain Idylle," an unknown voice interjected. "Planetary forces are mobilizing to secure planet-side teleport locations."

Edie cringed. Planetary forces? That would be whatever tiny fragment of the military that wasn't supporting the vaccination drive. And civilians ulcerating for some way to get their own back, whether against the Chekydran-hiin, the plague, or the former governor. The revolution had begun. Even if it was in support of the Claugh for the time being.

If it stopped Gliwt's entire command from teleporting into the station for her to have to chase down, all the better. She cast a look at the flare and gleam of Eilod's shuttle drawing nearer. Setting her teeth, she forced herself to look away. She couldn't do anything. Not for Eilod. But she could and should clear the route for the Chekydran delegates.

"Acknowledged. Fighters scrambling. First wave to Her Majesty's location in five. Do you copy *Dwyr Balen*? Keep it together for just another few minutes," Ari hollered.

"Acknowledged, *Dagger*. They won't get through," the shuttle pilot said. "Lunar station, lunar station, be advised that Her Majesty's transport will be coming in hot."

Edie snorted, but no relief cooled the heat clutching her chest. They weren't in the clear by any means.

"Jonas. Gallena. With me," Edie signed over her head as she ran for the emergency airlock. Troops closed around her, blood on clothes, some belonging to wearers, some not. A few limped or clutched at injury. Every single one scanned the open fields, weapons trained.

"Ambush between the docks and here," she said. "Delegates on the way. No response from dock team."

Jonas's features tightened. Gallena shifted her pulse rifle higher.

Edie shot a glance at Jonas. He lifted a brow in question.

"They knew," she said with her hands.

Jonas didn't ask about what. "About reviving the resistance? Your captain?"

Sighing, she lifted one shoulder, let it fall.

"It was predictable, right down to Gallena being the one to broach the subject," he said.

Edie gave up trying to tread water in her inadequacies. "Not to me."

He patted her shoulder. "Of course not. You're the epicenter of the storm. Be yourself, Firestorm, and let's make this mess messier."

The audio visualization on Edie's SEM climbed. Across from her, the main airlock opened.

People poured through at a dead run. Judging by the data the SEM sliced into Edie's skull, they were yelling. Maybe screaming.

Three seconds later, four Chekydran-ki swarmed through the hatch. Folded wings opened as they emerged from the airlock. The two leading Ki, smaller than the pair Edie recognized as the queen and her drone, launched into the air in pursuit of the fleeing humanoids.

Edie's nerves prickled anticipation.

V'kyrri.

Her pulse picked up speed.

Resistance fighters, V'kyrri in their midst, spilled through the airlock.

Weapons flashed to life, focused on the soldiers running from Chekydran. From across the pod, V'kyrri waved an arm overhead.

"Path from dock to pod clear," he said aloud.

So much for the ambush. The Chekydran-ki had driven them into the resistance's make-shift ambush. One more point for their side.

Edie shot a glance to the spot she'd last seen Eilod's shuttle. It wasn't there. Her Majesty's pilots had brought the shuttle much closer to station. Close enough that Edie could detect the attacking fighters.

"They're ours," Edie breathed. When she managed to pull air into her lungs, she bellowed, "Do you copy? Attackers are Nol Jakze interplanetary fighters."

Her team, Jonas, Gallena, Povora and the others stared, weapons going slack.

"Kartz." Whatever communicated from Admiral Seaghdh's single word through Edie's SEM, it dumped ice down her back and left her shivering.

"How the Three Hells did they access those fighters?" V'kyrri yelled. "You killed their codes."

"Fine question," Captain Idylle snapped.

"Captain," an unknown voice said. "Ships leaving atmosphere."

A stream of fire appeared against the black backdrop of space.

"Chekydran-hiin, Captain."

"Where are they coming from?" Ari bellowed. "Where? Mothership or planet side?"

Claugh short-range fighters swept into Edie's line of sight, peppering the Nol Jakze forces attacking Eilod's shuttle.

Edie ached for *t'Achreides-myn.* Her little boat would make short work of straightening out the nonsense. Course, it might also puncture a dome on station and murder everyone.

She frowned and pressed the heel of one hand against her aching sternum. Vibration settled deep inside, intensifying, mounting pressure upon pressure. Enough to make her bones ache. She gasped, head spinning. She'd been here before. Recognition burst inside her skull.

"Hiin on the platform. All parties. Chekydran-hiin attacking the platform," Edie yelled. Ferocity exploded into her chest. "Guard the Ki. Guard the Ki queen and her drone."

Resistance fighters converged on the gleaming

black queen and her drone. The pair rose to their full height, wings outstretched.

"All personnel to high alert. Get your shields up. We've got a Hiin mother ship in orbit somewhere," Ari said. "Camouflaged. Maybe hiding behind the moon. It's the only way they could get on the platform this fast."

"*Balykkal.* Initiating scans."

"The Ki confirm the advisory, Captain, and are moving to investigate."

The pressure in Edie's chest increased. Jonas, Gallena, and Povora closed ranks with her. She shot a glance at the dome and stumbled. Eilod's shuttle had drawn much closer. Single occupant fighters arced back and forth, strafing. The Nol Jakze fighters had taken hits. Their number had dwindled. The Claugh fighters had suffered no losses that she could see.

Good in that the Claugh were successfully defending their queen.

Bad in that the Nol Jakzian fighters weren't fighting back in favor of attacking the shuttle. Edie shook her hum-muddled head. "*V'kyrri.*"

"*Edie?*"

"*Nol Jakzian fighters can't hurt the shuttle. Why are they attacking*?" Jolted like she'd fallen off the bottom step of porch stairs at her parents' house, she gasped. "Get that shuttle docked," Edie screamed. "Get it docked. The attack is a delaying tactic."

"*Chekydran,*" V'kyrri snarled both in her head and aloud. Her SEM didn't sync with his internal voice. The mismatch gave her a headache.

"Get me weapons," Ari Idylle commanded, her audio signature a flat line on Edie's SEM.

Behind Edie, the emergency airlock exploded into the pod. A fist of a pressure wave slammed Edie. She landed face first in the dirt before she could register the need to catch herself. Spitting bitter soil, she rolled.

Chekydran-hiin, tentacles waving weapons, shoved one at a time through the airlock opening. Right on top of her and her cell. She jammed down the trigger of her gun.

"Bugs," Jonas shouted aloud. He grabbed Edie under the arms and hauled her backward as she sprayed the creatures emerging from the air lock.

"The Hiin have engaged Her Majesty's shuttle," Seaghdh said.

Gallena took up suppression fire.

Jonas hauled Edie upright.

"Scatter," Povora yell-signed.

There was nowhere to scatter to. Running zigzags, people took off in every direction. The Hiin hesitated in stomping over their own dead and dying, eye stalks swiveling as if surveying the lay of the land as well as the opposition.

"*Edie.*" V'kyrri yelped inside the confines of her skull. "*RUN.*"

The Chekydran-hiin turned en masse to stare at Edie. Her SEM erupted with data as if the Hiin relied on echo location to figure her out. She backpedaled, spun, and pelted for the center of the dome. Weapons fire salted the earth around her, lifting the hair on her arms.

"New contact," someone from either the *Dagger* or the *Balykkal* called.

A shot clipped her. Shrieking as every nerve screamed fire, she went down hard.

"*Edie*," V'kyrri's bellow resounded in her head.

She slid a meter. A blow and sting to her ankle jerked her into a fetal position. She spotted the source of her pain. Bug. Trying to grab her.

She shot it in what passed for a face. It collapsed, spraying dirt into the air. A ship soared out of the dust pall, arcing over the dome. Weapons hot. Recognition thumped Edie in the chest.

Trente.

Another Chekydran-hiin rushed her. Sobbing for breath, she shot it, too. Fear wrenched her to unsteady feet. Edie staggered, snarling and lobbing fire over her shoulder. The butt of her pistol grew hot.

"Shields buckling," caught her eye in the script rolling past on her SEM.

Ice filled Edie's veins. Another tentacle slapped beside her.

Edie ran.

Bugs cantered on her tail. Her pulse synced to the beat of their legs impacting soil. She had nowhere to run. No means of escape. She flashed back to fifteen years ago. She'd been a child pursued by a madman in a Claugh uniform—the madman who'd forced her to murder her parents. That day of running, her legs screaming, her lungs bursting, she'd been driven to become what she'd loathed in the Claugh. A monster. Long suppressed wounds in her psyche cracked, bleeding memory and panic into her system. Now it was Chekydran. Only she wasn't a child. Edie was the monster she'd been made.

With shaking hands, she loosed an explosive from her belt. It fell into the soil. She urged her aching body to go faster.

3, 2, 1.

POP.

SEM data stilled for a moment, then ragged, high-frequency data spikes lit up her visual field. For several seconds, the pattern of bug legs running, broke. When it resumed, a bug galloped up on her from the side. She half turned to deal with it. One of the bugs at her back wrapped a tentacle around her chest. It shook her. Edie lost her pistol.

The Chekydran jerked as if it had been stung. Eyestalks swiveled away from her. Pain wrapped her ribs. She couldn't breathe. Kicking the tentacle squeezing her did nothing. Eyesight hazing, she clutched for her tool belt. Then she arced through the air.

"Oof." Edie hit the dirt and slid. Her SEM glasses dislodged. It was all she knew for certain while her system registered and cataloged injuries and struggled to suck breath into achy lungs.

"*Edie*."

Sparks infused her blood. V'kyrri levered her upright and shoved lenses into her limp hands. He crouched, propping her against his body, lifted a rifle and fired into the oncoming ranks of Chekydran-hiin.

Color burst across her sight and the message seeped from V'kyrri into Edie. The Hiin were afraid of him. The Chekydran-ki wanted him off platform. They wanted—no—they needed him safe. Edie frowned, looked over her shoulder at the queen and her drone standing behind V'kyrri, their hind legs sawing their wings. Forcing lethargy away, Edie shoved the SEM to her face, and registered the vibration produced by the Ki. It rose and fell in soothing, rhythmic arcs.

Resistance fighters, bloody but upright, advanced, firing.

The number of Hiin didn't diminish.

At least Gliwt's troops had stopped teleporting.

"CLEAR," Edie sign-shouted. She threw a seeker. The metallic object hit the dirt halfway between her and the leading edge of Hiin where it rocked back and forth for a split second. Then it whirred to life and rushed the front line.

The bugs dove apart.

The bomb blew. A burst of static on the SEM. Ichor and chitin spattered the ground.

"Get her out," Seaghdh bellowed over the open channel. His terror and rage split Edie's skull through the SEM. "EILOD!"

The shuttle exploded.

Chapter Thirty-Five

The Chekydran-ki faltered. They, too, stared, wings slack.

Trente's ship arced through the leading edge of the burning gas ball and debris that had been the queen's shuttle, taking Edie's heart with it. She couldn't move. Couldn't breathe.

"Eilod," V'kyrri whispered.

Her SEM registered the timber of that single word and shoved it directly into her neural fibers. It might as well have been a scream. She gasped and wiped blood from beneath her nose. Jonas appeared and hauled her upright with shaking hands.

Povora, tears streaming down her face, fists clenched, stared at what remained of the queen's shuttle. Teeth bared, Gallena opened fire on Chekydran-hiin.

"*Dagger,*" Sindrivik yelled. "*Dagger.* Any responder."

Data blanketed the SEM field. Edie squinted.

Resistance and former military alike joined Gallena, creating a defensive line between Edie, V'kyrri, the Ki, and the Chekydran-hiin.

"Stand down, Major," a woman's voice said. Sorrow, thick and choking, weighted the frequency signature of the words. They stood on Edie's chest as they ran down her lenses.

"Stand down. We've lost her. We've lost Eilod Saoyrse." The SEM finally tagged the speaker. Princess Len af Baan. Eilod's aunt. "Captain Idylle. Acknowledge."

"What?" Ari snarled.

Stinging tears spilled over. Edie didn't bother swiping them away. Without a trigger to pull, she'd have to be content with blowing up every Hiin on station.

"By command of the combined councils, in the interests of the subjects of the Claugh nib Dovyyth Empire, we hereby remand His Imperial Majesty, Auhrnok Admiral Cullin Seaghdh nib Riorchjan, to your care. The queen is dead. Long live the king."

Edie winced.

"Belay that," a jumble of voices spilled words before Edie's eyes, almost obscuring a male voice screaming, "ALIVE ALIVE ALIVE!"

"Baxt'k," Ari whispered, then cleared her throat and bellowed. "What the Three Hells is going on?"

"The Ki," Jayleia shouted. "They have a line on her. Eilod is alive. Do you copy? She's alive."

Pandemonium.

V'kyrri's knees gave. Edie couldn't catch him in time. She ripped the SEM lenses from her face. Scrubbing moisture from her cheeks, she muttered, "Praise to all Twelve Gods."

Jonas tossed shots over her shoulder and mimed putting her glasses back.

She obeyed.

"Replay," Seaghdh snapped. "Get an analysis team on that attack. Pick apart every move every ship made. Analysis, projected trajectories, and stats on who's likely to have pulled her from the shuttle. I want it yesterday."

Edie eyed the path Trente had flown. Certainty flooded her system. Adrenaline threw her pulse against the inside of her skin. "He's got her."

Eyes turned to her before returning to the Hiin. The SEM field stilled.

"Edie?" Captain Idylle prompted.

"The *Erillian Aggressor* picked her up."

"Proof or conjecture?" Seaghdh demanded.

"A little of both."

"He hates her," Damen breathed, the ragged nature of his frequency data suggested he'd been the one screaming. Talk about the downside of being linked to a telepathic species.

"No," Edie and Jayleia said in unison. Edie waited for Jay to finish the thought. She didn't. Finally, surveying the battlefield and forcing her brain into gear, Edie shrugged. "He only thinks he does."

V'kyrri scrubbed his face with a sleeve, fired several rounds, and then climbed to his feet. "We're done here."

"We're being overrun," Jonas snapped.

Edie threw another bomb. "Can you get the Ki off station? Take as many resistance as you can. Use the Chekydran ships if you must. Get off. The resistance and the Ki have to survive."

Bug parts sprayed and arced back to the ground.

Jonas shook his head. "You're crazy."

"She's right," V'kyrri snapped back. "If Eilod is alive—"

A flash of weapons fire. Pain burst in her head. V'kyrri went down. Edie vomited into the dead soil right next to V'kyrri's prone, seizing body. Edie fell to her knees. She'd never gotten to say the words. Never gotten to see him say 'I love you'. Of course not. Everything she loved died. Goddess of Destruction, after all.

She'd led the Chekydran-hiin to him. She'd killed him. Just like she'd gotten her parents killed all those years ago. Her fault. Not because she'd wired them up and pushed the detonate button. Because when she'd run like the frightened child she'd been, she'd lost her mind and run straight to Mom and Dad. They'd died. And it was her fault. No one knew the forests and fields the way she had. She could have run anywhere. Hidden. Lost the soldiers in the trees. Led them into a grove of hone-fern trees and let the slug wasps handle them.

Repeated patterns.

As if she'd learned nothing, she'd led the enemy right to the person she most cared about in the world. Goddess of Destruction.

Fine. She'd embrace it.

"Edie," Jonas shouted from behind her.

Her friends. She was destroying them, too. Clean sweep.

Terrible burning sorrow expanded within her. It flashed to rage, bursting the confines of everything she was. She ripped V'kyrri's gun from his twitching corpse, yanked her spare free, and jammed down the triggers. Spraying plasma and laser-fire, she rose and waded into the oncoming wave of Chekydran. Weapons flashed. Tentacles flailed. Snarling, weeping, Edie plowed into the thick of the creatures. They parted before her.

She caught sight of her squad. Chaos reigned. Bugs

swarmed the empty fields.

Despair clogged her throat, and it took her seconds to raise her shaking fists to signal retreat.

Suspended from the noose of a tentacle around her neck, Gallena picked up the sign, and passed it. Beautiful blue eyes bulging, her face turning purple, she went limp.

Chekydran-ki soldiers arced through the dome, their forelegs dripping gore. They circled their queen and drone, then landed beside them. Teleport distortion enveloped them.

Edie slumped. Good.

The Chekydran-hiin holding Gallena shook the woman's body and flung it at the humanoid fighters flashing the retreat order to one another as they assembled at the main airlock. Their numbers had been halved. Teleport distortion grabbed a group of them. Another. The rest retreated.

Relief twined into her blood. Part of the team would survive. At least she hadn't gotten them all killed. Yet. Breathing hard, smearing moisture from her face with an impatient swipe of one sleeve, Edie slaughtered another bug. For Gallena.

Covered in bug parts and the blood of her squad, she spun a circle. Firing.

Tentacles slapped. One lucky blow swept V'kyrri's rifle from her grip and bloodied her hand. A roll of energy slammed into her back. Someone else on deck with explosives. Good. Maybe someone would think to puncture the dome. They'd all die, sure, but more importantly, the Chekydran-hiin would die.

A bug untouched by weapon or injury slumped to the ground. Her head pulsed. The beat and surge grew, filling her skull until it creaked. Teased by the familiar throb, hope blossomed out of the raw places in her soul.

The Chekydran-hiin around her erupted into roiling tentacles and legs.

"V'kyrri," Edie burst her throat screaming. She fought her way to him, shooting with one hand and lobbing munitions with the other.

Blood streamed from his face, his arms, his legs, and several open lash points across his torso. Where he'd been shot showed through the tatters of his uniform. The wound had turned purple. His limbs twitched, but impossibly, he was on his feet. Half a dozen Chekydran ringed him, writhing.

Headache assailed her. Nausea pressed the back of her throat. She staggered to the Chekydran farthest from V'kyrri, put the muzzle of her gun against the base of one eyestalk and pulled the trigger.

V'kyrri flinched. "Edie?" His knees gave. The storm clouds in his eyes cleared.

Chekydran at the edge of V'kyrri's mental killing field stirred.

Edie sprayed plasma.

One of the bugs swiped her off her feet. She went down hard. Oh good. More bruises. She didn't bother to rise, merely jammed down the trigger with one hand and grabbed an explosive from her belt with the other.

V'kyrri crawled to her side, claimed another gun and started firing.

She lobbed the bomb.

Three seconds later, it detonated. The pressure wave tore through bug bodies like a tidal wave. The problem was that it shoved the leading edge of Chekydran right at them. Ichor and bug bits splashed her.

"*We've done our duty, Edie.*"

"*Dagger. Balykkal. Sen Ekir.* Anyone with teleport power. Two to teleport at my location."

"Not yet," she said. Flat. Concentrating on mowing down bugs. "It's time to end this. Get me to the dome. Outer edge."

Power pulsed from him, setting her teeth on edge.

The Chekydran in the lead stumbled. Their companions washed up against their backs, a river newly dammed, rising and frothing in protest of restraint.

V'kyrri grabbed Edie under the arms and hauled.

Her eyesight dimmed in response to the jagged pain slicing her skull. Finally, V'kyrri stopped, scooped her into his arms and ran. Every step rattled her bones. Her teeth clacked, exploding hurt into her already aching head. Eyes watering, she caught a glimpse over his shoulder.

The Chekydran shook off his assault and began stutter-stepping in their wake.

He put her down.

Dirt under one shoulder and the dome force field at her back. She yanked explosives from her belt, shoved them all into a massive, untidy pile of SQ-9. In response to the force field, the SQ-9 changed color from green to the kind of yellow that promised sweet, ripe fruit.

"Hold them off," she bellowed and ripped open the pouch holding her triggers.

"Teleport in two," Ari said. "Hold on."

Edie didn't bother looking over her shoulder. Either they'd make this, or they wouldn't. She picked a metallic trigger with remote control ignition, set it, and bedded it into the SQ-9.

If she lived, she'd trip the trigger with her handheld. If she died, the timer would run down in ten minutes.

"Let's get out of here," she said, wrenching her handheld up to order evacuation.

Pieces came to her hand. Edie stared.

"Give the detonation code to *Sen Ekir*," V'kyrri said, his arms spread as if that alone held the Chekydran at bay. Maybe it did.

More bugs lusting for their blood poured through the air lock doors.

Edie shook her head. She'd managed to destroy most of this mission. The thought arrested her. She glanced at the innocent-looking bomb she'd glued to the force field and the dome. She could still do this. If she triggered the bombs manually.

Edie swallowed the reflexive surge of terror.

Goddess of Destruction, indeed, but she'd be damned before she'd destroy V'kyrri along with her. She spun and activated his com.

"*Dagger*. Get him out," Edie ordered. "Get him out."

"Edie," he protested. "No. There has to be another—"

Gods bless Ari. V'kyrri dissolved.

Edie's shoulders sagged, and she couldn't get her breath. For a split second, her eyes burned and stung so sharply, she suspected a slug wasp had survived on station. She closed her eyes and saw her parents. Bloody. Suspended between the porch support columns, her bombs at their feet.

They smiled. Perfect, beautiful smiles of compassion and knowing. Compassion for her sudden burst of understanding. Just like Edie could have done had she been thinking as a fourteen-year-old child, her parents could have run. They could have hidden and evaded the Claugh for a very long time in the wilderness. They hadn't. They'd sacrificed themselves. By choice.

All their suffering, all their pain. It had been worth it. Because every torture they suffered meant Edie was still alive and free.

Her turn.

V'kyrri was alive. He was free.

She loved him with everything she was. All the way down to some better part of her that had been buried by bitterness and the drive for vengeance. She loved him and wanted a future—a life with him. She craved what her parents once had.

The Chekydran weren't going to allow it.

They'd already tried to steal him from her. They'd ripped Nol Jakze from her people. Edie couldn't—wouldn't—let them do it to anyone else. This ended here and now.

For the surviving members of her displaced people.

For Eilod and her idealistic empire.

For the memory of everything Edie's parents believed and honored.

For every ounce of adoration in her soul for one smart-assed telepath with eyes like an ocean she'd never see. Edie opened watering eyes. People and creatures the known galaxy over would sleep easier.

Limbs trembling, she crawled to the explosives. It'd be quick, at least.

"*EDIE*!" V'kyrri's despairing cry shredded her soul.

"I love you," she said. "I love you." She chanted it inside her head without pause until it rang inside her body in time with the beat of her heart. Tears dried.

Bugs boiled into range.

Hand shaking, breath a rasp in her throat, she punched the flashing button.

Fire and agony blew her backward into the alloy glass of the dome, blood, her blood, arcing into the fireball of Chekydran-hiin weapons fire expanding in slow motion.

Eyesight fading, Edie slipped, smiling and boneless down the glass. She couldn't get her breath. Couldn't. S'okay. Didn't need to breathe. Not anymore.

3, 2, 1.

BOOM.

Torment yanked her backward, a kick from a massive foot to her blown-open chest. Pressure vanished, and Edie fell. And fell. The metronome of her pulse, ticking out the measure of her life, slipped. It faded to a whisper and stuttered, winding down.

Altheas. Her father's perfect face, sparkling, warm brown eyes, the straight, razor-thin nose, the faint white scar on his right cheek from a firework gone wrong in his apprenticeship, and his lips. Saying her name.

Hi, Daddy.

You have a choice to make, Sweetheart.

Chapter Thirty-Six

"Get her. Get her, now."

"I'm working on it," Pietre shouted. "Shut up."

"V'k." Damen grappled V'kyrri by his shoulders.

"They did it," a voice yelled via com. "They breached the dome. The station is tearing itself and the Chekydran to shreds."

V'kyrri fought off his best friend.

Damen tackled him.

The incidence field fired. Glowed.

V'kyrri threw Damen and scrambled for the incoming teleport. Edie materialized, slack, a hole in her chest. He crawled through the blood that had registered as a part of her and been teleported along with her.

Raj and Dr. Idylle went to work rapidly, barking orders at one another.

Dizziness swept V'kyrri. He ignored it. He took Edie's hand, touched her face, and sank into the dimming light of her. "*Edie. You aren't dying for me, damn it.*"

His mental voice echoed through the hollow confines of the temple he'd always envisioned her being. Cold panic drove him. He dove deep into the cooling ashes of Edie.

Ari's voice, thick with terror followed him. "Twelve Gods. V'k. He's going after her. He's forcing her heart to beat, controlling respiration."

"If he dies while connected to her…" Damen said.

"We die with him," Seaghdh finished.

V'kyrri shuddered. No. They wouldn't. He'd spared himself the moral conundrum of endangering his friends while fighting for Edie. By cutting them off during the crash of the *Rhapsody*, he'd saved their lives now. He could go after Edie with a clear conscience.

"*Edie. Firestorm. Altheas Drake. Come back. I need you. I love you. Come back or take me with you, but no leaving me.*"

Like a line jerking taut, his headlong dive into the dimming fire that was Edie bounced to a halt.

"*V'k,*" Ari said inside his head.

Snarling, every part of him burning, he turned on his friend and student. He struck. Power flared, snapping his blow right back at him. He reeled.

"*I'm helping, you Orhait's ass,*" she snapped, thrusting a filament of bright power at him. "*Here. Take it.*"

"*Danger,*" he responded, lit beyond capacity by the weird syncopated on, on, off pulse of Ari's energy. "*Go back.*"

"*You're too worn out for this, you stubborn bastard,*" she said.

"*No. Ari. You'll bleed dry. I can't…*"

Feathers caressed his physical face. Color exploded across all aspects of his perception. Alien thought patterns enclosed him, the ashes of Edie, Ari, and the Ki in a bubble—maybe a cocoon—of shifting light and energy.

Recognition swept him the way antennae swept his face. The Chekydran-ki. They'd teleported to the *Sen*

Ekir.

The kaleidoscopic cocoon might exist only in his mind, but the bubble tightened. It closed on him, scraping through him, pulling every mote of light and hope and love with it.

For a second, the bubble hesitated, wavering. It pulsed in time with Ari's on, on, off beat of power.

Refusal.

How he got that, he couldn't say. He knew only that the Ki gently shoved Ari out of the closing circle, leaving her to bleed energy and affront. The cocoon shrank to an orb he could wrap his arms around. It collapsed further still, brightening to the point that he couldn't bear to regard it with any sense, physical or mental.

The Ki queen nudged him with a thought. V'kyrri created a physical construct of himself, standing amid the fading embers of Edie. The queen set the gleaming orb in his palm, the way Edie had once tipped a fireball into his hand.

The orb wasn't Edie. It was the vital, burning essence of everything she was to him and maybe to herself.

V'kyrri knelt and nestled the orb into the ash heap.

Nothing happened. His eyes and chest burned. Air couldn't slip past the loss swelling within him.

"*Edie*."

The orb exploded.

In that flash, heat, light, and brilliant flames ripped past. Clutching a tiny filament of flame, V'kyrri fell out of Edie's psyche. He slammed into his own body with such force he found himself sprawled on the deck plates, staring at the *Sen Ekir*'s ceiling. He spared a moment to hook the flicker he'd brought with him, not into his consciousness, but into his soul.

"V'k." Jayleia rushed to his side, her voice thick. Moisture tracked her face. "Look at me. Are you…"

Blinking the whirl of fire and pain out of his mental eye he rasped, "Edie," and struggled to rise.

"Stay still," Jay commanded, shoving him flat. "Raj and Dr. Idylle are working on her, there's still a chance, V'k. Tell me you're okay."

He couldn't.

"What happened?" Jayleia demanded.

"I-I think the Ki tried to help me and Ari…get Edie back."

Jay's dark eyes widened.

"There was an explosion. I thought she was called Firestorm because of what she did during the war," he said and shook his head. "That's wrong."

Fresh tears tracked Jay's cheeks. She sat cross-legged on the deck beside him.

Fear constricted his chest. It powered him to sitting.

Jayleia smiled. "S'okay, V'k. She's still on the edge, but Linnaeus and Raj are pumping her full of blood products since we have a legion of donors. Internal damage from the chest wound is nearly repaired. They'll start closing…"

The Chekydran-ki queen stepped into V'kyrri's line of sight. She convulsed and spat a reddish-purple gelatinous substance onto her forelegs. She leaned past V'kyrri.

He scrambled to his knees.

Jay grabbed his wrist.

Dr. Idylle and Raj looked up.

The queen dumped the goo in the middle of Edie's open chest wound.

V'kyrri swayed. "What…"

Both doctors smeared the substance across the chasm in Edie. Raj and Dr. Idylle spoke over the top of one another, their words a jumble. "Healing. Damen. Proven efficacy. Fast. Healing."

He forced himself to breathe in time with the machine breathing for Edie. Through the window of gel, he detected the flutter of Edie's heart, intact now, and pink. He shook with a bitter laugh.

"When I said I wanted your heart," he murmured, "I didn't mean like this."

Laughing and crying at once, Jayleia punched his shoulder.

"V'k." Ari's voice via com.

"Ari. I'm sorry—"

"Don't," she said. "I get it. I'd have attacked, too, had you tried to get between me and Seaghdh. You're off duty. That's an order. But you might consider making a statement."

"What?" V'kyrri looked around, finally registering that far too many bodies had crammed into the *Sen Ekir's* tiny medi bay. He brushed fingertips across Edie's still cheek. Heat flooded his system. The chill of space had relinquished her. Warm skin met his touch. Her heart still beat, though he was losing visual on that as the Chekydran healing gel darkened.

Edie was alive.

"You have a crowd amassed outside," Seaghdh said. "One hundred thousand and growing."

"Eilod and her machinations," Ari muttered. "She couldn't have turned Edie into more of a legend if she'd tried. And she did try."

V'kyrri bristled. "She—"

"Stand down, V'k," Seaghdh said. "Edie's a hero. She's a symbol of courage and self-sacrifice to her people. The sagas are already being written."

"You're afraid this'll get dangerous," V'kyrri said.

"It already has," Seaghdh said.

"Get out there," Ari said. "Go covered in her blood and tell them."

"Tell them what?" he demanded.

"She's alive," Raj snapped. "I don't know how, but she's alive, and the longer that's true, the better her chances."

V'kyrri's knees didn't want to hold him.

It took Jayleia and Damen supporting him to get to the gate. Determined to address the crowd in their own language, he shook off his friends, and looked at Jonas, Povora, Raz, and the rest of the resistance. Tears streaked their faces. Holding his hands over head, V'kyrri said, "She lives."

As if saying those two words broke a vital part of him, tears burned his eyes and spilled over. "She lives."

Motion and the noise of cloth brushing cloth rose and crested like a wave running outward as the news rippled through the throng of people. Jonas came and clapped V'kyrri's shoulder.

"Praise to all Twelve Gods," Jonas said.

The crowd echoed him. As he scrubbed his face dry, V'kyrri did, too.

Chapter Thirty-Seven

"*Time to go, sweetheart,*" Edie's mother said.

"*Yes,*" Edie said. "*I love you. Dad, too.*"

Her mother's tender fingers slipped from Edie's cheek, her smile and face fading in a twist of color and light. So much color. It engulfed her. She breathed it, tasted it. More color than had ever existed. Some couldn't be seen, only experienced via all the other sensory inputs, some of which, she didn't possess. Intense. A SEM on overload. Or V'kyrri trying to hear for her.

Color brightened and dimmed in time with her pulse. Or maybe her pulse beat in time with the color. Dazzled by the play of rainbows and energy enclosing her in its grip, she sank, nestling into the buoying support.

I love you. I love you. The words resolved from the surge and recede of power. They washed the shores of her awareness, coaxing her to wake.

Huh. Her chest itched. Right on top of the hard, bony places. Her fingers twitched. In slow motion, her right hand flopped from her side to her sternum so she could rub away the sensation of things crawling on her skin.

Trembling fingers caught hers. "*No. No scratching. You're still healing.*" Warm lips brushed her forehead. Lazy curls of pleasure spun in the wake of that caress.

Edie opened her eyes and had to wait for them to focus away from what she'd seen while dying, so she could look on what was going to be the rest of her life.

Sea green eyes. Brown hair. Copper skin. The blinding light of hope.

"Can you give it a rest?" she tried to say. It came out a whisper. If it came out at all.

His brows came together.

"I love you, too, you crazy Claugh. But I heard you the first six thousand times you said it."

"*Good. Now look at me while I tell you aloud. I want to tell you often enough for you to memorize the shape of the words on my lips, starting now.*"

"I love you."

She stretched her fingers in his grip. He released her. Edie brushed his lips with quivering fingers. He said it again. The image seared a path straight to her stretched and too-full heart. Painful, yes, but it made her smile, nevertheless.

Finally, he stirred. The skin between his brows puckered. "*Ari and Seaghdh asked me to call when you woke. Do you mind*?"

She rolled her head as much to say no as to see if she could.

Straightening, he tapped his badge. "*Dagger*, Captain V'kyrri. I need your top two on private channel, please."

He piped the words into her head as he said them, as if aware that her acuity hadn't recovered to the point that she could read him. Especially not in the dim light of an active scan bed. The overhead lights were off, which meant he'd been sleeping beside her. Standing vigil.

He ordered the lights to quarter light. Enough for her to see him signing a translation for what was being said by his friends.

"V'k," Ari said.

"Edie is awake."

"Thank the gods." Ari again.

"Captain Idylle. Thank you for helping keep me alive," Edie whispered.

"You knew? That's…I didn't," Ari said through V'kyrri. "The Ki wouldn't let me."

"You know why," Edie said.

"What? No. I'm still pissed they shut me out."

Edie shifted the itch in her chest making her restless. "They couldn't risk you. Extra heartbeat in your field."

V'kyrri froze. His eyes went wide, and his jaw, slack. If Ari or Seaghdh had anything to say, V'kyrri did not translate it.

Edie laughed. Searing pain in her sternum cut it short.

"Still lobbing bombs," Ari said. "Thanks."

"At least it's a private line," V'kyrri said.

"Edie," the admiral interjected. "You single-handedly destroyed the entire attacking Chekydran-hiin force and the whole of the lunar agricultural station. We'd have been routed. Your people would have lost the greatest bulk of experienced fighters this world has known."

"Cravuul dung. Single-handed nothing. How long?"

"You've been out for two days," V'kyrri said.

She gasped and looked around as if Eilod might be hiding in the shadows. "Her Majesty?"

V'kyrri hesitated. His shoulders hunched. "Following up leads. No word."

Damn it, Trente. Edie frowned. If she got to her ship, she might have a shot at messaging him. Didn't mean he'd answer, but at least she'd let him know she knew. For all the difference it would make. She blew out a shaky breath. "Jonas?"

"Alive. Worried about you."

Relief stung her eyes. "Povora? Raz? The others?"

"I can't answer for all of them," V'kyrri said. "I'll have Jonas compile a list."

"Vaccination?"

"Underway," V'kyrri said. "Your pilots are heroes. Two developed symptoms in flight. They delivered their vaccines then flew themselves into the ocean to avoid infecting anyone else. Another half dozen…"

"V'kyrri. Edie. Later. You must be moved to a secure location," Seaghdh urged. "The Chekydran-hiin—"

"Are after V'kyrri," she said. "Not me."

V'kyrri stared at her, his brow furrowed.

"My team and I will need your analysis," Seaghdh said, "once you and V'kyrri are safe. Captain? It's time."

V'kyrri's hands fell slack. His presence in her head and heart muted. He spoke as he turned away, his features bleak. "Here's where I lose her."

Edie scowled. The itch in her chest deepened to an ache.

Raj edged into the bay. He and V'kyrri bundled her into an anti-grav chair. Raj hovered at her right side. As V'kyrri pushed her into the empty holding pen, the Chekydran-ki queen and her drone closed in on Edie's left. She extended a shaking hand.

The queen lowered her head, bringing her eyes level with Edie's. Her antenna brushed Edie's skin.

"Thank you," Edie said. For an instant, Edie's vision blurred into a wash of color that snapped back into hard focus. She had to blink away headache. The ache in her sternum wouldn't ease. Neither did the swirls of the sea green she associated with V'kyrri eddying inside of her.

Her hand fell out of contact with the queen.

V'kyrri had to help Edie get her hand back into her lap.

She huffed a shallow breath.

"You died two days ago," he said. "Give yourself some time."

She glanced at the gates. Physical transport. Not a teleport. Either she'd been more grievously injured than two days of regen implied, or the Claugh had a plan.

Awareness burst and expanded inside her skull. Nol Jakze needed to see her to be sure their mascot hadn't become their martyr.

"Let's do this," she managed. "Since you mean to use me without my consent, again."

The furrows in V'kyrri's forehead deepened and the blood ran out of his face. When she closed her eyes for a moment, the green of his eyes colored the inside of her eyelids. It eased her too-fast pulse and she opened her eyes.

If the Claugh intended to go on using her, she'd use them. She wasn't done making choices.

V'kyrri took her to the gates.

Soldiers snapped to attention and saluted. One wore a fierce grin. The other blinked reddening eyes.

Dread settled on her shoulders. Hero worship. This was going to be a zero-g, Port Poison, horned shark roundup, wasn't it? Scent hit her. Sweet, as nuanced and multi-faceted as the play of color she associated with the Chekydran-ki queen.

The gates opened. Lights flared. Edie squinted, lifted a hand in self-defense. As her eyes adjusted to the glare of holo-cameras, she managed a weak smile. Someone, most likely V'kyrri, had rallied the surviving members of her short-lived command. Jonas had them strung across the front lines of the crowd that stretched back as far as Edie could see.

Flowers, masses and masses of flowers mounded against the holding pen fence. Candles flickered. Papers fluttered in the breeze, most of them covered with children's drawings. A few toys had been sacrificed to the makeshift altar.

The ache in Edie's chest sharpened, and she pressed it with the heel of her palm. It did nothing to drive the pain back, only routed it to her stinging eyes.

Raj had allowed her a medical SEM for the duration of transport. Translation only. No enhancement. It registered the tidal wave of sound that was her people shouting with their hands over their heads.

Some offered praise to the gods. Some signed, "Firestorm." Others, "General." Jonas, positioned in front of the cameras, met her eye and spelled out, "Altheas Drake."

The weight sitting on her grew heavier.

Nol Jakze's surviving military leaders edged through the line of resistance fighters. They lined up at attention. The cameras could still see her and their hands.

"General Firestorm," the woman closest to her said. "I am Hynomo Nuwas, formerly a general under the auspices of the late governor." She gestured down the line. "We all were. Terrible things happened on our watch, betrayals we should have seen coming. Betrayals we should have stopped. We have a long road to redemption. We want to walk it among honorable companions. We hereby resign our commissions in the Nol Jakze Armed Forces. We'd like to join the resistance under your command. If you'll have us."

V'kyrri's grip on the arm of her chair tightened until all color left his knuckles.

"We also came on behalf of the citizens of Nol Jakze to ask you to step into the governorship," the former general said. "Elections must be held, yes. But until that time, Nol Jakze needs someone in the position who has proven she has the interests of the people at heart."

So it began. Flames danced across Edie's field of internal vision. She glanced to her right. V'kyrri had wiped every mote of expression from his face. His pallid, bloodless knuckles offered the only visible sign of distress. He'd put on a crisp, khaki uniform. It fit well enough to speed her pulse far more pleasantly than the first time she'd laid eyes on him. She wanted to enjoy the shift, but his eyes had gone flat. Chilly. Remote.

Edie shivered. Here they were. Zero hour.

Marshalling bits of strength and determination, she rocked to her feet.

Jonas bolted to her side and wrapped an arm around her waist, holding her upright, while the crowd cheered, hands overhead.

Uncertainty and disappointment scraped her bones. It should have been V'kyrri holding her. Was this his choice, then?

"I am honored and deeply grateful to each of you," she said. "Never have I been prouder to be Nol Jakzian. When the call to service went out, you did not hesitate. We have thwarted the first wave of Chekydran-hiin attacks."

"Plague was only the beginning," Jonas said when she had to rest a moment to gather strength.

"Yes. You ask me to act as interim governor," she said. "Had anyone asked me ten years ago, full of rage and ego, I would have accepted. Now, I cannot." Jonas's grip on her tightened.

"You need someone still in communion with the church," she said. "You need someone who comprehends the sanctity of your family farms and businesses. You need someone who will remind you of what's best about Nol Jakze."

"You…" several people began at once.

"Can't stay," Edie said with a slash of hands. "I can't stay. First, I am called to serve. Not just Nol Jakze, but anyone in the path of the Chekydran-hiin. Second and most importantly, I've spent the past decade searching for family. I never expected to love my enemy."

She shot a glance at V'kyrri.

The remote mask shattered. Dark, roiling storm clouds gathered in his expression, carving hollows into his cheeks.

Sea green surged within the confines of her soul. V'kyrri. He was there somehow, intertwined in the fabric of who and what she was.

Eyes stinging, she hastily looked back at the crowd. Tears on a few faces. Anger on others. A few smiles. Povora finally wore one when she looked at V'kyrri.

"It is among old enemies that I have found family at last," she said. "If they will have me. I pledge to do my utmost for Nol Jakze from within their midst."

V'kyrri swept her off her feet, into his arms. Pain stabbed her chest.

"Careful," Raj squawked.

Pain subsided.

"General. The governorship—"

"Jonas. You need Jonas."

V'kyrri's fierce grin justified her choice. "If you will excuse us. I am invested in getting the general to safety."

"Is that what you call it?" Povora quipped.

Edie and V'kyrri laughed.

V'kyrri carried her through the holding pen, past another section of fence to a tiny room formed from a set of prefabbed collapsible plates. Sealed, undoubtedly. Sterile.

"Hold still," he said. "Teleporting."

Nice. She'd been wrong. She wasn't so injured that she couldn't be teleported. Finally. Some good news.

"We'll match biofilters between teleporters," V'kyrri said. "If we're infected, we won't teleport. If we teleport, we aren't infected."

"Where?" she whispered.

"Rest easy."

Edie resorted to speaking with her hands. Even if they were rubbery and slow to obey. "Oh good. Claugh

Captain not answering my questions. My favorite."

His diaphragm bounced. Still he said nothing.

Come to think of it, where the Hells could they teleport? Her family farm? Not exactly the place to hide the two people the Chekydran-hiin seemed to want dead.

"Great. I've graduated from the top of the Claugh Most Wanted list to the number two spot on the bugs'."

V'kyrri's grin put a dimple in his cheek she'd never seen before. "At least you're used to it."

Teleport distortion spun her head. Icy claws dug at her still healing chest. They materialized in a spacious room flashing amber. She squinted.

Dizziness settled. The flash winked to normal pseudo-daylight. Edie frowned. The only places that bothered with mimicking natural daylight wavelengths were governmental buildings, corporations trying to impress clients, and massive spaceships.

None of those made sense.

"Where are we?"

Wrapped in a clean suit, a person Edie had missed seeing gestured. Possibly spoke, but the medical SEM Raj had lent Edie painted nonsense before her eyes.

V'kyrri didn't translate. Trembling hope and anticipation lit the connection thrumming in her head. He placed her on what was unmistakably a scan bed.

Edie rocked her head, looking for a location anchor.

"*Relax and let us take care of you.*" V'kyrri's mental voice said.

"*Us who?*" She sucked a shallow breath.

The medi came to Edie's side. She began pushing buttons, lifting the gown Edie was wearing to glance at whatever wound still marred her chest.

While the doctor worked, Edie registered the shimmer of force field hugging the inside of the walls and the gentle vibration of massive energy flowing through a ship. For a split second, fear sped her heart rate.

The *Dagger*.

Two figures wearing clean suits came into the room along with a rush of wind. Positive air flow followed. Keeping infection inside. She and V'kyrri were in quarantine.

Edie fumbled for controls for the scan bed.

"General Firestorm," the medical SEM printed out the words but offered no information about the voice saying her name, much less who'd spoken it. Not V'kyrri. The unit would have tagged his speech.

The pair of clean suits, one taller than the other, stood stiff. At attention. Facing her. A frisson of danger strolled Edie's nerve fibers.

"Do you understand me?"

"I see what you're saying, if that's what you're asking," Edie replied. She had no notion how her voice sounded, but it felt stronger. A little less like she might be pulling it up from the soles of her boots.

"Captain Ari Idylle." The shorter of the two clean suits lifted fingers. "Forgive the break in protocol. We wanted to be certain you could understand us without virtue of telepathic translation."

Edie nodded.

"Your Royal Highness, Admiral Aurnoch Riorchjan Cullen Seaghdh, I present General Firestorm, also known as Edie and Altheas Drake," Captain Idylle said, offering a brief bow to the taller, leaner figure beside her. She faced Edie once more. "General Firestorm, I present His Royal Highness, Regent of the Empire in Her Majesty's absence, Cullen Seaghdh."

Edie breathed a bitter laugh. Here she was in the one place in the universe she'd never expected to be unless she was blowing it out of the sky, facing people who should, and frankly, who probably still did, want her dead.

A dry, dusty husk of fear squirted weak adrenaline into her system.

The man Edie had thought of as the knife blade held up a hand. "General Firestorm." Another scribble of slow-poke Tagrethian strolled across lenses that had nothing to offer other than what featureless words were said. The weighted pause following that name she'd once hated made her scrunch her brows together.

She tapped the too thick frames holding her lenses. "Medical unit. If you're trying to influence, threaten, or scare me, this thing is useless to both of us."

V'kyrri pressed his lips tight, but the corners twitched.

"You've been in the top five of our most wanted lists for the last decade," Cullen Seaghdh said. "Your name frightens small children the empire over."

"Really?" She peered over the SEM frames at him. "We should compare boogeyman notes some time, Aurnoch Riorchjan."

The tall clean suit clenched his fists, but beside him, the shorter one shook with what looked suspiciously like laughter.

Edie frowned and glanced at all the players. Was that what this was? She tipped her head. "Are you looking for the monster your people made of me fifteen years ago, Your Highness? After you made sure your captain and your cousin muzzled her?"

"We baxt'kal did not." V'kyrri glared at her.

"What made Eilod trust you with protecting the treaty site and her life?" Seaghdh demanded.

"She risked her life for the benefit of Nol Jakze," Edie said, "and in doing so, she manipulated me into becoming what she wanted. What makes you think I can't see through you now?"

V'kyrri laughed.

Edie scowled at Cullen Seaghdh. "What the Hells were you thinking letting the queen into a quarantined city anyway?"

"There was no *let* to it," Captain Idylle grumbled. "She and the Chekyrdan-ki were on…"

The regent sliced a hand through the rest of the sentence. "You swore to destroy the empire."

Eilod and the Ki had been on world before the bombs, and the admiral didn't want her to know. Interesting.

"Yes, I swore to destroy the empire." More than once. No one needed to know that. "Then V'kyrri taught me trust and love. He charmed me into questioning and discarding my prejudices. Because of V'kyrri, I learned forgiveness. Both of people I'd thought of as enemies and of myself."

"You were the one who drew the teeth on old rage and fear," V'kyrri said aloud. His pride and love warmed her from the inside out.

Edie shrugged, or at least, tried. "I'm aboard the ship I most ached to destroy, and I have no plans to blow anything up any time soon. Unless you give me a team to take back to finish off the UMOPG base."

"Had you not found V'kyrri…"

"And him me," she asserted. "The better part of me."

He crept close enough to take her hand.

"You'd have made Nol Jakze a blood bath."

"Yes." Edie nodded.

They traded a look she didn't want to interpret.

"Instead we threw one another lifelines. I hauled him out of one death. He hauled me out of another. Is that enough protestation of how nice and civilized I've become?"

V'kyrri squeezed her hand.

"Civilized." The regent took a couple of steps closer. "You're going to run into people in this empire, in this very room, whose loved ones died by your hand."

Edie glanced at the medi. A woman with brown eyes looked back through the face mask.

"If I've manipulated you, General, it was to find out how you'll respond to that," the regent said.

"With condolences where I can," Edie said. "If you believe the science, the soldiers who came to Nol Jakze were lost the moment they set foot on world."

The medi nodded, the gesture so miniscule, Edie doubted she knew she'd moved at all.

"General—"

"Scrape that off. My name is Edie. We all know who and what I am. I'm no hero. The fact that you're not standing me up in front of a firing squad is enough."

The tall clean suit jerked as if stung. Edie's baxt'kal useless SEM registered a sound wave that it insisted was a laugh. From him. The Aurnoch Riorchjan. The stories told in TFC about him insisted the man had no sense of humor.

"You are indeed a hero, and were it not for quarantine, you and Captain V'kyrri would have been afforded a hero's welcome. Instead, we regret you'll be in quarantine for two weeks."

"Brace yourselves," Ari said. "You have a long list of visitors applying for access."

"My crew?" V'kyrri asked.

"Your crew."

Edie brightened.

"No firing squads, Edie," Seaghdh said. "Rest. Recuperate. Then we'll need every lead you can muster. It is vital we recover Eilod."

"More than vital," Ari echoed.

"Because until you do, you're carrying the heir apparent?" V'kyrri asked with a grin.

"You have no idea. I'm going to shoot the next person who offers me a pillow," Ari grumbled.

Edie laughed.

"Stop that!" the medi ordered, pointing at Edie. "Your heart, ribs, and surrounding tissue are still fragile. You are not clear for duty of any kind. Either of you." The doctor spoke Tagrethian that time. No mistaking it was she who spoke, not with her hands on her hips while she stood between Edie and the regent.

"This room is secure," the doctor said, turning on V'kyrri. "You will refrain from telepathy of any kind. The Chekydran-ki insist. To that end, the room is shielded."

V'kyrri jerked upright "What?"

"Shielded," she repeated, then spun on her heel and made a shooing motion. "Your Highness. Captain. You have exhausted my patient long enough. Time is up.

Please make your way to the airlock."

"We hear and obey."

Edie couldn't tell who'd muttered that. Ari, the medi, and His Royal Highness retreated to the airlock.

"One more thing," V'kyrri said, drawing her fingers to his lips. The skin of his cheeks darkened. "You'd think I'd have learned my lesson by now."

Edie lifted an eyebrow.

"You know about connections." He gestured between them.

"Yes."

He pulled in a long breath. "Right. There are different kinds based on…"

"You're working up to confess about the chip of you in here?" She curled fingers against the tender skin and bone of her upper chest. "Were you supposed to ask permission for that one, too?"

V'kyrri's hand shook. It looked to her like he'd stopped breathing. "I was. It's—Edie. My people have a pair bond. Friends bond mind to mind. You'd think lovers would bond heart to heart, and the gods know we tried in a terrible way."

"Soul to soul," she whispered.

He nodded. "I had no right…"

"You did," she said. "You do. Haven't you listened to a thing I've said? V'kyrri. If I am home, it is because you are my home."

Smiling, even as his eyes reddened, he leaned in to press his lips to hers. "Welcome home."

A word about the author...

Marcella Burnard graduated from Cornish College of the Arts with a degree in acting. She's a Tarot-reading third-degree Wiccan who knows far too much about space travel because she desperately wanted to be an astronaut when she grew up. Turns out, she gets airsick. She wisely decided to write space travel, instead.

Marcella writes science fiction romance, urban fantasy, paranormal, and fantasy. If a story brings the weird, Marcella's right there for it. She lives in Florida where she and her husband are outnumbered by cats. Marcella is actively involved in feline rescue in the Tampa Bay area, and you can always find cat photos and videos on her Facebook page or on her Instagram account.

Visit her at:

http://marcellaburnard.com

Thank you for purchasing
this publication of The Wild Rose Press, Inc.

For questions or more information
contact us at
info@thewildrosepress.com.

The Wild Rose Press, Inc.
www.thewildrosepress.com